Blood Marks

Ruby Scott

D&V

Ruby Scott

www.rubyscott.com

Edited by Em Kay
Cover Design by Lise Gold
Published by D&V Publishing (Scotland)

'In the fantastical creatures and impossible feats of folklore, we find the very real truths of human nature.'

— *Anonymous*

Author's Note

Origins of the Baobhan Sith

Before you embark on this journey, it's important to understand the origins of the pivotal characters: the Baobhan Sith and Babd.

In Scottish folklore, the Baobhan Sith (pronounced baa-van-shee or bow-an-shee) are seductive, dangerous creatures, often depicted as vampiric. Whilst the origins of the Baobhan Sith is shrouded in mystery, many think they are the risen souls of cursed women, banished from their villages, for unnatural acts, or being witches, often both.

Many of those accused and killed were midwives, working tirelessly in rudimentary conditions to save the lives of mothers and children. Their failures, in a time of high infant and maternal mortality, were often misinterpreted as malice and evidence of a pact with the Devil. These so-called 'unnatural acts' also included tragically mundane events like milk curdling inexplicably, a sudden illness in the village, or social and religious deviance. This deviance could include speaking out of turn, failing to attend church, or any behaviours deemed outside the strict norms of the time. Same-sex relationships, while considered sinful and against God's law, made up a smaller number of accusations.

The driving forces behind these accusations were complex and deeply rooted in the anxieties of the time. Fear of the unknown, fuelled by superstition and religious dogma, played a significant role. Personal vendettas also came into play, with accusations of witchcraft used as a tool to settle scores or eliminate rivals. Deep-seated misogyny was undeniably a factor, as the vast majority of the accused were women, particularly those who were older, independent, or otherwise marginalised. This phenomenon was exacerbated by a dangerous form of groupthink, where communities, gripped by fear and suspicion, would readily accept and participate in the persecution of their neighbours. This issue of group hatred, a willingness to condemn and destroy based on unfounded accusations, societal pressures and religious intolerance, is a chilling reminder of a darkness that, despite centuries of education, still lingers in human society to this day.

The Baobhan Sith are said to appear as beautiful women, dressed in flowing green gowns, their true nature concealed until it is too late. Their sharp, elongated nails are a tell-tale sign, used to deadly effect. They are known for their enchanting voices and their mesmerising dance, luring unsuspecting victims to remote locations with the promise of revelry. Once isolated, the Baobhan Sith would reveal their true form and drain their victims of blood, leaving them lifeless. These creatures are tied to the wild, untamed places of Scotland, of which there are still many.

There were, however, also whispers of another side to the Baobhan Sith. Some tales suggest that they were not merely bloodthirsty predators, but also guardians of the natural world, protectors of the very wilderness they inhabited. They were said to have an intimate connection with nature, embodying its fierce, untamed beauty and ruthless power. This duality - the dangerous seductress and the protector of the wild - is what makes the Baobhan Sith so fascinating and enduring in Scottish lore.

As the author of this novel, I have drawn on these traditional accounts of the Baobhan Sith. However, I have also taken some artistic liberties, weaving my own interpretations into the established folklore to serve the narrative of this story. Folklore is a living, evolving thing, and storytellers reshape these ancient tales to give them new meaning and relevance.

And, what a way to curse two women who loved each other physically but to give them long nails.

We also mention The *Badb* (pronounced bahv or bibe), in this book, a figure from Celtic and Scottish lore, is a spectral being tied to prophecy, battle, and death. Often depicted as a crow or raven, the *Badb* is said to foretell calamity with her cries, her presence a harbinger of bloodshed and chaos. She is related to the trio of sisters known collectively as the Morrígna, goddesses of war and sovereignty, embodying the fierce, untamed forces of nature and fate.

Legends describe the *Badb* haunting battlefields and wild places, her form blending seamlessly with the natural world. Some tales suggest she takes human shape, appearing as a mysterious woman whose words carry the weight of inevitability. The legend says *Badb* does not simply revel in destruction; she represents the cyclical nature of life and death, the destruction necessary for renewal. However, there is always the possibility that power can be corrupted.

While her connection to war is prominent, the *Badb* is also a guardian of the wild, tied to the untamed spirit of the

Highlands. Her dual nature, as both a fearsome omen and a force of transformation, makes her a compelling figure in Scottish mythology. The *Badb* reminds us of the fine line between beauty and ferocity, life and death, and humanity's fragile place within the natural world.

I hope you enjoy the dark tale of the forbidden 'unnatural' world.

Part One

Chapter One

The Scent of Attraction

The gallery pulsed with an energy Greer Morrigan Dubhán had long ago learned to filter out. Laughter bounced off the pristine white walls, punctuated by the chime of champagne glasses and extravagant use of words like 'transcendent' and 'provocative.' Greer positioned herself near the entrance, her lean frame impeccably dressed in tailored black trousers and a crimson silk blouse. The whole scene was like the start of a clichéd sapphic romance, she thought wryly.

She touched her dark hair, swept up in a simple yet elegant style, which hinted at an effortless sophistication. This was her trademark armour—minimalist, intentional, and alluring.

She rarely attended events like this. Galleries were often too crowded, too noisy, too pretentious, and too full of inflated egos. But tonight marked three hundred and ninety-one years since the torture of her transformation. Since hatred turned love into hunger. The date always drew her out of seclusion, as if her cursed body sought to commemorate its own making. Plus, Thomas, the beautiful soul he was, had promised there would be a buffet, and she was a sucker for a tiny canapé. She took a sip of red wine, its aroma hinting at blackberry and oak, as her eyes scanned the room, observing but never lingering.

Until she walked in.

Greer's attention caught on a figure across the room who seemed to shimmer. The woman was petite, but her presence filled the space like the comforting aroma of fresh bacon rolls – warm, inviting, and utterly irresistible. Her dress, a riot of colours that sang against the muted tones of the gallery, swirled around her ankles as she moved with a dancer's fluidity. Greer caught the glint of a silver pendant nestled in the hollow of her throat, and a delicate scent of sandalwood and paint clung to her. Chestnut hair, reminiscent of autumn leaves just before they fall, albeit less withered, framed a face alive with passion and a playful curiosity that made Greer smile.

Her heightened senses stirred. The air thickened, carrying a whisper of something warmer, more enticing. It wasn't just the woman's perfume – though undeniably intoxicating – but her energy, her vitality. Greer's heart raced, a rare and dangerous sign.

'Get it together,' she murmured, although she knew restraint may be nothing more than a memory tonight.

'Talking to yourself, Greer? The party must be a real thrill,' a voice interrupted from her left.

Greer turned, arching an eyebrow at the man who had sidled up next to her. Thomas, the gallery owner, moved with a grace that only their kind possessed. His expensive suit screamed wealth, and his perfectly practised smile held centuries of carefully maintained charm. Like her, he wore his humanity like a well-tailored mask though they had an unspoken agreement never to acknowledge their shared nature in public.

'Just taking in the sights,' Greer replied, her tone cool. Her eyes flicked back to the woman, who was now examining a large abstract canvas, blissfully unaware of the scrutiny.

Thomas followed her focus, to one of the three artists whose work was on display, his smile widening. 'Ah, Freya Solasta. The art world's new darling, so they say. Quite the talent, isn't she?'

'Talented, indeed,' Greer murmured, though her focus wasn't on the art.

Thomas laughed. 'I wouldn't get any ideas, Greer. She's far too gentle for someone like you.'

Greer's jaw tightened. 'And what exactly is that supposed to mean?'

'Only that you have a reputation for being rather... intense.' He gave a vague wave of his hand.

Greer didn't bother to respond. Instead, she finished her wine and set the empty glass on a nearby table, her attention drawn back to Freya. She had centuries of practice in the art of discretion, but tonight, she felt uncharacteristically reckless.

When Freya finally moved, it was with a dancer's deliberation, her dress swaying with each step as she moved to another display. Greer found herself gravitating closer, staying just out of sight, yet close enough to savour every detail: the way Freya's fingers grazed her lips in thought, the subtle curve of her mouth as she explained the intention behind each piece to an inquisitive potential buyer.

It wasn't until Freya paused at a smaller painting in the corner of the room that Greer's resolve wavered. The artwork was a chaos of blues and greens, turbulent yet strangely soothing. It was a submission from another artist. Freya cocked her head, her expression softening, and Greer couldn't resist.

'What do you see?' Greer's voice was low, smooth, and undeniably commanding.

Freya startled slightly but turned, her eyes meeting Greer's with a mix of surprise and intrigue.

'I'm not sure,' Freya admitted, her voice warm and melodic. 'It's reminiscent of... the ocean, but not quite. Something deeper.'

Greer nodded, stepping closer. 'I think it's meant to evoke the subconscious. A reflection of what we hide beneath the surface.' If anyone else had given that explanation, she'd have thought them pompous, but needs must.

Freya's expression brightened. 'You've seen it before?'

'Once,' Greer replied, which was true, and she hadn't rated it then. Neither had anyone else, given it was back on display, no buyer found. Her gaze dropped to Freya's hands, noting the faint smudges of paint on her fingers. 'Artist?'

A blush crept over Freya's cheeks. 'Is it that obvious?'

'It's in the details,' Greer said, her eyes steady. 'And the manner you look at the world.'

For a beat, silence stretched between them, as though the air was too charged for words. Greer could feel the pull, the magnetic draw that was as exhilarating as it was risky. She hadn't felt this way in years, and it terrified her.

Freya broke the quiet first, her eyes sparkling with amusement. 'And you? Let me guess. You're the mysterious type who prefers to observe rather than engage.'

Greer's lips curved into a small, almost predatory smile. 'Something like that.'

'Well,' Freya said, tilting her head, 'maybe tonight's the night you change that.'

Greer's pulse quickened. She wanted to believe it was just idle flirtation, the kind of casual banter she'd perfected over the years. But Freya's gaze was too sincere, too disarming. She was exposed.

But before she could respond, Thomas's voice sliced through the moment. 'Freya! There you are. I've been looking for you.'

Freya's expression shifted, the spell broken. 'Thomas. Hi.'

'You're the belle of the ball. Don't let this woman keep you to herself,' he said with a pointed glance at Greer.

Freya hesitated, her eyes darting back to Greer. 'It was nice meeting you...?'

'Greer,' she supplied, her voice steady despite the simmering irritation at Thomas's interruption.

'Greer,' Freya repeated, her lips curving into a smile. 'I'll see you around.'

And just like that, she was gone, swallowed up by Thomas and the swarm of admirers. Greer watched her disappear into the throng, her heart pounding with a mix of frustration and excitement.

She had witnessed countless lifetimes, encountered innumerable people. But something about Freya Solasta was different, risky, and compelling. Plus, she was hot as fuck.

Chapter Two

Studio Secrets

Greer hadn't planned to end up in Freya Solasta's studio. In fact, she hadn't planned much of anything after that electric moment in the gallery, when Freya's laugh had filled both the space and her soul. But the casual invitation to visit, extended with warm ease by Freya as they parted that evening, had proven impossible to resist.

Stepping into the artist's studio was akin to stepping into a dream – a vibrant, chaotic dream where colours exploded, and textures begged to be touched. Sunlight streamed through the skylight, illuminating dust motes dancing in the air and catching the edges of canvases stacked haphazardly against the walls. The aroma of oil paints, both fresh and drying, mingled with the sharper tang of turpentine and the subtle sweetness of linseed oil. Beneath it all, a faint hint of sandalwood and something uniquely Freya – a warm, earthy scent that reminded Greer of sun-baked clay and bare flesh.

'Cosy,' Greer remarked, her tone wry, although she had the first faint trace of a smile.

Freya returned the smile, a smudge of crimson paint on her cheek. 'Cosy is a diplomatic way of saying 'a bit of a tip,' isn't it?'

'Not at all,' Greer replied, venturing further inside. Her gaze wandered the studio, pausing on an unfinished painting—an explosion of colour that seemed to throb with feeling. 'Your work is very expressive.'

Freya cocked her head, her expression curious. 'And what do you think it's expressing?'

Greer's eyes met hers, and for a beat, the intensity of her stare made the air between them crackle. 'That you perceive things in ways most don't.'

A soft blush bloomed on Freya's neck, but she held Greer's gaze. 'That's high praise,' she said quietly, before adding with a playful smile, 'especially from someone so enigmatic.'

Greer chuckled, leaning casually against a nearby table. 'Enigmatic? I'm an open book.'

'Right,' Freya countered, her tone light but her eyes dancing with mirth. 'Because mysterious strangers who radiate brooding confidence are so typical.'

Greer laughed, the sound low and rich. 'Maybe I prefer to let my actions do the talking.'

Freya's eyes flicked momentarily to Greer's hands, resting on the table's edge, then back to her face. 'Mm, perhaps, but I'm intrigued by you, Greer Morrigan Dubhán.'

Greer arched an eyebrow. 'Full name and everything? Impressive.'

'Google,' Freya said simply, her grin impish. 'It's a wondrous thing.'

'And what did Google reveal?' Greer kept her tone

light, but her body tensed subtly as she waited for the response.

'That you're an architect. Accomplished. Private. You don't publish details of your commissions in any of the usual journals, and your client list seems to be more confidential than the Swiss banking system, although everyone wants you— And your personal life is even less documented. You are—fascinating,' Freya said, her tone dipping slightly as she turned her attention back to her canvas.

'Fascinating,' Greer echoed, her smirk softening. 'Diplomatic way of saying I keep myself to myself.'

Freya peeked over her shoulder, her eyes twinkling. 'Not entirely. It's more like... you're the kind of person with stories. Lots of them. I think you just choose carefully who gets to hear them.'

There was something unnervingly perceptive in Freya's comment, an insight that cut through her meticulously crafted veneer. 'And what about you?' she asked, her tone gentler now as she deflected the focus. 'What compels you to create?'

Freya paused, her brush suspended above the painting. 'It's like there's something inside me that has to come out. Stories, emotions, moments... Art helps me understand it all.'

'And do you?' Greer asked, genuinely curious. 'Understand it?'

Freya turned fully now, resting lightly against her easel. 'Not always. But sometimes the journey is the answer.'

For a heartbeat, the studio seemed frozen, the air between them humming with unvoiced tension. Greer's gaze drifted briefly to Freya's mouth before darting back to her eyes, a hushed, transient confession of her thoughts.

Freya noticed—she must have noticed—but instead of

retreating, she moved closer. 'You're different,' she said, her tone quiet but unwavering.

'So are you,' Greer replied, her words tinged with the faintest hint of vulnerability.

Their eyes locked, and for a moment, it felt as if the existence beyond the studio ceased. Greer's instincts clamoured for her to go, to shield herself—and Freya—from the peril she harboured. But she remained still. Instead, she allowed the moment to stretch, inhaling the charged air between them, aware she was flirting with danger... and not giving a damn.

Chapter Three

Bound by Curiosity

Greer hadn't anticipated this—neither the tender weight of Freya's interest that seemed to hover like an unvoiced promise, nor the magnetism that drew them together once more, a mere day later, at the quaint café Freya had mentioned in passing.

The coffee house was nestled in a tranquil nook of Edinburgh, accessed via an inconspicuous passage off West Bow in Edinburgh's old town. Its eclectic furnishings and bohemian ambience were a perfect mirror of Freya's effervescent spirit. Greer had selected a table by the entrance, her back to the wall by instinct, and found herself uncharacteristically toying with the corners of her napkin. She never fidgeted.

When Freya breezed in, her presence suffused the space as effortlessly as morning sun. Her bright smile was disarming, tugging Greer from her typical composure. Freya's paint-splattered canvas tote, adorned with patches and delicate painted blossoms, slid from her shoulder to the ground with a casual thump as she took her seat.

'I hope you haven't been waiting too long,' Freya said, her tone warm as she settled into the chair opposite Greer.

'Not at all,' Greer replied, though her heartbeat told a different tale. She'd spent the past ten minutes envisioning how this encounter might unfurl, an uncommon indulgence for someone so adept at restraint. 'But I wasn't entirely certain you'd show.'

Freya laughed, a gentle, lyrical sound that seemed to capture the attention of the entire café. Other patrons turned and smiled. 'Why wouldn't I? It's not every day I get to unravel the enigma of Greer Morrigan Dubhán over coffee.'

Greer arched an eyebrow, her lips curving into a subtle smirk. 'Unravel? That sounds perilous.'

'Only if you allow it to be,' Freya teased, leaning forward, her chin resting on her hand. Her eyes glimmered with mischief, and Greer felt a pull—an invisible thread connecting them, luring her closer despite the warnings resounding in the recesses of her mind.

Their conversation began as playful repartee, weaving between wit and inquisitiveness. Freya posed questions—bold and unguarded—and Greer, atypically, found herself responding. She spoke of her work as an architect, how she crafted buildings that stood as testaments to both form and function, spaces that could inspire and shelter in equal measure. But when Freya inquired about her personal life, the answers became more challenging to provide. The centuries behind her felt too weighty, too delicate for this instant.

'So,' Freya said eventually, her tone light but her gaze keen, 'are you always this mysterious, or is it just for me?'

Greer's smirk deepened. 'Perhaps you draw it out of me.'

'Lucky me,' Freya replied, though her tone softened as her eyes dipped, lingering on Greer's fingers, long and slender. 'You have this manner of making everything feel intentional, like you've already mapped out ten steps ahead.'

Greer paused, the words that followed feeling like a gamble. 'And you seem determined to steer me off course.'

Freya's eyes widened slightly, but instead of withdrawing, she smiled. 'Maybe that's not such a bad thing.'

For a heartbeat, silence stretched between them, the murmur of the café fading into the background. Greer's instincts cautioned her to take a step back, to safeguard herself from the attraction she felt toward this woman. But instead, she leaned in, her tone low as she said, 'Maybe not.'

The moment held, suspended like a taut wire. Greer's gaze flickered briefly to Freya's lips, a fleeting thought flashing through her mind before she could halt it. Freya's hand went to her cheek, as though searching for a speck of paint she hadn't managed to wash off, a flush of crimson rising.

'I... I probably look a mess,' she said, a self-conscious laugh escaping her lips. 'Studio life, you know?'

Greer smiled, the sound deep and rich. 'You look beautiful,' she said, allowing her guard to slip.

Freya's eyes held a glimmer of something unspoken, something that promised this was far from the conclusion of their tale.

As their conversation meandered on, Greer found herself increasingly drawn in by Freya's vibrant spirit and quick wit. They spoke of art, of the city, of the tiny moments that made life worth savouring. And with each passing minute, Greer felt the walls she'd so carefully constructed begin to crumble, brick by metaphorical brick.

Greer knew the risks, knew the potential for devastation

that lurked beneath the surface of this connection. But as Freya's laughter filled the air, as her hand brushed Greer's arm in a moment of shared amusement, Greer found herself willing to play with fire.

They lingered in the café long after their cups had run dry, the outside fading into irrelevance. It was only when Freya glanced at her watch, her eyes widening at the hour, that reality seeped back in.

'I should get going,' Freya said, though her tone held a note of reluctance. 'I have a commission I need to finish.'

Greer nodded, her own responsibilities tugging at the edges of her mind. 'Of course. I won't keep you.'

But as they stood, as Freya gathered her things, Greer felt a sudden, irresistible urge to prolong this interlude. 'Freya,' she said, her tone quieter than she intended.

Freya paused, her eyes meeting Greer's with a silent question.

'Thank you,' Greer said, the words feeling inadequate but necessary. 'For this. For...' She gestured vaguely, encompassing the café, the conversation, the intangible something that had sparked between them.

Freya's expression softened, her smile turning gentle. 'You don't have to thank me, Greer. I wanted to be here. With you.'

The words hung in the air, a confession and a promise all at once. Greer felt her pulse quicken, her carefully maintained control slipping dangerously.

'Will I see you soon?' Freya asked, her tone lilting with hope.

Greer nodded, a smile playing at the edges of her lips. 'Soon,' she agreed.

And as Freya slipped out of the café, the bell above the entrance signalling her departure, Greer knew with a bone-deep certainty that this was only the beginning. Whatever this was, whatever it could become, she was irrevocably, undeniably hooked.

The trouble was, she couldn't bring herself to care about the consequences. Not when Freya's scent still lingered in the air, a tantalising reminder of the fire she was all too willing to burn in.

Chapter Four

The Crimson Sanctuary

Greer stood before the unassuming door, its plain exterior revealing nothing of the realm within. The only indication she was in the correct location was a subtle emblem carved into the frame—an intricate entanglement of roses and thorns. A deep breath centred her, though her heightened senses were already attuned to the rhythm of the space beyond: muffled, pulsing music intertwined with the soft murmur of hushed voices.

She rapped twice, confident and purposeful. The door cracked open, and a woman's face emerged, half-concealed by the shadowy illumination spilling out from inside.

'Password?' the woman inquired, her tone neutral yet resolute.

'Crimson Sanctuary,' Greer replied, with a roll of her eyes. She'd been going through this charade with Maeve twice a week for the last fifteen years. They needed security, but she was sure the beautiful butch just loved the clandestine theatrics.

Maeve gave a slight nod and stepped aside, granting her entry.

'Love the new DM's.' Greer nodded to the boots with rainbow laces, noting her reflection in the shine. Whilst Maeve wasn't her type, she knew the woman would be a very thorough lover. Without waiting for a reply, the blush was sufficient, Greer made her way to the heart of the sanctuary.

The heavy velvet curtains swallowed the outside, ushering Greer into a realm of hushed whispers and heightened senses. The air thrummed with a suppressed energy that made the fine hairs on her arms stand on end. The scent of leather and expensive perfume mingled with the muskier aroma of arousal and the faint metallic tang of blood. Candlelight flickered, casting dancing shadows across the hardwood floor; illuminating the curve of a bare shoulder, the glint of a piercing, the fleeting touch of a hand on a thigh. A low, pulsing beat vibrated under her soles, mingling with the soft murmur of conversations and the occasional gasp of pleasure that cut through the air.

This was no common club. It was a haven, a space for those seeking exploration and trust, where consent was revered, and desires were given voice. For Greer, it was also one of the rare places where she could feed without fear of harm.

The hostess, Gillian, a tall woman with a commanding presence and a cascade of platinum hair, approached her. 'Welcome back, Ms Dubhán. We missed you on Thursday.'

Greer offered a polite smile. 'Life's been busy.'

The woman's gaze lingered, assessing, but not intrusive. 'Understood. Your usual preferences?'

'Yes,' Greer replied, her tone even. 'Someone who understands my needs and is... discrete.

The woman nodded and gestured toward a corner of

the space. 'Hannah. She's new, but I think you'll like her. You'll find her... attentive.'

Greer inclined her head in thanks and made her way across the area. As she approached, the woman looked up, her striking green eyes meeting Greer's with a mix of curiosity and confidence. She was dressed simply, but her allure was in her confidence, her posture relaxed yet inviting.

'Mind if I join you?' Greer asked, her tone polite but carrying an undertone of command.

Hannah's lips curved into a small smile. 'Please do.'

The initial conversation was light, an exchange of names and boundaries. Hannah's tone was smooth, her words laced with intrigue but grounded in certainty. Greer appreciated that. She needed someone who understood the importance of trust, of clarity.

'What brings you here?' Hannah asked after a moment, her gaze steady.

Greer hesitated, choosing her words carefully. 'Sometimes, it's about finding connection in a manner that doesn't require explanation.' *A connection that isn't you, Freya.* The thought flashed, unbidden.

Hannah nodded slowly, her eyes searching Greer's face. 'I can understand that.'

The conversation ebbed and flowed until Hannah leaned closer, her tone dropping to a conspiratorial whisper. 'Shall we?'

Greer allowed Hannah to lead her further into the private alcove. The younger woman reached out, her fingertips grazing Greer's cheek with a feather-light touch. Greer leaned into the contact, her eyes fluttering closed for a brief moment. When she opened them again, Hannah had moved closer, her lips hovering a mere breath away.

'Tell me what you want,' Hannah murmured, her tone low and inviting.

Greer's gaze darkened, the hunger within her stirring to life. *Not you,* a traitorous voice whispered, *it's not you.*

'I want to taste you,' she replied, ignoring the inner monologue. 'But only if you desire it too.'

Hannah's smile widened, her eyes sparkling with anticipation. 'I do. I want everything you have to offer.' *Everything? Could you handle everything*? The thought flickered, but she pushed it down.

Permission granted, Greer closed the gap between them, capturing Hannah's lips in a searing kiss. It started slow, almost tentative, but quickly deepened as their bodies melded together. Hannah's hands roamed Greer's back, sliding under her shirt to caress the smooth skin beneath.

Greer broke the kiss, trailing her lips down the column of Hannah's throat. She paused at her pulse point, feeling the rapid flutter beneath the delicate skin. The scent of Hannah's arousal mixed with the tantalising aroma of her blood, making Greer's head spin with want.

'May I?' Greer asked, her tone loaded with desire as her fingertips brushed the top button of Hannah's blouse.

'Please,' Hannah breathed, her chest heaving.

Greer made quick work of the buttons, parting the fabric to reveal the smooth expanse of Hannah's chest, and a delicate lace bra. She dipped her head, trailing kisses along Hannah's collarbone before moving lower. With a rough tug, she released Hannah's breast from the lace. Hannah arched into the touch, a soft moan escaping her lips as Greer's mouth closed around a taut nipple.

As Greer lavished attention on Hannah's hardening pink nipples, her hand slid lower, slipping beneath the hem of Hannah's skirt. Hannah's hips pressed forward, seeking more contact as Greer's fingers brushed upwards against the dampness of her underwear.

'Tell me if you want me to stop,' Greer murmured against Hannah's flesh, her fingers teasing the sensitive skin through the fabric.

'Don't you dare,' Hannah gasped, her hand fisting in Greer's hair.

Greer smirked, slipping her hand inside to stroke the slick heat of her folds. Hannah's head fell back against the wall, her mouth falling open in a silent cry of pleasure as Greer's fingers circled her most sensitive spot.

Greer worked her hand in tandem with her mouth, sucking the erect pink bud, teasing it with her teeth, building Hannah higher and higher. Her fingers slid inside, fluttering against the tension coiling in Hannah's body, the telltale tightening of her inner walls signalling her impending release.

Just as Hannah was about to climax, Greer pulled back slightly. Hannah whimpered at the loss of contact, her eyes flying open to meet Greer's heated gaze.

'I want to taste you,' Greer repeated, her tone a low, urgent whisper. 'All of you.'

Hannah's eyes widened, understanding dawning. She tilted her head to the side, exposing the graceful line of her neck. 'I trust you,' she breathed.

As Greer's arousal heightened, she felt the familiar sensation of her razor-sharp nail emerging on her forefinger, a unique trait of the Baobhan Sith. With practiced control, she grazed the nail along Hannah's throat, applying just enough pressure to create a thin, shallow cut. Hannah gasped, her body trembling with a mix of anticipation and pleasure as a small bead of blood welled up from the cut.

The first taste of Hannah's blood hit Greer's tongue like

dark wine, rich and heady. She licked at the shallow wound, savouring each drop as her fingers resumed their skilful ministrations, bringing Hannah closer and closer to the edge.

Just as the pleasure was becoming too much to bear, Greer sealed the small cut on Hannah's neck with a final brush of her tongue, thrust her fingers deep, curling them just so and used her thumb to tease her clit. Hannah shattered with a hoarse cry, her release crashing over her in wave after wave of ecstasy. Greer held her through it, easing her down with gentle caresses and soothing words.

When Hannah finally stilled, her body going lax in Greer's arms, Greer pressed a soft kiss to her forehead.

'That was incredible,' Hannah murmured, her tone hazy with satisfaction.

Greer smiled, tenderness softening her sharp features. 'You were exquisite,' she replied, adjusting Hannah's clothing and guiding her to the plush chaise in the corner of the alcove.

But as Hannah drifted in the afterglow, Greer's thoughts turned unbidden to Freya. The memory of her energy, her intoxicating scent, the way she made Greer vibrate in her presence... it all crashed over Greer like a tidal wave.

She knew it was dangerous to want more, to crave the kind of connection that went beyond fleeting pleasure and carefully controlled feeding. But as she looked down at Hannah's sated form, Greer couldn't help but imagine what it would be like to share this part of herself with Freya – not just her body, but her heart and soul as well.

It was a terrifying thought, one that threatened to shatter the carefully constructed walls Greer had built around herself over the years. But as she slipped out of the alcove and made her way back into the night, Greer knew one thing for certain: Freya had awoken something within her, something that refused to be ignored or denied.

Chapter Five

The Shadows Beneath

The flat was quieter than Greer anticipated, yet it matched her contemplative state as she lingered in the doorway, absorbing the understated refinement of Freya's home. Welcoming, unpretentious, with just a hint of bohemian artistry, it mirrored its occupant perfectly. Shelves overflowed with well-worn novels and art theory books, lining the walls. An assortment of cushions adorned the comfortable, lived-in sofa. A partially completed painting rested against one wall, and the subtle scent of sandalwood permeated the air, soothing and inviting.

'So, what's your verdict?' Freya asked as she placed two steaming mugs of tea on the low coffee table, her tone cheerful yet laced with a hint of nervous curiosity. She'd insisted Greer come over after their café rendezvous the previous day, expressing a desire to share 'something inspiring.'

Greer offered a gentle smile. 'It's very... you.'

'I'll interpret that as a compliment,' Freya teased, her grin broadening as she settled onto the sofa. She motioned to the space beside her. 'Come on. Make yourself comfortable.'

Greer paused briefly before sinking into the sofa. It was more inviting than she expected, the tension she usually carried in her shoulders easing. Freya's proximity, a mere breath away, sent a subtle yet palpable physical exhilaration through her.

'So, this piece you wanted to share?' Greer inquired, as she glanced toward the canvas.

Freya blushed, and she waved a dismissive hand. 'It's not finished. But...' Her gaze softened as she turned toward the painting. 'It's something I've been working on for a while. But it feels like it's lacking something. I thought perhaps viewing it through someone else's perspective might provide some insight.'

Greer's eyebrow arched. 'And you selected me?'

Freya's smile turned contemplative. 'You perceive things differently to most, and you're an architect, so you understand structure, form, balance. Maybe you'll spot something I've overlooked.'

The vulnerability in her tone stirred something profound within Greer, a pull she couldn't resist. Standing, she approached the canvas, her steps measured, as if nearing something sacred. The painting was a maelstrom of colours—fiery reds bleeding into cooler blues, punctuated by bold black lines that seemed to anchor the chaos. It was simultaneously beautiful and unsettling, evoking an emotion Greer couldn't quite articulate.

'It's raw,' she said finally, her tone hushed. 'Intense. Like it's striving to communicate something but hasn't discovered the right language yet.'

Freya joined her, standing near enough that Greer could feel the subtle warmth radiating from her body. 'Precisely,' she murmured. 'That's how it feels to me, too. Like it's just beyond my grasp.'

Greer's gaze flickered to Freya, her breath catching at the way the other woman's eyes shimmered with passion and frustration. 'Maybe it's not about finding the words. Maybe it's about allowing the silence to speak.'

Freya blinked, her lips parting as if to respond, but no words emerged. Instead, she smiled softly, her gaze exploring Greer's face. 'You're far more profound than you let on, you know that?'

Greer's lips curved into a subtle smirk. 'Don't let it shatter the mystique.'

Freya laughed, a sound that sent warmth unfurling through Greer's chest. The moment lingered, charged yet tender, until Freya broke the spell by stepping back. 'I'll consider your advice,' she said, her tone playful as she returned to the sofa.

Greer followed, though her mind was still entangled in the threads of their interaction. As she settled back into her seat, Freya handed her one of the mugs, their fingers grazing briefly. The contact was fleeting, yet it sent a spark racing up Greer's arm.

They sipped their tea in companionable silence for a while, the distant hum of the street filtering through the windows. Greer found herself sinking deeper into the sofa, soothed by Freya's presence and the unspoken connection that seemed to weave itself tighter with each passing moment.

'You're difficult to read,' Freya said suddenly, her tone piercing the quiet. Her tone wasn't accusatory, merely inquisitive. 'It's like you've got walls within walls. But then, every now and then, I catch a glimpse of something beneath. Something... softer.'

Greer's fingers tightened slightly around her mug. 'That's a perilous habit, peeking beneath people's walls.'

Freya's smile didn't waver. 'Only if they have something to conceal.'

Silence stretched between them, not awkward but weighted. Greer considered deflecting, guiding the conversation back to safer territory, but something in Freya's gaze held her captive.

'Maybe I do,' she admitted quietly. 'But not all walls are meant to keep people out. Sometimes they're there to keep things in.'

Freya's expression softened, and she leaned forward slightly, her hand resting on the edge of the sofa cushion. 'And maybe some things aren't meant to stay hidden forever.'

Greer's breath hitched, her pulse thrumming in her ears. God, this conversation was infuriatingly cryptic. Every instinct in Greer's body screamed at her to close the distance, to feel Freya's warmth against her skin again. Her hand twitched with the urge to reach out, to trace the delicate line of Freya's jaw.

Freya's gaze dropped briefly to Greer's lips before meeting her eyes again. Her tone, when she spoke, was barely above a whisper. 'Tell me if I'm wrong.'

Greer's control wavered, her carefully constructed barriers trembling under the weight of Freya's quiet intensity. 'You're not,' she murmured.

The words hung in the air like a challenge, a confession, and an invitation all at once. Freya moved first, closing the space between them with a tentative yet purposeful kiss. Her lips were warm, soft, and utterly disarming, and for a moment, Greer allowed herself to sink into the sensation, to forget everything but the woman in front of her.

But then, as though she'd been zapped with a cattle prod, reality struck back. Greer pulled away, and rose abruptly from the sofa. 'I should go,' she said, her words clipped and hurried.

Freya blinked, confusion and hurt warring with a flicker of something else in her eyes—a spark of understanding, perhaps, or maybe even a touch of anger. 'Did I...?'

'It's not you,' Greer interrupted, her tone softer now but still firm. 'I just... I need time.'

Without waiting for a response, she moved toward the exit, her movements brisk and deliberate. The weight of Freya's gaze followed her, and it took every ounce of strength Greer had not to look back.

As the door shut behind her, Greer exhaled, her heart pounding as she stepped into the cool night air. She'd let herself get too close, too exposed. And yet, as she walked away, she couldn't shake the thought that some things were worth the risk.

The shadows of her past, the hunger that lurked beneath the surface, the walls she'd built to protect herself and others—they all seemed to pale in comparison to the light Freya had ignited within her. It was a dangerous game, this dance of vulnerability and desire, but for the first time in centuries, Greer found herself wanting to play.

She knew there would be consequences, that the truth of her nature would eventually come to light. But in that moment, as she walked the quiet streets of Edinburgh, Greer allowed herself to hope. Hope for a future where she could be seen, truly seen—her darkness and her light—and still be accepted, as Freya, with her open heart and perceptive gaze, seemed capable of doing. Hope for a connection that went beyond the physical, beyond the hunger that drove her.

Chapter Six

A Friend from the Shadows

Pushing open the heavy oak door, Greer was greeted by the familiar chime of a bell that sounded like it had been forged in a forgotten century. The air inside Diorbhail's Antiques was thick with the scent of history – aged wood polished to a gleam, the patina of leather worn soft by countless hands, the metallic tang of tarnished silver, and the earthy aroma of ancient coins. Sunlight filtered through the grime-coated windows, illuminating a chaotic tableau of artefacts and relics. A suit of armour stood guard in one corner, its metal cold and unforgiving to the touch. A tapestry depicting a hunt hung on one wall, its faded threads whispering of forgotten pastimes and long-dead prey. Each object in the shop seemed to vibrate with a silent energy, a story waiting to be unearthed.

'If you're here to gripe about my exorbitant prices, Greer, save your breath,' Dior called from behind the counter, not looking up from the small, intricate clock she was cleaning. 'And if you're here to actually purchase something for once, I might just faint from the shock.'

Greer smirked as she sauntered in, running a finger

along the cold metal of the suit of armour. 'Wouldn't dream of depriving you of such entertainment, Dior.'

Dior turned, her sharp green eyes glinting with mischief as her dark hair caught the light. Her tailored jacket and fingerless gloves lent her the air of a rogue rather than an antiquities dealer. She leaned back, resting a hip against the counter. 'You're a nuisance. But I suppose even nuisances need company, especially such beautiful ones.'

Greer approached, her gaze drifting over a delicate silver drinking quaich displayed on velvet. She picked it up, turning the cool metal over in her hands. 'This new?'

'A George III Scottish provincial drinking quaich,' Dior said, adopting a theatrical air of grandeur as she placed a hand on her hip. 'Inverness, circa 1800, by Alexander Stewart. And before you ask, yes, some bloody know-it-all customer had the audacity to correct me on it. Can you imagine the arrogance? Correcting me on something I crafted with my own hands.'

Greer laughed, setting the quaich back on the counter, her fingers lingering near Dior's, almost, but not quite, touching. 'You never let them live it down, do you?'

'Never,' Dior replied with a dramatic wave of her hand, her eyes sparkling. 'If I had a shilling for every self-important collector who thought they knew more than me, I'd...' She paused, grinning. 'Well, I'd have enough to buy that yacht I've always wanted.'

She'd never buy a yacht. The thought brought a smile to Greer's face as a comfortable silence settled between them, filled only with the rhythmic tick of the clock Dior was cleaning.

But Dior's expression shifted, her gaze sharpening as she leaned forward, her arm brushing Greer's in a way that was too deliberate to be accidental. 'You've got that look again,' she said, tilting her head. Her eyes, usually sparkling with amusement, now held a serious glint. 'The one from the fifties, when you were obsessed with that Robertson woman. The scientist with the political aspirations?'

Greer's brow furrowed. 'I don't have a look.' *Not one she can see, anyway.*

Dior raised an eyebrow, stepping closer, invading Greer's personal space in a manner only she was allowed. 'Oh, but you do. A certain intensity in your eyes, a kind of... restless energy. You went on and on about how exquisite she'd taste, drove me mad with it. And when you finally got your reward, what was it you said? Battery acid mixed with spoiled meat? You were ill for weeks, scrubbing your mouth with carbolic until you sneezed bubbles.'

Greer winced at the memory, the phantom taste of bitterness and decay lingering on her tongue. 'It's not like that.'

Dior's eyes narrowed knowingly, her hand coming to rest on Greer's arm, a silent acknowledgment of their shared intimacy. 'Worse, then.'

Silence stretched between them, heavy with unspoken truths. Greer looked away, her fingers tracing the edge of the counter, a knot of unease tightening in her stomach. Dior was right. This was worse.

This time, instinctively, Greer knew Freya would satisfy her in a way no one else ever had—body, mind, and soul. The thought terrified and thrilled her in equal measure, a heady cocktail of anticipation and dread.

'Want my advice?' Dior said, her tone softer now, her fingers tracing small circles on Greer's arm, a gesture both comforting and possessive.

Greer met her gaze, arching a brow. 'I'm afraid to ask.'

'Get yourself a Greggs sausage roll,' Dior said with a

smirk, stepping back and breaking the tension. 'Always hits the spot.'

Greer barked a laugh, shaking her head. 'You're incorrigible.'

'And you're predictable,' Dior shot back. She leaned in, her tone dropping to a more intimate level. 'Just be careful, Greer. Obsession... it's not always kind to us.'

Greer nodded, her humour fading. She reached out, her hand briefly covering Dior's in a silent acknowledgment of their shared history, the lovers they'd had, the dangers they'd faced. 'Thanks, Dior.'

As she turned toward the exit, the bell chiming above her, Greer couldn't shake the weight of Dior's words. Obsession. A risky game, one she'd played before with disastrous consequences. But this felt different. Freya felt different.

It wasn't just the allure of her scent, the promise of her taste. It was the way she made Greer feel, the way she seemed to see beneath her carefully constructed façade to the vulnerabilities beneath. The way she made her want to be seen. It was terrifying and exhilarating, a rush unlike anything Greer had experienced in her long life.

As she walked, her mind drifted to their last encounter, to the softness of Freya's lips and the warmth of her touch. It had been a moment of weakness, a slip in her ironclad control. But it had also been a glimpse of something more, a tantalising hint of the connection she craved.

Greer knew she was walking a thin line, balancing on the edge of a precipice that could lead to either ecstasy or ruin. But as she wove through the crowded streets, the memory of Freya's smile, her laughter, her gentle understanding, refused to fade. What was it about Freya that made her believe this time might be different? Was it her open heart, her perceptive gaze, the way she seemed to accept both the darkness and the light within Greer?

Perhaps Dior was right. Perhaps obsession was too dangerous. But Greer found herself willing to play, consequences be damned. Because in the end, the promise of Freya's light, the chance to bask in her radiance, to be truly seen by her, was worth any risk.

Chapter Seven

The Art of Hunger

The invitation beckoned from Greer's desk like a beautifully crafted trap. Heavy cream card stock, embossed with dark green lettering: 'The Emergence of Freya Solasta - Solo Exhibition' She'd been staring at it for twenty minutes, her finger tracing the elegant script while her mind wandered to less elegant places—Freya's lips parting for her, the heat of her breath on Greer's neck, the intoxicating scent of her studio clinging to her skin.

Fuck it, she muttered, reaching for her mobile.

Three missed calls from Dior. *Predictable.*

The phone barely rang once before Dior's voice cut through. 'Please tell me you're not going.'

'Hello to you too,' Greer said, leaning back in her chair. 'And why wouldn't I?'

'Oh, I don't know,' Dior's sarcasm crackled through the line. 'Maybe because the last time you got this obsessed with someone, the Great Fire of London of 1666 mysteriously started?'

'That wasn't my fault,' Greer protested. 'And I helped rebuild. Eventually.'

'You're missing the point, darling. This—'

'Woman,' Greer inserted, before Dior could.

'—woman, has you acting like a lovesick teenager.'

Greer glanced at the invitation again. Eight o'clock. The gallery would be packed—Thomas would have made sure of that. The thought of him hovering around Freya made something dark and possessive curl in her chest.

'I have to go,' she said finally. 'It's important to her.'

'Important to her, or important to your libido?'

'Goodbye, Dior.'

She hung up before her friend could protest further, but Dior's words lingered. She was right—this was dangerous. Every time Greer got close to Freya, her control frayed a little more. The hunger, usually so carefully managed, grew sharper, more demanding.

But the alternative—staying away—felt impossible.

❄

The gallery was filled with a cacophony of sounds—the gentle clink of glasses, the scrape of shoes against polished floors, the murmur of conversations punctuated by the occasional burst of laughter. The air was thick with the scent of expensive perfume, vying with the sharp scent of paint from Freya's new works and the subtle tang of nervous sweat. Greer made her entrance fashionably late, her heels clicking a confident rhythm against the polished floor, the scent of her own perfume—dark and musky—trailing behind her like a predator's scent.

She'd chosen her outfit carefully: a black suit that exuded power, tailored to emphasise every curve, the sharp lines a deliberate contrast to the softness she knew Freya preferred. The jacket hugged her shoulders, the trousers...

well, they'd made more than one head turn as she walked in. The fabric felt like a second skin, a reminder of the hunter she was trying to keep contained. Her hair fell in dark waves past her shoulders, and her lipstick was the exact shade of fresh blood—a private joke she couldn't resist.

'You came.' Thomas materialised from behind a particularly noisy group, his smile as artificial as his tan. 'I wasn't sure you would, after... everything.'

Greer took a slow sip of wine. 'Wouldn't have missed it for the world.'

'No,' he said, his tone dropping, a hint of menace in his tone as he moved closer. 'You wouldn't, would you? Even though you know you should stay away.'

Before she could respond, a wave of movement parted the crowd. Freya had emerged from the back room, a vision in midnight blue, and Greer's breath caught.

She wore a dress the colour of midnight, dotted with tiny crystals that caught the light like stars. Her hair was swept up, exposing the elegant line of her neck. People turned to watch her as she moved, drawn in by her energy—she radiated excitement and nerves, her cheeks flushed, eyes bright.

Their gazes met across the space, and for a moment, everything else fell away. Freya's smile small and private, sent heat coursing through Greer's body. Then someone called Freya's name, and the moment broke.

'Stunning, isn't she?' Thomas murmured, his tone a little too close to her ear. 'So full of life.'

The threat in his voice was subtle but clear. Greer's fingers tightened around her glass. 'Careful, Thomas.'

'Or what?' His smile never wavered. 'You'll show everyone exactly what you are?'

She turned to face him fully, letting the shadows

around them deepen unnaturally, her tone taking on a low, almost inhuman resonance. 'Do you really want to find out?'

He stepped back, instinct overriding bravado. 'Just stay away from her, Greer. She's not for you.'

'That's not your decision to make.'

She moved away before he could respond, drifting through the crowd toward the main exhibition space. And there, taking up the entire back wall, was a painting that stopped her dead in her tracks.

It was massive, easily eight feet tall, dominated by swirling shades of darkness. But within the darkness, something moved—a figure composed of shadow and hunger with eyes that seemed to burn right through you. Around it, splashes of crimson bloomed like drops of blood in water. *Herself.*

She saw herself in the painting, or rather, the monster she feared she was.

The plaque beside it read simply: 'Hunger.'

'What do you think?'

Greer hadn't heard Freya approach—a rare feat that spoke to how captivated she'd been. The artist stood close enough that Greer could smell her perfume, the usual undertone of sandalwood to which she had become accustomed. Freya's gaze flicked from the painting to Greer.

'It's...' Greer swallowed hard as she focused on the painting. *You've been watching me. Seeing me. The real me.*

'You're hard to look away from.' Freya's tone was soft, meant only for her. 'Even when you're trying to disappear.'

Greer turned to face her, and the air between them stirred with possibility. 'Freya...'

'Don't.' Freya stepped closer, her hand reaching out to brush a stray strand of hair from Greer's cheek, her touch sending shivers down her spine. 'Don't pull away again. I'm tired of playing this game.'

'It's not a game.'

'Then what is it?'

The question hung between them, laden with unspoken truths. Greer could hear Freya's heartbeat, smell the warmth of her skin, feel the pull that grew stronger every time they were near each other. *She wanted to lean in, to close the distance, to taste her again, to feel her hands on her body, to lose herself in the moment and forget all the reasons why she shouldn't.*

'It's dangerous,' Greer said finally, her tone rough.

Freya's laugh was low, knowing. 'Good.'

Before Greer could respond, a group of critics descended on Freya, pulling her away with effusive praise and pointed questions. But as she was led away, she glanced back over her shoulder, and the look in her eyes made Greer's centuries-old heart skip a beat.

She was in trouble. Deep, exquisite trouble.

Dior was going to kill her.

Chapter Eight

Echoes of the Past

Sleep had always been more of a luxury than a necessity for Greer, but tonight it eluded her entirely. The painting haunted her—not just its imagery, but what it meant. Freya had seen her, truly seen her, even if she didn't understand what she was seeing yet.

Greer paced her penthouse, the lights of Edinburgh twinkling below like earthbound stars. The city, like her, had a way of holding onto its soul even as the centuries swept by, a familiar ache that never quite faded.

Edinburgh, 1636. The candlelight had caught Jean's hair just so, turning it to spun gold. She'd been beautiful, passionate, and utterly fearless. 'I know what you are,' she'd whispered that first night, pressing Greer's hand to her throat, her pulse a frantic drum against her skin. 'Take what you need.'

Greer squeezed her eyes shut against the memory, her hand going to her own throat, as though she could still feel the ghost of Jean's touch. Jean had been the first to offer herself freely, to understand that the taking wasn't just about hunger, but a strange, intimate kind of exchange—a sharing of life force, a fleeting glimpse into each other's souls. She'd also been the first to die—not by Greer's hand, but by time's inevitable march. That was the curse of it all—not the hunger, but the loss.

Fuck, Greer muttered, rubbing a hand over her face, the phantom scent of Jean's lavender perfume lingering in her memory. She needed a drink. Something stronger than wine.

Her mobile buzzed—Dior.

'I can feel you brooding from across town,' Dior's voice was sharp, but tinged with amusement. 'Stop it.'

'I'm not brooding,' Greer lied, pouring herself a generous dram of whisky. 'I'm... reminiscing.'

'Even worse. Is it Margaret again? Or Catherine? Don't tell me it's the insufferable poet from the 1890s—what was her name?'

'Alice,' Greer supplied, a reluctant smile tugging at her lips. 'And she wasn't insufferable. Just... intense. And a bit melodramatic, if I'm honest.'

'Melodramatic? She wrote an entire sonnet about your kiss. I believe my favourite line was, 'Within my soul I hear the spring rain fall, and feel the kiss...'

Despite herself, Greer chuckled. 'You're never going to let that go, are you?'

'Never,' Dior agreed cheerfully. 'Someone has to remember your embarrassing phases. Speaking of which, this current one...'

'Don't.'

'I've been to the gallery. I've seen what she did. She painted you, Greer. She painted your hunger.' Dior's tone was serious now, all traces of humour gone.

The whisky burned going down. 'She painted what she thought she saw.'

'And what happens when she sees more?'

Paris, 1832. Anne-Marie's screams echoed through the years, the terror in her eyes as she finally understood what Greer was, what they'd been sharing. The taste of fear in her blood that last time, bitter and wrong, had stayed with Greer for decades.

'It won't come to that,' Greer said quietly, her voice barely a whisper. 'I won't let her get close enough.'

'No,' Dior's tone softened, as if she could see the memories playing in Greer's mind. 'You won't. Because you're going to walk away. Aren't you?'

The question settled between them, weighted with centuries of similar moments, similar choices. But this time...

'I can't,'. Greer admitted. 'God help me, Dior, but I can't.'

She could almost hear Dior's sad smile. 'I know, darling. I know.'

After hanging up, Greer moved to her desk, pulling out a leather-bound journal—one of many she'd kept over the centuries. Inside, sketches and photographs traced the path of her existence: Margaret's delicate profile, Catherine's laughing eyes, Alice's dramatic poses, Anne-Marie's final terrified expression.

And now Freya. She'd started appearing in Greer's sketches weeks ago—the curve of her neck, the way her hands moved when she talked about art, the fearless light in her eyes when she'd said 'Good.' in answer to the danger.

The hunger stirred, different from the physical need she satisfied at the Crimson Sanctuary. This was deeper, more dangerous—the hunger for connection, for understanding, for someone to see her, the way the painting had, and not recoil. *For something real in a world that felt increasingly artificial.*

Her mobile buzzed again—a text this time. Freya.

'The painting isn't finished yet. I need your muse.'

Greer stared at the message, her finger hovering over the reply button.

Edinburgh, 1923. Clara's gentle voice: 'We all need someone to see us as we are, love. Even monsters like you and me.'

Clara had been different—not a lover, but a friend. Another of their kind who'd taught Greer that control was possible, that hunger didn't have to mean destruction. Until Clara herself misplaced her faith in a young nurse. An iron bar to the heart had brought their love affair to a dramatic end. The nurse had spent the next twenty-six years in Broadmoor, while Clara was nothing more than dust—but her wisdom remained.

What was it Clara had said? Something about the heart being a compass... An ironic smile touched Greer's lips.

'On my way,' she typed, her heart pounding an uneven rhythm against her ribs, then pressed send before she could change her mind.

Some hungers, she was learning, couldn't be denied. The trick was surviving them.

Chapter Nine

Shadows and Light

Freya stood in front of the unfinished painting, brush suspended mid-stroke, remembering how Greer had looked at her gallery piece two weeks before. Not just *looked*—recognised something in it. Something that had made her pale, made her pull back even as her gaze had darkened with what Freya could only describe as hunger. *What had she seen in it?*

There had been no contact since that night, despite Freya's efforts. 'Shit,' she muttered, lowering the brush. A drop of crimson paint, like blood, splattered onto the drop cloth. Three hours, and she'd managed to add exactly two brushstrokes. Both wrong.

Her phone sat silent on the paint-splattered table nearby. No response from Greer since their late-night session, when she'd finally shown up looking devastating in that same black suit, her hair slightly wild as if she'd been running her hands through it. They'd stood in front of the painting together, not quite touching, while Freya tried to explain her vision. But what had come out instead was more like a riddle: 'It needs more shadow,' she'd said. 'More depth. Like there's something moving beneath the surface.' The memory made her shiver—her own words had sounded strange, almost obssessed.

Greer had made a sound—not quite a laugh, not quite a groan. 'You see too much,' she'd said, and then she'd left, her exit as abrupt as every other time they'd gotten close to... whatever this was between them. An understanding, a precipice, a connection that defied logic.

The buzz of the studio doorbell jolted her from her thoughts. For a heartbeat, her pulse quickened—*but no, it was just Thomas*, looking irritatingly pleased with himself.

'Darling,' he said smoothly, carrying what looked like gallery contracts. 'We need to talk about the showing. The response has been phenomenal. Simply phenomenal.'

'Thomas,' Freya sighed, wiping her hands on her already paint-stained jeans. 'I'm working.'

He glanced at the painting, his expression shifting, a flicker of something unreadable in his gaze. 'Ah yes. Your... portrait.'

'It's not a portrait,' she said.

'No?' he said, his smile turning knowing. 'Then why does it look so much like her? The way she moves, the way she watches. It's all there.'

Freya turned back to the canvas, frustrated because he wasn't wrong. Every brushstroke had been an attempt to capture something she'd glimpsed in Greer—that careful grace, that contained power, that sense of something ancient and dangerous lurking just beneath the surface. A shudder ran through her as she stared at the canvas. She still hadn't managed to capture it.

'I'm worried about you,' Thomas said, his words taking

on a lecturing quality that made her want to throw something. 'Getting involved with Greer Dubhán... it's not wise.'

'I'm not involved with her,' she said, a beat too late.

'No?' He raised an eyebrow. 'Then why is she in every piece you've painted for the past month?'

Freya stared at her studio walls. He was right again, damn him. The smaller studies, the sketches, even the abstract pieces—they all held echoes of Greer. The curve of her neck, the line of her jaw, the intensity of her gaze. She had become her unintentional muse, whether she liked it or not.

'She's interesting,' Freya said finally, lamely. 'Artistically.'

'She's dangerous,' Thomas said, his words sharp. 'More than you know.'

Something in his manner, a hint of genuine warning, made Freya turn to face him fully. 'What does that mean?'

'Just be careful,' he said, setting the contracts down with a pointed look. 'Some mysteries aren't meant to be solved.'

After he left, Freya grabbed her phone and keys, a sudden surge of determination coursing through her. She'd had enough of mysteries and warnings and people talking around whatever truth they were all so careful to avoid.

Greer's architecture practice occupied the top floor of a renovated Georgian building in New Town. The receptionist—young, nervous, and clearly trained well—tried to stop her.

'I'm sorry, Ms. Dubhán isn't taking visitors today. Or... most days, actually.'

'Tell her it's Freya Solasta,' Freya said.

'I... she's very clear about interruptions—'

'Tell her,' Freya said, her words sharper than she

intended, 'that if she doesn't want to see me, she can tell me herself.'

The receptionist hesitated, then pressed a button on her desk phone. After a moment of hushed conversation, she looked up with surprise. 'Go on in. End of the hall, black door.'

The office suited Greer perfectly—minimalist, elegant, with large sash windows offering a stunning view of the city. Greer stood by those windows, her back to the entrance, a sight that stopped Freya in her tracks.

'You're avoiding me,' Freya said, proud of how steady she sounded, despite the way her heart hammered against her ribs.

'Yes.' Greer didn't turn around.

'Why?'

Now Greer did turn, and the look in her eyes, a mix of longing and something darker, made Freya's breath catch. 'Because you're starting to see me.'

'Is that such a bad thing?'

Greer moved then, crossing the space between them with that fluid grace that had first caught Freya's attention. She stopped just short of touching, close enough that Freya could smell her perfume—something dark and complex, a subtle reminder of her presence.

'What do you see?' Greer asked, her words low and intense, a hint of vulnerability in her gaze. 'When you paint me, what do you see?'

Freya met her stare, refusing to back down. 'Power. Mystery. Hunger.' She took a breath, her heart pounding. 'Pain.'

Greer's laugh was soft and bitter. 'And you're not afraid?'

'Should I be?'

Instead of answering, Greer reached out, her fingers hovering just above Freya's cheek without making contact. They stood close enough to feel the heat from each other's skin, neither willing to step back.

'You should run,' Greer said, her hand trembling slightly. 'Far and fast.'

Freya leaned in, closing that last fraction of space, until Greer's fingers, cool and smooth, brushed her skin. Trails of fire followed in their wake. 'I'm not going anywhere,' Freya said firmly. 'So you can either keep running, or you can trust me enough to stay.'

I can't. The words splintered in Greer's throat. 'Please, Freya. Just... let it go.'

'No.' Freya took a step closer, until they were almost chest to chest. 'You don't get to look at me the way you do, to inspire everything I create, to make me feel like this, and then just... disappear.'

'Freya—'

'I'll figure it out eventually,' she said, her gaze not leaving Greer's face. 'Whatever you're hiding. I'm good at seeing what others miss. You said so yourself.'

Something flickered in Greer's eyes—fear? Admiration? Desire? Before Freya could decide, the insistent buzz of the intercom broke the silence. Greer's assistant announced her next call was on the line.

'Go,' Greer said softly, her gaze dark and unreadable. 'Please.'

Freya turned to depart, but at the exit, she paused, her hand on the doorknob. 'The painting really isn't finished, you know. Come by tonight. After dark.' She smiled slightly, a challenge in her eyes. 'That's when you prefer to move anyway, isn't it?'

She left before Greer could respond, but she felt those

dark eyes following her all the way out of the building. In her studio, she'd solve this mystery one brushstroke at a time. On canvas, truth had a way of revealing itself, even if it killed her.

Chapter Ten

Patterns in the Dark

Dreams bled into the corners of Freya's darkened bedroom, turning familiar shadows strange. Beneath a silver moon, Greer swayed, her movements as fluid as water. Intricate patterns adorned her skin, flowing from her exposed feet, swirling up her legs and disappearing beneath the hem of her dress. The marks pulsed with a soft, dark light, shifting and changing like shadows underwater. A whisper of wind carried the scent of damp earth and distant music, a haunting melody that seemed to beckon Freya closer.

Freya woke with a gasp, the remnants of the dream clinging to her like cobwebs. Her heart hammered against her ribs, a frantic drumbeat against the silence of her studio. She sat bolt upright, reaching out to switch on the bedside lamp, dispelling the lingering shadows. The moonlight through the window seemed to mock her, a pale imitation of the dream's intensity.

Her studio clock read 3:17 a.m. With shaking hands, she reached for her sketchbook, desperate to capture the patterns before they faded from memory. *'Tea,'* she muttered, pushing back the duvet. *'I need tea.'*

Her grandmother's package still sat unopened on the kitchen counter. She put the kettle on, the familiar hum a small comfort in the unsettling quiet. While it boiled, she finally tore open the brown paper wrapping. Inside was a leather-bound book, its spine cracked with age, pages soft and yellowed. A note fluttered to the floor.

'Found this clearing the attic. Your great-gran's last sketchbook. Remember how you used to sit for hours looking at her illustrations? Maybe it'll inspire something. Love, Gran x'

The kettle clicked off. Freya poured the water over the tea blend, the scent of chamomile, hibiscus, and rose momentarily soothing her racing thoughts. She curled up in her battered armchair, the warm mug a comforting weight in her hands, and opened the sketchbook.

The first few pages held familiar sights—selkies emerging from waves, kelpies with seaweed-tangled manes, pixies darting between flowers. Katherine's distinctive style brought each creature to vivid life, her notes scattered around the margins in elegant script.

Then she turned a page and the mug slipped from her numb fingers, clattering onto the floor, the sound lost beneath the sudden roar in her ears.

There, rendered in precise ink strokes, was Greer. Not exactly Greer—the drawing was dated 1947—but the likeness was uncanny. The same proud tilt of the head, the same dangerous grace in the pose. And there, wrapped around the figure's feet and ankles, were the exact patterns from Freya's dream.

Below the drawing, in Katherine's flowing hand, was a

single phrase: *Baobhan Sith—She who dances in the moonlight.*

The margin notes were sparse but specific:

Marks appear only in moonlight or moments of true nature.

Each pattern unique as a fingerprint.

Beautiful, deadly, eternal.

Freya's fingers traced the inked lines, her artist's eye noting every detail. The way the marks seemed to flow like water, the subtle suggestions of movement in static lines. She could almost feel them writhing beneath her touch, mirroring the way they had pulsed and shifted in her dream.

Laptop open, she found herself researching, her fingers flying across the keyboard. Keywords spilled across the search bar: *Baobhan Sith, Scottish folklore, night dancers, marking patterns.*

Time dissolved. Each click led her deeper, each source opened new questions. Stories of beautiful women who danced with travellers by moonlight. Tales of blood and seduction, of eternal hunger wrapped in eternal beauty. She stumbled upon a digitised version of an a digitised version of an old Gaelic ballad, its words transcribed in faded ink. The ballad told the tale of Isla, a Baobhan Sith who fell in love with a mortal fisherman named Callum. They met under the silver light of the moon, their passion as wild and untamed as the sea itself. Isla, consumed by her love for Callum, defied the ancient laws of her kind and revealed her true nature. Callum, initially entranced by her beauty and power, eventually succumbed to fear. He betrayed Isla, driving a blessed iron nail through her heart as she slept. The ballad ended: *'The sea remembers Isla's tears, and whispers her name on the wind. Beware the Baobhan Sith's love, for it burns with an eternal flame.'*

Dawn painted Edinburgh's rooftops in rose and gold, erasing the darkness. A shiver ran through her. Her phone had been buzzing periodically, but she'd been too absorbed to check it. Now, in the growing light, she saw the messages:

Greer [3:47 a.m.]: Still want me to see the painting?

Greer [4:15 a.m.]: Freya?

Greer [5:30 a.m.]: Everything all right

The last message had come just minutes ago:

Greer [6:03 a.m.]: Dawn's coming. Another time, perhaps.

Freya looked from the phone to the open sketchbook, to her own dream-inspired drawings scattered across her desk. Then back to Katherine's detailed rendering of a woman who could have been Greer's twin. The woman's expression was unreadable, her lips curved in a way that could be interpreted as a smile or a smirk, her eyes holding secrets Freya was suddenly desperate to uncover.

'Oh,' she whispered to her empty studio, a sudden, terrifying understanding dawning on her. 'Oh, fuck.' She grabbed her phone, her fingers fumbling as she typed out a reply.

Chapter Eleven

Blood and Ink

Sleep wasn't an option. Not with her mind racing and her great-grandmother's sketchbook burning a hole in her consciousness. Freya watched night turn to day, cradling her fourth cup of tea while surrounded by printouts, sketches, and her laptop's harsh glare. The Baobhan Sith. Beautiful women who danced with travellers in the moonlight. Who moved with inhuman grace, attuned to nature through every sense. Who hunted with eternal hunger.

Who never aged.

Freya's hands moved across her sketchpad almost unconsciously, recreating the strange markings from both her dream and Katherine's drawings. She'd tried Googling them—'supernatural birthmarks,' 'Celtic fairy markings,' 'Scottish vampire symbols'—but found nothing that matched exactly. These seemed unique, personal. Like Katherine had drawn them from life.

Her phone buzzed again. Thomas.

'Lunch? We need to discuss the exhibition.'

She ignored it, instead opening Katherine's sketchbook

again. The resemblance to Greer was uncanny—not just in the features, but in the essence. The way Katherine had captured that predatory stillness, that contained power. Had her great-grandmother known what she was drawing? The sparse notes suggested she might have.

A note fell from between the pages: an address in Old Town and a name—Dr Simon McKay, Folklore Studies.

Freya's heart jumped. She checked the time—10:47 a.m. Early enough.

She sent a message to Thomas, giving him the address from where he could pick her up and then wasted no more time.

The Celtic Studies department was housed in a glorious, Gothic building. Dr McKay's office was tucked away in a corner that smelled of must and coffee. The man himself matched his surroundings—older, tweed jacket, wire-rimmed glasses, beard more grey than brown.

'Katherine Solasta's granddaughter?' His eyes lit up when she introduced herself. 'Please, come in. I've been hoping someone from your family would find me.'

Freya blinked. 'You knew my great-grandmother?'

'Knew of her. Studied her work extensively.' He gestured to a shelf lined with familiar spines—Katherine's published works. 'Her illustrations weren't just art, you see. They were documentation.'

Freya's mouth went dry. She pulled out the sketchbook, opening it to the Baobhan Sith drawing. 'Documentation of what?'

McKay's expression shifted, becoming more guarded. 'Ah. You found that one.'

'What was she documenting, Dr McKay?'

He sighed, removing his glasses to clean them—a gesture that seemed more about buying time than improving visibility. 'Your great-grandmother had a gift. She saw things others missed. Things that preferred to remain hidden.'

'Like the Baobhan Sith?'

'Among others.' He replaced his glasses, studying her carefully. 'Why this sudden interest?'

Freya hesitated. 'The markings in her drawing—I've seen them. In dreams, at first, but...' She pulled out her own sketches. 'They're exact matches.'

McKay went still. 'When did these dreams start?'

'After I met...' Freya swallowed. 'Someone.'

'Someone beautiful? Graceful? Almost ethereal?'

She nodded.

'Miss Solasta.' His voice was gentle but urgent. 'These markings are unique to each individual. Like fingerprints, as your great-grandmother noted. If you're seeing the exact same patterns she drew in 1947...'

'Then it's the same woman,' Freya finished. Her head spun with the implications.

McKay pulled a book from his shelf, old and leather-bound. 'The Baobhan Sith were said to be irresistible to artists, poets, musicians. Something about the creative spirit calls to them.' He opened to a marked page. 'Your great-grandmother theorised they fed on more than just blood—they consumed inspiration, passion, the very essence of creativity.'

'But they didn't kill their...' Freya searched for the word.

'Lovers?' McKay suggested. 'Not always. Some stories speak of long relationships, of mutual exchange. The human offering blood and inspiration freely, the Baobhan Sith offering... other things in return.'

'What things?'

'Immortal love,' he said simply. 'And a muse that never dies.'

Freya thought of her paintings, how they'd come alive since meeting Greer. How colours seemed sharper, ideas flowed faster, her work deeper and more profound than ever before.

'There's more,' McKay said, pulling out another book. 'But perhaps—'

A shadow fell across the doorway. 'That's quite enough, Simon.'

Freya turned. Thomas stood there, his usual smooth charm replaced by something colder.

'Miss Solasta was just leaving,' he said, his tone brooking no argument.

'Like hell I am,' Freya began, but McKay cut in.

'Perhaps he's right.' He slipped a card into her hand. 'Come back tomorrow. Alone,' he said under his breath as he turned his back on Thomas.

Thomas's grip on her arm was firm but not cruel as he led her out. Once outside, she wrenched away. 'What the hell, Thomas?'

'You're playing with fire,' he said. 'And you're not the only one who could get burned.'

'What do you know about this?'

His laugh was bitter. 'More than I ever wanted to. Go home, Freya. We can discuss the exhibition another day. Paint your pretty pictures. Leave the monsters in the dark where they belong.'

He turned and walked away, angry, leaving her with more questions than answers. But one thing was becoming clear—Greer wasn't the only one keeping secrets.

Freya clutched the sketchbook tighter and headed

home. She had research to do, and a very specific painting to finish before the day ended.

Chapter Twelve

Hunger Games

The back room of Dior's Antique shop smelled of beeswax and old wood, with undertones of copper that made Greer's teeth ache. Both women wore sunglasses despite the dim lighting, a private joke about their shared nature that had long since lost its humour.

'You look like shit,' Dior observed, sprawled in her favourite Victorian armchair. 'Did our artist keep you up past sunrise?'

'I didn't see her.' Greer paced the confined space, her movements tight with restrained energy. 'She didn't answer my messages.'

'Probably for the best.'

Greer shot her a look over the rim of her Wayfarers. 'Don't start.'

'Me? Never.' Dior's smile was sharp. 'Though I notice you're wearing a groove in my eighteenth-century Persian carpet. Hungry?'

The word made Greer's stomach clench. Since meeting Freya, her hunger had become more insistent, harder to ignore. The controlled feeding at the Crimson Sanctuary barely took the edge off anymore. She wanted... more.

'It's not just physical hunger, is it?' Dior's tone softened with rare sympathy. 'You want to consume her completely. Art, passion, everything she is.'

'I want to protect her,' Greer corrected, but the words rang hollow.

'Hannah,' Dior called out. 'Come here, dear.'

The door opened, and Greer stiffened as a familiar figure entered—the woman from the Crimson Sanctuary. She looked different in the crisp blouse and pencil skirt, professional, but her eyes held the same knowing look. *Hannah.* Greer hadn't expected to see her here, and a flicker of surprise crossed her face.

Dior, ever observant, caught the flicker. 'I've had to feed and take comfort elsewhere, with your head so consumed by your latest fancy,' she said, her tone light but her eyes serious. She turned her gaze to Hannah, her tone hardening with command. 'Take off your clothes.'

The command wasn't for Greer's benefit—this was Dior and Hannah's own dance, practised and familiar. But as Hannah began unbuttoning her blouse, Greer caught the faint scent of her skin, the quickening of her pulse. Dior motioned for her to join them.

Any other night, it might have been enough. Any other hunger, it might have satisfied.

'No,' Greer said quietly, already moving toward the exit. 'But thank you for the offer.'

'Greer.' Dior's words stopped her. 'She's researching us. Your little artist. She visited Simon McKay today.'

Greer's hand froze on the doorknob. 'How do you know?'

'I know everything that happens in my city.' Dior waved

dismissively. 'The question is, what are you going to do about it?'

Through the door, Greer could hear the subtle sounds of Hannah undressing, the whisper of silk against skin. Behind her sunglasses, Dior's eyes would be darkening with hunger.

'Nothing,' Greer said finally. 'She deserves answers.'

'Answers get humans killed.'

'Not always.' Greer's tone was quiet but firm. 'Sometimes they just need to understand.'

Dior's laugh followed her out into the shop. 'Love makes you philosophical, darling. It also makes you stupid.'

Greer didn't bother responding. Outside, Edinburgh's twilight was gathering, shadows pooling in ancient corners. Freya was probably painting, her hands stained with colours that reminded Greer of blood. The thought made her hunger twist inside her, a living thing with claws and teeth. But beneath it was something deeper, more terrifying than hunger—a desperate need to be known, to be seen, even if that seeing might destroy them both.

She took off her sunglasses, letting the last rays of sun burn her sensitive eyes. Sometimes pain helped clear the mind, serving as a reminder you were still capable of emotion.

Chapter Thirteen

Shadow Dance

Greer had watched enough bad American true crime documentaries to know she shouldn't be there.

The rough grit of the rooftop scraped against her palms as she settled into her usual position, the chill night air biting through her thin jacket. Below, Freya's studio glowed with warm light, a beacon in the sea of Edinburgh's darkened rooftops. Greer could see her every move through the large windows—the way her brush danced across the canvas, the frustration in the clench of her jaw, the way she periodically ran a paint-stained hand through her hair, leaving streaks of colour against her forehead. The faint sounds of Freya's movements drifted up—the scrape of a stool against the wooden floor, the clink of a brush against a water jar, the soft sigh of frustration that made Greer's heart ache with a longing she couldn't name.

Tonight, Freya seemed possessed by some new energy. She moved between canvases with urgent purpose, consulting what looked like an old book, then returning to her work with renewed intensity. Even from this distance,

Greer could sense her focus, could almost taste the passion rolling off her in waves.

'This is getting pathetic,' she muttered to herself, but didn't move.

Her phone buzzed. Dior, of course. 'Stop stalking her and make a decision.'

Greer typed back: 'I'm not stalking. I'm protecting.'

'From what? The only danger to her is you.'

Ouch, thought Greer. She had already packed a bag, researched properties in remote parts of Scotland. She could disappear tonight, let Freya's fascination fade into memory. It would be cleaner, safer, kinder in the long run.

But then Freya brushed her hair back from her face, and Greer's resolve crumbled. Dior bid her goodnight. It seemed her friend and lover had given up trying to talk sense into her.

Movement in the studio caught her attention. Freya had stopped painting and was now pacing, talking on her phone. Her free hand gestured animatedly, and even without being able to hear, Greer could read the agitation in her movements.

Before she could stop herself, Greer pulled out her phone and called Thomas.

'What do you want?' His voice was clipped.

'She seems upset.'

A pause. 'Are you watching her? Christ, Greer.'

'What did you say to her, Thomas?'

'Only the truth. That some mysteries should stay buried. That some creatures should stay in the shadows where they belong.'

Greer's grip tightened on the phone. 'You had no right.'

'I had every right. Someone has to protect her since you clearly can't control yourself.'

In the studio Freya had ended her call and returned to painting, but her strokes seemed angry now, almost violent.

'She's not yours to protect,' Greer said softly.

'No? Then whose is she? Yours?' Thomas laughed bitterly. 'We both know how that ends. Or have you forgotten Anne-Marie?'

The name froze the breath in her lungs. 'That was different,' she said in barely a whisper.

'Was it? A talented artist, fascinated by darkness, drawing you out of the shadows... sounds familiar, doesn't it?'

Greer watched as Freya stepped back from her canvas, studying whatever she'd created with an intensity that made Greer's skin prickle. 'I won't hurt her.'

'Too late. You already are.'

He hung up before she could respond. Below, Freya had moved to her window, staring out into the night. For a moment, Greer could have sworn their eyes met across the darkness, but that was impossible. Wasn't it?

Her phone buzzed again—Dior sending an address. 'My contact at the airport can have papers ready by morning. New identity, clean start for us. Say the word.'

It would be so easy. She'd done it before, dozens of times over the centuries. Cities blurred together after a while, faces faded, connections broke clean when you moved fast enough.

But as she watched, Freya returned to her painting with renewed determination. There was something different about her movements now, something almost ritualistic. She kept consulting that book, then making marks on the canvas that Greer couldn't quite see.

The sight filled her with an unfamiliar emotion—not just hunger or desire, but fear. Not of discovery, but of loss.

The thought of never seeing Freya again, never knowing what she was creating, never feeling that raw connection… it was unbearable.

'No,' she typed back to Dior.

'Stupid girl,' came the instant response. 'At least tell me you're not going to do anything dramatic.

Greer watched as Freya finally stepped away from her canvas, exhaustion evident in the slope of her shoulders. A new day would arrive soon enough.

'No promises,' she wrote, then turned off her phone.

She had decisions to make. But for now, she stayed, a shadow amongst shadows, watching over the woman who might destroy everything she'd built, everything she was. The woman who, despite every instinct for survival, she couldn't bear to leave.

Chapter Fourteen

Half Truths

The knock came at midnight. Freya knew who it was before she opened the door—no one else moved that quietly, yet made the air vibrate with such presence.

'You've finally decided to stop avoiding me,' she said as Greer stepped into the studio. The woman wore dark colours as usual, but something about her seemed different tonight. Less controlled, perhaps. More dangerous.

'Yes.' Greer's eyes swept the room, lingering on the covered canvases. 'You've been busy.'

Freya watched as Greer moved through the space while she deliberately kept her back to Katherine's sketchbook on the desk. 'I've been learning.'

'Have you?' Greer's voice was soft, but there was an edge to it. She stopped in front of Freya's newest piece—the one she'd been working on all week. 'Show me.'

Freya hesitated. The painting was different from her others—darker, more primal. She'd worked on it in a kind of fever, guided by Katherine's drawings and her own haunting dreams. 'It's not finished.'

'Show me anyway.'

With steady hands, Freya pulled away the covering. The canvas was huge, dominated by a figure dancing in moonlight. But unlike her previous paintings of Greer, this one showed the dancer's skin covered in swirling patterns, marks that seemed to move in the dim studio lighting.

Greer went very still. 'Where did you see these?'

'You know where.'

'Tell me anyway.'

Freya moved closer, close enough to feel the chill that always seemed to emanate from Greer's skin. 'In my dreams at first. Then in old drawings. They appear in moonlight, don't they? When you dance?'

Greer turned to face her, and for a moment, Freya saw something primordial and wild in her eyes. 'You've been speaking to Thomas.'

'And Dr McKay.' Freya lifted her chin. 'And I have my great-grandmother's sketchbook.'

Greer's expression tightened almost imperceptibly. 'You've been thorough in your research.'

'My great-grandmother was Katherine Solasta.' Freya watched Greer's face carefully for any sign of recognition, but saw none. 'She documented things others couldn't see.'

'Some things,' Greer said quietly, moving to the window to stare out at the moonlit city, 'are better left undocumented.'

'Tell me the truth, Greer.' Freya's voice was steady despite her racing heart. 'Tell me what you are.'

'You've already decided what I am.'

'I want to hear it from you.'

Greer was silent for a long moment, turning away. When she spoke, her voice was distant, as if recalling something ancient. 'There are places in Scotland where the veil between worlds is thin. Where the old magic still lingers. I was born in such a place, a long time ago.'

'How long?'

A ghost of a smile touched Greer's lips. 'Long enough to see Edinburgh built stone by stone. Long enough to watch empires rise and fall. Long enough to learn that connection is dangerous, and trust is a luxury I cannot afford.'

Freya stepped closer. 'Yet here you are.'

'Here I am.' Greer turned back to her, and something in her expression made Freya's breath catch. 'Because you've done what only one other person ever managed—you've seen me. Really seen me.'

'Katherine?'

'No.' Greer's laugh was soft and bitter. 'Someone else. Someone who paid dearly for that sight.'

The implications hung heavy in the air. Freya thought of Thomas's warnings, of Dr McKay's careful words. But she couldn't stop herself from asking, 'What happened to them?'

'I destroyed her.' Greer's voice was barely a whisper. 'Not intentionally. Never intentionally. But my nature... it demands things. Dangerous things.'

'Like blood?'

Greer's eyes snapped to hers, darkening. 'You know too much.'

'The Baobhan Sith,' Freya said, testing the words. 'Beautiful women who dance in moonlight. Who feed on—'

'Stop.' Greer held up a hand. 'Don't say it. Don't make it real.'

'It's already real.' Freya moved closer still, close enough to touch. 'I'm not afraid.'

'You should be.' But Greer didn't move away. 'I can hear

your heart racing. Smell the adrenaline in your blood. Sense the heat of your skin.'

'Is that all you feel?'

The question staggered Greer, shattering her careful control. She closed her eyes, her composure cracking. 'No,' she whispered. 'That's the problem.'

Before Freya could respond, Greer was at the door, her movements too quick to follow. 'I've said too much.'

'Or maybe not enough.'

Greer paused, her hand on the doorknob. 'Full truth is dangerous, Freya. For both of us.'

'More dangerous than half-truths and shadows?'

'Yes.' Greer looked back one last time, and for a moment, Freya could have sworn she saw those mysterious markings shimmer across her skin. 'Because once you know everything, there's no going back. For either of us.'

Then she left, leaving only the faint scent of night air and ancient magic. Freya turned back to her painting, to the swirling marks she'd captured in paint and shadow.

She'd learned enough tonight to know she was right about what Greer was. But more importantly, she'd seen something in Greer's eyes—not just hunger or ancient power, but fear. Fear of connection, of being known.

Of being loved.

Chapter Fifteen

Blood Ties

The woman appeared at Freya's studio door the following day, just after sunset, sleek, confident, and well-dressed. 'Hannah,' she said simply as she invited herself in. 'We should talk.'

'I'm working.' Freya returned to her canvas.

'Yes, I can see that.' Hannah moved closer, studying the painting with knowing eyes. 'The markings are wrong, by the way. They flow the other direction when she's hungry.'

Freya's brush clattered to the floor. 'What did you say?'

'Greer.' Hannah's smile was gentle but knowing. 'Her markings. You've got the basic pattern right, but they change direction based on her need. Dior sent me to explain.'

'Dior?'

'The antique dealer. She and Greer...' Hannah settled onto Freya's paint-splattered sofa, her movements languid. 'Well, that's quite the story.'

Freya's hands shook slightly as she wiped them on her jeans. 'You know what they are.'

'Intimately.' Hannah's smile turned wicked. 'I feed

them both sometimes. Though Dior's my primary... let's call her patron.'

'You what?'

'Feed them. They need willing donors to survive.' Hannah pulled down her top, revealing a small, neat scar on her breast, just above her nipple. 'It's a mutually beneficial arrangement. Though I suspect you're more interested in their history than my current role.'

'Their history?' Freya was painfully aware that her shock at this woman inviting herself into her studio meant she just kept repeating the woman's words back to her.

Hannah's expression softened. 'They were lovers, still are, although it's—an open relationship I suppose you could call it. But when it began for them, they were young and foolish and desperately in love in a time when such things were unforgivable. Dior was married—an arrangement made by her family. Her husband found them.' She paused, letting the weight of history settle. 'Neither he nor the villagers were... understanding. The curse was meant as punishment.'

'Curse?'

'The Baobhan Sith aren't born, Freya. They're made. By hatred, by fear, by the kind of righteous anger that turns ordinary villagers into monsters while claiming to fight monstrosity.' Hannah's eyes grew distant. 'They cursed them to feed on passion, to hunger eternally for what they'd 'sinfully' shared. Rather poetic, really.'

'Thomas knows,' Freya said slowly. 'That's why he's been trying to protect me.'

Hannah laughed softly. 'Thomas has his own reasons for understanding forbidden love. And his own pretty young men he's trying to protect from this world. He's not your enemy, Freya. Just someone who's seen too much pain.'

Before Freya could process this, Hannah had produced a small, elegant knife. The blade caught the studio lights as she drew it across her own wrist, barely breaking the skin. A thin line of blood welled up, bright as paint.

'The first taste is always offered freely,' she murmured. 'That's the rule. After that... well, consent becomes more complicated. But always necessary. They learned that lesson the hard way. Ask Greer about Anne-Marie.'

Freya watched, transfixed, as a drop of blood rolled down Hannah's wrist. She was torn between wanting to know more and wanting to remove this mentally ill stranger from her home. Curiosity won out. 'Does it hurt?'

'Only in the best way.' Hannah's smile was dreamy. 'Greer is particularly skilled. She knows exactly how much to take, how to make it feel like floating. Like dying and being reborn at once. Dior's more... intense. Together, they're divine.'

'You've been with them both? Together?'

'Occasionally. On special nights. When the hunger and the memories become too much for them to bear separately.' Hannah dabbed at her wrist with a handkerchief. 'They try not to feed together anymore. Too many old wounds, too much history. But sometimes... well, centuries of love don't just disappear, even when they end badly.'

The image of Greer and Dior together, bound by tragedy and eternal hunger, sent a complicated surge of emotions through Freya—sympathy, jealousy, and fascination.

'Why are you telling me this?'

'Because Dior thinks you deserve to know what you're walking into. Because Greer is too haunted by the past to tell you herself.' Hannah stood, smoothing her dress. 'And because sometimes love survives even the darkest curses. If you're brave enough to face it.'

She moved to the door, then paused. 'Oh, and Freya? When you confront her—and we both know you will—remember this: she's not pulling away because she doesn't want you. She's pulling away because the last time she loved someone that deeply, *they* died.'

Then she was gone, leaving Freya with the scent of blood in the air and determination building in her chest. She grabbed her keys and phone. Enough half-truths and shadows. It was time for answers.

Chapter Sixteen

Confessions

Greer was standing at her office window when she heard the elevator ping. Even before her door burst open, she caught Freya's scent—paint, passion, and rage rolling down the hallway like a storm.

'Your pet donor paid me a visit,' Freya said without preamble, letting the heavy office door slam behind her. The receptionist had already left for the night.

Greer didn't turn around, she didn't need to. She could see Freya's reflection in the glass—beautiful and angry. 'Hannah isn't my pet.'

'No? Just your willing blood bank? Yours and Dior's?'

Greer turned slowly, taking in Freya's flushed cheeks, her paint-stained hands clenched into fists. 'What exactly did she tell you?'

'Everything you wouldn't.' Freya moved closer, her eyes fierce. 'About the curse. About you and Dior. About what you are.'

'Did she now?' Greer's voice was dangerously soft. 'And did she explain why we keep these secrets? Why we stay in the shadows?'

'Because you're cowards?'

Greer moved then, too fast for human eyes to track. Suddenly she was inches from Freya, close enough to hear her heart racing, to smell the adrenaline coursing through her veins. 'Because we're monsters.'

But Freya didn't flinch. Instead, she lifted her chin defiantly. 'You're not monsters. You're victims. Cursed by small-minded people who couldn't bear to see love that didn't fit their rules.'

Something cracked in Greer's carefully maintained control. 'Is that what you think? That we're just tragic romantic heroines? We kill to survive, Freya. We feed on passion and blood and—'

'And consent,' Freya cut in. 'Always with consent. Even cursed, even hungry, you never take what isn't freely given.'

'Until we lose control.' Greer's laugh was bitter. 'Until the hunger becomes too much and we—'

'Like with Anne-Marie?'

Greer recoiled as if struck. 'Don't.'

'No, let's talk about it. Because that's what this is really about, isn't it? Not just the curse, not just what you are. You're afraid of history repeating itself.'

'You don't understand what you're talking about.'

'Then make me understand!' Freya stepped closer, eliminating what little space remained between them. 'Stop protecting me and tell me the truth. All of it.'

For a moment, they stood frozen in tableau—the hunter and the willing prey, though it wasn't clear which was which. Then Greer spoke, her words hollowed by endless years.

'The curse didn't make us monsters. It just gave us the means to become them.' She turned away, moving back to the window. 'What Dior and I had... it was beautiful. Pure.

The curse twisted that, turned love into hunger, desire into need. We feed on passion now because that's all we have left of what we once were.'

'And Anne-Marie?'

Greer let out a huff of air. 'I thought I could love again. Thought I'd learned control.' Greer's reflection showed a sardonic smile. 'I was wrong. The hunger... it doesn't care about love. About intentions. One moment of weakness, one slip in control...'

'She died?'

'Worse. She lived. Long enough to see what I really was. Long enough to fear me. To hate me.' Greer turned back to face Freya. 'Is that what you want? To see the monster beneath the woman?'

'I've already seen you,' Freya said quietly. 'In my dreams. In my art. The markings that appear when you feed, when you dance. I'm not afraid.'

'You should be.'

'Let me see who you are.'

The words hung in the air between them, heavy with challenge and possibility. Greer's eyes darkened, and for a moment, Freya thought she saw something shift beneath her skin—like tattoos coming alive.

'You don't know what you're asking.'

'I'm asking for truth.' Freya reached up, her fingers hovering just above Greer's cheek. 'I'm asking for trust.'

'And if the truth destroys you?'

'Then at least it will be my choice.' Freya's pulse quickened. 'Hannah survives. Why?'

'Because she feeds me.' Greer's reply was instant. 'Because she understands what that means.'

'She said...' Freya swallowed hard. 'She said you and Dior feed together sometimes.'

Greer went very still. 'Did she?'

'I want to see.' The words came out before Freya could stop them. 'I want to watch.'

'You have no idea what you're asking of me.' But Greer's eyes had taken hold of hers, and something dark unfurled in their depths.

'Show me.' Freya stepped closer until she could feel the chill emanating from Greer's skin. 'Let me understand.'

'If you see that,' Greer whispered, 'you can never go back. Never unsee what we are, what we do. What it means to feed us.'

Freya met her gaze steadily. 'I don't want to go back. I want to go forward. With you.'

Something shifted in Greer's eyes—resignation, acceptance, or perhaps just surrender to the inevitable. She released Freya's gaze and stepped back.

'Tomorrow night,' she said softly. 'Under the full moon. I'll show you everything.'

'Promise?'

Greer's smile was sad and ancient and beautiful. 'I promise. But Freya?' Her voice dropped to a whisper. 'Pray you don't regret it.'

The sound of Freya's footsteps faded as she walked away, leaving Greer alone.

Chapter Seventeen

Threshold

The text from Greer had been cryptic: an address in Old Town, a password ('Crimson Sanctuary'), and a time (midnight). Nothing else. Just those three pieces of information that had burned in Freya's mind all day as she waited for darkness to fall.

Now she stood before an unmarked door in a quiet street, wondering if she had the right place. The only sign she might be where she was meant to be was a subtle etching in the doorframe—roses and thorns intertwined in an endless knot.

Her knock echoed slightly in the empty street. The door opened just enough to reveal a woman with close-cropped silver hair and arms corded with muscle. She wore tailored black trousers and a made-to-measure waistcoat that did nothing to diminish her distinctly butch presence. Her eyes, sharp and assessing, took in every detail of Freya's appearance.

'Password?' The woman's voice was deep, touched with an accent Freya couldn't quite place.

'Crimson Sanctuary.'

The woman's stern expression softened into something like sympathy. 'Ah. You must be Freya. We've been expecting you.' She stepped back, opening the door fully. 'I'm Maeve.'

The entrance opened into a space that seemed to absorb light, all dark woods and deeper shadows. Music played somewhere, so faint it was more feeling than sound. The air was warm, heavy with incense and something else—something that made Freya's pulse quicken.

'This way.' Maeve's Doc Marten boots made no sound on the hardwood floor as she led Freya deeper into the building. 'Greer said you might come.'

'What is this place?'

Maeve's smile was knowing. 'A sanctuary. For those with... particular appetites.'

They passed rooms with doors slightly ajar, offering glimpses of scenes that made Freya's cheeks flush. Soft gasps and lower sounds, almost growls, emerged from behind others, mixed with the occasional sharp intake of breath.

'Are they all...?' Freya couldn't finish the question.

'Like Greer?' Maeve shook her head. 'No. Most are just seeking pleasure, release. Connection. The others... well, they keep to their own spaces. You never know where you truly belong unless you test your boundaries.'

They stopped before a door different from the rest—older, made of darker wood, with that same rose-and-thorn pattern carved into its frame.

'Last chance,' Maeve said quietly. 'Once you go through that door, once you see what's beyond it... there's no unknowing. No going back to your normal life of mundane desire.'

Freya thought of Greer's markings in the moonlight, of

Hannah's knowing smile, of the hunger that seemed to radiate from this entire building.

'I don't want normal,' she said. 'I want truth.'

Maeve studied her face for a long moment, then nodded. 'They're waiting for you.' Her hand settled on the doorknob. 'But remember—you chose this. Whatever happens next, you walked through this door willingly.'

Freya thought of Hannah's words, *'Together, they're divine.'*

'Open it,' she said, her tone leaving no doubt as to consent.

The door swung open onto darkness and the scent of night air. As Freya stepped forward, she heard Maeve's voice behind her, soft and almost sad: 'Welcome to the Crimson Sanctuary, little one. Remove your shoes on entering and... May you survive what you find here.'

Chapter Eighteen

Marked by Moonlight

The door swung open, revealing a circular chamber bathed in moonlight that streamed through arched windows set high in the walls. Hannah's comment—'divine'—came back to her mind.

As instructed, she kicked off her shoes. The air within was still and heavy, scented with jasmine incense and the faint metallic tang of anticipation. Smooth, polished flagstone was cool and comforting beneath her bare feet. Hannah reclined on a pile of velvet cushions scattered across the floor, her pale skin almost gleaming, the discarded crimson robe pooling around her like spilled blood. The silence was absolute, broken only by the soft whisper of what Freya assumed was their own breathing.

'Brave girl,' Dior's voice came from somewhere behind Freya, rich with amusement. 'Or foolish. Sometimes it's hard to tell the difference.'

A beat of silence, and then Greer shot her former lover a warning look. Though Freya couldn't make out what was passing between them, she felt the change in atmosphere.

'She deserves to know,' Greer said.

'Oh, darling.' Dior moved past them, and Freya turned to catch the movement. 'She deserves so much more than just knowing.'

The air seemed to thicken as Dior approached Hannah, running a finger down her throat. Freya watched Hannah's head tilt back, exposing her neck in a gesture that made her breath hitch.

'Watch,' Greer murmured, her lips close to Freya's ear. 'Watch what we are.'

Freya's gaze was fixed on the scene before her, her heart pounding in her chest. She watched as Dior's fingers trailed along Hannah's collarbone, lingering on a faint, silvery scar. It had to be a mark of past feedings, a testament to the countless nights Hannah had offered herself to these two beautiful, dangerous creatures.

A sudden wave of understanding washed over Freya. It wasn't just about the blood, or the pleasure, or even the connection. It was about surrender. About giving oneself over completely to something larger, something more powerful. She remembered how Hannah had spoken of Greer and Dior, the mixture of awe and longing in her voice. It wasn't love, not in the way Freya understood it. But it was something... else. Something that bound Hannah to these women in a way that went beyond words.

As Dior moved, her flesh seemed to change, shapes appearing like faint tattoos created from shifting ink. They swirled around her arms, her throat, disappearing beneath her robe.

Then Greer stepped into the dim moonlight, naked, and Freya gasped. Her body was exquisite—tall and lean, with the kind of fluid grace that made even stillness seem like dancing. Shadows were carved beneath her collarbones, tracing the elegant line of her throat, highlighting the subtle curves that her tailored clothes usually concealed. She moved like a predator, contained power and deadly elegance, yet there was something vulnerable in the way she held herself, as if expecting Freya's judgement. The combination made Freya's heart race—this beautiful, dangerous creature who could break her in an instant, yet looked at her with such uncertainty.

Freya had dreamed of these markings, painted them obsessively, but nothing had prepared her for the reality. They were alive, writhing across Greer's skin like living shadows, each unique yet somehow harmonious with Dior's.

'The curse marks us,' Greer said. 'Shows our true nature when darkness and desire touches us. When we hunger.'

Freya's attention turned back to Hannah, who moaned in anticipation. Her body was lined with faint white scars—beautiful, deliberate patterns. As Dior's fingers traced them, they seemed to echo the markings on her own flesh.

'They feed together,' Hannah's voice was dreamy, 'when the hunger becomes too much to bear alone. When the memories of what they once were...'

'Quiet,' Dior commanded, her voice a low caress as she bent to kiss her.

Freya couldn't look away. The kiss was beyond passionate—it was primal, hungry. When Dior's lips moved to Hannah's throat, Freya noticed a small, sharp, pointed nail at the end of her forefinger.

'This is what we are,' Greer's voice coiled low in Freya's ear. 'What we need to survive.'

The nail flashed, quick and precise. A line of blood welled. When Dior's tongue caught the first drop, Hannah moaned—a sound of pure surrender. Her body went pliant, her head falling back, and from their movements, Freya knew this was a well-practiced dance.

Greer's nail traced a delicate line across Hannah's breast, drawing another thin crimson line. The precision of it, the control even in this moment of primal need, made Freya's breath hitch. As they fed, Hannah's moans grew deeper, more desperate. Freya could see her skin flushing, her body arching into their touch.

What followed made Freya's cheeks burn and her heart race. The feeding transformed into something else entirely —a dance of pleasure and power that left Hannah crying out in ecstasy. They coaxed her, teased her, fingertips gliding over the most sensitive areas of her body, her breasts, her nipples, down further. Hannah arched as though aching for their touch. Dior's fingers moved in swift circles, now playing with her clit. Then Greer's hand took over as Dior slipped inside, all the while they continued to feed. Their combined strength held Hannah down as her body writhed and thrashed beneath them, calling out, begging them not to stop. Her climax came with an earth-shattering scream of deliverance, then she slipped into what seemed like blissful unconsciousness, a smile of utter satisfaction on her lips.

When Greer lifted her head, her lips stained dark and her eyes heavy-lidded, Freya had to grip the doorframe to keep herself upright. There was something terrible and magnificent in seeing them like this—these creatures of darkness, so captivating in their hunger, and the rapture they brought with it. It was sublime and terrible and the most erotic thing Freya had ever seen.

'Now you understand,' Dior's voice was thick with blood and satisfaction, the words directed at Freya. 'Why we can never truly be human again.'

'I understand,' Freya whispered, but her eyes were fixed

on Greer, on the way her tongue caught the last drops of blood from Hannah's skin. 'I understand everything.'

Greer looked up then, her eyes dark with hunger and something else—shame, perhaps, or fear of judgement. But the expression on Freya's face seemed to catch her breath, her gaze intense.

Because Freya wasn't watching with horror or disgust. She was watching with an artist's eyes, with a lover's eyes, with the gaze of someone seeing beauty in darkness.

'Feed from me,' Freya demanded, ripping her blouse open. 'I want to know how it feels to surrender to you.'

Greer was on her feet in an instant, moving with inhuman speed. 'No.'

'Why not? I'm offering freely.'

'Because,' Greer's voice shook, 'if I taste you, I'll never be able to stop. You're not just dinner, Freya. You're...'

'Everything,' Dior finished, rising from beside Hannah. She had moved so silently, Freya hadn't realised she was there. 'You're everything she's been hungry for since they cursed us. And that makes you far more dangerous than any blade.'

Hannah sat up, adjusting her robe, the cut on her throat already clotting. 'The hunger never truly dies,' she said, her gaze meeting Freya's. 'But it can be managed. Contained. Unless...'

'Unless there's love,' Dior's smile was sharp with memory. 'Love makes the hunger impossible to control. Isn't that right, my dear?'

Greer's markings were still writhing, but slower now, like waves calming after a storm. 'Leave us,' she said, her voice strained.

Dior helped Hannah to her feet, leading her toward the door. But she paused beside Freya, her lips close to her ear.

'Be very sure, little artist. Once you offer, once you taste this darkness... there's no going back.'

Then they were gone, leaving Freya alone with Greer. The markings seemed to reach for her, like shadows seeking warmth.

'Why did you want to see this?' Greer asked, her eyes fixed on Freya.

'Because,' Freya stepped closer, close enough to trace one of the moving patterns with her finger, 'you can't create art without understanding shadow. And I want to understand all of you. Even the dark parts. Especially the dark parts.'

Greer shuddered at her touch. 'And if the darkness consumes you?'

Freya smiled, tilting her head to expose her throat. 'Then I'll paint with it.'

Chapter Nineteen

Echoes of Truth

Sleep was impossible. Freya sat in her studio as dawn crept over Edinburgh, her sketchbook open before her, pages filled with fevered drawings of swirling markings and shadows. When she closed her eyes, she saw Greer, those living patterns writhing across her skin. The memory of what she'd witnessed at the Crimson Sanctuary made her hands shake—not with fear, though perhaps it should have, but with a desperate need to capture it, to understand it more deeply. Her great-grandmother's sketch-book lay open beside her own, and now she saw the patterns there with new eyes. Katherine had known. Had seen them, documented them, tried to understand them, just as Freya was doing now.

Her phone buzzed—a message from Dr McKay. 'Found something interesting in the archives. Come when you can.'

Freya wasted no time. The Celtic Studies department was quiet this early. Simon McKay didn't look as if he had slept either.

'You've seen them,' he said without preamble, studying her face. 'The markings.'

Freya hadn't intended to admit it, but something in his expression made her nod.

'Good.' He turned to a stack of papers on his desk. 'Then you'll understand these.'

The pages he spread out were old, the paper yellowed and delicate. Sketches, like Katherine's but older, showed the same swirling patterns Freya had seen last night. But these were annotated in faded Gaelic, with English translations squeezed into the margins.

'These date back to 1634,' McKay said quietly. 'A village minister documented a series of… incidents. Two women, cursed by their community for a forbidden love affair. The markings appeared in the nights that followed their transformation.'

Freya's fingers traced the drawings. 'Greer and Dior.'

'I believe so.' McKay pulled out another document. 'The curse was specific—to feed on passion, to hunger eternally for what they'd shared. But there's something the modern accounts miss.' He tapped a particular passage. 'The markings aren't just decoration. They're a map.'

'A map of what?'

'The curse itself. Each pattern shows how it binds them, how it transforms love into hunger.' He hesitated. 'Your great-grandmother had a theory. She believed the curse could be broken if someone could understand the patterns fully enough.'

Freya thought of how the markings had moved, how they'd seemed to reach for her when she'd stood close to Greer. 'Did she figure it out?'

'She died before she could.' McKay's voice was gentle. 'But she left notes. Theories. And more importantly…' He pulled out a small, leather-bound journal. 'She left this.'

The journal was newer than the sketchbook, dated just

months before Katherine's death, and was one of the many papers Freya's family had donated to the university upon her great-grandmother's death. Inside, the patterns were drawn with precise detail, annotated with what looked like mathematical formulae and snippets of old Gaelic.

'She believed the curse worked like a lock,' McKay explained. 'And these patterns are the key. But understanding them requires more than just observation. It requires...'

'Connection,' Freya finished. 'Someone who sees them with more than just their eyes.'

'Yes.' McKay watched her carefully. 'But getting close enough to study them comes with obvious risks.'

Freya thought of Hannah, of the ecstasy on her face as Greer and Dior fed from her, of the way they'd satisfied her before she'd passed out from pleasure. It hadn't looked like a risk. It had looked like *transformation.*

'What happens if the curse is broken?' she asked.

'No one knows. It's never been done.' McKay closed the old documents carefully. 'But consider this—a curse born of love, twisted by hatred. What might happen if love were to untwist it?'

Freya gathered Katherine's journal and her own sketchbook. 'Thank you.'

'Miss Solasta.' McKay's voice stopped her at the door. 'Your great-grandmother was brilliant, but she was also an observer. You... you're something else entirely. Just remember—understanding a curse doesn't make you immune to it.'

Outside, the morning sun was fully up, warming Edinburgh's ancient stones. Greer would be sleeping, those beautiful, terrible markings hidden until the next time she hungered.

Freya opened her sketchbook to a fresh page. She had patterns to map, a curse to understand, and a woman to save—even if that woman might destroy her in the process. She wouldn't be the first Solasta woman to risk everything for forbidden knowledge. But she might be the first to succeed.

Chapter Twenty

Are You Sitting Comfortably?

Stepping out of the lift, Freya was greeted by a breathtaking panorama of Edinburgh spread out beneath a sky dusted with stars. Floor-to-ceiling windows framed the cityscape, the twinkling lights reflecting off the polished surface of the grand piano in the corner. The air hummed with a subtle energy, a blend of ancient power and modern luxury. The scent of expensive perfume hung in the air. Everything spoke of careful curation, of centuries of collected beauty.

But it was Greer herself who drew Freya's eye. She stood by the windows in a black silk robe, her hair loose around her shoulders, looking somehow both vulnerable and dangerous in the filtered light.

'Your markings,' Freya said, crossing the room without conscious thought. Her fingers found the edge of Greer's robe, pushing it open slightly. The skin beneath was flawless, bare—no trace of the swirling patterns she'd seen before. 'They're gone.'

'They only appear when...' Greer's voice caught as

Freya's fingers traced her collarbone. 'When certain needs arise.'

The silk parted further under Freya's eager hands, revealing more unmarked skin. But as her fingers explored, something began to change. Beneath her touch, shadows stirred, patterns emerging like frost spreading across winter glass.

'Like now?' Freya whispered, fascinated by the transformation.

'Yes.' Greer's smile was predatory. 'You could say it's our version of...' Her hand slipped beneath the waistband of Freya's loose trousers, fingers finding heat. 'Arousal.'

Freya gasped, her hips moving involuntarily. Pleasure sparked through her body, instant and overwhelming. The markings on Greer's skin writhed faster, responding to their shared desire.

'We just show it differently,' Greer murmured, her fingers moving with practised skill as Freya moaned, clutching at her shoulders.

'Well,' came Dior's amused voice from the doorway. 'This is cosy.'

Freya froze, but Greer's hand didn't withdraw. If anything, her smile widened. The markings on her skin pulsed with a hunger that was suddenly all too obvious.

'Perfect timing,' Greer said. 'We were just about to discuss origins.'

Dior settled onto one of the leather chairs. 'Were you now? And here I thought you were just seducing our little artist.'

Greer's hand withdrew slowly, deliberately, making Freya bite back another moan. The loss of contact left her trembling, but the heated look in Greer's eyes promised this wasn't over.

'Get dressed, darling,' Dior said to Greer. 'This story requires... distance.'

Chapter Twenty-One

Origins

Greer slipped away to change, giving Freya a moment to collect herself. She smoothed her clothes and ran fingers through her tousled hair. When Greer returned, she wore silk pyjamas that draped her body with casual elegance, her skin now unmarked, the strange patterns gone.

'It wasn't magic,' Greer began, settling onto the couch beside Freya. 'Not in the way you might think. It was... a change. A fundamental shift within us.'

Dior's fingers found Greer's across the back of the couch. 'They tried to break us,' she continued, her voice taking on an ancient cadence. 'Publicly shamed us, whipped us, stoned us... left us for dead. But they didn't succeed. The pain became a catalyst.'

'It was 1634,' Greer's voice took on a distant quality, her fingers intertwining with Dior's. 'A time when women had little power, little voice. We were possessions, defined by our relationships to men. Wives, daughters, mothers... nothing more. To step outside those boundaries, to claim any kind of autonomy, was to invite suspicion, even damnation. And to love another woman...' She swallowed hard. 'That was considered an abomination, a direct challenge to God's order.'

'They called us witches,' she continued, her voice dropping lower. 'It was an easy label to apply to any woman who dared to be different, who possessed knowledge or skills that were deemed unusual, or simply who didn't conform to their expectations. And the punishment for witchcraft... well, you know the stories.'

'My husband dragged us, Greer and I from his marital bed,' Dior added softly. 'Naked and exposed, onto the cold cobbles by the harbour.'

Greer's hand tightened on Dior's. 'The cold stone bit into my skin, but it was nothing compared to the chill in the air, the weight of their hatred. Ewan, Dior's husband, led the charge, his voice hoarse with rage, calling us unnatural, abominations. The crowd...' She closed her eyes at the memory. 'Their faces were contorted with disgust, with a kind of righteous fury that was terrifying to behold. They truly believed they were doing God's work.

'The whipping came first,' her voice grew pained. 'The lash tore at our skin, each strike a searing reminder of our transgression. I could feel Dior's pain as if it were my own, a shared agony that bound us together even as they tried to tear us apart.'

'Then came the stones,' Dior whispered. 'Small ones at first, thrown by children with wide, frightened eyes.'

'Then larger ones,' Greer continued, 'hurled by the adults, their faces hardened with judgement. The impact... the blood... the taste of it in my mouth... It was like they were trying to erase us, to obliterate us from existence.' Her voice broke at the edges. 'But they didn't leave us there, not in the village. They wouldn't risk the taint of our wickedness polluting their homes. They dragged us further, beyond the village limits, up past the cemetery, to Gallow Hill. They dumped us there, like rubbish, like something to be forgotten, banished. Left us for dead, thinking they'd finished the job. Broken, bleeding, barely clinging to life.'

'The silence after,' Dior added, her tone raw with memory. 'That was almost worse than the pain.'

'No village doors slamming shut, no retreating footsteps,' Greer nodded. 'Just the wind whistling through the trees, the distant cry of a bird, and the sound of our own desperate breaths. We were utterly alone, abandoned to the elements, left to die a slow, agonising death.'

'Witches,' Dior's laugh was bitter. 'Any woman loved differently...'

'But they didn't burn us,' Greer said softly. 'We were too unnatural even for burning.'

'The pain was...' Dior's voice caught. 'Beyond anything human. But underneath it...'

'Something stirred,' Greer finished. 'Something ancient. The earth drew the pain away, replaced it with... a life of its own. The night became our companion, our mother.'

'We felt ourselves changing,' Dior continued. 'Senses sharpening, wounds healing differently. The hunger came last—the need for blood, for passion. For everything they tried to deny us.'

'Time became meaningless,' Greer's voice was barely a whisper. 'We watched seasons change, generations rise and fall. But we remained.'

'Not unchanged,' Dior added. 'But unbroken.'

Silence fell. Freya could almost see it—two women, broken and abandoned, transforming not through magic but through sheer will to survive, through pain and rage, and a love that refused to die.

'The markings?' she asked softly.

'They appeared with the first hunger.' Greer touched her own skin. 'Like the curse writing itself on our flesh. Reminding us always of what we lost, what we became. People thought we had hooves, like deer.' She gave a gentle laugh. 'They didn't understand the patterns on our skin.'

Dior's eyes grew distant. 'There was a time,' she said, 'when beings like us were not feared, as stories go. Centuries ago, in the most rural parts, the Baobhan Sith were revered. We were the protectors of the land, the guardians of the forests and streams. Our connection to the moon was seen as a blessing, our dances a celebration of life and fertility. We lived in harmony with the humans, offering our gifts of healing and protection in exchange for their respect and offerings. But that time had passed before we were born. Ròs is the only one who remembers. But the Burning Times took over, and the rest was lost to the mists of time. Fear was all that surrounded our kind after that. Profit and industry replaced the need to be at one with the land. People changed. But we didn't. They couldn't break our love of women. They only transformed it into something eternal.'

'But dangerous,' Greer turned to Freya. 'Now you understand why we keep our distance. Why we feed only on those who understand the risk. Why I tried to stay away from you.'

'Did you ever...' Freya swallowed. 'Did you ever try to break the curse?'

The two women exchanged a look heavy with history. 'The curse is part of us now,' Dior said gently. 'To break it would be to break ourselves.'

'Unless,' Greer's voice held a note of something like

hope, 'someone found another way. A way to transform it again, through love freely given instead of hate.'

The implications hung in the air. Outside, the sun was setting, and Freya could feel the subtle shift in both women as darkness approached—the gathering hunger, the promise of night.

Greer's markings began to stir beneath her skin again, responding to the growing darkness. When her eyes met Freya's, they held both warning and invitation.

'Now you know everything,' she said softly. 'What happens next is your choice.'

Dior rose gracefully. 'Choose carefully, little artist. Some hungers, once awakened, can never be put back to sleep.'

She left them alone, the door closing silently behind her. In the growing darkness, Greer's markings grew more visible, more alive.

'Stay,' Greer whispered. It wasn't clear if it was a request or a warning.

Freya's answer was to reach for her.

Chapter Twenty-Two

Boundaries

After Dior left, silence settled over the penthouse. Freya's fingers traced the place where she'd seen the patterns moving under Greer's skin.

'They respond to you,' Greer said softly. 'The markings. They've never done that before.'

'Because I'm beginning to understand them now.' Freya's touch grew bolder. 'Each line, each swirl—they're not just scars. They're a record of your transformation.'

'Understanding doesn't make them less dangerous.' But Greer leaned into her touch. 'If anything, it makes you more vulnerable.'

'Then help me understand the danger.' Freya moved closer, watching dark veins of power ripple beneath Greer's skin. 'What happens when you feed?'

Greer's hand caught hers, stilling its exploration. 'It's intimate. More intimate than sex. When we take blood, we take essence. Energy. Life force. It creates a connection that's hard to break.'

'Like with Hannah?'

'No.' Greer's smile was sad. 'Hannah feeds us to experience a heightened state. It's a transaction, consensual but limited. What you're suggesting... it would be different. Because of how I feel about you. Because of what you mean to me.'

'Tell me how.'

Greer stood, moving to the windows. Her reflection was ghostly against the city lights, the patterns now clearly visible on her skin. 'When we feed from someone we... care for, it's harder to control. The hunger becomes tangled with emotion. With need. If I started feeding from you, I don't know if I could stop.'

'What am I to you?' Freya asked, moving closer still.

The patterns on Greer's skin seemed to freeze mid-swirl. 'You're the moon pulling at my tides. The hunger beneath the hunger.' Her fingers traced Freya's jaw. 'Something I can't name without breaking its power.'

'Then don't name it.' Freya leaned into her touch. 'Show me.'

'It isn't that simple.' But Greer turned into her touch. 'The first time... it changes things. Creates a bond. You'll feel what I feel, need what I need. The hunger becomes shared.'

Freya tilted her head, exposing her throat. 'Give me just a taste.'

Greer's hands came up to frame her face, and Freya could feel the slight elongation of her nail—not quite a claw, but sharp enough to draw blood. 'Not like this. Not here.' Her voice was pained with restraint. 'If we do this, we do it properly. Safely.'

'The Crimson Sanctuary?'

'Yes.' Greer's thumbs stroked Freya's cheekbones. 'With Dior present, to stop me if...'

'If you lose control?'

'If I love you too much to stop.'

Those words changed everything—a seduction and a warning wrapped in one. Beyond the windows, clouds filled the night sky, yet Greer's flesh shone.

'Tomorrow night,' Freya said. It wasn't a question.

'Are you sure? Once we start...'

'Your patterns,' Freya touched Greer's chest, where the markings spiralled over her heart. 'They tell the story of how you were transformed by pain and hatred. Maybe...' Her fingers traced the swirling lines. 'Maybe they can be transformed again. By choice. By love.'

Greer caught her hand, pressing it harder against her chest. Beneath Freya's palm, the patterns moved like living things, responding to their shared touch.

'Tomorrow night,' Greer agreed softly. 'But Freya?' Her eyes held centuries of hunger and fear and something far deeper than mere emotion. 'Remember that you chose this. Whatever happens next, remember you walked willingly into our darkness.'

Chapter Twenty-Three

First Taste

The Crimson Sanctuary's circular room thrummed with expectancy, while jasmine and wildness filled the air, making Freya's pulse race. The clear night sky bathed the room in deep blue. Freya stepped onto the cool stone and let her dress slip from her shoulders. The material fell away, abandoning her skin to the night. The only sound to break the anticipation was her heartbeat.

Greer watched from the shadows, her markings already writhing beneath her skin, responding to desire and hunger intertwined. 'Are you sure?' Each word cost Greer visible control. 'You can change your mind.'

Freya's answer was to tilt her head back, exposing the elegant line of her throat. In the dimness, the hollows of her collarbone, the fullness of her breasts were visible. She was a living canvas, pale and perfect, waiting to be marked.

Greer circled her. When her nail traced the curve of Freya's breast, they both shuddered. The point was sharp now, transformed by hunger, leaving the faintest red line.

'Here,' Greer murmured, positioning her nail just above

Freya's nipple. 'The skin is sensitive here. The blood flows close to the surface.'

The first cut was exquisite—a bright flash of pain that transformed instantly into pleasure as Greer's mouth found the wound. Freya gasped, her body arching. The sensation was unlike anything she'd imagined—pleasure so intense it bordered on pain, every nerve ending suddenly, impossibly alive.

Greer's markings writhed faster as she fed, dark patterns flowing like ink across her skin. Her usual careful control cracked, revealing something primal beneath. When she looked up, her eyes were black with hunger and need, blood staining her perfect lips.

Freya's legs gave way, but Greer caught her, lowering them both to the cushions. Each point of contact between them blazed with need. The room began to spin, not from blood loss—from overwhelming sensation. She could feel everything Greer felt: the hunger, the desire, the desperate need for more.

'Please,' Freya whispered, though she wasn't sure what she was begging for.

Greer's mouth found her throat, not cutting, not yet—just tasting, teasing. Her tongue traced invisible patterns that matched the ones writhing across her skin. When her nail drew another line, this time along Freya's inner thigh, the moan that escaped was barely human.

She arched as Greer moved lower, her lover's head sinking between her thighs. The second taste was deeper, hungrier. Freya's consciousness began to fragment, pleasure building in waves. She was distantly aware of her body responding, arching and trembling, everything dreamlike and distant. There was only Greer's mouth, Greer's hands, the sharp perfection of her nail drawing lines of fire across sensitive skin. She widened her legs, inviting more, and Greer answered—moving from the tiny cuts on her inner thighs to her swollen clit, her tongue swirling and pressing until Freya shattered into pure sensation.

Through half-closed eyes, she watched the markings dance across Greer's flesh, beautiful and furious. They seemed to reach for her, wanting to map themselves onto her skin, to claim her as their own. She wanted it too—wanted to be written into their story, to be part of this primal dance.

The pleasure crested suddenly. Freya cried out as her body convulsed, the exhilaration almost too much to bear. Above her, Greer's markings pulsed in time with her heartbeat, their patterns merging and separating like lovers embracing.

As consciousness began to fade, Freya felt Greer gather her close, felt soft lips press against her temple.

'Sleep,' Greer whispered, her voice still rough with satiated hunger. 'Sleep, my wild heart. Dream of our darkness.'

Freya's vision blurred as sleep claimed her, the patterns on Greer's skin fading like a dream.

❄

From the shadows, Dior watched, her own markings writhing beneath her skin, her hunger as fierce as Greer's, though she remained still in her chair. The scent of Freya's blood, the sound of her pleasure, the raw intimacy of the feeding—it stirred memories of when she and Greer had first shared such moments. Her nail lengthened, pricking her own palm as she maintained her control.

She would feed later. Hunger demanded it. But for now, she was guardian and witness to this new becoming, this fresh transformation. Someone needed to stay alert, to ensure the feeding didn't go too far, to pull Greer back if necessary. Though, from the way Greer cradled Freya's sleeping form, such intervention hadn't been needed. Not this time.

Chapter Twenty-Four

Surrender

Consciousness returned slowly, like swimming up through dark water. Freya felt Greer's body pressed against hers, every curve and plane of immortal flesh igniting memories of what they'd shared. She sensed the subtle pulse of her lover's markings even before opening her eyes—they seemed to reach for her through layers of skin, calling to something newly awakened in her own blood. The circular chamber was bathed in pale light. How long had she been lost to sleep?

'You're awake.' Greer's voice was soft against her skin, her breath teasing the sensitive spot beneath Freya's ear where she'd fed earlier. The memory alone made Freya shiver with renewed desire.

'Mm.' Freya turned into her embrace, every nerve ending singing with remembered pleasure. Her body felt different—more alive, more sensitive, as if Greer's feeding had awakened parts of her she never knew existed. 'I want more.'

Greer's markings stirred faster at the words, writhing

beneath her skin like living shadows. Where their bodies pressed together, Freya could feel them reaching for her, hungry for more than just blood.

'It's addictive,' Greer warned softly, but her hands were already starting to wander, tracing forms that made Freya arch into her touch. 'The feeding, the intensity... it can consume you.'

From the shadows came a slight movement—Dior shifting in her chair, her own designs now visible, dancing beneath her skin with barely contained hunger. In the moon's glow, she was devastating—all dangerous curves and ancient power, her eyes reflecting centuries of desire. Freya watched her, remembering how Greer had spoken of their shared past, their eternal connection.

'Dior's hungry too.'

A low growl rumbled in Greer's chest, possessive and warning. Her arms tightened around Freya, a nail tip lengthening against sensitive skin.

'No,' Freya touched Greer's face, turning it toward her. Her fingers traced the sharp line of her jaw, feeling the tension there. 'Listen. You told me the feeding is deeper when there's... feeling behind it. You love her. Have for centuries.' She traced one of Greer's markings, watching it writhe beneath her touch. 'Wouldn't that make it more powerful? More meaningful?'

The shapes beneath Greer's skin pulsed with something beyond hunger—recognition, need, centuries of complicated emotion. She looked at Dior, and in that glance passed volumes of shared history, shared pain, shared love that had survived even the darkest curse.

'It's dangerous,' Greer whispered, but her resolve was weakening. Freya could feel it in the way her body responded, the way her markings reached not just for her now, but for Dior too. 'The three of us... the hunger could overwhelm us all.'

'Then let it.' Freya's voice was growing more urgent with need. She could feel her own hunger building—not the same as theirs, but something new, something that made reality glimmer around them with possibility.

Dior rose from her chair, her movement as fluid and quiet as that of a shadow. Her markings were fully visible now, dancing across her skin in forms that complemented Greer's perfectly. They spoke of shared history, shared curse, shared hunger that had bound them together through centuries. When she knelt beside them, Freya felt the air thicken with power.

'Are you sure?' Dior's eyes grew darker. 'Once we start...'

Freya's answer was to reach for her, pulling her down into their embrace. 'Undress,' Freya said, and Dior didn't hesitate.

The moment their bodies met, power surged between them. Freya gasped as feeling overwhelmed her—Greer's cool skin against her back, Dior's heat against her front, their markings reaching through her flesh to touch something deeper than blood.

What followed exploded beyond ordinary pleasure. Two sets of sharp nails traced lines on her skin, trails of exquisite ecstasy that made her writhe between them. Two mouths found different pulse points, each cut bringing its own unique rapture. The markings seemed to flow between them all, binding them together in an ancient dance that spoke of curse and blessing, hunger and satisfaction, love that survived centuries of darkness.

Freya lost track of whose hands were where, whose mouth drew what sounds from her throat. Every touch was intense, every taste a new revelation. Greer's passion complemented Dior's precision, their styles different but harmonious. They possessed her completely—tongues exploring where their nails had cut, fingers delving deep inside her, their bodies moving together in a rhythm of pleasure and hunger. Greer's mouth was at her breast, Dior's tongue between her thighs, while their fingers claimed her in ways that made her cry out for more. When one fed from the cuts they'd made, the other would drive her higher with knowing touches, building climax upon climax until Freya thought she might shatter from the intensity of being so thoroughly claimed, so completely taken, so utterly possessed by them both.

Each trickle of blood drained from her brought a different wave of feeling—Greer's fierce and passionate, making Freya cry out with the intensity of it. Dior's slow and methodical, drawing moans that seemed to come from her very soul. Their combined hunger wrapped around her like dark wings, lifting her into undiscovered realms of bliss. She felt everything they felt: centuries of desire, of restraint, of love twisted by curse but never broken.

Reality began to blur at the edges as pleasure built to impossible heights. Freya could see their markings now, really see them—designs of ancient power writing themselves through all three of them, binding them together in ways that moved beyond flesh and blood.

When the final wave of ecstasy crashed over her, Freya saw their forms merge into one perfect, infinite design. It was beautiful and terrible, this joining of cursed and blessed, mortal and immortal, love and hunger and power all wound together into something entirely new.

Then darkness claimed her again, but gently this time,

cradled between two immortal hearts that beat in time with her own transformed pulse.

Her last conscious thought was that she finally understood—some hungers went deeper than blood, some feelings were worth any price, and some loves could surpass even the darkest curse.

Chapter Twenty-Five

Afterglow

As Freya stood at her easel, draped in morning light, brush suspended, she was distracted by the tiny cuts that mapped last night's pleasure across her skin. Each one was already healing, pink and delicate, but when she traced them with her fingertips, a surge of desire shot through her.

Above her nipple, where Greer had first tasted her, the skin was particularly sensitive. Just touching it brought back a flood of sensation—the exquisite pressure of that sharpened nail, the heat of Greer's mouth, the way pleasure had exploded through her like starbursts.

Her inner thigh bore Dior's touch, a delicate constellation of cuts that made her catch her breath when she ran her fingers over them. The memory of both women feeding from her simultaneously made her knees weak even now. She had to steady herself, amazed that something so intense could have been real.

Everything was different this morning. Colours seemed sharper, more vivid. She could hear the whisper of wind around the building's corners, smell paint and turpentine with new clarity. Even her own heartbeat felt stronger, more purposeful, as if her blood now carried some echo of their power.

The canvas before her reflected these changes. She'd been painting since dawn, unable to sleep, trying to capture what she'd experienced. The work was different from anything she'd done before—darker, more primal. Patterns emerged in the brushstrokes without conscious thought, not quite the same as their markings but clearly inspired by them.

Her phone buzzed—a text from Greer: 'How do you feel?'

Freya smiled, touching her breast. 'Alive,' she wrote back. 'More alive than I've ever been.'

The response came quickly: 'It only gets stronger.'

A shiver ran through her at the promise in those words. She could still feel them both somehow, like shadows at the edges of her consciousness. When she closed her eyes, she could almost see their designs dancing beneath her eyelids.

Her phone buzzed again—Dior this time: 'The hunger will come soon. Be ready.'

Freya's body responded to the word 'hunger', with instant arousal. She steadied herself against the easel again, wondering if this was how they felt all the time—this constant awareness, this simmering need just beneath the surface.

Turning back to her canvas, she loaded her brush with crimson. The colour reminded her of blood in moonlight, of the way it had looked on Greer's lips, on Dior's fingertips. She began to paint with renewed intensity, letting the sensations flow through her into the work.

Something had changed inside her, something fundamental and irreversible. Her body thrilled with new awareness, her art was transforming, and a deep, primal hunger had begun to stir in her core.

They had marked her in ways that went far deeper than skin. And despite Greer's warnings about addiction, despite Dior's cautions about hunger, she knew with absolute certainty that she would never want to go back to the life she had before last night.

The canvas before her bloomed with dark beauty, capturing something of what she'd become. Not quite human anymore, perhaps, but not quite their kind either.

Chapter Twenty-Six

Sweet Blood

The bedroom vibrated with a primal energy that made Freya's skin prickle with anticipation. A silvery glow illuminated three figures intertwined on a bed of silk cushions. The air was thick with the scents of arousal—musk and sweat and the metallic tang of blood that made Freya's mouth water. She watched, mesmerised, as the patterns on Greer and Dior's skin writhed and pulsed. This was only her third night with them, and yet she couldn't imagine any other life.

'Pleasure changes the blood,' Greer murmured, trailing sharp nails lightly down Freya's torso. 'Makes it sweeter, richer. The more intense the pleasure...' She smiled against Freya's throat. 'The more exquisite the taste.'

Dior's hands joined Greer's exploration, her touch knowing and deliberate. 'Shall we show her?'

What followed was an education in ecstasy. They took their time, drawing out every sensation. Greer's mouth traced patterns that matched her markings, while Dior's fingers found places that made Freya arch and gasp. When the first wave of pleasure crashed over her, they didn't stop

—they simply changed rhythm, building her toward another peak.

‘Again,’ Greer commanded softly, her nail tracing circles around Freya’s breast. ‘Let us taste how sweet you can become.’

The second climax was stronger than the first, leaving Freya trembling. The third made her cry out, clutching at them both. By the fourth, she was incoherent, lost in sensation. Only then did Greer’s nail finally break the skin, drawing a thin line above her breast. The first drop of blood welled.

‘Delicious,’ Greer breathed, before lowering her mouth to taste.

The pleasure of the feeding was different now—deeper, more intense. Freya could feel both their hungers, their shared desire. When Dior’s nail opened another cut along her inner thigh, the sensation was exhilarating.

‘You’ll always be mine,’ Greer whispered against her skin between tastes. ‘But sharing you.’ Her markings pulsed faster. ‘Sharing makes the pleasure sweeter for us all.’

Dior hummed in agreement, her tongue busy leaving marks of her own.

Freya surrendered to them completely, understanding now why they called it a dance. Three bodies moving in perfect rhythm, pleasure and hunger intertwined. Greer’s fingers moved lower, tracing the sensitive skin of her inner thigh, sending shivers through her. Dior’s tongue flicked against the curve of her breast, a counterpoint to the sharp pressure of Greer’s nail. Freya’s breath hitched, her body tightening, arching, seeking something she couldn’t name but desperately craved.

‘So close,’ Greer murmured, her voice a low thrum

against Freya's skin. 'Let go, my wild heart. Let us taste your surrender.'

Dior's hand slipped between Freya's legs, her fingers finding the slick heat, mirroring the rhythm of Greer's movements. Freya cried out, her vision blurring as another wave of pleasure built, stronger than any before. It was too much, too intense, yet she wanted more, needed more, craved the dizzying spiral that promised to consume her completely.

Just as she felt herself teetering on the edge, about to shatter into a million pieces of pure sensation, the door burst open, shattering the intimate moment.

Hannah stood there, her face a mask of hurt and rage.

'How could you?' Her voice cracked with emotion. 'Both of them? You have no idea what you've done.'

Greer moved with supernatural speed, placing herself between Hannah and Freya. Dior reached for a silk robe, draping it over Freya's exposed body.

'Hannah—' Dior began, but Hannah cut her off.

'No, she needs to hear this.' Her eyes, wild with a desperate kind of knowledge, were fixed on Freya. 'You think you can just go back to normal after this? Try to have regular sex with regular people? Nothing will ever compare. Nothing will ever be enough.' She laughed, bitter and broken. 'The hunger doesn't just belong to them anymore. It's in you now. And it will eat you alive.'

The pale light caught the silvery scars that mapped Hannah's skin—countless feeding marks, each one a testament to her addiction. Her voice dropped to a whisper. 'I tried to warn you. But you'll learn, just like I did. There's no going back from this. No escaping what you've become.'

Chapter Twenty-Seven

Aftermath

The air in the circular chamber crackled with a tension unconnected to pleasure. Still reeling from the abrupt end to their encounter and Hannah's fierce warning, Freya lay cradled in Greer's arms. Dior had led Hannah away, for now.

'Nothing will happen to you,' she heard Greer murmur, her voice low and intense. 'You're a part of me now, Freya. You make my heart beat.' It was a confession, a promise, and Freya's own pulse echoed the frantic rhythm of Greer's words. The connection between them, forged in darkness and sealed in blood, felt stronger than ever. The patterns on Greer's skin, though less pronounced now, still seemed to reach for her, a visible testament to their bond.

'But there is something I need to attend to,' her lover said, releasing her from the embrace. Greer moved towards her desk, the laptop's screen casting a cold, blue light across her face. Freya watched her log in to her banking app. With a few precise keystrokes, she initiated a substantial transfer of funds.

'We take care of our own,' she explained, sensing

Freya's unspoken question. 'All arrangements must be... suitably compensated.' It was clear this was more than a financial transaction. It was about obligation, protection, ensuring the silence and cooperation of those who knew their secret.

'I doubt Hannah sees it as a mere business transaction.' Freya's voice was soft, but her gaze was direct as she joined her lover.

'No.' Greer's hand found Freya's, her fingers interlacing with hers. 'But we need her. All of them, in truth. We can't...' She searched for the right words. 'Imagine feeding only from you. As much as I desire it, it would be like trying to exist solely on the rarest, most exquisite wine—too potent, too intoxicating. It would consume us both.'

A shiver of disappointment preceded Freya's understanding. 'You require variety.'

'We require balance,' Greer corrected gently, drawing Freya closer. 'And Hannah... she's been loyal, discreet. A valuable asset. We can't afford to lose her, especially now.'

'How did you meet her?'

'Through a specialised agency. One of Victoria Fraser's businesses, as it happens.' Greer's other hand traced patterns on Freya's arm, mimicking the movements from before.

'Victoria Fraser?' Freya knew the woman; in fact, she had purchased two paintings from the exhibition on the night she first met Greer. 'Is she...?' Freya let the question hang, momentarily distracted by Greer's touch.

A genuine smile lit Greer's face. 'A Baobhan Sith? Not in this lifetime. The mere sight of blood makes her queasy. She would laugh at the mere suggestion. But Victoria is a special woman. She understands people's needs, their desires—she understands our needs, and helps facilitate...

arrangements. She never judges. The world could use more individuals like her.' Her expression sobered as she gazed at Freya, one hand coming up to trace the delicate skin of her throat where she'd fed earlier. 'You know there's a marked difference in how we react to you, compared to Hannah. It's visible in the skin.'

Greer's finger traced the place where she'd cut Freya during their passionate encounter. 'See—Hannah's skin shows faint white lines where we've fed. But your cuts...' She smiled, a hint of ancient wonder in her eyes. 'They've already vanished completely.'

Freya looked down in amazement. Where marks should have been, there was only smooth, flawless flesh. The implication made her heart race—this was tangible proof that their connection extended beyond mere feeding.

Without warning, Dior and Hannah came back into the room. Greer jumped in surprise, her elbow catching a crystal tumbler on the desk. It crashed to the floor, the sharp sound slicing through the quiet intimacy. As she bent to clear the broken pieces, a jagged edge caught her palm, drawing blood.

'Let me help,' Freya offered instinctively, reaching for Greer's bleeding hand, still lost in the tenderness of their conversation.

In an instant, she found herself roughly pulled back, Dior's grip like iron around her waist. Greer had recoiled, pressing herself against the wall, her eyes wide with a primal fear that sent a chill down Freya's spine. Her markings writhed frantically beneath her skin, reacting to a deep, instinctive terror.

'Never,' Dior's voice was harsh in Freya's ear, her own patterns pulsing with alarm. 'Never attempt to taste our blood. Not under any circumstances.

Chapter Twenty-Eight

Shattered

The taxi ride home had been a blur. Dior had practically carried her out, bundled her into the cab, and ordered the driver to take her home. No explanation, no goodbyes. Just the lingering image of Greer's terrified face and the echo of that harsh warning about blood.

Sleep had been impossible. Every time she tried to sleep, she was consumed by the patterns writhing beneath Greer's skin, felt the phantom touch of their shared passion. Her body still hummed with the memory of their feeding, of pleasure so intense it bordered on pain. The cuts they'd made had healed completely, but she could map each one from memory, each point where their hunger had marked her.

Now, standing before Greer's door in the harsh light of morning, Freya's hands shook as she knocked. The sound seemed too quiet, too polite for the storm raging inside her. She knocked again, harder this time.

Nothing.

'I know you can hear me,' she called out, her voice cracking. 'Both of you. Your hearing is too good to pretend otherwise.'

Silence answered.

Something snapped inside her. Her fists pounded against the door, no longer caring who might hear. 'You don't get to do this! You don't get to share what we shared and then just... disappear!' Her throat was tight with unshed tears. 'Please,' she pressed her forehead against the cold wood. 'Please, I'm dying out here. I can feel you both on the other side of this door. I can feel the marks you left on my soul, even if they've faded from my skin.'

More silence.

'Fine.' Her voice dropped lower, knowing they could still hear every word. 'Then I'll tell everyone in this building exactly what you are. I'll scream it from the street. I'll—'

The door opened so suddenly she nearly fell forward. Dior stood there, perfect, yet terrible in her anger. 'Are you insane?' she hissed, pulling Freya inside roughly before slamming the door.

'Whatever it takes,' Freya said, fighting to steady herself. 'I won't be dismissed like this. Not after everything.'

'This isn't about dismissal.' Dior's markings were visible even in the daylight, writhing with agitation. 'This is about protection. Survival.'

'Mine or yours?'

'Both.' Dior moved to block her path further into the apartment. 'Go home, little artist. This isn't a path you want to walk.'

'I'm not leaving.' Freya's hands were shaking, but her voice held firm. 'Not until you explain. Not until I understand why one drop of blood could possibly be worth this pain.'

'This will destroy you both,' Dior said softly, something like sympathy crossing her features.

'Let her in.' Greer's voice drifted from somewhere in the shadows, rough as though from crying. 'She won't leave us be until she understands.'

The penthouse was darker than usual, all blinds drawn against the morning light. Greer sat curled in a leather chair, looking wrecked. Her usual grace was gone, replaced by a kind of brittle stillness. Her markings were barely visible, more like bruises beneath her skin. When Freya moved toward her, Dior's arm shot out, holding her back.

'You need to understand why we can't be together,' Dior said, her voice gentle but firm. 'If you had touched her blood last night... your life as you know it would be over.'

'What does that mean?' Freya couldn't take her eyes off Greer's hunched form, her heart aching to comfort her.

'There's no single answer.' Dior's markings stirred as she spoke. 'For some, it's instant death. For others... it's worse. They share our curse, bound to darkness and hunger for eternity. I've seen both. Neither is a fate I'd wish on anyone.'

'Remember Isabella?' Greer's voice was barely a whisper, but it carried across the room like a blade. 'She lasted three days, screaming the whole time as the curse ate through her body.'

'And Mary,' Dior added, pain evident in her voice. 'Transformed but trapped between worlds, neither human nor fully cursed. She hammered an iron nail into her own wrist, unable to bear it any longer.'

'I promise,' Freya said desperately, fighting against Dior's restraining arm. 'I swear I'll never touch your blood. Just let me feed you, be with you. We were perfect together, you felt it too. I know you did. You both did.'

Dior's laugh was sad. 'Oh, little one. You taste so sweet.' Her own markings pulsed, and across the room, Greer's responded. 'Your blood sings to us like nobody before you. But that's not the only problem. Do you know what it's like to love a mortal? To watch them age, fade, die? While we remain unchanged, carrying the weight of their memory through endless nights?'

'But I see you,' Freya stepped closer to Greer, her voice breaking with intensity. 'Both of you. I see past the curse, past the hunger. I can read your markings, understand their patterns. I know I can break this curse—

'Stop.' Greer's voice was stern. 'Do you think you're the first to say that? To think love could overcome this curse?' She finally looked up, her eyes aged with pain. 'They all died, Freya. Every single one who tried. Their bodies twisted, their minds shattered. I won't have that for you.'

'Greer, please—'

'No.' Greer stood, her movements jerky and unnatural. 'You need to leave. Now. Don't go back to the Sanctuary. Don't come here. Don't try to contact us. This ends here.'

Freya felt the words slice into her. 'You're making the same mistake they made all those centuries ago. Banishing love out of fear.'

'Perhaps.' Greer's smile was bitter. 'But at least you'll be alive to hate me for it.'

'You're creating your own curse,' Freya said softly. 'Choosing loneliness out of fear, just like they chose hatred. Don't you see? The curse isn't just what they did to you—it's what you keep doing to yourselves.'

For a moment, something flickered in Greer's eyes—recognition, perhaps, of the terrible symmetry. Then her expression hardened. 'Better cursed than watching you die.

Dior, show her out.' Greer turned away, her shoulders rigid with tension.

'Please,' Freya's voice broke on the word. 'Please don't do this. I can't—' She pressed her hand to her chest, trying to contain the physical pain of this rejection. 'I can't breathe without you now.'

'You'll learn to breathe again.' Dior's grip was gentle but implacable as she guided Freya toward the door. 'The human heart is remarkably resilient.'

'No.' Freya tried to dig in her heels, to resist, to catch one last glimpse of Greer. 'You don't understand. Everything feels different now. Colours are wrong without you. The air tastes empty. How am I supposed to paint when all I can see are your markings? How am I supposed to sleep when I can still feel your hunger inside me?' Her voice had risen, catching with desperation. 'Greer, look at me. Please. Just look at me.'

But Greer remained turned away, though her markings writhed with grief beneath her skin. Only Dior saw the single tear that traced down her cheek.

'Try to understand,' Dior murmured as she opened the door. 'Sometimes love means walking away.'

The door closed behind her. Freya stood in the hallway, staring at the solid wood that now separated her from everything that mattered. Her legs gave way and she slid down the wall, unable to comprehend how she was supposed to leave this building, go home, continue existing in a world that no longer held Greer's touch, Dior's hunger, or Greer's love.

The lift dinged cheerfully at the end of the hall, obscenely normal. Inside, she pressed her forehead against the cool metal wall, watching her reflection fragment in the polished surface. She looked the same as yesterday, and that seemed wrong somehow. Shouldn't there be visible evidence of this devastation? Shouldn't her skin show the absence of their markings, the void where their hunger had lived?

Outside, Edinburgh continued its morning routine, oblivious to her world shattering. People hurried past, clutching coffee cups, checking phones, living their mundane lives. How did they do it? How did they breathe this empty air and not collapse under the weight of such ordinary existence?

She made it three steps from the building's entrance before the sobs overtook her. Ducking into a nearby close, she pressed herself against cold masonry and let grief consume her. Each breath was an effort, each heartbeat a reminder of what she'd lost.

They thought they were protecting her, saving her life. But as she slid down the rough stone, legs unable to hold her, Freya wondered if there would be enough of her left to save. How could she return to her old life when every canvas would show only Greer's patterns, when every shadow would hold Dior's grace, when every moonrise would remind her of what she'd glimpsed and lost?

The marks they'd left on her skin might have healed without a trace, but the ones they'd left on her soul felt like open wounds, bleeding and raw. She had no defence against this pain, no way to process the magnitude of this loss.

They'd shown her a world of primal passion, then cast her back into ordinary darkness.

Above her, a sliver of morning sun caught the building's windows, and for a moment, she thought she saw movement behind the pulled blinds of the penthouse. But it was probably just wishful thinking, just her heart trying to find hope where there was none.

She should go home, try to sleep, to eat, to pretend she could rebuild some semblance of normal life. But home was up there now, in that darkened penthouse with two immortal hearts that had chosen loneliness over love.

Chapter Twenty-Nine

Starvation

Greer saw a stranger reflected in the penthouse windows: a gaunt, hollow-cheeked figure, her usual intensity gone. Her skin, once vibrant and alive, now held the greyish pallor of a long-dead corpse. The scent of decay clung to her, a faint but persistent aroma of must and week-old road kill, all of which made her stomach churn. Her reflection shimmered slightly, the edges blurring as her control wavered. Even her markings, once so vibrant, had faded to faint shadows, tattoos born of youth now withered with age, testament to her diminished state. Even her expensive silk robe hung loose now, draped over shoulders that had grown too sharp, too angular.

The city lights blurred before her eyes. When was the last time she'd moved from this spot? Hours? Days? Time had lost meaning, become fluid and uncertain like everything else in her life. Empty wine bottles littered the floor—not that alcohol could actually intoxicate her, but she kept trying, desperate for any escape from the constant ache of absence.

The painting dominated the wall opposite her bed,

impossible to ignore. She'd bought it the day after sending Freya away, had it delivered. Now it watched her, accused her. In it, her true nature writhed across the canvas in sweeping strokes of black and crimson. Freya had seen her, really seen her, and still wanted to love her. That was the real curse—not just that they brought pain to everyone they loved, but that they were loved anyway, despite their darkness.

Her fingers traced the glass, leaving smudges on the smooth surface. Somewhere out there, Freya was living, breathing, creating. Perhaps even healing. The thought should have brought comfort, but instead it carved fresh wounds in her already ravaged heart. Every heartbeat felt like a betrayal—how dare she continue existing when she'd torn such a hole in both their lives?

'You can't even properly die of a broken heart,' she muttered to her reflection. The curse's cruel joke—they could starve themselves to the edge of death, but never cross over. Only iron through the heart would end it, and only when wielded by someone who loved them. A final twist of the curse—death only by betrayal of love.

She'd tried once, centuries ago, to end it herself. The memory of that failed attempt still burned—the iron blade turning to smoke in her hands, the curse laughing at her presumption. They were bound to this existence, forced to watch everyone they loved either die or turn away. At least she'd spared Freya both fates.

The hunger gnawed at her constantly now, a hollow ache that had nothing to do with food. She hadn't been to the office in weeks letting emails pile up unanswered. What did architecture matter when the only thing she wanted to build was a bridge back to that last night, before everything shattered?

The lift's soft ping announced visitors. Dior's scent reached her first, followed by Hannah's familiar warmth. Even in her weakened state, Greer could hear their sharp intakes of breath at her condition.

'Jesus Christ,' Hannah breathed, taking in Greer's deteriorated state. 'She looks worse than last week.'

'She hasn't fed.' Dior's voice was sharp with worry. 'She's being melodramatic.'

'I can hear you both,' Greer said without turning, her voice rough from disuse.

'Good. Then hear this—you need to feed. You're making yourself ill.'

A bitter laugh escaped Greer's cracked lips. 'But never ill enough to die. That would be too merciful, wouldn't it?'

'Enough.' Dior crossed the room, her own markings dark with anger. She stopped short when she saw the painting. 'You bought it.'

'Of course I bought it.'

'To punish yourself?' Dior's voice softened. 'Or because you couldn't bear anyone else having it?'

'Both. Neither.' Greer finally turned from the window. The movement cost her more energy than it should have. 'Because she saw me. Really saw me. Not just the hunger or the curse, but everything beneath it. And I sent her away.'

'To save her life!'

'Did I?' Greer gestured to the painting, her hand trembling with the effort. 'Look at how she painted the patterns. She understood them, Dior. Really understood them. Maybe she could have—'

'No,' Dior said. 'We've been down this road before. Remember Vienna? Remember what happened to Charlotte when she thought she could break the curse?'

'This is different. Freya is different.'

'It's always different! Every time we let ourselves hope, it's different. And every time, we end up watching someone we love die in agony.' Dior moved closer, gripping Greer's shoulders. Her fingers could span the bones too easily now. 'You're not just punishing yourself. You're punishing me too. Making me watch you waste away over a love you chose to end.'

'I didn't choose—'

'You did. And you're choosing this pain now. You could feed. You could learn to live with the ache, like we always do. But instead you're wallowing in this... this performance of grief.'

Greer sagged in Dior's grip, too weak to maintain even the pretence of strength. She hadn't looked this bad since those first days after the curse, when they'd lain broken and transformed on the hill.

'Hannah,' Dior's voice was gentle now. 'Go prepare yourself. She needs to feed.'

'I won't—' Greer started to protest.

'You will. Because I won't watch you do this to yourself anymore. Because she wouldn't want this for you.'

A pounding at the door interrupted whatever Greer might have said next. Thomas's voice carried through the heavy wood, sharp with fury.

'Open this door right now! What the hell have you done to Freya?'

Greer's markings stirred for the first time in weeks, responding to the threat in his voice. But it was his words that made her heart clench—what had happened to Freya?

Chapter Thirty

Blood and Paint

Thomas stalked across the penthouse floor like a caged animal, his usual polished demeanour cracking with every step. The morning light caught his movements, making him seem almost human in his agitation. Almost.

'She's destroying herself,' he said, his hands clenching and unclenching at his sides. 'I've never seen anything like it. She paints for days without sleeping, without eating.' His voice caught as he ran his hands through his perfectly styled hair. 'When I try to bring her food, she just...' The helplessness in his expression was painful to witness. 'She says she can't taste anything anymore. That everything tastes like dust compared to—'

'Don't,' Greer whispered, but the word was barely audible, a breath of pain in the quiet room. Her markings stirred weakly beneath her grey-tinged skin, responding to even this indirect mention of Freya.

Thomas continued relentlessly, his words tumbling out like poison that needed releasing. 'She's obsessed with blood now. Mixing different shades of red, trying to capture something she says she saw in the two of you. The new paintings...' His whole body shuddered, and for a moment his own carefully maintained glamour slipped, showing something afraid beneath. 'She won't let anyone see them, but I caught a glimpse. Something's twisted inside her, something dark and hungry. It's like she's trying to paint her way back to you, but she's losing herself in the process.'

Dior had arranged herself on the leather sofa with casual elegance, Hannah draped across her lap like a Renaissance painting of decadence. Her fingers traced idle patterns on Hannah's skin, each touch making the woman shiver. 'Aren't we all beyond redemption?' she mused, her nail lengthening to a deadly point as it trailed along Hannah's inner thigh.

The nail pressed deeper, drawing a thin line of perfect crimson. Hannah's moan filled the room, a sound of pure submission as Dior bent to taste, her tongue following the blood's path with practised precision. The scent overwhelmed Greer's senses, her markings rippling with sudden life as the hunger she'd been denying surged through her veins.

'Oh, for—' Thomas threw up his hands, his disgust almost convincing if she didn't know better. 'I haven't even eaten yet.'

Without breaking her attention from Hannah's thigh, Dior reached into her designer bag and tossed him a grease-stained paper wrapper 'Greggs. Still warm.'

'A sausage roll? Really?' He caught it with unconscious grace, betraying his inhuman reflexes.

'You prefer blood pudding?' Her smile was red-stained and wicked, droplets of blood catching the light like rubies.

'I need to go to her,' Greer said suddenly, pushing herself up from her chair. Her legs trembled with weakness, but determination drove her forward, each step a battle against her own deteriorating body.

Dior's head snapped up, blood dripping from her chin in a way that should have been grotesque but somehow remained elegant. 'Over my dead body.'

'That can't even be arranged,' Greer shot back, the ghost of their old banter flickering between them.

Hannah whined at the interruption of her feeding, the sound purely human and oddly out of place. Everyone turned to look at her, their expressions a mix of amusement and exasperation before collectively shaking their heads.

'She has a show in six weeks,' Thomas said, delicately wiping pastry crumbs from his fingers with a silk handkerchief. The mundane gesture seemed absurd against the backdrop of blood and hunger. 'Her first major exhibition since... well. She'll lose everything if this doesn't happen. She's not established enough to survive a cancellation.' He moved closer to Greer, his voice softening with genuine concern. 'If I tell her you'll be there... it might be the only thing that will keep her going until then. Give her something to work toward instead of this endless spiral.'

'No.' Dior stood in one fluid motion, her markings dark and writhing with anger beneath her skin. 'Absolutely not. You've seen what separation has done to them both. Bringing them together again—'

'I'll do it,' Greer interrupted.

'Greer—'

'But,' she turned to Dior, something of her old strength returning to her voice, drawing her spine straighter, 'only if you let me feed now. I need to be stronger. Need to be able to face her.'

Dior's eyes narrowed, the patterns beneath her skin shifting with calculation as she recognised the manipulation but also its necessity. After a long moment, she nodded to Hannah, who shifted eagerly on the sofa, her skin already flushed from Dior's feeding.

'Your terms are acceptable,' Dior said formally, then added with a hint of her usual sardonic humour, 'Though I do enjoy watching you bargain with what you should have been doing anyway.'

Thomas headed for the lift, his movements once again precise and controlled. He paused only to say, 'Six weeks. Try not to waste away completely before then.'

As the lift doors closed, Greer sank to her knees beside Hannah, her movements both graceful and desperate. Her markings began to darken, spreading across her skin, responding to the scent of blood and the promise of relief.

'She won't be the same,' Dior warned softly, her voice carrying centuries of hard-earned wisdom. 'Neither will you.'

'We were never meant to stay the same,' Greer replied, letting her nail lengthen. The sharp point caught the morning light like a promise, or perhaps a threat. 'That's what got us cursed in the first place.'

Chapter Thirty-One

The Opening

Steam filled Freya's bathroom, turning the mirror opaque as she emerged from the shower. Her skin tingled where the hot water had traced paths that reminded her of other touches, nights past. She caught herself pressing fingers to the places where Greer's marks had been, remembering the exquisite pressure of that sharpened nail, the heat of that hungry mouth.

The memory made her gasp, her hand sliding lower of its own accord. Ten weeks without Greer's touch had left her hypersensitive, every sensation amplified by absence. In her mind, it was Greer's cool fingers tracing patterns on her heated skin, Greer's tongue following the path of water droplets down her throat. She braced herself against the sink, lost in the memory of pleasure, of twin hungers satisfied in darkness.

'Focus,' she whispered to her reflection, now visible through the clearing steam. But focusing was dangerous too —every time she closed her eyes, she saw Greer's markings writhing beneath pale skin, felt the ghost of that hunger answering something wild in her own blood.

The dress she'd chosen hung on the back of her bedroom door—black silk that would shift like shadows when she moved. She'd spent hours selecting it, knowing every detail mattered. The neckline dipped just low enough to show where those first precious cuts had been made, while the slit in the skirt would reveal flashes of thigh where Dior had marked her. Let them see the places they'd claimed, the skin that had healed too perfectly.

As she applied her makeup, her hands steady despite her racing heart, Freya studied herself critically. Six weeks of obsessive painting had left their mark—she was thinner, her cheekbones more pronounced, her eyes burning with something that might have been inspiration or madness. But there was power in her stance now, certainty in her movements. She'd poured everything into the new collection, every drop of passion and pain transformed into art that would make Greer understand.

The perfume she chose was new—nothing that would remind them of previous encounters. Tonight needed to be fresh, unprecedented. As she traced it along her pulse points, she imagined Greer's reaction to the scent, how her eyes would darken with recognition of the message in her choice: blood and roses, darkness and desire.

Her fingers trembled slightly as she fastened the delicate silver chain around her neck. The pendant nestled in the hollow of her throat—a small piece she'd found in Dior's shop, even though the woman herself hadn't been there. An intricate knot of thorns and roses.

'You're inside me now,' she whispered to her reflection, practising the words she'd been holding close. 'You flow through my veins like a second pulse. How can you deny this connection when I can feel your hunger in my dreams?

When your patterns write themselves in my art without conscious thought?'

Her phone buzzed—Thomas. 'I'm outside. The meter is running. Don't make me come up there and get you.'

A smile curved her carefully painted lips. Nothing could keep her from tonight. Not after weeks of working in a fever state, channelling every moment of passion and pain into canvases that would make them understand. The gallery walls would be hung with evidence of their connection—not just the obvious pieces they'd expect, but the subtle ones, the dangerous ones. The paintings that showed what she'd glimpsed beneath their curse, the true nature of their markings, the key to unravelling centuries of pain.

She slipped into heels. Let them see she'd changed, that she wasn't just the willing prey they'd left behind. She'd learned their dance, mapped their patterns, understood their hunger from the inside out. Tonight wasn't about begging to be taken back—it was about showing them they'd never truly let her go.

One final check in the mirror. The woman who stared back was both familiar and strange—still Freya, but with a delicious darkness moving beneath her skin. The understanding of how a curse could become a choice, how pain could transform into power.

Her phone buzzed again. 'I mean it, Freya. We have a schedule.'

She grabbed her phone, took one last breath of perfumed air. Inside her chest, her heart beat out a rhythm that felt like destiny. Tonight would change everything. Not because she would beg them to reconsider, but because she would show them what she'd become in their absence. What their curse had created in her.

The paintings waiting at the gallery would speak for her

—canvases that held more than just images, or memories. They held truth, transformation, and the key to their salvation. Once Greer saw them, once she understood what Freya had discovered...

'Coming,' she texted back, already moving toward the door with deadly grace. Tonight wasn't an ending. It wasn't even a beginning.

It was a becoming.

Chapter Thirty-Two

Revelation

The gallery was closed for their private viewing. The spotlights cut sharp shadows across the empty space. Greer moved with deadly grace, stopping only when the first painting stopped them in their tracks.

'My God,' Hannah breathed, but Greer and Dior stood silent, transfixed.

The initial pieces were studies in shadow and transformation—figures emerging from darkness, patterns suggesting movement captured in mid-flow. But to their ancient eyes, each canvas held deeper truths. Freya had captured their markings with devastating accuracy, showing how they shifted and changed, how they responded to hunger and night air.

'She saw everything,' Dior murmured, her own markings stirring beneath her skin in response to their painted counterparts. 'Every detail, every subtle change.'

As they moved deeper into the gallery, the paintings grew more complex. One massive canvas showed their patterns as they appeared during feeding—but Freya had revealed something they'd never noticed. The markings weren't random; they formed intricate geometries, mathematical progressions that spoke of logic rather than curse.

'Look,' Greer traced the air above one painting, following the flow of patterns. 'She's shown how they're connected. How they echo each other.'

The next section made even Dior catch her breath. These pieces showed their markings as part of something larger—reflecting patterns found in nature, in healing, in growth. One canvas depicted their curse marks transforming like flowers opening to moonlight, while another showed them flowing like river networks, like blood vessels, like life itself.

But it was the final triptych that brought them to a gasping halt.

The first panel, titled 'Diorbhail', showed Dior in her true form. The markings on her skin were rendered in oils so rich they seemed to move in the light. But rather than showing them as scars of punishment, Freya had captured them as marks of survival, of strength. Dior's painted form emerged from darkness like a goddess of night, beautiful and terrible and utterly sublime.

The second, 'Greer', was almost too intimate to bear. Greer saw herself as Freya saw her—powerful and vulnerable at once, her markings not a curse but a chronicle of love that refused to die. The painting captured the exact moment of feeding, but transformed it into something sacred rather than profane.

The third piece, 'Rapture', stole the very air from their lungs. It showed all three of them entwined, but abstracted into swirls of colour and shadow that somehow captured the essence of their connection. Greer and Dior's markings reached across the canvas like living things, while Freya's form arched in ecstasy, caught in a moment of perfect surrender. It was feeding and sex and love and transformation all at once, rendered with such raw honesty it was almost painful to witness.

'This is...' Hannah's voice cracked. 'I've never seen anything like this.'

'Magnificent, isn't it?' Thomas appeared beside them, practically vibrating with excitement. 'Almost everything's sold already. The critics are calling it a breakthrough show.'

'Who?' Greer's voice was tight. 'Who's buying them?'

Thomas consulted his tablet. 'Various collectors for most pieces, but the triptych...' He scrolled through his notes. 'I didn't deal with that one myself... Hold on, I've got it here, all three pieces to one buyer— Thomas looked up, stunned. 'Agnes Lasair.'

The temperature in the gallery seemed to drop. Dior's markings darkened visibly beneath her skin.

'No,' Greer breathed.

'You know her?' Hannah asked.

But Greer was already moving, her grace turned predatory. 'Where is Freya?'

'Getting ready for her grand entrance.'

'Why?' asked Hannah. 'What's wrong?'

'Because,' Dior's voice was sharp with fear, 'Agnes doesn't buy art. She collects secrets. And power.' She caught Greer's arm. 'She's seen what these paintings reveal.'

'We have to protect Freya.' Greer's markings writhed with barely contained panic. 'Agnes can't be allowed anywhere near her.'

'Who is Agnes Lasair?' Hannah asked, but the look Dior and Greer exchanged silenced her question.

'Find Freya,' Greer ordered Thomas. 'Now. Before—'

The gallery lights dimmed slightly, signalling the arrival of guests. Somewhere in the building, a door opened.

They were out of time.

Chapter Thirty-Three

The Arrival

The gallery doors opened and the first guests began to filter in, their excited murmurs echoing off white walls. But Greer barely registered their presence. Her entire being was focused on the scent that had just hit her—Freya's perfume, but different now, mixed with something darker, richer.

'Spread out,' Dior commanded, her voice low enough that only Baobhan Sith ears could catch it. 'Thomas, keep Agnes away from her if she shows.' Then she turned to Hannah, taking her hands. 'Hannah, stay close to the exit. I want you out of harm's way.'

Greer wasn't listening. The crowd had parted, and there was Freya.

The black silk dress flowed around her body, revealing teasing glimpses of the skin they'd once marked. She'd lost weight, but it had transformed her into something ethereal, dangerous. Her eyes burned with a fever brightness that Greer recognised—the same fire that had consumed countless others who'd tried to unravel their curse.

Their gazes met across the gallery, and the world seemed to stop.

Freya moved through the crowd with a predatory grace she must have learned from them, making her way toward the triptych. She knew they'd be there, knew they'd understand what she'd created. Each step was deliberate, a performance for them as much as the admiring crowd.

'Ladies and gentlemen,' Thomas's voice cut through the tension, professional and polished. 'If I could direct your attention to our artist...'

But his words faded to background noise as Freya reached them. This close, Greer could see the subtle changes in her—not just physical, but something deeper. The way she held herself, the knowing look in her eyes. She'd crossed some threshold in their absence, moved beyond simple humanity.

'Do you understand now?' Freya asked softly, her voice meant only for them. 'What your markings really are?'

'Stop,' Greer breathed. 'You don't know what you're dealing with.'

'Don't I?' Freya's smile was sharp as a blade. 'Look at what I've painted. Really look. Your patterns aren't a curse—they're a map. A way back to what you were before hatred twisted you.'

'A map that others can now read,' Dior cut in, her voice urgent. 'Do you have any idea what you've done? Who you've exposed us to?'

But before Freya could respond, a new scent cut through the gallery—old and cold as midwinter frost. Greer's markings writhed beneath her skin in instinctive recognition.

'Darling girl,' came a voice deadly in its softness. 'What remarkable insight you have.'

They turned to find a woman standing before the triptych. She was beautiful in the way that arctic wastelands were beautiful—pristine and deadly. Her dress was white as bone, her hair black as pitch. When she smiled, her teeth glistened. Surprising for a woman who'd never visited a dental hygienist.

'Agnes,' Dior's voice held centuries of carefully controlled fear.

'The paintings are exquisite,' Agnes said, running one perfectly manicured finger along the frame of 'Rapture.' 'Such... understanding. Tell me, my dear,' she turned to Freya, 'how did you learn to see so clearly?'

Greer moved without thinking, placing herself between Freya and Agnes. Her markings were fully visible now, a body cloaked in living tattoos, responding to the presence of something far older and more dangerous than herself.

'She's mine,' Greer growled, the words torn from some primal place.

Agnes's laugh was like breaking ice. 'Oh, sweet child. Nothing is truly yours. Not your curse, not your patterns...' Her eyes glittered with ancient malice. 'And certainly not this fascinating little artist who's learned to read our oldest secrets.'

The gallery lights flickered, just for a moment. In that instant of darkness, Agnes's own markings became visible—patterns so complex they hurt to look at, writing themselves across her skin in scripts that predated humanity.

'Now then,' she said pleasantly, 'who will do the introductions?'

Chapter Thirty-Four

The Minister's Wife

The silence stretched, thick and heavy with unspoken history. Agnes's voice, when it finally broke the quiet, was like ice cracking on a frozen lake. 'Silence? That's not in the least hospitable. The least you can do is introduce me to this creature.' Her accent was the crisp, cultured tone of Edinburgh's elite, but beneath it lurked a guttural echo that made the hairs on Freya's neck stand on end. 'I'm Agnes.' She extended a hand towards Freya, her fingers long and pale, tipped with nails that gleamed like polished bone. The scent of frost and grave dirt clung to her, a chilling contrast to the warmth of the gallery.

Her beauty was severe—high-cheekbones sharp enough to slice bread, grey eyes the colour of fishermen's nightmares. She wore cream, a dress that seemed to absorb light rather than reflect it, and her silver hair was swept up in a style that hadn't been fashionable since the 1630s.

But it was her smile that made Greer's markings writhe in recognition. The same smile that had once greeted them at Bible study, innocent and devout, before they'd destroyed her life with their sins.

'Agnes,' Dior breathed, the name falling like a stone into silence.

'I am Badb,' Agnes corrected, her voice now resonating with an unnatural depth, a sound that vibrated the very bones of the gallery. The air around her shimmered, and for a fleeting moment, her form flickered, revealing the shadow of a crow's wing. 'Agnes died at the stake, burned by her husband's congregation, because of you.'

The woman turned her attention to Freya. 'They needed someone to blame for harbouring witches. They blamed you for the storms that sunk the boats, for the famine that followed. They blamed me for allowing the two of you to— do the unnatural.' Her gaze fixed on Greer, hatred burning beneath the polite veneer, now intensified by an ancient, primal power. 'You used me. My kindness, my ignorance. Made me complicit in your corruption.'

Freya stepped forward, but Greer caught her arm. The gallery guests continued their conversations, somehow blind to the supernatural presence now unveiled in their midst.

'We never meant—' Greer started.

'What you meant doesn't matter,' Agnes cut her off. 'I was innocent. Devoted to God, to my husband—your minister. I thought you came to study scripture, to find His light. Instead, you brought darkness into my home, made me an unwitting party to your sins.' She gestured to the triptych. 'And now you flaunt that darkness as if it were beautiful.'

'You died because of us,' Dior's voice was heavy with old guilt. 'But we can't undo what they did.'

'I became this,' Agnes corrected, her perfect composure cracking to reveal the raw power beneath. 'Do you know what it's like, feeling the flames consume you, the very essence of your being transformed by fire and hatred? Hearing him pray for your soul as your flesh burns? All because I was too naive to see what was happening under my own roof. Under God's roof!'

She moved closer, and now they could see what lay beneath—skin that rippled like wax about to melt, eyes burned with otherworldly light. Feathers, dark as night, briefly sprouted from her back, only to recede just as quickly.

'I made a vow as I burned, a vow that became my very being,' she continued. 'To cleanse this world of creatures like you. To punish those who corrupt His natural laws. And the flames... they answered. They gave me purpose. Power. I became the very force I was accused of consorting with.' Her smile widened. 'The power to hurt even those who cannot die.'

'The paintings,' Freya said suddenly. 'You bought them because they show—'

'How to unmake you? Yes, clever girl. Your art reveals so much—the patterns of their curse, the way it flows through their bodies.' Agnes's hand moved faster than human eyes could track, producing something that gleamed dully in the gallery lights. 'And where to strike to cause the most pain.'

The iron blade plunged toward Greer's heart, aimed at the exact spot Freya had painted where her markings spiralled most densely. Freya moved without thinking, putting herself between Greer and the blade. Time seemed to slow as metal met flesh, as Agnes's smile turned to surprise, as Greer's scream of denial shattered every window in the gallery.

Chapter Thirty-Five

Blood and Iron

Chaos erupted as the gallery windows imploded. Screaming guests fled through shattered frames, their exodus punctuated by the sound of crunching glass underfoot. Freya lay crumpled in front of the triptych, blood spreading around her body like spilled wine. Greer's cry of rage still echoed off the walls as Agnes spun away from her failed strike, iron blade gleaming.

'Your pet's blood smells divine,' Agnes taunted, her form flickering between elegant woman and something darker, crow-wings shadowing the air around her. 'But it's not the sacrifice I came for.'

She lunged at Greer, the blade whistling through air. Greer barely dodged, the iron passing close enough that her skin blistered from its proximity. Behind her, one of Freya's smaller paintings fell, its frame splintering.

'You corrupted everything you touched,' Agnes snarled, pressing her attack. 'Made me complicit in your sins.' Each word was punctuated by another strike, driving Greer back through the gallery. 'Made them burn me for your crimes.'

Dior moved to flank her, but Agnes was too quick. She

kicked a broken frame into Dior's path, forcing her to vault over it. The movement brought her too close to Hannah, who had been trying to reach Freya's prone form.

'No—' Dior's warning came too late.

Agnes's blade found Hannah's heart with surgical precision. 'Another heathen banished,' she crowed as Hannah's eyes widened in shock. 'Another soul cleansed by iron and righteousness.'

Time seemed to slow as Hannah crumpled, her expression more surprised than afraid. Her hand reached toward Dior as she fell, her mouth open as though making a silent plea for help. Then the light left her eyes, and she was gone.

'You revel in it,' Dior's voice was barely human, her markings writhing like living shadows across her skin. 'You dare speak of righteousness while glorying in death?'

She dropped to her knees, movements precise despite her rage. From the pocket of her evening dress, she produced a handful of ancient runes that gleamed dully in the emergency lights. With practised speed, she began placing them in a circle around herself and Greer.

Agnes laughed, from the deepest hollows of her empty soul. 'Celtic trinkets won't save you from God's judgement.'

But her laughter died as Dior set the last piece. Each rune began to glow: the Triquetra pulsing with protective power, the Triskele spinning with ancient motion, the Ailm burning with silver light, the Ngetal whispering secrets in forgotten tongues. Circles and spirals wove between them, creating a barrier of light and symbol that Agnes could not breach.

'These are older than your borrowed divinity,' Dior said, rising. 'Older than your hatred. They remember when the Badb served nature's balance, not religious zealotry.'

Agnes struck the barrier with her blade, sending sparks

flying. But she could not cross it. 'You think this will save you? Save her?' She gestured to Freya, still bleeding outside their circle. 'Iron has tasted her blood now. The curse will take her, one way or another.'

'The only curse here is you,' Greer snarled, moving toward the barrier's edge. But Dior caught her arm.

'She's baiting you,' Dior warned. 'We need to think.'

Around them, the gallery lay in ruins. Paintings were shattered, the revelations of their secrets scattered across blood-stained floors. Only the triptych remained intact, its images of transformation and possibility now watching over Freya's still form like silent witnesses.

Agnes began to circle their magical barrier, her movements predatory. With each pass, her human guise slipped further, revealing more of the corrupted deity beneath. Feathers sprouted from her arms, her eyes burned with unholy fire.

'I can wait,' she said. 'The girl bleeds. Your pet is dead. How long before your conscience forces you to leave your sanctuary?' Her smile was cruel. 'Sometimes the greatest torment is watching others suffer for your sins.'

Dior's hand found Greer's, their markings synchronised in shared grief and rage. Outside their circle of ancient symbols, Freya's blood crept closer to the barrier's edge, while Hannah's cooling body bore silent testament to the price of Agnes's righteousness.

They needed a plan. But first, they needed to survive.

Chapter Thirty-Six

Chaos and Control

The wail of police sirens pierced the night. Greer's gaze darted between the approaching lights and Freya's crumpled form, a worrying amount of blood surrounding her body.

'Go,' Dior said, her voice tight with fury. 'I'll handle our righteous friend.'

Greer didn't hesitate. She burst through their protective circle, the ancient runes flaring as she passed. Agnes lunged for her, but Dior was faster, hurling a broken frame that forced the furious deity to dodge.

'Your fight's with me now,' Dior snarled, her markings writhing like living shadows. 'I owe you for Hannah.'

Greer reached Freya in three desperate strides, gathering her into her arms. The iron wound was deep but had missed her heart. Blood stained Greer's hands, but Freya's pulse was still there, weak but present.

Armed police burst through the gallery doors, weapons raised. But instead of chaos, there was calm. Thomas stood among them, his usual perfectly-tailored suit incongruous among tactical gear.

'Area secure,' he commanded, his voice carrying unnatural authority. 'Perimeter established. No one enters or leaves without my authorisation.'

The officers moved with mechanical precision, following his orders without question. Greer had never seen this side of him—the power he wielded over mortal authorities.

'The girl needs medical attention,' he called out, but his eyes met Greer's with clear meaning: *Get her out. Now.*

Agnes's laughter echoed as she traded blows with Dior, their forms blurring with supernatural speed. 'Thomas can't control them forever. My followers are coming—true believers who'll cleanse this city of abominations.'

As if summoned, figures in black gathered at the shattered windows, brandishing iron weapons, their crosses gleaming at their throats. But they couldn't enter—Thomas's police had the building locked down, their minds bound to his will.

'Not tonight, they won't,' Thomas said smoothly, adjusting his cuffs. 'Edinburgh is my city. You're trespassing.'

Dior seized her moment. As Agnes turned to snarl at Thomas, Dior struck. Her nail—lengthened to a deadly point—raked across Agnes's face. Corrupted blood, obsidian-black, spattered the ruined gallery floor.

Agnes unleashed a scream, a sound that shattered what remained of the windows. Her form flickered violently—woman, crow, something older and more terrible. Then she was gone, leaving only feathers and the scent of burning hatred.

'This isn't over,' her voice echoed from everywhere and nowhere. 'The girl's blood is tainted now. Iron-touched. She'll never be the same.'

Greer clutched Freya closer, feeling the heat of fever already building in her skin. 'Stay with me,' she whispered. 'Please. Just hold on.'

'Greer, get her to the sanctuary,' Dior ordered as she knelt beside Hannah's body, gathering her fallen lover in a final tender embrace. 'I'll handle things here.'

Thomas was already creating their cover story, his voice smooth as he directed his enthralled officers. 'Gas leak... structural damage... no casualties...'

'The paintings,' Freya mumbled against Greer's chest, barely conscious. 'They show... how to break...'

'Shh,' Greer pressed her lips to Freya's burning forehead. 'Save your strength. Stay with me.'

She carried Freya's injured body toward the service exit, using shadows to hide their passage. Behind them, Dior's wail of grief for Hannah pierced the night.

The war wasn't over. Agnes would return, with her zealots and her iron and her twisted righteousness. But tonight, Greer had only one priority—saving the woman who'd risked everything to save her.

Chapter Thirty-Seven

Iron's Touch

Frantic energy filled the Crimson Sanctuary's circular room, the usual scents of arousal and anticipation giving way to the sharp tang of fear and adrenaline. Greer stumbled through the doorway, Freya's limp form cradled in her arms. Her own markings writhed beneath her skin, a frantic dance of desperation. Dior followed close behind, her voice sharp as she barked orders, clearing the space with a ruthless efficiency that chilled the very bones of those present. Greer lurched towards the cushions, every movement desperate. She would not let Freya fucking die. Not here, not now not ever.

'Hold on,' Greer whispered against Freya's hair. 'Just hold on.' But Freya's skin was already too cool, her breathing too shallow.

Maeve appeared with medical supplies—mortal solutions for an immortal problem. There wasn't a bandage or antibiotic in this world that could counter blessed iron. Her usual stoicism fractured for a moment at the sight of Freya's wound. 'Oh fuck,' she breathed. 'Is that—'

'Iron,' Dior confirmed, her voice tight with grief. 'Blessed iron.'

Greer laid Freya on the cushions, her movements gentle despite her trembling hands. 'I can't lose her,' she said, the words torn from somewhere deep and primal. 'I won't.'

'Your markings,' Dior noticed suddenly. 'They're reaching for her.'

The patterns beneath Greer's skin did indeed seem drawn to Freya, writhing toward her like living things seeking connection. But where they usually brought pleasure, now they brought only pain—Freya whimpered at their proximity.

❄

Freya's breath hitched, a rasping, shallow gasp that echoed in the sudden hush. The iron's touch had been like a brand, a searing cold that had burrowed deep, not just into her flesh, but into something far more vital. Her vision blurred, the room's familiar shadows dissolving into grey mist.

The wound wept dark, viscous blood—nothing like the bright crimson that had once fed their passion. It felt wrong, tainted. A chill deeper than any winter frost spread through her limbs, numbing her fingers and toes.

She could hear Greer's frantic whispers, feel the desperate pressure of her hands trying to staunch the flow, but it was like trying to hold back the tide. Life seeped away with each dark drop that fell to the floor. Her heart fluttered weakly, a dying bird trapped in a cage.

A tremor ran through her body, her eyes fluttering closed. The pain had receded, replaced by a strange, unsettling calm. It was seductive, this gentle pull toward oblivion.

She felt Greer's face against hers, a whisper of a kiss on her forehead—a silent farewell.

She tried to speak, to offer some last word of comfort, of love, but her voice was gone, lost somewhere in the growing darkness.

❄

'Greer...' Dior's voice cut through the encroaching darkness, sharp and urgent. 'Look at her blood! It's... it's reacting to the iron. It's not just a physical wound.'

Greer's head snapped up, her eyes widening as she looked at the dark blood pooling on Freya's chest. It wasn't clotting properly. It seemed almost inert, as if the iron had somehow poisoned it, stopped it from fulfilling its natural function.

But there was something else—where Greer's tears had fallen, mixing with the tainted blood, strange patterns began to form. Like her markings, but different, a new language searing through her flesh.

'She's dying,' said Dior, as she knelt beside them, studying the strange patterns forming in Freya's blood. 'But there might be a way...'

'No.' Greer's arms tightened around Freya. 'Our blood could kill her.'

'She's dying anyway,' Dior's voice was gentle but firm. 'The iron is stealing her life, drop by drop. Our blood might transform her, might save her—'

'Or torture her,' Greer's voice cracked. 'You've seen what happens when mortals taste our blood. The agony they suffer. And we can't... we can't ask her. She hasn't given consent. I won't do that to her, won't take that choice away—'

A single word, barely a whisper, stopped them both. Freya's lips moved, forming the word with the last of her strength.

'Please.'

Greer looked down into Freya's eyes, seeing in them not just pain and fear, but trust. Absolute trust.

The time for choices had come.

Chapter Thirty-Eight

Blood Bond

Greer cradled Freya's limp body while Dior prepared what they needed—a silver bowl, ancient and etched with symbols akin to those that had protected them in the gallery. Only the gasps of Freya's shallow breaths and the frantic pounding of Greer's own heart broke the silence.

'It has to be both of us,' Dior said, her markings beginning to stir beneath her skin. 'Our blood combined might be strong enough to counter the iron's poison.'

Greer nodded, unable to tear her gaze from Freya's face. The iron's corruption had spread—dark lines traced paths through her veins, visible beneath her increasingly translucent skin. She fought for each breath, every inhale a battle.

'If this goes wrong...' Greer couldn't finish.

'She chose this,' Dior reminded her. 'She's always chosen us.'

Their working was centuries old, though neither had performed it before... not with intent. But they had no choice now—Freya's pulse weakened with each passing moment.

Dior's nail lengthened, sharp as a surgeon's blade. She drew it across her own wrist, letting cursed blood fall into the bowl. The moment it struck the metal, her markings flared bright beneath her skin, responding to old magic.

Greer's hand trembled as she held out her own wrist. When Dior's nail split her skin, the pain was nothing compared to the fear churning in her chest. Their combined blood swirled in the bowl, forming and dissolving like living things.

'Now,' Dior whispered.

Greer lifted Freya's head, supporting her while Dior brought the bowl to her lips. The moment their blood touched her tongue, Freya's body arched violently. Her eyes flew open, unseeing, rolled back to show only whites.

'Hold her,' Dior commanded, continuing to tip the bowl. 'She has to take it all.'

Freya convulsed in Greer's arms, her skin burning hot then ice cold. Where their blood traced paths down her throat, lines began to appear—not like their markings, but a new language, as though combining their ancient curse with Freya's mortal essence.

'Please,' Greer whispered against Freya's hair. 'Please stay with me.'

The bowl emptied. For a moment, nothing happened. Then Freya screamed—a sound of such agony it shattered the mirror above, raining glass down like deadly tears.

Dior threw the runes to protect them, dispersing the falling shards.

'Is it killing her?' Greer's voice broke.

'No,' Dior watched, fascinated, as new lines etched themselves across Freya's skin. 'It's changing her.'

Freya's body temperature fluctuated wildly as she thrashed in Greer's arms. The iron wound on her chest began to smoke, dark blood turning silver where it met their combined essence. Her fingers clawed at air, leaving trails of luminescence in their wake.

❄

Freya's blood was on fire, every vein, every cell in her body screaming in protest and… elation? It was agony, yes, but an agony intertwined with something else, something that felt strangely like power. A power that was both terrifying and exhilarating. Was this what Greer and Dior felt every time they fed? This desperate, overwhelming need, this sense of being consumed by something larger than themselves?

She could feel the lines as she drifted in and out of consciousness, not just on Greer's and Dior's skin, but inside her, as if their essence was rewriting her own, transforming her into something… other. Something new. It was as if she was being unmade and remade, atom by atom, into a being that could exist in both realms, a bridge between the mortal and the immortal.

❄

Greer and Dior took turns to sit with Freya as she shifted between screaming agony and deathlike stillness, holding her, whispering ancient words of comfort. Their own markings responded to each phase of her transformation, reaching toward her with every convulsion.

Just before dawn, Freya's eyes opened. They were her own, yet different—flecked with silver like starlight on water. She looked at Greer with perfect clarity.

'I can see them,' she whispered, reaching up to trace one

of Greer's markings. Where their skin met, a spark danced. 'I can see everything now.'

Greer caught her hand, pressed it to her lips. 'What do you see?'

But before Freya could answer, her eyes rolled back again. This time when unconsciousness took her, it was gentle—her breathing deep and even, her skin cool but not cold.

'Will she...' Greer couldn't finish the question.

Dior touched Freya's forehead, reading the new lines that had settled beneath her skin. 'She's not Baobhan Sith,' she said slowly. 'But she's not mortal anymore either. She's something new.'

Chapter Thirty-Nine

New Beginnings

Thomas arrived at the Crimson Sanctuary three days after the gallery incident, looking as impeccable as ever despite having spent those days managing police, press, and public perception. The ease with which he controlled mortal minds no longer seemed amusing—it was a power that demanded respect or, in the wrong hands, fear.

'The official story is holding,' he said, accepting a glass of wine from Dior. 'Gas explosion. Tragic accident. Insurance will cover everything.'

'And the real story?' Greer asked, not moving from her vigil at Freya's bedside. She hadn't left since the transformation, her devotion as clear as the markings that stirred beneath her skin whenever Freya stirred in her sleep.

'Is spreading through certain circles.' His expression grew serious. 'Agnes has everyone frightened. The community as a whole is... unsettled. Then we have a mortal who can read our patterns, now transformed by ancient blood magic?' Thomas glanced at Freya, raising an eyebrow. 'It changes things.'

As if responding to his words, Freya stirred. She'd been sleeping more than not these past days, her body adjusting to its new reality. The lines beneath her skin were unlike anything they'd seen—not the curse-marks of the Baobhan Sith, but something more fluid, more alive. Sometimes they shifted with her dreams, creating images of impossible beauty.

'She moved a cup yesterday,' Greer said softly, her voice full of wonder and love. 'Without touching it. Just... wanted it, and it came to her.'

'Telekinesis?' Thomas raised an eyebrow.

'More like... reality bending to her will. I had to duck out of the bloody way,' said Dior as she watched the tender way Greer smoothed Freya's hair. 'She's carrying part of our curse now, but filtered through her artist's soul. She sees patterns in everything—not just our markings, even in the energy of her surroundings.'

The air around them seemed to thicken with possibility. Their blood had changed Freya, but she was changing them too.

'You two seem... different,' Thomas observed, his gaze moving between Greer and Dior.

'We've found peace,' Dior said simply. 'The curse twisted what we once were into darkness. But Freya might show us a different way.' She smiled at Greer, then turned her attention back to Thomas. 'And I've not been to Greggs since this happened. It's probably my svelte curves you're noticing.' She struck a pose to prove her point.

Thomas exchanged a weary glance with Greer.

'Everything with Dior comes back to food,' said Greer, 'and yet she never puts on a single pound.'

'What can I say when you have something to flaunt...' Dior chuckled.

'Speaking of flaunting—I managed to save one piece from the gallery. The triptych's centrepiece,' said Thomas with a flourish.

'"Rapture",' Dior said, impressed.

'It's being delivered to your penthouse,' he said to Greer. 'Seemed fitting, given recent developments.'

A soft sound from the bed drew their attention. Freya's eyes fluttered open, silver-flecked and knowing. When she saw Greer, her whole being seemed to light up, their connection almost visible in the air between them. Around her, reality rippled slightly, responding to her joy. A nearby vase of flowers suddenly bloomed more fully, their colours deepening.

'Now that's just downright weird,' said Dior.

❄

'I feel... different,' said Freya, her voice thick with sleep. 'Like every nerve ending is on fire. But it feels good.'

She stretched, her body tingling with a strange new energy. She sniffed, suddenly aware the air was alive with a thousand different scents, each one distinct and vibrant – the fragrance of the flowers on the table, Thomas's overuse of cologne, the exhaust fumes from passing buses.

'It's the blood,' Dior said softly, coming to stand beside Greer. 'It changes you. Heightens your senses, awakens your potential.'

Freya turned her head, meeting Dior's gaze. The older woman's eyes, usually so guarded, now held a warmth, a tenderness, that Freya had rarely seen before, even when they made love.

'How long was I out?' she asked, her voice still hoarse.

'A few hours,' Greer replied, squeezing Freya's hand. 'You needed to rest. To heal.'

Freya tried to sit up, but a wave of dizziness washed over her, forcing her to lie back down. Her body felt both heavy and strangely light, as if she were floating just above the surface of the bed.

'Easy, love,' Greer said, her voice laced with concern. 'It takes time to adjust. The transformation... it's a lot for the body to process.'

'She'll need to feed soon,' Dior added thoughtfully, as she studied Freya's face. 'The hunger will be different for her, but it will come.'

The word 'hunger' sent a jolt through Freya's system, a primal echo of the need she had felt during her transformation. But this was different, subtler, a gentle hum beneath the surface rather than an all-consuming fire.

'I'm not sure I'm ready for that yet,' she admitted.

'There's no rush,' Greer said, sensing her apprehension. 'We'll be here to guide you, every step of the way.' She held up her phone. 'I've downloaded the *Just Eat* app, so I'm going nowhere. Did you know that Harvey Nichols Brasserie can bring your dinner to you by moped!'

Freya laughed, reassured by their presence, by the unwavering support that radiated from them both.

'What happens now?' she asked, her voice barely above a whisper.

Greer and Dior exchanged a look, a silent conversation passing between them. It was a look of determination, of resilience, of a love that had endured for centuries.

'Now,' Greer said, her hand finding Freya's, their fingers interlacing. 'We face the future. Together.'

Chapter Forty

Interwoven

Freya woke to an overwhelming hunger. It wasn't just a single craving but two distinct needs that twisted within her transformed body—a sharp, primal thirst for blood and a deeper, molten desire for flesh. These new sensations were accompanied by a subtle hum beneath her skin, a chorus of energies she was only just beginning to understand. Her markings, still new after three weeks, pulsed with a light that seemed to answer the faint thrum, their glow mirroring the soft hues of civil dawn. Dusky blues and blush pinks crept across the penthouse bedroom, bathing the space in a muted, tranquil glow, yet beneath that serenity, Freya sensed a complex tapestry of energies, interwoven and alive.

She was no longer just human, no longer just an observer. The blood of the Baobhan Sith flowed through her veins, a potent elixir that had rewritten her very being. Greer and Dior had explained some of what was to come in the hours following her transformation—the heightened senses, the shifting hungers, the pull of the supernatural realm that now lay within her reach. But nothing could have prepared her for this.

The city was a cacophony of sound twenty floors below, each noise distinct and vibrant, almost tangible. Freya could isolate the rumble of early buses, the rhythmic tap of footsteps on pavements, even the delicate flutter of pigeons' wings on the breeze. Each sound seemed to carry its own unique signature, a thread in the larger tapestry of the city's awakening. The scents were even more overwhelming, a vibrant kaleidoscope. She could pinpoint the rich aroma of coffee from a café half a mile away, the warm, yeasty scent of fresh bread from the bakery down the street, and, strongest of all, the intoxicating, coppery tang of her lovers' skin—each scent a distinct note in a powerful chord.

Greer's arm, a warm, grounding weight, tightened around her waist, a subconscious reflex in her sleep. Freya turned, drawn in by the subtle energy that shimmered around her lover, even in slumber. As she studied Greer's face in the dim light, she saw not just the physical form but the intricate patterns of energy that flowed beneath the surface, revealing a peacefulness, a vulnerability that was masked in waking hours.

A sudden surge of desire, hot and intense, pulsed through Freya, a tangible wave that seemed to ignite the very air around them. It was more than just physical need—it was a hunger for connection, a yearning to weave their energies together in the unique, intimate tapestry that only they could create.

She leaned down and kissed Greer, softly at first, then with more urgency. Her tongue traced the line of Greer's bottom lip, tasting the lingering sweetness of their shared pleasure.

Dior shifted, already reaching for her. 'If you're hungry, the glasses are ready in the kitchen—'

'No.' Freya turned to capture Dior's mouth in a desperate kiss, tasting the last remnants of darkness and ancient magic on her tongue. 'I want it from you. Both of you. Like this.' The thought of cold blood in crystal glasses seemed obscene when she could feel their pulses calling to her, their markings reaching for hers in the subdued pre-dawn light.

'Are you sure, love?' Greer asked. Freya noticed a slight unease in her tone. 'It's... different, feeding like this. More intense.'

'I know,' Freya said. 'But I need it. I need you. Both of you.'

'You'll need to fully transition onto human blood eventually,' she heard Greer say softly.

'Eventually.' Dior's smile was visible in the muted glow, her markings brightening with anticipation. 'But if she wants to feed from us right now, she can. And bypassing the glasses saves on the washing up.'

Freya found herself cradled between them, their breasts pressed against her, Dior's hand sliding between her legs. She could feel their heartbeats, smell their arousal, see the way their markings reached for her like living things. She could see intricate patterns there too, swirling beneath their skin like rivers of silver light.

'Take your time,' she heard Greer say, and noticed her nail lengthen. 'One hand for feeding, one hand for pleasure.'

'Or it'll get messy,' Dior added, her fingers playing gentle circles on Freya's inner thigh.

Freya whimpered. Her nail extended, a physical manifestation of the energy shifting within her. As she tentatively drew a small line above Greer's left breast, she felt a subtle resistance, a boundary between their energies, before the skin parted easily. A thin crimson line welled, and Freya watched, mesmerised, as the patterns beneath Greer's skin responded, shifting and flowing towards the small wound like quicksilver, drawn in by an invisible current.

The first taste of Greer's blood was an explosion of sensation, an explosion of flavour, rich and complex, carrying echoes of centuries, of power, and of passion. It was more than just taste; it was a rush of energy, a cascade of information that flooded her senses. She moaned, not just from pleasure, but from the sheer intensity of the connection, as patterns of sensation spiralled through their linked energies, a vibrant dance of light and feeling.

'Tell me what she tastes like?' Dior asked, her hand teasing its way up soft skin to the centre of Freya's arousal.

Freya allowed her head to roll back in pleasure before she answered. 'Like a Château Lafite Rothschild 1869.'

'Let me try.' She watched Dior swipe her finger through a stray droplet, place it on her tongue, then pull a face as though she'd sucked a lemon. 'She's corked!'

Greer's laugh turned to a gasp as Freya's tongue found the small wound again. Dior's nail extended, cutting a thin line across her own breast, and Freya turned and latched on eagerly. She could see the patterns now, intricate swirls of silver and shadow that connected them all. They seemed to pulse with a life of their own, extending beyond the boundaries of their bodies, weaving through the air around them. When she touched them, they resonated like plucked strings, sending waves of pleasure, each a distinct note in a complex chord, through all three women. She was learning to play them like instruments, her fingers tracing the intricate lines, each touch, each caress, creating new harmonies of sensation, new melodies of pleasure that echoed around them. And likewise, when she responded to the pleasure of Dior's touch toying with her clit, they too felt the surge of need.

'Want to taste how sweet Greer's blood is when she is pleasured?' asked Dior as she moved positions, the bed dipping under her weight as she moved. Freya watched as Dior positioned herself between Greer's legs, pushing her knees apart and leaning forward to place light kisses on her stomach.

'Keep feeding,' she said to Freya, as she glanced up through hooded eyes. 'This will blow your mind.' She flashed a wicked grin then moved down Greer's body.

Freya ran her tongue over the shallow wound she had made earlier, teasing the ragged edges in the same way as Dior was teasing Greer's clit. Their lover's body arched, twisting in delight, a low moan escaping and filling the room.

Greer's hand grabbed the back of Freya's head, guiding her mouth down a fraction. Freya responded immediately, her tongue swirling around the pink bud, before gently sucking then grazing her teeth over the hardened nipple. Greer cried out in appreciation.

Out of the corner of her eye, she caught movement. Greer reached down for Dior's head, weaving her fingers through dark hair. Greer's back arched as she pressed herself against Dior's face, her mouth, her tongue – screaming out, begging them for more, her body thrashing.

'Taste her as she climaxes,' gasped Dior as she briefly came up for air, but her reprieve was short-lived.

'Don't stop. Fuck, don't either of you stop.'

Freya felt Greer's grip tighten, pushing her down to feed, and every nerve in Freya's body came alive, tingling, a rush of euphoria. Greer's orgasm, Dior's wild arousal all multiplied with her own – she was exploding into a million colours all at once.

'Feed!' The order was short and sharp from Dior, and in her dizzy state, she latched onto the line of oozing crimson. Her body, her mind, her world, immediately intensified with the most divine sensation – a hundred orgasms crashed through her body – relentless, without mercy, ravaging her senses as Greer's orgasm hit with full force.

Her hands grabbed for Greer, for the sheets beneath, desperately clutching for anything to ground her, exhilarated but terrified to allow herself to surrender to the abyss of pure ecstasy.

'Let go. Feed.' Dior instructed again, as her fingers eased their way up her thigh, caressing her arousal. Deftly easing through her folds, fingers sliding inside, a firm thumb over her clit, demanding she yield to the ultimate high, and she did.

Freya came apart, hollering, as she fractured into streams of unadulterated joy. Her head rolled back, her body riding out surges of pleasure – and they kept coming.

Eventually, everything slowed, an awareness of her body, her breathing returned and she lay panting, her heart fluttering in her chest.

'That was—' she couldn't begin to find the words to describe what had happened.

Dior chuckled. 'That's what happens when you've been making women come for nearly four hundred years. I don't mean to boast, but I'm pretty damned—'

A pillow swiped across the bed, hitting her on the side of the head.

'Stop taking all the damned credit,' said Greer, lying

back against the pillows, a look of satisfaction relaxing her features, her cheeks flushed.

'The patterns,' stuttered Dior, looking between their naked bodies. 'It's as though they are singing. Moving together, reaching for each other.'

Freya touched Dior's skin, drawing her fingertips along the markings that spiralled over her hip. The touch sent sparks of pleasure through their connection, making Dior arch and cry out. Wild living patterns, glowed brighter, became more defined. Fascinated, she pushed herself up, turning her attention to Dior.

'You know what this means,' she said, as though she were Einstein having a eureka moment.

Dior and Greer exchanged a cautious glance between each other.

'We need to keep doing this... and it may take a while to fully learn the intricacies of this new language,' she said with a smile.

'Oh, is that right?' Greer sat up, putting her hands on Freya's shoulders, pushing her back down onto the bed. 'Then I think that can be arranged.'

They moved together in the vast bed, hands and mouths exploring familiar territory made new by Freya's deepening powers. She could feel everything now—every touch magnified, every pleasure shared three ways through their connection. In the absence of words, they instinctively moved in harmony, hands, tongues, and mouths in constant movement to maximise pleasure. When Dior's fingers curled inside her, Greer's circled her clitoris, the sensation echoed through all of them like ripples in a pool. When she sucked harder at the wound on Dior's breast, they all tasted blood, all felt the rush of power and pleasure.

Time lost meaning. They fed and fucked and fed again,

the crystal glasses in the kitchen forgotten. Freya learned she could intensify their pleasure with just a touch, sending patterns of ecstasy spiralling through their markings. She learned that her own climax could trigger theirs, creating a cascade of shared sensation that left them all trembling and gasping.

Finally, sated, they lay tangled in the ruined sheets. Sunlight streamed through the windows now, illuminating the room, making Freya's new markings shimmer with an almost ethereal light as she studied them in the mirror beside the bed.

'That bloody sun,' said Dior, as she reached for the remote to lower the blinds. 'Honestly, Freya, you are obsessed with light from those damned windows and your markings.'

'But they seemed more intricate today, after— You know,' she said with an edge of self-consciousness. She ran a hand over her body, feeling the vibration beneath her fingertips. 'I feel connected to everything...'

She turned to see another strange glance pass between her two lovers.

'Tell her,' said Dior. 'If anyone can make sense of it, Freya will.'

'Tell me what?' She cocked her head, unsure of what they were about to reveal.

Greer let out a sigh. 'We don't know if it is significant or not, but Dior and I have been researching, digging through old texts, trying to find anything that might help us understand what's happening to you. To us.'

'What have you found?' Freya asked, with a hesitant anticipation.

'Fragments,' Dior said, her voice low. 'Ancient memories of what we once were, before the curse twisted our purpose. Stories passed down through generations of beings who guarded the connections between all living things.'

Freya's chest tightened. 'Guardians?'

'It's just a legend,' Greer said quickly, seeing the look on Freya's face. 'A story to frighten children.'

'But what if it's not?' Dior countered. 'What if Freya is something more than just a new kind of Baobhan Sith? What if she's the key to everything?'

The buzz of Greer's phone interrupted the moment. She reached for it, frowning at the screen. 'It's Ròs. She wants to meet.'

'All of us?' Dior asked, tension creeping back into her shoulders.

'Yes,' Greer said, sitting up. 'She says it's urgent. Something about attacks in other cities. Sanctuaries targeted.'

Freya felt it then—a shift in the patterns that wove through reality, a sense of something dark gathering on the horizon. Her markings pulsed once, responding to the danger not yet arrived. She could taste it in the air like approaching thunder, see it in the way their markings dimmed slightly, preparing for a threat.

As Freya lay between her lovers, their blood still singing its unique melody in her veins, she wondered if she was ready. The power that flowed through her was intoxicating—and she was already craving more, a thirst that seemed to grow with each passing moment. A faint, almost imperceptible flicker of something dark and hungry stirred beneath her skin, a subtle reminder of the precipice she now walked, a path where power and hunger danced a dangerous duet.

The game had begun anew. And this time, they would rewrite the rules.

Part Two

Chapter Forty-One

Whispers of War

The Dark Vault lived up to its name. Dior descended the worn stone steps into Edinburgh's underbelly, where the ancient walls still whispered secrets. The private club occupied one of the city's oldest vaults, its entrance concealed behind a fashionable wine bar's vintage stock. The faint scent of ancient decay clung to the damp air, a contrast to the polished veneer of the establishment above.

Music pulsed through the stone—something with a bass line that throbbed like a heartbeat. The sound grew stronger as Dior approached the heavy oak door, its surface carved with symbols that shifted and changed when viewed directly. Runes, she recognised, from a time before the Baobhan Sith, before the curse. They spoke of protection, of secrecy, of a power that predated even their kind. She pressed her hand against one, letting her markings flare briefly. The door swung inward.

Inside, darkness and intimacy reigned. The air was thick with the scent of blood, musk, and expensive perfume — a heady mix that spoke of pleasures both ancient and new. Booths carved from the rock walls offered privacy for feeding and other delights, their velvet curtains drawn just enough to hint at the activities within. The low lighting, provided by flickering gas lamps that cast long, dancing shadows, added to the atmosphere of clandestine indulgence.

It hadn't always been like this. Dior remembered its beginnings—a dark, damp pit where she'd first suggested they create a haven for their kind. Back then, they'd scrubbed blood and grime from the stone floors and hung velvet curtains with their own hands, transforming abandoned space into something sacred in its own way. They'd promised each other they'd never become the monsters humans feared - that feeding would always be about willing sacrifice, about pleasure freely given. Now, watching donors and Baobhan Sith move through their eternal dance of hunger and satisfaction, Dior wondered if they'd kept that promise. The Sanctuary had evolved, become more sophisticated with its leather booths and crystal glasses, but the core remained the same - a place where their kind could feed without fear, where the hunger could be sated without shame. Where the line between predator and prey blurred into something more complex, more consensual.

Dior had understood that need better than any of them. She'd seen how isolation twisted their nature, how hunger denied led to violence. 'We're not meant to be alone,' she'd said, hanging those first velvet curtains. 'Even in darkness, we need each other.' She'd been right, as she so often was about matters of the heart.

The Vault wasn't just a feeding ground. It was a hub, a marketplace of sorts. Here, deals were struck, alliances forged, secrets traded. Along one wall, a fiddler sawed at his instrument, weaving a tapestry of ancient folk tunes that spoke of forgotten magic and hidden glens. Beside him, a singer with a voice like the wind through the heather, both wild and captivating, added her own haunting verses, her lyrics laced with coded messages and veiled warnings understood only by those who knew how to listen. This was more than mere music; it was a subtle exchange of information, a sharing of secrets under the guise of entertainment.

To the left, a smaller, more secluded area held bookshelves filled with ancient tomes and modern grimoires. A seer offered glimpses of possible futures, while a scholar of ancient lore traded information for blood. It was a place of whispered conversations and carefully guarded secrets, where the currency was often more than just money.

Movement near the entrance caught Dior's attention. A woman entered, moving with unnatural grace. Her eyes held an unsettling gleam that Dior recognised from Thomas's reports – possibly one of Agnes's enhanced followers? The woman chose a donor with predatory efficiency, leading him to a booth. What happened next made even Dior's ancient blood ran cold. The feeding was violent, primal - nothing like their usual careful exchange of pleasure and sustenance. The man's rapturous screams turned to real ones, but a subtle manipulation of energy, a cold, precise control she'd only ever seen in Agnes's followers, kept other patrons from noticing. When the woman emerged, she showed no sign of the ecstasy that usually followed feeding. Only a cold, calculated satisfaction that spoke of darker hungers.

Thomas sat at his usual corner of the bar, elegant as always in his tailored suit. Behind the bar, James moved with practised grace, his eyes finding Thomas's every few moments. The boy couldn't be more than twenty-five, but there was a quiet strength in how he handled the Vault's unique clientele. The way his gaze lingered on Thomas spoke volumes, a silent conversation passing between them in the midst of the surrounding chaos. A small, silver band on his left ring finger glinted in the low light - a recent addition, Dior noticed. A complication, Dior thought, but a genuine one.

Perhaps that will be its strength.

'Just you tonight?' Thomas asked as Dior approached, gesturing to the empty seat beside him. His gaze flicked to the door. 'No lovely young artist in tow?'

'Greer's keeping her occupied.' Dior settled onto the barstool, watching as the enhanced follower slipped out into the night. 'She's still learning to control her hunger in crowds.' She paused for a beat and reflected. 'She's still learning to control her hunger at home. It's insatiable. All she does is sleep and feed. I'm knackered.'

Thomas gave a shudder. 'Too much information. I'm a very visual gay man...' He held up his hand and then placed the other over his lips as though the image made him queasy.

Dior rolled her eyes. 'A very dramatic gay man,' she muttered.

James set fresh glasses of Mortlach before them with quiet efficiency. His hands shook slightly - he'd noticed the earlier violent feeding, too. He caught Thomas's eye, a silent question passing between them, then he set down a small, velvet pouch beside Thomas's glass. Thomas, ever observant, reached out and caught his fingers briefly, the tender gesture in contrast to the darker activities happening around them. It was a small touch, a silent reassurance, but it spoke volumes about their connection. 'It's all right, love. She can't harm you here.'

'But she could harm you,' James murmured, his voice

tight with a worry that seemed to age him beyond his years. He glanced towards the door, his anxiety palpable. He opened the pouch, revealing a delicate silver chain holding a pendant shaped like a raven's feather. 'Happy anniversary. Two years,' he murmured, his voice thick with emotion. 'There isn't anything I wouldn't do for you, Thomas. Remember that.'

'James...' Thomas's voice was husky, his usual composure cracking for a moment. He looked at the pendant, then back at James, his eyes filled with a depth of emotion that few ever saw.

'I've heard things, working here,' James continued, his gaze fixed on Thomas. 'About what they did in Glasgow.'

'Agnes isn't the only one watching us closely,' Thomas replied, his expression darkening, his hand still resting over James's. It was a protective gesture, a silent vow. 'There's been increased interest in your new protégé. The kind of interest that makes Glasgow look like a warning shot.' He leaned forward, lowering his voice, his fingers tightening almost imperceptibly around James's. 'I hear she prefers to feed from the two of you rather than taking donors. Quite unusual, that. And certain parties find unusual things... fascinating.'

Dior accepted the glass he offered - Mortlach 47-year-old, known as 'The Beast of Dufftown'. The whisky did little to ease the tightness in her chest. The news from Glasgow and Aberdeen had shaken her more than she wanted to admit. Three nights ago, they'd attacked a sanctuary much like this one. Five donors dead, their bodies arranged in a mockery of ancient feeding rites. In Aberdeen, they'd nearly taken one with a blessed iron blade. *And it wasn't just the violence*, she thought, the images flashing before her mind's eye. *It was the precision, the knowledge.*

'You hear a lot, don't you, Thomas?' She asked.

His expression grew serious. 'More than I'd like. The Glasgow attack... it wasn't just violence. They knew exactly where to strike, how to disable the wards. And Aberdeen?' He took a slow sip of his whisky, his gaze fixed on James. 'They had inside help. Someone gave them the sanctuary's layout, the security protocols.'

Dior's nail lengthened instinctively before she caught herself. 'Agnes.'

'Her fingerprints are all over it. Though you won't find that name in any news reports.' Thomas produced a tablet, sliding it across the bar.

Dior scanned the articles. Agnes stared out from each one, elegant and untouchable in designer suits. These days, she went by Agnes Lasair, not Sinclair, as she was back then. Tech CEO, philanthropist, rising star in right-wing politics. She was particularly vocal about 'moral decay' and 'traditional values.'

'She's building a power base in the human world,' Thomas continued, his voice low, almost a murmur. He finally released James's hand, the absence of contact seeming to leave a void between them. 'The Righteous Assembly is just the beginning. She's got politicians in her pocket, civil servants, police. Most of her followers are human zealots, though she keeps a few enhanced ones like that creature we just saw. But it's the humans who are the real threat - they can move freely in daylight, infiltrate anywhere.'

'Let me help,' James interjected, his voice low but determined, a spark of defiance in his eyes. He stepped closer to Thomas, his body language a mix of youthful bravado and genuine concern. 'I can get close to them. They won't look twice at another human who shares their...

values.' His lip curled in disgust. 'They're always recruiting for their cause.'

'No.' Thomas's voice was sharp, the word laced with a fear that was almost tangible. He reached for James's hand again, his fingers interlacing with the younger man's in a gesture of desperate affection. 'You've seen what they do to those they consider traitors.'

'The orders are scattered, divided,' Dior cut in, before their argument could escalate. She recognised the fear in Thomas's eyes, the desperation in James's voice. It was a dangerous combination, one that could lead to reckless decisions. 'You know how they are—too proud to work together, too arrogant to believe they could fall.'

'Something's coming,' Thomas said, his gaze fixed on the far wall, his grip on James's hand tightening almost painfully. 'Something worse than—'

The door swung open. Mànas entered, chief of the Northern Order, bringing with him the sharp bite of Highland winter and the thick scent of fox musk that made him instantly recognisable among their kind. He was a mountain of a man, his weathered face framed by a thick mane of red-brown hair streaked with grey. His eyes, the colour of aged amber, held a wisdom that came from centuries spent navigating the treacherous landscape of both human and Baobhan Sith worlds.

'I should go,' Dior said, finishing her whisky. The pleasant warmth had faded, replaced by cold certainty that time was running out. 'Greer will want to hear this.'

'Dior.' Thomas caught her arm as she turned to leave. 'Be careful who you trust. Agnes isn't working alone.'

She looked pointedly at his hand until he released her. 'I only trust two people in this world, Thomas. You know that.'

As she climbed the steps back to the street, Dior couldn't shake the memory of the enhanced follower's cold eyes. In her mind, she saw Freya's markings, silver and new, unlike anything in their long history. Change was coming, whether they were ready or not.

Her phone buzzed. A text from Greer. *F had a vision. Get back here.*

Dior started running, the chill night air whipping past her face. *A vision*, she thought, her pulse racing. *From Freya? What did she see?*

And as she ran, a single, terrifying thought echoed in her mind: *What if Freya's vision was not just a glimpse of the future, but a catalyst?*

Chapter Forty-Two

Whispers of War

The suffocating darkness of the Black Mausoleum in Greyfriars Kirkyard, heavy with the scent of damp earth and forgotten prayers, was a balm to Agnes's soul, in much the same way the curing yard in Pittenweem, with its sharp, acidic tang of salt and smoke, had been all those years before. She'd told herself it was duty that brought her there. The salt-rough women with their coarse laughs and capable hands needed guidance, needed saving from their earthly weaknesses. That's what she told herself as she watched Dior moving among them, touching shoulders, easing aches with gentle hands. She remembered the day she'd brought tallow for Dior's cracked hands, how her own fingers had trembled as she worked the salve into each salt-burned crevice, how Dior's pulse had fluttered beneath her touch like a trapped bird. 'Just helping a sister in Christ,' she'd whispered, more to herself than to Dior. But even then, she'd known it for a lie.

Now, centuries later, she'd realised the spell that had been cast upon her as righteous fire burned away the memory of gentle touches and forbidden wants. She'd learned to embrace the flame, to let it consume everything soft within her. Everything weak. Everything that still remembered the scent of salt and tallow and the way Dior's hands had felt beneath her own. Those memories haunted her still, even here.

But standing in this tomb, in the heart of forgotten suffering, she found a sliver of peace that eluded her in the world of the living. The chill that seeped from the ancient stones didn't frighten her; it was a familiar embrace. They whispered to her, the ghosts of the Covenanters, their voices a chorus of sorrow that echoed her own pain. 'Bluidy' Mackenzie, their tormentor, lay entombed nearby, his power extinguished, his cruelty a distant memory. In this unholy sanctuary, surrounded by the spectres of the persecuted, Agnes was not alone. The darkness was her friend, her confidante, the only place where she truly felt understood.

Fury built in her chest as she remembered the gallery, the way that mortal girl had interfered. The iron should have found Greer's heart. Should have ended centuries of abomination.

Lying back on her narrow bed, Agnes closed her eyes. When rage threatened to overwhelm her, she always returned to this memory - the moment of her transformation. The source of her power. The birth of her purpose.

The flames had started at her feet. She remembered how the villagers had been methodical about it, constructing the pyre with careful precision. Her own husband had arranged the kindling, tears streaming down his face as he whispered prayers for her soul. *Hypocrite*, she thought, the word a venomous hiss in the darkness. *He condemned me to save his own skin.*

'Thou shalt not suffer a witch to live,' he had quoted, his voice breaking. 'Forgive me, Agnes.'

But she hadn't been a witch. She had been innocent - a minister's wife who had welcomed two women into her home to study scripture. Who were these people to say she had not seen the darkness in those women's souls?

The flames licked higher, and with them came the first whispers. Ancient voices speaking in tongues that predated Christianity, offering power in exchange for pain. As her flesh blackened and peeled, she saw visions of Greer and Dior dancing in moonlight, their unholy markings writhing beneath their skin. She saw their secret meetings in her home, their unnatural love defiling the very scriptures they pretended to study.

Her screams turned from agony to rage. The voices grew louder, weaving themselves into her burning soul. They showed her the truth - that she had been chosen. That her suffering would forge her into a weapon of divine retribution.

As the flames consumed her mortal form, something else was born in the inferno. The last traces of Agnes burned away, replaced by an ancient power that sang of vengeance and righteous fury. Her beauty wasn't destroyed but transformed, becoming something sharp and terrible - a blade forged in holy fire.

The villagers watched her burn until nothing remained but ashes. They buried what little was left of her in unconsecrated ground, an unmarked grave that would deny her soul rest. But they had not understood - her soul was no longer her own.

She rose from her own ashes as Badb, a creature of divine vengeance. Her purpose was clear, burned into her transformed being - to hunt down all such creatures who corrupted God's natural order. To cleanse the world of their taint.

Now, centuries later, Agnes opened eyes that held the pain of fire. Her followers had arranged sacred objects around her room - crosses, holy water blessed iron. But these were mere trinkets compared to the power that burned in her transformed soul.

She rose from the bed and moved to the window. They were gathering strength. She could feel it— the shift in ancient powers, the way their corrupted love twisted reality.

'Soon,' she whispered, and her breath frosted the glass. Her form flickered, showing glimpses of what lurked beneath her beautiful mask - feathers black as sin, teeth sharp as judgement, eyes that held the memory of holy fire.

The girl's interference had only fuelled her rage. Their love for each other would be their undoing. She would make them watch as she destroyed everything they held dear, just as they had destroyed her innocent faith.

In the city, her followers began their evening prayers. Their devotion fed her power, their absolute belief strengthening her purpose. They understood as she did - that sometimes God's work required terrible deeds. That divine love sometimes wore the face of vengeance.

She smiled, and in the window's reflection, her teeth were daggers.

'Burn with me,' she whispered. 'Burn with me—and know true divine fire.'

Chapter Forty-Three

The Old One

Freya recounted the vision of destruction and persecution she'd seen in her mind's eye to Dior. Scarcely had she finished when there was a knock at the door. Not a buzzer from street level to gain access, but a literal rap of knuckles against hardwood—three sharp raps that echoed through the silent penthouse. Greer poured Dior another glass of wine.

Freya looked at her with a quizzical expression. But Greer looked knowingly at Dior. There was only one person who it could be.

Unlocking the door and sliding back the bolts, Greer opened it to find Glicia wearing a charity shop cardigan and sensible shoes, looking like someone's grandmother who'd lost her way. But no mortal grandmother had markings that shifted like smoke beneath their flesh, or eyes that held centuries of secrets.

'First Bearer,' Glicia's voice was soft, yet it carried the weight of ages as she addressed Greer. 'The years have been kind.'

'I'm hardly the first anything these days.' Greer touched

the fine lines at the corners of her eyes then stepped back, formally inviting her in. 'What brings you from your solitude?'

Glicia crossed the threshold, her gaze taking in every detail of the penthouse. When her eyes fell on Freya, something flickered in their depths - recognition, perhaps, or a hint of something more complex. *She knew what Freya's becoming*, Greer thought, a shiver of apprehension tracing her spine.

'Change brings me. As it brought you to her.'

'You've heard about the attacks,' Dior interjected, her voice tight. She'd barely made it back from the Vault before Freya's vision struck.

Glicia nodded, her movements economical, precise. 'Word travels fast in our circles. Agnes is making her move.' She moved into the room with a grace that belied her apparent age, stopping before Freya. 'So, you're the one who sees the patterns.'

Freya straightened, though Greer noticed she kept hold of Dior's hand. 'And Dior tells me you're the one who reads the old books.'

A smile, fleeting yet profound, touched Glicia's lips. 'Books? Child, I was there when they were written.' She reached up her sleeve and withdrew something wrapped in a once-white tissue that had been used more times than Greer dared to think about.

'Here.' Glicia unfurled the wrapping to reveal a brooch, crafted from old silver, its Celtic knots cradling an Elie ruby at its heart. 'You'll need this. It was found on Elie's shores in 1634, not a mile away from where this all started.'

Unlike ordinary garnets, this one held an inner fire that seemed to dance between blood-red and twilight-black. The metalwork around it writhed and shifted, ancient patterns protecting the stone like loving hands. A strange sense of recognition stirred within Freya as she took the gift from Glicia, her fingers tracing the cold silver and warm stone. A faint energy thrummed beneath her touch, resonating with the patterns on her skin.

'But understand - its power can be used only once,' the old one warned. 'The stone was found the very night they tried to destroy love with hatred. It holds both sides of that power within it. When the moment comes - and your heart will know when - it will spend itself completely. Choose wisely. Use it only when everything rests on love's truth.'

'How will I know?' Freya asked, her eyes fixed on the way the garnet seemed to pulse in time with her own heartbeat.

'Protection. Focus. Memory.' Glicia's expression grew serious. 'This stone channels the natural energies of the earth, the very powers you are now learning to wield. The Elie ruby holds a magic that predates even the oldest Orders.' She met Freya's gaze, her eyes filled with a knowing that spanned centuries. 'Agnes isn't the only one who'll want to study your gift. The Orders remember too much and understand too little.' Her gaze shifted to Greer. 'You remember the last Convocation, fifty years past.'

'I remember the price of change,' Greer said, her voice heavy with frustration. She hated committees. 'We were fools,' she said, her voice barely above a whisper. 'We thought the two of us could face down the others, that truth and love of two would be enough. We didn't understand the true nature of politics in play.'

'And now?' Glicia's gaze was sharp, piercing, demanding honesty.

'Now we know better,' Dior interjected, stepping

forward, her voice firm, resolute. 'We know that two isn't enough. We need allies, knowledge, strategy.'

'And luck,' Freya added, her fingers tracing the intricate metalwork of the brooch, her touch gentle yet purposeful.

'Luck is for the unprepared,' Glicia countered, her voice a low, resonant hum. 'You need to understand what you're dealing with. Agnes isn't just a vengeful spirit. She's become something... darker.'

'You know her weakness,' Dior said to Glicia, her tone leaving no room for evasion. It wasn't a question.

'I know many things.' Glicia turned toward the door, her movements deliberate, each step echoing with purpose. 'Including why she fears what your Freya might become.' She paused, one hand on the doorframe, her silhouette framed against the light. 'The patterns aren't just markings, child. They're memory. History. Power. Shame.' Her eyes, ancient and knowing, met Freya's. 'And they remember being something else entirely.'

'What aren't you telling us?' Greer asked, sensing the weight of unspoken truths.

'Only that which you need to work out for yourself.' Glicia's voice was soft, yet it carried an undercurrent of urgency.

'Agnes was innocent once,' Greer said softly, her gaze distant, lost in the echoes of the past. 'Before we destroyed her life.'

'No.' Freya moved to her lover, her hand coming to rest over Greer's heart, her touch a silent reassurance. She traced the markings on Greer's skin with a delicate touch. 'She chose hatred. Chose to become this twisted thing. Just as I chose love.'

'We can't fight a corrupted deity,' Dior argued, but there

was less conviction in her voice now, a hint of uncertainty creeping in.

'Can't we?' Freya smiled, a slow, knowing smile that sent a shiver down Greer's spine. Shadows danced at her command, responding to her unspoken will. 'I'm not just seeing the patterns any more - I'm learning to reshape them. And together...' She gestured, and their markings all began to glow, resonating in harmony, light and energy. 'Together we're stronger than she could ever imagine.'

Greer opened her mouth to argue but stopped when she saw the look in Freya's eyes. Determination, yes, but also something else. Something that spoke of knowledge and a power that was still unfolding. It was both terrifying and exhilarating.

'The curse,' Freya said, her voice taking on a new resonance, a depth that seemed to echo from the very stones of the building. 'It was meant to punish you, to turn your love into a weapon against you. But what if...' She paused, her gaze turning inward as if she were reading something written on the air itself. 'What if the patterns hold the key to breaking it? To transforming the curse into something... else?'

'You're talking about rewriting centuries of magic,' Dior said, her voice a mixture of awe and apprehension. 'It's never been done.'

'Maybe it's time to try,' Freya said simply. As if in agreement, the silver brooch in her hand pulsed with a soft, inner light. The stone at its centre seemed to deepen in colour, reflecting the hues of the twilight sky. Freya's own markings responded, their silvery light echoing the brooch's glow.

'But how—' asked Greer, but Glicia held up a hand, cutting off her question. 'There's no time for explanations now. Agnes is coming. And she's not alone.' Glicia looked back, and for a moment Greer saw past the grandmother disguise to something primal and terrible. 'Everything burns, First Bearer. The trick is knowing which fires purify and which merely destroy.' She smiled again, sad and knowing. 'Keep her close. Keep both of them close. The Orders will try to separate you, but only together will you survive what's coming.'

Then she disappeared, leaving behind only the scent of M&S rose talcum powder and the garnet brooch in Freya's hand.

'Well,' Dior said into the silence. 'That was cryptic as fuck.'

Freya looked down at the brooch, her fingers tracing its intricate design. The stone seemed to pulse in time with her heartbeat, a silent rhythm that echoed the patterns on her skin.

'She's right,' Freya said softly. 'About the patterns. They're not just markings. They're a language. A story. And I think...' She paused, her brow furrowing in concentration. 'I think I'm starting to understand what they're saying.'

As if to underscore her words, she raised her hand, and the shadows in the room responded, swirling around her like living things. The air crackled with a sudden burst of energy, and a nearby glass of water floated gently into her outstretched hand.

Greer and Dior exchanged a look of mingled awe and apprehension. Their little artist was gone, replaced by something far more powerful.

Dior hoped she might use that same power on the overflowing laundry basket.

Chapter Forty-Four

A Gathering of Shadows

The entrance to the Old Chamber, where the first Convocation in fifty years was to be held, lay beneath Calton Hill, concealed behind a nondescript door that belied the ancient power it guarded. As they descended the steps, a sense of stepping back in time, of entering a place where the veil between worlds was thin, settled over Freya. She felt the weight of history pressing down, intensified by the proximity of Greer ahead and Dior behind, their markings casting a faint, silver glow in the darkness. Her own patterns pulsed in response to the power layered into the walls; older than time, a complex web of memory and magic that made her head spin. She forced herself to focus on the reassuring sway of Greer's hips, on the steady rhythm of their footsteps.

At the bottom of the stairs, massive oak doors stood open. The chamber beyond flickered with candlelight, illuminating stone walls carved with symbols that seemed to writhe and shift as Freya tried to focus on them. Her gift showed her the truth beneath the glamour—these weren't just decorative markings but a record of centuries of Baobhan Sith history, treaties sealed in blood and sex, alliances forged and broken.

The chamber was already half full. Baobhan Sith gathered in clusters, their markings flaring like quicksilver as they caught sight of the new arrivals. Whispers followed their progress, voices hushed but carrying clearly to Freya's newly sensitive ears.

'The exiles and their lover...'

'...changed her, broke all the laws...'

'...sees the patterns themselves...'

The whispers seemed to follow them, and Freya felt a prickle of unease. A woman, her movements like a cat stalking prey, detached herself from one of the groups. Freya noticed her markings first, elaborate spirals that seemed to pulse with a hidden energy. *Ambition and desire*, Freya thought, remembering Greer's lessons. The woman's hair was black, pulled back from a face that was both beautiful and severe—an economical facelift. The smile she offered was sharp, cold and as inviting as a morgue freezer.

'Greer, darling.' She pressed close, markings brightening as she kissed Greer's cheek. Freya felt a surge of something hot and possessive at the contact. 'And Dior.' Another kiss, lingering longer on Dior's cheek, making Freya's jaw tighten. When she turned to Freya, the woman's pupils dilated, taking in every detail. 'So, this is your artist. I see why you broke tradition for her.'

Before Freya could respond, the temperature in the chamber seemed to drop. The crowd parted as a man entered. A whisper from Greer told her this was Mànas. Freya stared, momentarily stunned by his appearance. His dark markings were unlike any others in the room. Where female Baobhan Sith bore silvery patterns, his markings were savage things - black vipers thrashing beneath his skin, tearing to break through flesh from within, desperate to strike. The wave of his power shook Freya, making her grab Dior's arm for balance, her gift overwhelmed as she tried to process his design of violent chaos. She shuddered, wondering how Greer and Dior could stand to be near him.

Every eye in the chamber followed his progress. Freya saw hunger in those looks, desire and fear in equal measure. His beauty set him apart, the only male leader of their kind, a deep brass note in a symphony of silver.

Freya noticed Bethia's markings flickered as he passed. Even Greer and Dior seemed affected, their shoulders tightening, though their expressions remained carefully neutral. Freya found herself wondering how many of these powerful women had sealed alliances with him in the traditional way.

'Interesting, isn't it?' A voice purred near her ear.

Freya turned to see a woman with flaming red hair standing beside her. She moved with a fluid grace that reminded Freya of Greer. *Ròs*, she remembered, from Dior's lessons. The head of the Stone Order. The woman's markings formed precise geometric patterns, and Freya sensed a mind that valued structure and organisation.

'This is Ròs,' Dior confirmed, 'head of the Stone Order, known for their steadfast loyalty and unwavering principles.'

'How they all react to him. Even after centuries.' Her eyes, intelligent and sharp as emeralds, met Freya's. 'But you see more than most, don't you? They say you see beyond the patterns themselves.'

Mànas turned then, his attention falling on their small group like a sudden, sharp chill. 'Shall we begin?' His voice was surprisingly soft, but it carried to every corner of the chamber. 'We have much to discuss.'

The gathered Baobhan Sith moved toward the ancient stone table that dominated the centre of the chamber. Freya noticed how they arranged themselves - Mànas at the head, Bethia and Ròs taking positions that formed a triangle of power. Others filled in according to some hierarchy she couldn't quite grasp, though she saw how their markings brightened or dimmed as they claimed their places.

Greer guided Freya to a spot between herself and Dior, slightly apart from the main table. They were exiles, after all. In the shadows behind them, Freya glimpsed a familiar figure. Glicia watched silently, her own markings barely visible, a subtle reminder of the ancient power she wielded.

'The world is changing,' Mànas began, his voice a low rumble that vibrated in Freya's very bones. 'Our kind faces threats we haven't seen in centuries.' His black markings writhed faster, a silent storm beneath his skin, making several younger Baobhan Sith flinch. Freya felt a tremor of unease ripple through the room. 'Agnes Lasair grows bolder. The Righteous Assembly spreads. And now...' His gaze fixed on Freya, intense and unwavering. 'Now we have something unprecedented.'

'Abomination,' someone muttered, the word seeming to hang in the air. Freya couldn't identify the speaker, but she saw how the word rippled through the patterns in the room, creating discordant waves.

'Opportunity,' Bethia countered, her spiralling markings flaring with interest as she studied Freya. 'When was the last time our kind saw true change? Perhaps this is exactly what we need.'

'Need?' Another voice, sharp with scorn. Freya turned to see a severe-looking woman whose markings formed rigid, unyielding lines. *Morven*, she remembered, a leader known for her strict adherence to ancient laws. 'We need to maintain our traditions, not corrupt them with human blood.'

'Careful, Morven,' Ròs's voice was mild, but her patterns pulsed with warning. 'Some of us remember when those traditions were new. Change isn't always corruption.'

Mànas raised a hand, silencing the growing murmurs. 'The question isn't whether we accept change, but how we survive it.' His dark gaze swept the room, taking in every face. 'Agnes doesn't distinguish between traditional and progressive. She'll burn us all equally.'

Freya watched the patterns shift and swirl as alliances formed and reformed in the space of heartbeats. She saw how Bethia's spirals reached toward Mànas's darkness, how Ròs's geometric shapes tried to impose order on the chaos. Beneath it all, she sensed something else - a deeper pattern, ancient and vast, that seemed to pulse in time with her own heartbeat, and with the subtle vibration of the brooch hidden beneath her clothes.

'Show us,' Mànas commanded suddenly, his gaze locking with Freya's. 'Show us what you see.'

The chamber fell silent. Greer tensed beside her, but Freya stepped forward. She could feel every eye on her.

'Your markings aren't just decorative,' she said, her voice steadier than she felt. 'They're alive. Connected. Every alliance you've made, every oath sworn, every pleasure given or taken - it's all there, written in silver and shadow.' She turned slowly, taking in the whole room, her gaze lingering on the intricate patterns woven into the stone walls. 'And underneath it all, there's something older. Something that remembers when the markings meant something different entirely.'

'Different?' Bethia leaned forward, her spiralling patterns quickening with interest. 'Different how?'

'What do you mean, *remembers*?' Ròs's geometric patterns flashed with sharp angles of suspicion.

Freya opened her mouth to respond, but found she couldn't explain what she sensed. The knowledge was there, just beyond her reach, like a word on the tip of her tongue. The brooch pulsed faintly against her skin, a silent echo of the ancient power she was struggling to articulate. She felt Greer step closer, protective, but before she could try to answer, Mànas cut through the rising murmurs.

'And Agnes?' His black vipers writhed faster, their movements almost frantic. 'What do you see of her?'

'Fire,' Freya said, the word escaping her lips like a sigh. 'But not just the fire that burned her. She's found something else, something that burns hotter than revenge or rage.'

A commotion at the chamber entrance scattered Freya's thoughts. A young Baobhan Sith stumbled in, her clothes torn and bloody. One arm hung useless at her side, and deep gashes across her torso still wept crimson. Her markings flickered erratically, like a candle in a harsh wind, suggesting whatever had attacked her had come terrifyingly close to finding its mark with blessed iron.

'The Dark Vault,' she gasped, swaying on her feet. Blood trickled from the corner of her mouth. 'They found it. They're attacking now.'

The patterns in the room exploded into chaos. Freya saw Greer and Dior exchange a look of horror.

'Thomas,' Dior whispered. 'James.'

But as the chamber erupted into action, Freya caught Glicia's eye in the shadows. The old one's expression was grim, knowing. Whatever was happening at the Dark Vault, Freya realised, was only the beginning.

The patterns didn't lie. Change was coming, riding waves of blood and fire. Her visions were coming true, and somewhere in the city above, Agnes was smiling. But was she orchestrating it, or merely a pawn in a larger game? The question echoed in Freya's mind as the chamber erupted around her, the fragile peace shattered, the future uncertain.

Chapter Forty-Five

Echoes of Violence

The entrance to the Dark Vault had been ripped open like a festering wound. Dior took the steps three at a time, Greer and Freya close behind. The elegant wine bar that concealed the club lay in ruins - shattered bottles leaked expensive vintages across the floor, mixing with darker liquids Dior refused to contemplate.

Silence. After centuries of existence, Dior knew silence rarely meant safety.

The heavy oak door hung from one hinge, the centuries-old wood splintered and charred. The scent of burnt flesh and something else - something chemical and acrid - stung her sensitive nose. No music pulsed through the stone now. No whispered conversations or gasps of pleasure echoed from the booths.

'Thomas?' Her voice sounded thin and fragile in the dead air. 'James?'

The main chamber was a scene of carnage. Broken furniture, shattered glass, bodies - some stirring, some terrifyingly still. The bar where James had served them whisky hours ago was split in two, its polished marble top cracked like shattered bones.

A sound caught her attention - ragged breathing from behind an overturned table. Dior moved swiftly, shoving the heavy wood aside. A donor lay curled in a protective ball, his throat bearing the marks of a feeding interrupted. But it wasn't the donor she focused on.

James crouched over him, shielding the human with his own body. Blood matted his dark hair, and his clothes were ripped, arms scored with bleeding gashes, but his eyes were alert, blazing with a fierce, protective light.

'Where is he?' she demanded, already knowing the answer wouldn't be good.

'They took him.' James's voice shook with rage rather than fear. 'Four of them grabbed Thomas while the others...' He gestured at the destruction, his voice thick with barely suppressed fury. 'He fought. God, he fought so hard. But they knew exactly what they were doing. Knew exactly where to find us.'

Greer's sharp intake of breath mirrored Dior's own sickening realisation. Someone had betrayed them. Someone who knew the Dark Vault's defences, its schedules, its weaknesses.

Freya moved through the carnage, her markings pulsing with a soft, silver light, the stone in her brooch a steady, calming presence beneath her clothes. 'The patterns here are wrong,' she said. 'Broken. Like someone took a knife to a tapestry and just...' She touched one wall and jerked back as if burned.

A groan from one of the booths caught their attention. Dior recognised the figure sprawled across the velvet cushions - one of Mànas's favourites, a young man who'd been there just hours ago, eager for the Order leader's attention.

'What happened?' Dior demanded, her voice sharp with urgency.

The young man's eyes were glazed with pain and something else - a lingering terror that made his words stumble. 'They knew us. Called us by name. Knew who we fed from, who we...' He coughed, blood staining his lips a gruesome crimson. 'Said we were corrupted. Addicts of our pleasure.'

'How many?' Greer asked, helping him sit up, her touch surprisingly gentle.

'Twenty, maybe more. Humans, mostly, but different. Wrong.' His fingers brushed the wounds on his chest, a tremor running through his body. 'Stronger than they should be. And their eyes... like they were burning from the inside.'

Freya knelt beside a fallen donor, her hand hovering over the woman's forehead. 'They're all marked with the same pattern. Not like ours, but...' She closed her eyes, her brow furrowed in concentration. 'Fear. Hatred. But underneath that, there's something else. Like they've been touched by fire.'

'Agnes,' Dior spat the name like a curse. 'She's found a way to enhance them. Make them strong enough to hunt us.'

'We need to tell the Orders,' Greer said, her voice calm but edged with steel. 'Call another Convocation. Plan a response that won't start a war.'

Dior whirled on her, her control snapping. 'A war? They just attacked our sanctuary. Took Thomas. How many more have to die before you'll act?'

'And how many will die if we don't think this through?' Greer's voice remained steady, a stark contrast to Dior's rising fury, which only fuelled Dior's anger. 'If we rush in without understanding what we're facing?'

'I understand perfectly.' Dior gestured at the destruction around them, her voice thick with barely suppressed rage. 'Agnes is done playing politics. She's showing us exactly what she thinks of diplomacy.'

'All the more reason to be careful.' Greer reached for her, but Dior stepped back, her body rigid with tension. 'Love, please. We need allies. Strategy.'

'We need to find Thomas.' Dior's nail lengthened, a sharp, dangerous point glinting in the dim light as her control slipped. 'Before they...'

'Turn him,' Freya finished softly, her voice cutting through the tension like a knife. Both women turned to her. She stood amid the wreckage, her markings bright with a newfound understanding, the brooch a faint, pulsing light beneath her shirt. 'That's what the pattern means. The fire in their eyes. She's not just killing our people. She's transforming them. Making them hate what they once were.'

A sound from James made them all turn. He stood straighter, chin lifted, his earlier fear replaced by a steely resolve. 'I can help. I'm human - I could go to their meetings, pretend I'm interested in their cause. They'd never suspect me.'

'No.' Greer's tone was final, brooking no argument. 'It's too dangerous.'

'They took Thomas.' James's voice cracked, but his gaze remained steady, locked on Greer's. He took a step closer, his voice dropping to an urgent whisper. 'I won't just sit here and do nothing. I can get inside in a way none of you can. I can find him. I have to.'

Dior met his eyes, seeing the same desperate determination she felt mirrored there. *He loves him,* she realised, a pang of empathy piercing her grief for Hannah. *Just as fiercely as we love each other.*

'He's right. We need every advantage.

'You're letting your feelings cloud your judgement.' Greer's words were sharp, each one a stinging blow.

'And you're letting your caution kill the one we love.' Dior knew she'd gone too far even as the words left her mouth, but she couldn't stop, the fear and anger a toxic cocktail in her veins. 'While you plan and strategise, Agnes is building an army. One sanctuary at a time, one victim at a time. And now she has Thomas.'

Freya moved between them, one hand extended toward each, a calming presence in the storm of their emotions. 'Stop. Your patterns... you're tearing something that shouldn't be torn.'

The truth in her words doused Dior's anger like cold water. She looked at Greer - really looked - and saw the fear beneath her lover's careful control. The same fear that churned in her own gut, threatening to consume her.

'I can't lose him,' Dior said quietly, her voice raw with emotion. 'Not like this.'

Greer's expression softened, her anger giving way to a deep, aching sadness. 'Then we find him. Together. But smartly.'

A crash from upstairs interrupted any response. Footsteps - multiple sets - pounded on the floor above, descending toward them.

'They're back,' James whispered, his eyes wide with alarm.

Dior's nail lengthened, this time with deadly purpose. No deity was going to fuck with her friends.

Chapter Forty-Six

Aftermath and Alliance

Freya focused on keeping her breathing steady, her heart hammering as footsteps pounded down the stairs toward the devastated sanctuary of the Dark Vault. Beside her, Dior and Greer tensed, falling into fighting stances as naturally as dancers taking their marks. She could see their patterns writhing beneath their skin, ancient curses responding to the threat of violence. The faint pulse of the brooch beneath her shirt was a steady, calming rhythm in the chaos.

The smell of blood and burnt flesh still hung in the air, making Freya's newly transformed senses reel. She tried to centre herself, reaching for the strange new power that had begun to awaken within her since the night Greer and Dior's blood had mingled with her own. If she concentrated, she could see the energy that connected everything in the room—the complex web of alliances and animosities that had shaped Baobhan Sith society for centuries, now twisted and torn by violence.

A flash of movement in her peripheral vision made Freya turn just as a figure burst through the shattered doorway. But instead of Agnes's fanatical followers, she found herself staring at a bloodied Ròs.

The leader of the Stone Order moved with deadly grace despite her wounds, her geometric markings pulsing with barely contained power. 'They hit the Old Chamber,' Ròs said without preamble. 'Minutes after you left. They knew exactly when we'd be distracted.'

'Casualties?' Dior asked, though the tightness around her eyes suggested she already knew the answer wouldn't be good.

'At least a dozen. Mostly the younger ones who hadn't fed recently.' Ròs's gaze cut to Freya. 'Your little display riled them up. Made them careless.'

Freya flinched but held her ground. 'I didn't mean to—'

'What's done is done,' Greer cut in, her voice firm. 'Right now we need to focus on what comes next.'

Dior's nail lengthened, the sharp point gleaming in the low light. 'Revenge.'

'Retaliation,' Ròs corrected. 'Strategic retaliation.' Her eyes narrowed as she took in the destruction of the Dark Vault. 'Though I wouldn't say no to a little revenge on the side.'

'They took Thomas,' James said quietly from where he crouched beside the fallen donor. He'd torn strips from his ruined shirt to bind the man's wounds. 'We need to find him before they—'

'We will,' Dior promised, her voice fierce. She turned to Ròs. 'What about the other orders? Mànas? Bethia and the Shadow Order?'

Ròs's lip curled. 'The Shadow Order are fighting back, but they're outnumbered. They won't be able to hold out alone for long.'

Greer's brow furrowed. 'And Mànas?'

'No sign of him or any of his order. It's like they vanished into thin air.' Ròs's tone made it clear she found this deeply suspicious.

'We need to regroup,' Greer said, her expression grave. 'Gather what's left of our forces, reach out to Bethia—'

'And do what?' Ròs challenged. 'Keep fighting separately until Agnes picks us off one by one?' She shook her head. 'No. It's time to do what we should have done centuries ago - unite the orders against a common enemy.'

Dior and Greer exchanged a long look, centuries of history passing between them. Freya could feel the weight of old wounds and complicated loyalties vibrating through the patterns that bound the three of them together.

'Look, we can forget 1692, let bygones be bygones. I hereby lift the exile,' said Ròs with a roll of her eyes. 'That selkie had it coming anyway!'

'Ròs is right,' Dior said at last. 'We're stronger together than we ever were apart.'

Greer sighed but nodded. 'Then we'll need neutral ground. Somewhere safe to gather, to discuss terms now that the Old Chamber has been destroyed.'

'I can help with that,' Freya offered, the words out of her mouth almost before she'd consciously decided to speak. 'My studio. It's private, secure, and empty now that I'm with you—' She glanced at Greer and Dior. 'It's not being used. Also, Agnes and her followers would never think to look for us there.'

For a long moment, no one spoke. Freya saw surprise, hesitation, and calculation flit across the faces around her. She held her breath, half-expecting to be dismissed out of hand. After all, what did a newly transformed human know of Baobhan Sith politics?

But to her shock, it was Ròs who nodded first. 'It's a

good plan,' the order leader said. 'Neutral ground, hiding in plain sight.' Her gaze sharpened as she looked at Freya with new interest. 'You're full of surprises, aren't you, little seer?'

She met Ròs's eyes steadily, even as she felt Greer and Dior's surprise and cautious approval pulsing through their bond.

'You have no idea,' she said softly.

Ròs's smile was a slash of red in the gloom. 'I look forward to finding out.'

❄

Freya's studio was a haven of ordered chaos. The large windows were covered with heavy, blackout curtains, shielding the space from the harmful rays of the sun. The room was filled with canvases in various stages of completion, their vibrant colours contrasting with the muted tones of the Baobhan Sith. The air hummed with a faint energy, a lingering echo of Freya's own magic. It was different from the oppressive weight of the Old Chamber or the raw, violent energy of the Dark Vault. Here, the patterns felt more fluid, more open to interpretation.

'It's...unexpected,' Ròs said, her gaze sweeping over the paint-splattered easels and shelves overflowing with art supplies. The leader of the Stone Order seemed out of place amidst the vibrant clutter, her geometric markings alien to the organic forms of Freya's art.

'It's perfect,' Dior countered, her eyes scanning the high ceilings and reinforced doors. 'Plenty of space, and only one entrance to secure. We can set wards here to prevent unwanted entry. They are powerful sigils, woven from magic, that can deter or even harm those who try to cross them without permission.'

Greer was studying the layout, her expression thoughtful. 'The wards will need to be set,' she said echoing Dior's words. 'Agnes's followers might be hesitant to enter a human space, but Agnes herself...' She trailed off, her gaze drawn to a half-finished canvas depicting a swirling vortex of colours. 'What do you see here, Freya?'

Freya followed her gaze, her fingers tracing the edge of the canvas. 'Possibilities,' she said softly. 'The patterns aren't fixed here. They're still forming, still shifting.' She looked up, meeting Greer's eyes. 'It's like the energy here is more...malleable.'

Before Greer could respond, a low groan echoed from the far side of the room. A makeshift cot had been set up near one of the covered windows, where the injured young man from the Dark Vault lay, his breathing laboured. James, ever vigilant, hovered nearby, his face etched with worry. The young man was one of the few survivors from the brutal attack, and the weight of that hung heavy in the air.

'He's one of ours,' James was saying to Glicia, who had made her way over to the two men. 'Not a donor. They'd never have let him live this long if he was. But Thomas—' his voice broke on the name, '—he insisted. Said it was important to offer sanctuary to those who needed it, even if they weren't of your kind.'

'That sounds like him,' Dior said, a ghost of a smile touching her lips. 'Always the protector.' But her eyes were filled with a fierce determination that spoke of retribution.

James nodded, his gaze fixed on the injured man. 'He would have protected me, too. With his life, if necessary. I should have stopped them.'

'Enough,' Greer said, her voice gentle but firm. 'There's no use in blaming yourself. We'll find him, James. I promise you.'

Freya felt a surge of empathy for the young man. She knew what it was like to feel helpless, to watch someone you cared about being taken away.

Freya moved closer to James, and lay a hand on his arm, a silent offer of comfort.

'Thank you,' James said, his voice thick with emotion. 'Thomas... he means everything to me.'

Freya nodded, understanding the depth of his unspoken words. She turned to Greer and Dior, her own resolve hardening. 'We need a plan.'

'Agreed,' Greer said, her gaze taking in the assembled group. 'We need to work together. All of us.'

Mànas emerged from the shadows, his movements fluid and silent. His viper-black markings writhed, and his gaze was fixed on Freya, a mixture of curiosity and something darker, something that made her skin crawl.

'And what do you propose, little seer?' he said, his voice a low, resonant hum.

'Ròs had the right idea,' Freya said, ignoring his question. 'We unite the orders. A united front against a common enemy.'

'Easier said than done,' Morven scoffed, her rigid markings flashing like warning signs. 'The orders have never been united. Not truly.'

'Then it's time we changed that,' Freya countered, with conviction. 'We need to put aside our differences, our old grudges. We need to work together, or we'll all fall.'

'Ròs is right,' Dior said at last. 'We're stronger together than we ever were apart.'

She looked at each of them, her gaze lingering on Mànas, who watched her with an unreadable expression. 'We need to find Thomas,' she added, her voice softening

'And then we need to stop Agnes. Before she destroys everything we hold dear.'

A murmur rippled through the room, a mixture of agreement and apprehension. Freya could feel the patterns shifting, the old alliances and rivalries being re-evaluated in the face of this new threat.

'And how do you propose we do that, little seer?' Mànas asked, his voice laced with a hint of mockery.

Freya met his gaze, her own eyes blazing with determination. 'By using our strengths,' she said, 'our pure hearts... Together.'

Chapter Forty-Seven

Crimson Bonds

Ròs's residence was a stark contrast to Freya's chaotic studio. Stepping across the threshold was like entering another world, a world of old money and even older secrets. This Georgian townhouse, nestled in the quiet affluent Edinburgh neighbourhood of The Grange, exuded an air of elegance. High ceilings, ornate cornices, and tall, shuttered windows hinted at hidden depths within, breathtaking in their elegance. The polished wooden floors gleamed in the soft light, and the air was subtly perfumed with a scent Freya couldn't quite place – but she had no doubt was expensive. It created an atmosphere of refined sensuality, a stark contrast to the raw energy of her studio.

'Impressive,' Dior murmured, taking in the elegant furnishings and discreetly placed artwork. 'Very... understated.'

Ròs smiled in the dim light. 'A leader must maintain a certain image,' she said. 'Besides, after centuries, one develops an appreciation for the finer things.' She gestured towards a deep blue velvet sofa that dominated the centre of the room. 'Shall we?'

Freya, Greer, and Dior exchanged a look. The tension in the room was palpable, a mixture of anticipation and apprehension. They knew what was expected, what was required to solidify the alliance. An ancient tradition, a ritual as old as the Baobhan Sith themselves: the bonding of pleasure.

'Before we begin,' Greer said, her voice firm, 'we need to talk about Thomas.'

Ròs's smile tightened almost imperceptibly. 'Of course. The missing one weighs heavily on our minds. Especially on young James. We can only hope he understands the necessity of this... union.'

'He will,' Dior said, her voice hard. 'He knows what's at stake. We all do.'

'Indeed,' Ròs said. 'The fate of our kind may very well rest on this alliance. And on your...' She paused, her eyes lingering on Freya, '...unique abilities, little seer. Agnes has shown her hand. Now it's time to show her ours.'

Freya felt a shiver run down her spine, a mixture of excitement and trepidation. She knew that what they were about to do was more than just a symbolic gesture. It was a merging of power, a sharing of essence, that would bind them together in a way that words never could. A necessary step to gather their strength and find Thomas.

Ròs closed the space to stand directly in front of Freya, her hand lifting to stroke her face. 'You look scared, little one,' she said, as she tilted up her chin. Freya's mouth opened as their gaze met. The intensity of the older woman's eyes stripped her of everything except desire. 'We won't hurt you. The pain will be a pleasure from which you'll never want to be released.' A slow smile crept over

Ròs's face. 'And once we make this union, you will never be released.'

A shudder sped through Freya's body.

'Watch, then join us.' Ròs stepped back and shed her emerald green dress with a grace that whispered of centuries of practiced seduction. Her geometric markings, stark and precise against her pale skin, seemed to pulse with an inner light as she approached the sofa. She reclined on the plush surface, her body a study in languid elegance.

Dior and Greer followed, their movements mirroring Ròs's, a slow, deliberate shedding of inhibitions along with their clothes. Dior, always bold, was the first to reach for Ròs, her fingers tracing the intricate patterns on the other woman's skin. Greer, more reserved, hesitated for a moment, her gaze meeting Freya's across the room. A silent question, a silent reassurance.

Freya stepped forward, her heart hammering in her chest. A surge of desire hit her, hot and intense, as she watched the three women. But beneath the desire, there was something else, something deeper. A sense of connection, of shared purpose, that went beyond the physical.

Freya's breath caught as she watched Greer kneel before Ròs, then devour the woman with increasing hunger. Ròs's hips rolled against Greer's mouth, her fingers twisted in Greer's hair, forcing her deeper. Through their connection, Freya felt Greer's struggle to breathe, tasting Ròs's sweet essence on her tongue as though it were her own mouth pressed there.

Heat pooled between her thighs as Greer slipped two fingers inside Ròs. The sensation of being filled, echoed through Freya's body. She felt Ròs's pleasure spike as Greer curled her fingers, hitting that perfect spot while her tongue circled, then flicked relentlessly.

Dior straddled Ròs's face, trembling as that skilled tongue found her centre. Freya gasped, overwhelmed by the dual sensations - Ròs's mouth on Dior, Greer's mouth on Ròs, all of it reverberating through her own body. Dior's thighs quivered, her control slipping as Ròs sucked her clit.

'Please,' Dior begged, her voice breaking. 'I need—'

'Not. Yet.' Ròs's command vibrated against Dior's flesh.

Greer thrust deeper, faster, her mouth never leaving Ròs's clit. Ròs bucked wildly, coating Greer's face as she came. Freya couldn't tear her eyes away from the scene before her. Her pulse raced as she watched Greer's face buried between Ròs's thighs, jealousy and desire warring in her chest. Each moan, each movement sent jolts of pleasure through her body. The connection between them let her experience everything - Greer's tongue sweeping against Ròs's clit, Dior's mounting need, Ròs's commanding pleasure. The force of Ròs's second orgasm triggered Dior's release, as silver essence flowed from both women in waves of shared ecstasy, leaving them all gasping, connected, transformed.

As their pleasure subsided, Ròs's eyes locked onto Freya. 'Strip.' A command that brooked no argument.

Freya's fingers trembled at her buttons while Ròs reclined. She watched Ròs slide her hand down to touch herself. The leader of the Stone Order circled her own clit with practiced strokes, then slipped two fingers inside, her breath hitching. Dior and Greer latched onto her breasts, tongues swirling around hardened nipples.

Freya's breath came in short gasps as she watched. Heat flooded her body at the sight of those skilled fingers. The sounds of Ròs's pleasure, low moans, made Freya's own arousal heighten.

Dior and Greer's mouths on Ròs's breasts nearly tipped

her over the edge as her desire built again - Ròs's fingers moving faster, Dior and Greer's tongues growing more demanding. Through their connection, each sensation echoed in Freya's body until she could barely stand.

'Come here,' Ròs ordered. 'Show us how ready you are.'

Freya's hand found her own wetness, fingers gliding through slick folds to her swollen clit then deeper. Every touch sent sparks through her body.

'Show me.'

Freya raised her glistening fingers and Ròs beckoned her forward. Ròs's hand closed around hers, her touch sending a jolt of desire through Freya's body. The patterns on Ròs's skin seemed to reach out to her own, intertwining with the newly formed markings that were still learning the language of her power.

'Now,' Ròs whispered, 'let us begin.'

Ròs watched her, her eyes dark with a hunger that went beyond the physical. She was a predator, a queen, and they were hers to command. Her hands moved over Freya's body, her touch both a caress and a claim, igniting a fire that threatened to consume her.

Freya arched beneath their touch, her own desire now raging. She felt herself losing control, surrendering to the tide of sensation that washed over her. Her markings pulsed with light, responding to the touch of the other women, weaving themselves into the tapestry of their shared pleasure. She felt Ròs's fingers slip inside her, filling her, claiming her. Freya cried out, her body arching, her senses overwhelmed by the intensity of the sensation. Dior's mouth found hers, swallowing her cries, her tongue a demanding presence that mirrored the rhythm of Ròs's movements.

Greer's hands moved over Freya's breasts, her touch

igniting a firestorm of pleasure. Ròs moved within her, her rhythm slow and deliberate, each thrust a spark that ignited a new inferno. Freya felt herself spiralling out of control, her body responding instinctively to the wisdom and rhythm of these women.

And then, with a cry that echoed around the room, she shattered. It was a climax unlike any she had ever experienced before, a blinding explosion of light and energy that seemed to tear her apart and put her back together again, stronger, more complete.

As the waves of pleasure subsided, 'I want you to taste me,' Ròs said. Then she glanced at Dior. 'You know what to do.'

Freya knelt before Ròs whose legs were wide, her arousal obvious. 'Thank you,' she said, her eyes cast down.

'Greer, my darling. I want everything you have.' Ròs held out her hand gently drawing Greer closer, and guiding her into position above her head. Then there were no words. They simply moved as one.

Freya's world narrowed to pure sensation as they joined together. Ròs's essence flooded her mouth - sweet, tangy, intoxicating. Her tongue found Ròs's clit, swollen and pulsing beneath her lips. Dior, behind her, filled her completely, while that probing tongue sent sparks of forbidden pleasure through her body. Ahead, she felt Greer's thighs trembling as Ròs's tongue slipped inside her lover.

The connection between them let her experience everything - the way Greer's clit hardened impossibly against Ròs's mouth, how Ròs's skilled tongue drove deeper, making Greer whimper. Each sensation echoed through Freya's body. She felt herself growing wetter, tighter around Dior's thrusting fingers.

Her own tongue moved faster against Ròs, drawing out more of that addictive sweetness. Through their bond, she felt Ròs's building pleasure as though it was her own - the tension coiling tighter, every nerve ending singing with need.

As they moved, their bodies intertwined, Freya felt herself ascending to a higher plane of existence. *This is it,* she thought, as a sense of wonder washed over her. *This is what it means to be truly connected, to be part of something larger than myself.* It was a world of pure sensation, where pain and pleasure blurred, where boundaries dissolved, and where only the present moment existed.

Their pleasure built together, higher and higher still, and then, with a cry that echoed they came as one. Silver essence flowing between them, sealing their alliance in waves of ecstasy.

Freya's body was sated, yet it vibrated with connection. But Ròs was far from done.

When dawn finally broke, the four women lay intertwined, their bond now unbreakable. Ròs traced the newly formed markings on Freya's skin.

'This is proof you belong to us, young seer. We have each claimed you, branded you as our own. And now,' Ròs whispered, 'we are ready to face Agnes.

Chapter Forty-Eight

Redemption's Eve

In a shadowed alley, Agnes surveyed the pitiful remnants of her faithful. So many lost to Baobhan Sith depravity, their blood soaking into the cobbled stones, a grim testament to the night's violence. *But not as many as those foul creatures had sacrificed in turn.* Her lip curled into a sneer at the thought. She had seen their wretched sanctuaries, watched as her followers purged the blight of their existence with fire and blessed iron. The memory of the Dark Vault's destruction, in particular, brought a sense of satisfaction.

And yet, she had seen something else, something that threatened to unravel every carefully laid plan. A tentative truce, an unlikely alliance between the fractious orders. And it was all spearheaded by that thrice-damned human, an interloper playing at immortality.

Freya Solasta. The name curdled on Agnes's tongue like spoiled eggs. She'd dismissed the girl as an inconsequential pawn, a passing fancy that would soon fall victim to the Baobhan Sith's fickle hungers. But the chit was proving far more resilient than expected. More dangerous, too, with her uncanny gift for uniting those wretched creatures under a common cause.

But she had Thomas, her captive. A pawn she could use to her advantage, perhaps, or a sacrifice to fuel her growing power. *What leverage does he offer?* she wondered, her mind already calculating the possibilities. *What secrets does he hold that could be turned against them?*

Well, Agnes had a cause of her own. And she had nurtured it in blood and pain and righteous fury for centuries, biding her time until the moment was ripe for vengeance.

That moment, she sensed with rising certainty, was nearly upon them.

'Rest now, my faithful,' she crooned to her ravaged followers, her tone bringing a promise of retribution. She ran a hand over the hilt of her iron blade, the metal cold and comforting beneath her touch. 'Gather your strength. For the reckoning draws nigh.'

The answering growl that rose from the assembled throng was more beast than human, a feral promise of violence to come, a chorus of hatred that echoed her own.

Oh yes, the reckoning was coming. Her ideal world, the one she envisioned, was a world cleansed of unnaturals. A world where humans, guided by true faith, lived without fear of the shadows. A world where the ancient evils were not just suppressed but eradicated. And when the dust settled and the blood dried, it would be the righteous who stood victorious. Agnes had made a vow on the pyre that consumed her mortal flesh. She had sealed it with her dying breath and the first bitter taste of her new birth as the instrument of divine wrath. And by all the powers that now coursed through her veins, powers granted by the very flames that had forged her anew, she would see it through.

The Baobhan Sith would burn.

And from their ashes, a new world would rise—one purified by righteous fire and washed clean in the blood of the fallen. She would see to it, even if it took an eternity. For she was no longer Agnes, the minister's wife. She was Badb, the instrument of divine wrath, and her vengeance would be absolute.

Chapter Forty-Nine

The Pattern's Truth

Freya stood in her studio, surrounded by paintings that glowed with energy, each canvas a testament to her journey, a visual echo of the transformation she had undergone. Her markings pulsed with silver light as she traced patterns in the air, leaving trails that hung like luminous cobwebs in the pre-dawn darkness. Dior and Greer watched from the doorway, transfixed by the display of power.

'It's like a language,' Freya said, her fingers dancing through the light, weaving intricate shapes that seemed to shift and change even as they formed. 'Not just symbols, but a whole system of meaning. The markings aren't random—they're sentences, paragraphs, entire stories written in silver and shadow.'

She moved to one of her canvases - the one she'd painted of Greer feeding. 'Look here,' she pointed to a particular swirl of colour, a vibrant splash of crimson and gold. 'This pattern appears whenever you feed, but it's not about hunger. It's about connection. The markings are trying to create bonds, to forge links between souls.'

'The curse twisted that,' Dior said softly, staring at the painting. 'Made those bonds into chains.'

'Exactly.' Freya's eyes lit up with a fierce, inner determination. 'But the original purpose is still there, underneath. When I drink from you both, when we share pleasure and power, the patterns try to flow the way they were meant to. That's why it feels so different - we're not just feeding, we're reconnecting with our true nature.'

Greer moved closer, studying the painting with a critical eye. 'And Agnes? What does she see when she looks at the patterns?'

'She sees corruption because that's what she wants to see.' Freya's hand traced the air again, drawing complex geometries of light on her skin. 'But look—when you follow the lines back to their source, before the curse warped them, they're all about unity. Connection. Love freely given and received.'

She turned to face her lovers, her expression intense, her voice filled with a newfound conviction. 'The villagers didn't create these markings—they only twisted what was already there. The Baobhan Sith were never meant to be creatures of darkness. You were meant to be guardians, protectors of sacred bonds between souls.'

'That's why feeding feels like ecstasy,' Dior said, understanding dawning in her eyes. 'It's not just about blood or hunger—it's about sharing life force, connecting on the deepest level possible.'

'Yes!' Freya's markings flared brighter, casting intricate shadows on the walls. 'And that's why Agnes is so dangerous. She's not just using hatred and religious fervour - she's corrupting our original nature even further, turning sacred bonds into weapons.'

She moved to another canvas, this one showing the

complex web of connections between all three of them, a shimmering tapestry of silver, crimson, and gold. 'But we've already started undoing her work without realising it. Every time we make love, every time we feed from each other in trust and passion rather than mere hunger, we're rewriting the patterns. Restoring them to what they should be.'

Greer's eyes widened. 'That's why your transformation was different. You didn't just receive our curse—you received the ancient energy, filtered through our love.'

'And that's why Agnes fears you,' Dior added, her voice hushed with awe. 'You're not just seeing the patterns—you're actively changing them back to their true form.'

Freya nodded, her hands weaving light into increasingly complex shapes, a silent conversation between her will and the raw energy that flowed through her. 'The key isn't fighting her hatred with more hatred. It's showing the magic itself a different way. Every time we choose love over fear, pleasure over pain, willing sacrifice over forced submission, we create a template for what the patterns should be.'

She turned to face them fully, power radiating from her transformed flesh, her eyes blazing with an almost unearthly light. 'I think that's why I can see the patterns so clearly—because I chose this. I walked into your darkness willingly, offered myself freely. There was no curse, no coercion, just... love.'

Greer moved next to her. 'And you think we can use this? Turn Agnes's own power against her?'

'Not against her, through her.' Freya caught Greer's hand, guiding it through one of her glowing patterns. Greer gasped as a surge of energy, and tingling warmth spread through her entire body. 'The fire that transformed her, the hatred that drives her—it's all built on a foundation of perverted love. She didn't hate you because you were monsters. She hated you because she envied your freedom to love as you chose.'

'So how do we stop her?' Dior asked, joining them in the web of light, her own markings pulsing in response.

'We show her the truth. All of us. Every order, every ally. We create a pattern so pure, so true to the original magic, that it burns away the corruption of centuries.' Freya's voice grew stronger, more certain, fuelled by a conviction that went beyond logic or reason. 'Not with blessed iron or righteous fire, but with the very thing she fears most—love freely given, bonds freely chosen, pleasure untainted by shame.

The patterns around them pulsed and swirled, responding to the power of revelation. In that moment, all three women could see it. The possibility of transformation, of curse becoming blessing, of ancient wrongs finally set right. They thought, too, of Thomas, held captive by a creature of darkness. It was imperative that they used their newfound unity to save him from whatever fate awaited him.

'It's dangerous,' Greer warned, though her eyes shone with hope. 'If we fail...

'Then we fail together,' Freya said firmly. 'But I don't think we will. The patterns want to be whole again. They're just waiting for someone to show them how.'

In the studio, three women stood surrounded by living light, their love a defiance of hatred's power. Tomorrow would bring war and fire and the clash of ancient energies. But now they had something they hadn't before—understanding. And with it, the key to their salvation.

Chapter Fifty

Blood and Strategy

The penthouse bedroom still reeked of sex and power, the scent a thick, intoxicating mix. Freya lay sprawled between her lovers, their markings casting a shifting glow across sheets that bore the evidence of their earlier passion. But despite the languorous pleasure that still pulsed through her body, her mind raced with plans and possibilities, fuelled by a potent cocktail of fear, determination, and the lingering echoes of their shared climax.

'We need to move soon,' Dior said, as she traced the curve of Freya's hip, her fingers lingering on the still-sensitive flesh. 'Every hour gives Agnes more time to break him.'

'Or turn him,' Greer added quietly, her breath warm against Freya's neck. 'You didn't see what she did to the others. How she corrupted their very nature, twisting their desires into something monstrous.'

Freya closed her eyes, letting her gift expand, seeking solace and clarity in the patterns. The room shifted and swirled around her, revealing echoes of their recent joining. Not just the raw, physical pleasure, but the deeper connections, the bonds of love and trust, strengthened by choice and sealed in blood. But beneath that, she sensed darker currents, the looming threat that hung over them like a shroud.

'She'll expect us to rush in,' she said, opening her eyes. 'To let emotion override strategy. That's what she's counting on.'

Dior's nail lengthened, scraping against Freya's skin, a sharp, possessive touch that sent shivers down her spine. It was a reflexive response to the thought of Agnes, a silent promise of vengeance. 'Then we don't give her what she expects.'

'No,' Greer agreed, sitting up, the sheet falling away to reveal the elegant lines of her body, damp with sweat, marked with fresh evidence of their shared passion, a living canvas of their love. 'We give her something else entirely.'

A knock at the bedroom door, sharp and insistent, shattered the intimate silence. 'It's me, Ròs,' a familiar voice called. 'I have news you need to hear.'

They dressed quickly, a practiced efficiency born of necessity. Freya noticed how both her lovers positioned themselves between her and the door, their bodies a living shield—protective instincts that ran deeper than conscious thought, a silent testament to their fierce, unwavering devotion.

When Ròs entered, her geometric markings were pulsing with barely contained urgency, her usual composure fractured by the night's events.

'James made contact,' she said without preamble, her voice tight with tension. 'He's infiltrated one of their prayer meetings. Says they're planning something big. Something that involves Thomas.'

Dior's growl vibrated through the room, a low, guttural sound of barely restrained fury. 'When?'

'Tomorrow night. Some kind of ritual cleansing.' Ròs's lip curled in disgust. 'Apparently Agnes plans to make an example of him. Show how even the most 'corrupted' can be purified through righteous fire. She's developed some sort of conversion therapy.'

The temperature in the room seemed to drop several degrees as Greer's power responded to her fury, a tangible chill in the air that had nothing to do with the night outside. 'Where?'

'That's the interesting part.' Ròs moved to the window, looking out over the sleeping city, a silhouette against the faint glow of dawn. 'She's not using her usual church. She's taking him to Arthur's Seat.'

Freya felt it then, a shift in the patterns, a sense of ancient power stirring, a resonance with something deep within her, a primal energy awakening.

'It's not random,' she said, her gift showing her threads of connection she hadn't seen before, a tapestry of interwoven energies, a map of power and intent.

'That place has history. Old magic. She is summoning the power of the seventeen,' said Greer.

Freya looked at her in bewilderment.

'The seventeen are trapped souls of those burned as witches, innocents corrupted by flames, confined to tiny coffins, no bigger than the size of your palm—and only one of their own can free them. It was said the coffins lay buried deep within Arthur's seat. She must have them. She is looking to amplify her power.' Greer said, grimly.

Dior began pacing, her markings writhing with barely contained violence, a storm brewing beneath her skin, a predator unleashed. 'So we go in hard. Hit them with everything we have. Between the orders—'

'No.' Freya's voice cut through the tension, sharp and decisive. 'That's exactly what she'll expect. What she wants.' She moved to the window beside Ròs, studying the distant bulk of Arthur's Seat, her mind racing, calculating, her gift revealing the hidden currents beneath the surface. 'We need to be smarter. More subtle.'

She turned back to her lovers, power crackling along her skin, her eyes shining with a terrifying ferocity. 'James is already inside. Let him be our eyes. Meanwhile, we gather our forces, but not for a frontal assault. We divide them, separate her from her power base.'

'How?' Greer asked, but her expression suggested she was already following Freya's logic, her mind already calculating angles and strategies, a general planning her campaign.

'By giving her a more tempting target.' Freya flashed an inhuman smile, the predator within breaking free. 'Me.'

The silence that followed was charged with possibility and fear. Finally, Dior spoke. 'Absolutely not. You're not offering yourself as bait.'

'Why not? It's perfect.' Freya moved between them, letting her power flare. 'She's obsessed with what I represent. A human transformed by choice rather than curse. A threat to everything she believes about corruption and sin.'

'She'll kill you,' Greer said flatly, her tone devoid of emotion.

'No.' Freya caught their hands, forming a circuit of power that made their markings blaze, a trinity, a bond unbreakable. 'She'll try to turn me. To prove that even willing transformation leads to corruption. And while she's focused on that...'

'We strike from the shadows,' Ròs finished, a cold, calculating satisfaction flashed across her face. 'Using the very darkness she thinks is our weakness.'

The plan took shape between them like a deadly dance, a tapestry woven from strategy and desperation, fuelled by love and a thirst for vengeance. James would continue his infiltration, gathering intelligence, a lifeline in the heart of the enemy's camp. Freya would present herself as a target too tempting to resist, a lamb to the slaughter, drawing Agnes's attention, her power, her focus. And in the chaos that followed ...

'It's risky,' Greer said at last. 'So many things could go wrong.' Freya could see the fear in her eyes.

'Everything worth doing is risky,' Freya replied, her voice soft yet firm. She pulled her lovers close, letting their energies mingle, their heartbeats syncing, their bodies pressed together in a fierce embrace. 'But together? Together we're stronger than she could ever imagine.'

Ròs, as though sensing that she was no longer needed, slipped silently from the room, her geometric markings fading into the shadows. The Stone Order leader understood the power of such intimate moments, the need for privacy to forge bonds stronger than iron.

Their kiss was raw, desperate, a fusion of fear, need and a burning, all-consuming passion. A promise and a prayer all in one. When they broke apart, the decision was made.

Tomorrow would bring blood and fire, blessed iron and righteous fury. But tonight...

Tonight was for preparation. For strengthening bonds that would need to hold against the coming storm. For reminding themselves of the power of their love, a weapon Agnes could never comprehend.

They fell into bed together, their bodies a familiar

haven, hands and mouths relearning that intimate terrain with a new urgency. Each touch was a vow, each shared breath a reaffirmation of their love, each whispered moan a prayer for strength and survival. Each thrust, each caress, each shared pleasure was a seal on their commitment to face whatever came as one.

Outside, Edinburgh slept on, unaware of the forces gathering in its midst. But in a penthouse high above the city, three women wove patterns of power and pleasure that would change everything.

The rescue would come.

Chapter Fifty-One

Into the Lion's Den

James adjusted his tie, checking his reflection in the polished brass plaque of the converted church.

'RIGHTEOUS ASSEMBLY—ALL WELCOME' gleamed in fresh gold lettering. His hands shook slightly as he smoothed down his carefully pressed shirt. Thomas had always been the one to help him make sure he looked his best. He'd always had impeccable taste. The memory, once a comfort, now felt like a punch to the gut.

The thought of Thomas gave him strength, a renewed sense of purpose. Whatever horrors waited inside, they couldn't be worse than the gnawing fear, the icy dread, of what Agnes might be doing to the man he loved.

Inside, the church had been stripped of its traditional Christian imagery. The walls were bare except for modern abstract paintings that seemed to pulse with barely contained flame, their vibrant colours a mockery of sanctity. The pews had been replaced with hard wooden chairs arranged in a circle, and the altar... James swallowed hard, bile rising in his throat. The altar was now a stark steel table. Strange devices were arranged with surgical precision—things that looked medical but felt wrong, twisted versions of healing tools turned to darker purposes.

'Welcome, brother.' A woman in an expensive suit approached, her smile not quite reaching her eyes, which gleamed with an unsettling intensity. 'I'm Margaret. First time?'

'James.' He forced his voice to stay steady, injecting a hint of nervous enthusiasm into his tone. 'I... I saw things. At the Dark Vault. Things that made me question everything.'

Margaret's expression sharpened with interest, her smile becoming more predatory. 'You were there? During the cleansing?'

He nodded, letting real trauma colour his words, the memory of the carnage still fresh in his mind. 'I worked the bar. I thought they were just eccentric customers, you know? Rich people with weird tastes. But then I saw...' He shuddered, a genuine reaction to the horrors he'd witnessed. 'What they really were. The way they fed. The things they did to people who trusted them.'

'The Corrupted prey on innocence,' Margaret said softly, her voice a silken whisper. 'They seduce us with pleasure, make us complicit in our own damnation.' She touched his arm, and James noticed her skin was unnaturally warm, almost feverish. 'But you're safe now. Agnes will show you the truth.'

Other members began filtering in, each moving with that same unnatural grace that marked them as different, enhanced—Agnes called them improved. James noted how they moved, too smooth, too controlled for normal humans. Their eyes gleamed, and when they spoke, their voices carried undertones that made his skin crawl, a subtle dissonance that set his teeth on edge.

He recognised some faces from the attack on the Dark Vault. A man whose hands had thrown blessed iron with deadly accuracy. A woman who'd moved faster than any human should be able to. They nodded to him politely, these monsters who'd helped destroy his world, and he fought the urge to retch.

The meeting began with what seemed like normal support group activities. People shared stories of encounters with the Baobhan Sith, each tale more horrific than the last. A woman described how her sister had been 'enslaved' by a Baobhan Sith's pleasure. A man spoke of finding his daughter in thrall to their unholy appetites.

James listened, memorising details, building a picture of Agnes's network, his mind cataloguing every fact, every nuance. He heard the truth beneath their twisted versions of events—how many of them had actually been willing participants until shame or society turned their pleasure to hatred, their fear to righteous fury.

Then the tone shifted.

'Brothers and sisters,' Margaret announced, 'we have a special guest tonight.'

The door opened, and James's heart stopped.

Agnes Lasair entered like a CEO arriving at a board meeting wearing a designer suit, perfect makeup, elegant heels clicking on polished floors. But there was something else, something that made the air itself seem to shrink away from her. Power radiated from her in waves of invisible heat, a tangible aura of command and menace.

'Welcome, seekers of truth,' she said, and her voice carried echoes of burning wood and screaming flesh, a subtle reminder of her origins. 'Tonight we begin the next phase of our holy work.'

James kept his expression carefully neutral as she outlined their plans. Cleansing rituals. Training for enhanced soldiers. Locations of unnatural gatherings marked for purification. She spoke of their mission with the fervour of a true believer, but beneath her words, James sensed something darker—a personal vendetta masked as religious crusade, a deep-seated hatred that went far beyond any doctrine.

But it was when she mentioned Thomas that his control almost slipped.

'Our special guest continues his conversion,' Agnes said, satisfaction dripping from every word, her smile a chilling parody of warmth. 'Soon he will be our strongest argument against their corruption. A living testament to the power of righteous fire.'

James's fingers curled into fists under the cover of his jacket, his nails digging into his palms. He forced himself to breathe normally, to nod along with the others' murmurs of approval. Inside, his heart was breaking, shattering into a million pieces. *What were they doing to Thomas? How much of him would be left when they found him?*

After the meeting, he lingered, helping stack chairs and dispose of paper cups. His careful helpfulness caught Margaret's attention.

'You seem eager to serve,' she observed, her eyes studying him with unsettling intensity.

'I want to help,' he said. 'After what I saw... I need to do something. They need to be stopped.'

She studied him for a long moment, her gaze piercing. 'There might be a place for you. We need people who understand their ways, who've seen their corruption first-hand.' Her smile turned predatory, a hunter about to ensnare its prey. 'Would you like to see more?'

This was it, the opening he'd been hoping for, the chance he'd been praying for. 'Yes,' he said fervently, with a false conviction that matched their own. 'Show me everything.'

Margaret led him deeper into the building, past offices and meeting rooms, down stairs he carefully counted, each step taking him further into the heart of the beast. The air grew colder, heavy with the scent of sanctified iron, with a chemical edge that burned his nose. The walls here were reinforced, marked with symbols that seemed to twist in his peripheral vision.

They passed guards whose eyes glowed with unnatural fire, watching every move they made. James noted their positions, their patterns, the way they communicated through subtle gestures. Everything could be useful. Everything could help bring Thomas home. Each level they descended made him more uneasy, as though reality itself was being warped by whatever power Agnes wielded, a subtle distortion of the natural order.

Finally, they reached what had once been the crypt deep in the bowels of the rock from which the city arose. Now it was a high-tech containment facility, steel finished with harsh lighting and the constant hum of power. James's skin prickled, a tangible manifestation of the unholy work being done within.

'This is where we keep those who still have hope of salvation,' Margaret explained, leading him past cells each containing a cowering figure. *What were they doing to them? To Thomas?* 'Through righteous fire, they can be cleansed.' Her voice was filled with a stomach-churning pride.

James saw things that would haunt his nightmares,

beings in various stages of 'conversion' their natural powers twisted and corrupted by Agnes's unholy fusion of pseudoscience and zealotry.

But he didn't see Thomas.

When Margaret had finally given him the grand tour, and he had assured her he'd help in whatever way he could, James finally escaped back to his tiny flat. His hands shook so badly he could barely type his message to Dior. He coded it carefully, including everything he'd learned: guard rotations, security systems, building layouts. But the most important part was the last line:

He's not in the church. They're holding him somewhere else. But I'm close to finding out where. Don't move yet. Trust me.

He sent the message and immediately deleted all trace of it. Then he sat in the dark, trembling with delayed reaction to the horrors he'd witnessed. The memory of those cells, those twisted experiments, would stay with him forever, etched into his soul.

'Hold on, love,' he whispered to the empty room, his voice choked with emotion. 'I'm coming. Whatever it takes, I'm coming for you.'

In the distance, church bells tolled midnight, a mournful sound in the stillness of the night. Tomorrow, he would go back, dig deeper, risk more. He would smile and nod and pretend to believe their twisted gospel. He would earn their trust, piece by piece, until they led him to Thomas.

For now, he allowed himself one moment of weakness, one quiet sob in the darkness, a single tear tracing a path down his cheek.

Chapter Fifty-Two

Whispers in the Dark

The patterns wouldn't let Freya sleep. They danced behind her closed eyelids, silver threads weaving stories she wasn't sure she wanted to see. Between Greer and Dior in bed, she tossed restlessly, their markings pulsing in response to her distress.

When the first vision hit, it felt like drowning. She was in a village square in the East Neuk of Fife, but not as a spectator—she was Greer, centuries ago, the hunger a sharp ache in her belly. Beside her, Dior her hands caressing Aileen's body, fingers slipping beneath her skirts, seeking the soft, yielding flesh within. Aileen moaned softly, her head thrown back, lost in the throes of ecstasy. In the distance, villagers, alerted by the sounds of pleasure, were gathering, their faces grim – the doors to the barn burst open. Eyes watching them, the intimate sharing of blood and pleasure.

The vision shifted. Now she was Dior, scrambling through the narrow streets of Pittenweem, her markings burning with grief and rage. Behind her, she could hear the villagers' cries, a cacophony of righteous fury. They had driven them out, away from the safety of their home, away from Aileen. Aileen who had come to them willingly, offering her blood and her body with a joyous abandon that had terrified the superstitious villagers. Now, smoke rose in the distance, carrying with it the sickeningly sweet smell of burning flesh.

'Freya!' Greer's voice pulled her back, a lifeline to the present. She was trembling, her markings blazing so bright they illuminated the whole room. 'What did you see?'

'The past,' Freya gasped, struggling to catch her breath. 'When they tried to destroy you.'

Dior's arms tightened around her, a silent reassurance. 'That was centuries ago, love. We survived.'

'But not all of us.' Freya turned to face them. 'There was another. Someone you loved, before. I felt her name, but I can't...'

'Aileen,' Greer whispered, and the name carried centuries of pain, a wound that had never fully healed. 'We don't speak of her.'

'She is one of Agnes's seventeen,' she said, but the patterns were already pulling her under again. This time she was somewhere else—a church, but not as it was now. She was Agnes, but not the creature of righteous fire she'd become. She was young, innocent, serving God with an open heart. Until the night she discovered what her new friends truly were.

The memory fractured, showing her glimpses of what followed: Agnes's horror at finding her husband participating in their demise. The shame that turned to rage. The villagers who listened to her tales of corruption and sin. The stones they threw, the building of the fire, the flames, the pain, not understanding that their hatred would forge something far worse than what they sought to destroy.

'She was innocent,' Freya said, surfacing from the vision, her voice hoarse with emotion. 'Before the fire changed her. She truly believed she was serving God's will.'

'Many monsters begin as innocents,' Dior said quietly. 'It's what they choose to become that matters.'

The next vision slammed into Freya without warning. Future possibilities exploded through her mind like shattered glass: Edinburgh in flames, beings hunted through streets where their sanctuaries once stood.

Thomas, his eyes burning with righteous fire, leading Agnes's soldiers against his former kind.

James, broken on a steel altar, his love turned to weapon against all he once held dear.

Seventeen spectral figures materialised, their features twisted with malevolent rage. Hellfire danced across their forms, consuming flesh that liquefied and reformed not to heal but to prolong their victims' suffering. Their hatred burned as fierce as the flames that wreathed them, each apparition locked in an eternal cycle of destruction and rebirth, existing only to magnify the torment of those they chose to destroy.

But worse were the personal visions: Greer, wounded and bleeding, her markings fading as her life force ebbed away. Dior, cornered by Agnes's enhanced followers, her eyes filled with a desperate defiance. And Freya herself, transformed into something that no longer remembered love or mercy.

'No!' She jerked upright, power crackling around her like lightning, a physical manifestation of her fear and determination. 'I won't let that happen. Any of it.'

'Tell us,' Greer commanded softly, her hand finding Freya's. 'Show us what you saw.'

Freya reached for them both, letting her gift flow

through their connection. Their markings synchronised, creating a circuit of shared vision.

When it was done, they lay in stunned silence, processing the magnitude of what they'd witnessed.

'If she succeeds,' Dior said finally, her voice heavy with dread, 'it won't just be us she destroys. She'll remake the world in her own image. Turn every pleasure into sin, every love into corruption.'

'The patterns know,' Freya said. 'They remember what we were before the curse, but they also show what we could become—both the light and dark possibilities.' She traced a complex whorl on Greer's skin, making their markings flare in harmony. 'We're at a turning point. What we do now will echo through centuries to come.'

'No pressure then,' Greer said dryly, but her eyes were serious, reflecting the gravity of their situation. 'Did you see any futures where we win?'

Freya hesitated. 'A few. But they all require something impossible.'

'What?'

'We have to make Agnes remember who she was. Who we all were, before hatred twisted everything.' Freya sat up. 'The fire that transformed her. It didn't just burn away her humanity. It burned away her ability to see beauty in darkness, to understand that not all hungers are evil.'

'You want to save her?' Dior's sounded incredulous.

'Not save. Remind.' Freya's markings pulsed with new purpose. 'Remind her that she once lived a life of love, not hatred. That the same power she uses to corrupt could be used to heal.'

'And if she won't remember?' Greer asked quietly, her gaze searching Freya's face.

The patterns shifted again, showing Freya one final

vision - a confrontation, not on Arthur's Seat, but in the ruins of the Dark Vault, amidst the echoes of violence and betrayal, ancient power against ancient power, love against hatred burning with equal fire.

'Then we fight,' she said simply. 'But at least we fight knowing the truth, and fight for love, not fear.'

Silence fell as the implications of her words sank in. The city was waking, unaware of the forces gathering in its midst, the choices that would determine not just its fate, but the fate of all who walked in darkness.

Greer pulled Freya back down between them, wrapping her in an embrace. Dior pressed close on her other side, their markings creating patterns of protection and fierce devotion.

'Whatever comes,' Greer said softly, her voice a vow, 'we face it together.'

'Always,' Dior agreed, her hand finding Freya's.

Freya closed her eyes, letting their love anchor her against the tide of visions still threatening to pull her under. The patterns sang around them, showing possibilities that branched and branched again, a dizzying array of potential futures.

But through all the possible futures, one truth remained constant: together they were stronger than any righteous fire. Together, they might just change everything.

Chapter Fifty-Three

Seeds of Doubt

Freya sat in her studio, surrounded by half-finished paintings that seemed to glow in the dim light. She hadn't been able to sleep, not properly, since the attack on the Dark Vault. Every time she closed her eyes, she saw fractured visions of the future, felt echoes of past betrayals, and sensed the ever-shifting patterns of the present, a kaleidoscope of energies that threatened to overwhelm her. But it was Mànas's patterns that troubled her most. Something about his movements, his energy, had been nagging at her since the meeting in the Old Chamber. His patterns were... wrong. Not just the dark, violent energy she'd seen before, but something more insidious, like a rot beneath the surface.

'You're certain?' Greer asked, studying the security feed over Freya's shoulder. The footage showed Mànas pacing in the main area of the studio, his movements agitated, his markings a restless tide beneath his skin. 'Mànas is many things, but a traitor?'

'Glicia warned us,' Freya reminded her, her fingers tracing the lines of a charcoal sketch she'd made, a quick impression of Mànas's aura. 'And look! There.' She pointed at the screen, isolating a moment where Mànas paused, his markings flaring briefly. 'The patterns can't flow naturally. They're fractured, like they're fighting against themselves, like something is trapped within, struggling to break free.'

Dior paced behind them, her own markings writhing with tension, a mirror of Freya's unease. 'He's been around for centuries. If he were working with Agnes, surely we'd have seen signs.'

'Unless that's exactly why we missed them,' Freya said, her voice low and thoughtful. 'We see what we expect to see. We trust what we think we understand. But what if he's learned to mask his true intentions? What if Agnes has found a way to corrupt even the patterns themselves?'

'And if you're wrong?' Dior asked, watching Freya work. 'If we accuse him without proof, we risk shattering the alliance before it's even begun.'

'I know,' Freya said. 'But if I'm right...' She didn't finish the sentence, but the unspoken threat hung heavy in the air.

'We need to involve Bethia and Fòs,' Greer said, ever the strategist. 'If we're going to confront Mànas, we need their support. Or at least, their neutrality.'

Dior nodded in agreement. 'They may not see what Freya sees, but they trust us. To a point.'

'They need to understand the patterns,' Freya added. 'Not just *see* them, but *feel* the dissonance, the way the energy is fractured.'

'Easier said than done,' Dior said, sighing. 'Most of us experience the patterns on a purely physical level. You're asking them to trust something they can't perceive.'

'Then I'll have to find a way to make them *feel* it,' Freya said, determination hardening her voice.

It took hours of careful planning and preparation. Freya

focused her gift, channelling the energy of the patterns into a tangible form, a subtle vibration that even those without her sight could feel. She practiced modulating her power, weaving it into the very air of the studio, a silent symphony of energy that gave life to the hidden truths she knew existed.

Finally, they summoned the leaders of the Shadow and Stone Orders to the studio. The atmosphere was tense, a mixture of apprehension and anticipation, as Freya explained her suspicions. She spoke not just with words, but with the raw energy of the patterns themselves, letting the subtle vibrations she had woven into the room speak for her.

Bethia, ever pragmatic, listened with a sceptical frown, her spiral markings pulsing slowly. 'Freya's gift is unique, that much is certain. But to accuse Mànas of treachery based on fragmented patterns...' She shook her head. 'It's dangerous. We need proof, something concrete.'

Ròs, however, seemed more open to the possibility. She knew, more intimately than most, the power and the truth that Freya's gift could reveal. The echoes of their shared experience still lingered in her own patterns. 'Mànas has always been ambitious,' she said, thoughtfully. 'And his order has been strangely absent since the attacks. It's worth investigating.'

'But how?' Bethia asked. 'We can't just march in there and demand answers. He'll deny everything, and we'll be back to square one.'

'We need to be subtle,' Freya said. 'We need to give him a chance to reveal the truth himself.'

'Or hang himself with it,' Dior added, a dark glint in her eyes.

The decision was made. They would approach Mànas,

not with accusations, but with questions. They would express their concerns, share Freya's insights about the corrupted patterns, and offer him a chance to explain. And Freya, with her unique ability to perceive the hidden language of the Baobhan Sith, would be watching, listening, feeling for any flicker of deception, any hint of the darkness that lurked beneath the surface.

The meeting was set for the following evening. As Freya prepared, she couldn't shake the feeling that they were walking into a trap. But the thought of Thomas, held captive by Agnes, spurred her on. They had to uncover the truth, no matter the cost. The patterns demanded it. And Freya, for better or worse, was finally learning to listen.

Chapter Fifty-Four

A Traitor's Confession

The sprawling mansion was a testament to Mànas's power and refined taste, but offered no comfort. He stood amidst the grandeur, surrounded by Freya's paintings of betrayal. Ornate furnishings and elegant decor mocked the raw, primal energy that filled the space. His dark markings writhed beneath his skin as he studied the evidence she'd uncovered, his expression unreadable. The air crackled as the scent of blood-infused paint mingling with the metallic tang of barely suppressed fear and rage.

'Interesting interpretation,' he said. He moved closer, his gaze sweeping over the canvases as if searching for a hidden meaning. 'But you're seeing patterns where none exist. Your gift makes you overconfident, little seer. There is no treachery in this order.'

'These aren't interpretations.' Freya moved to the largest canvas, where she'd attempted to capture the twisted dance of corruption she sensed in his lieutenant's energy. She hadn't painted the patterns themselves—that would have been too dangerous—but she had hinted at them, suggested their dissonance through abstract forms and clashing colours. 'Look closer. The coordinates of every safe house we've lost. The timing of each attack. All hidden in their patterns, waiting for Agnes to exploit.'

Mànas's laugh was as cold as winter, chilling as it echoed through the high-ceilinged room. 'You dare accuse me—'

'She's right.' Greer's voice was sharp and decisive. She and Dior emerged from the shadows, their markings bright with contained fury, their bodies radiating a palpable threat. 'We've lost too many sanctuaries too quickly. The enemy knows things only someone close to the order leadership could know.'

'And your evidence is paint and paranoid speculation?' Mànas sneered, his gaze shifting between them, his black viper markings thrashing beneath his skin, their movements agitated, betraying a hint of unease beneath his facade. 'You forget your place—'

'No.' Freya's power flared, making the paintings around them pulse, momentarily revealing the hidden energies beneath the surface. Raw energy emanated from her, pressing against them like a physical force. 'You forget yours. The patterns don't lie, Mànas. If you are not betraying us, then you are hiding something. Your patterns speak of fear, of deceit.'

A flicker of something—surprise, perhaps, or grudging respect—crossed his face. He stood, his movements deliberate, and moved towards the window, his back to them. 'I have led my order for centuries. I have made difficult choices, choices that have not always been popular,' he said. His voice was heavy. 'But I have always acted in what I believed to be the best interests of our kind.'

'And yet,' Dior interjected, her voice sharp, 'we are losing.'

Mànas turned back to them, his eyes blazing. 'Losses are inevitable in war. But they do not mean we are defeated.'

'These losses are too precise,' Greer said. 'The attacks are too well-informed. Agnes knows our movements, our safe houses, our weaknesses.'

'And you believe this knowledge comes from within my own ranks,' Mànas said, the smallest hint of pain in his voice.

'Yes,' Freya said. She stepped forward, her own markings pulsing in response to the energy in the room. 'And I can prove it.'

For a long moment, Mànas was silent, his gaze fixed on Freya. Then, he sighed, the sound heavy with resignation. 'I have had my own suspicions,' he admitted, as though the words were forced from him. Beneath his stoic facade, his markings betrayed a flicker of uncertainty, a subtle disharmony that spoke of internal conflict. 'There have been whispers, inconsistencies... things I could not explain. But to suspect is one thing. To know, another.'

'Who?' Dior pressed, her voice urgent. 'Who do you suspect?'

Mànas hesitated, then spoke a name that made Freya's blood run cold. 'Bran.'

'Bran.' Greer's voice was flat, but her markings flared, betraying her shock. He was Mànas's second-in-command, his most trusted lieutenant. The idea of him being a traitor seemed unthinkable.

'He has always been ambitious,' Mànas said, his voice low. 'Perhaps too ambitious.' He turned to Freya, his dark eyes filled with a sudden intensity. 'Can you confirm that it is him? Through his patterns?'

'I can try,' Freya said. She closed her eyes, reaching for the familiar hum of energy that thrummed beneath her skin. 'But I'll need to see them all. All your lieutenants.'

Mànas nodded. He gave a sharp command into the intercom, his voice echoing through the mansion. Within minutes, five figures assembled before them, their expressions a mixture of curiosity and apprehension. They were a diverse group, their markings ranging from intricate swirls to sharp, angular designs, but all bore the dark, unmistakable hue of Mànas's order.

Freya stepped forward. She could feel their power, their barely leashed control, but beneath it, she sensed something else—a subtle dissonance, a discordant note in the symphony of their energies.

'I need you to lower your shields,' she said, her voice ringing with newfound authority. 'Let me see your true patterns.'

They hesitated, glancing at Mànas for confirmation. He gave a curt nod, his face unreadable. One by one, they complied, their markings flaring as they dropped their mental defences.

Freya focused, extending her awareness beyond the physical realm. She saw the intricate tapestry of their energies, the way their patterns intertwined and diverged, a complex movement of light and shadow. She searched for the tell-tale signs of corruption, the fractured lines, the dark, discordant energy she had seen in her sketches.

Her gaze lingered on each lieutenant in turn, her heart pounding. She saw ambition, loyalty, fear, even a flicker of resentment in some, but not the deep-seated corruption she sought. *Could I be wrong?* she wondered, a chink of doubt piercing her certainty. *Was Mànas the traitor after all?* Then she saw him.

Bran stood at the back of the group, his expression carefully neutral, but his markings... they were different. Beneath the surface, she saw it—the rot, the twisting of the natural flow, the subtle but unmistakable signature of Agnes's influence. It was faint, almost imperceptible, but it was there, a hidden dissonance that screamed of betrayal. *There,* she thought, with a mixture of dread and grim satisfaction. *The fracture in the pattern, the hidden darkness.*

Before Freya could speak, before she could even form the words of accusation, Bran moved. He launched himself at her, his markings blazing with that same corrupted light she'd seen on Agnes's enhanced humans.

'You see too much, little seer,' he snarled, his voice distorted, a terrifying blend of his own voice and a spirit far more malevolent.

But Freya had seen this, too, in the patterns, moments before he moved. She twisted away, letting his momentum carry him past her.

'Clever bitch. You have no idea what's coming. What she's planning,' he said.

'So it's true.' Mànas's voice had gone deadly quiet, a stillness that was more terrifying than any shout. 'You betrayed us to that zealot.'

Bran's harsh laugh shattered the room's tense silence. 'Betrayed? I gave us a chance at real power. Agnes knows what we could become if we stopped cowering in shadows, feeding on human dregs.'

His markings blazed with unnatural light as he spoke, showing how deeply Agnes's influence had worked into his being. 'She can purify us. Burn away the curse and leave only power behind.'

'You fool,' Dior spat. 'She's destroying everything we are.'

'Everything we were forced to be!' Bran's face twisted with fanatic fervour. 'Why should we hide? Why should we pretend to be less than what we are? Agnes offers us freedom from old chains—'

The rest of his speech ended in a gurgling scream as Mànas struck.

The order leader moved faster than any human eye could track, his dark markings becoming living weapons that tore into his former lieutenant. Bran fought back against the serpents with enhanced strength, Agnes's corrupted power making him formidable. He landed blows that would have killed a normal Baobhan Sith, his nails leaving burning wounds that smoked with righteous fire.

But Mànas's rage was terrible to behold. It was the fury of a leader betrayed, a predator wounded, a king dethroned from his own sense of control. His markings writhed like living things, becoming teeth and claws and instruments of exquisite agony. Each strike carried centuries of fury, each wound he inflicted was designed to maximise pain.

'I trusted you,' he snarled between savage attacks. 'Made you my sword, my shield—'

'You made me your slave!' Bran's counterattack sent them both crashing through Freya's easels, scattering canvases and paint. 'Agnes showed me the truth—showed all of us what freedom could taste like!'

The room became a battlefield. Paintings were shredded, furniture toppled, walls cracked under the force of bodies being thrown against them. Freya tried to track the patterns of their combat, but the energies were too chaotic, too corrupted by hatred and betrayal. Even through her horror, a part of her, the artist, couldn't help but be fascinated by the raw display of power, the terrible beauty of their markings in the throes of combat.

'It's too late,' Bran spat, blood running from wounds that wouldn't heal properly—another sign of how Agnes's corruption had weakened him. 'I've already given her everything she needs. When the time comes...' He laughed. 'When the moment comes, you'll wish you'd chosen differently.'

Mànas moved with a predator's grace, as he circled his former lieutenant. Bran attempted to back away, to escape the inevitable, but iron-strong hands seized him, one at his throat, the other plunging deep into his chest, seeking the corrupted heart within.

The sound of breaking ribs echoed through the studio as Mànas tore through bone and tissue. Bran's scream cut off in a wet gurgle as his former leader extracted his still-beating heart, holding it up so the traitor could see his own life pulsing in those merciless fingers.

But Mànas wasn't finished. With methodical precision, he dismembered the betrayer limb by limb, each separation accompanied by the crack of bone and the tearing of flesh. Bran's markings flickered and died as pieces of him scattered across the polished floor. When Mànas finished, what remained bore no resemblance to anything that had once been a Baobhan Sith—just a twisted mass of meat and bone, dissolving into corrupt shadows.

The silence that followed was absolute. Even the usual sounds of the city seemed muted, as if Edinburgh itself held its breath, horrified. Blood dripped from Mànas's hands, each drop hitting the floor with the sound of thunder.

Freya stood frozen, her gift revealed the patterns of death and power still dancing in the air. She could see how Mànas's dark markings had changed during the execution, becoming something that predated their curse. *A primal darkness,* she realised, *a rage that went deeper than bone, a hunger that transcended even their cursed existence.*

'Now you see,' Mànas said quietly, turning to face her, his form shifting back into something more human, though his eyes still held centuries of violence barely contained. 'This is what we truly are beneath the veneer of civilisation. This is the power Agnes hopes to corrupt.'

Greer moved closer to Freya, protective but also shaken. Dior's nails had lengthened unconsciously, her body responding to the display of dominant power.

'You could have just questioned him,' Dior said, rolling her eyes.

'No.' Freya surprised herself by speaking, not looking away from the gruesome remains. Even as she recoiled from the brutality, a part of her, the artist, analysed the scene, the way the crimson stains caught the light, the stark contrast between life and death. 'His patterns were already too corrupted. Agnes's influence had reached his core. There was nothing left to save.'

Mànas studied her with new respect. 'You understand then. The price of power. The necessity of violence.' He gestured at the remains of his lieutenant. 'This is what awaits any who betray our kind. Remember that, little seer, as your own power grows.'

'Is that a threat?' Greer's voice carried a dangerous edge, her markings flaring in response.

'A warning.' Mànas began cleaning his hands with methodical care, wiping away the blood and viscera as if it were mere paint. 'Power like hers attracts attention. Makes enemies. The next time someone tries to take her from you, it might not be so... obvious.'

The implications hung heavy in the air. Freya felt the weight of it settle into her bones—the understanding that her gift made her both valuable and vulnerable. She looked at the scattered remains of Bran and knew there was more to come.

'Agnes will know what happened here,' she said softly. 'She'll feel the death of her agent.'

'Good.' Mànas's smile was terrible to behold, a chilling expression that sent shivers down Freya's spine. 'Let her know the price of turning our own against us. Let her wonder how many more of her corrupted followers we've identified.'

But as they began cleaning up the evidence of the execution, Freya couldn't shake a deeper unease. Yes, they'd eliminated one threat, but at what cost? The brutality she'd witnessed showed her a side of their nature that no amount of willing sacrifice or sacred pleasure could disguise. *Have we become the monsters they feared?* she wondered, the question echoing in the sudden silence.

And somewhere, Agnes waited. Waited with her righteous fire and her promises of purification. Waited with more converts hidden in their ranks, watching, gathering intelligence, preparing for the moment when betrayal would hurt most.

The enemy wasn't just at their gates anymore. The enemy was everywhere. And victory, Freya realised, might require becoming the very monsters Agnes claimed them to be.

Chapter Fifty-Five

The Artist's Refuge

The attack on the *Moonflower and Thistle* tea shop happened without warning. The small sanctuary, known only to a select few Baobhan Sith, had stood peacefully on Victoria Street for over a century. Tonight, its wards shattered like glass as an enhanced human smashed through the door, blessed iron gleaming in both hands.

The young Baobhan Sith behind the counter, barely a century old, didn't stand a chance. Her eyes, still bright with youthful curiosity, widened in shock as the attacker moved with unnatural speed. *There wasn't even time for a scream,* Freya thought, her stomach clenching with a sickening mix of horror and rage as she watched the scene unfold through the patterns. Blessed iron found her heart with surgical precision. She had time for one shocked gasp before her body began to crumble.

'Unclean,' the attacker whispered, his eyes burning with righteous fire. 'Purify all that is unclean.'

He methodically worked his way through the building, slaughtering the small group that had gathered for their nightly tea ritual. When he finished, he used the victims' blood to paint the Righteous Assembly's symbol on the wall —a burning sword piercing a heart.

Across Edinburgh, and cities across the world where the Baobhan Sith had migrated, similar scenes played out with terrifying efficiency. In her studio, Freya doubled over as the patterns around her fractured and screamed. The pain dropped her to her knees, her markings flaring with reflected agony.

'Freya!' Greer caught her before she hit the floor. 'What is it?'

'Death,' she gasped. 'So much death. The patterns are being torn apart—'

Dior's phone buzzed. The colour drained from her face as she read the message. '*The Moonflower and Thistle* is gone. And the *Silver Thorn. The Cave*. They're hitting every sanctuary in the city.'

'*The Crimson Sanctuary*?' asked Greer, an edge of trepidation in her tone.

'Still safe,' said Dior. 'Maeve has twenty-three souls seeking refuge, and counting. I've told her to lock the doors and not to allow anyone in who she doesn't know. I don't want to turn any of our own away but with Agnes turning our own against us... with her conversions...' she allowed her words to trail off. 'We won't be able to save everyone.'

Sirens began to wail in the distance. Then more sirens, until the night was filled with their urgent chorus. Through the covered windows, they could see smoke rising from multiple locations.

'It's starting,' Freya said, struggling to her feet. *This is what the patterns showed me,* she realised. *The flames, the chaos, the city torn apart.*

❄

On Rose Street, Sarah Robertson, a human shop assistant, was walking home from her late shift when she saw it—a figure moving too fast to be human, pursuing something that flickered at the edge of her vision. She ducked into a doorway just as they passed, witnessing a battle that defied explanation. The pursuer's hands glowed with strange fire. His quarry, beautiful and terrible, fought with inhuman grace until a rusty sword found its mark.

The sight of supernatural combat in the middle of her familiar street broke something in Sarah's understanding of the world. She wasn't the only one. All across Edinburgh, the veil between worlds was tearing, forcing humans to confront truths they weren't prepared to face.

❄

The Baobhan Sith fought back where they could, but they were overwhelmed. Centuries of hiding, of maintaining secrecy, had left them ill-prepared for open warfare. Regular humans panicked and fled, while Agnes's enhanced soldiers seemed to be everywhere at once.

When the mobile phones received emergency alerts in the form of a unified broadcast, the chaos paused briefly. Agnes Lasair appeared on screen, elegant and commanding in a tailored suit.

'Citizens of Edinburgh,' she began, 'Join us. Help us cleanse our city of this plague. The Righteous Assembly welcomes all who stand for purity and human dignity.'

'We need to get people out,' Greer said as the broadcast ended. 'The orders, the lone practitioners, anyone who might be targeted.'

'The studio can serve as a waypoint,' Freya suggested. 'I can adjust the patterns, create a temporary sanctuary before we move them somewhere safer.' She looked around, her gaze lingering on the reinforced doors and high ceilings. 'We set wards here to prevent unwanted entry.'

Freya reached out, her fingers tracing the air where she saw the studio's energy patterns humming. With a gentle tug, she pulled the silver threads tighter, weaving them into a shimmering barrier that solidified into an invisible shield, its edges marked by a faint, silver glow. The air inside the sanctuary glowed.

They worked quickly, reaching out to allies, organising evacuations. Some humans, despite their fear, chose to help. A taxi driver made multiple runs, ferrying Baobhan Sith refugees to safety. A nurse treated wounds without asking questions. Small acts of courage flickered like stars in the growing darkness.

Freya used her gift where she could, calming panic, easing pain, guiding people to safety. But the growing sense of threat wove its way into the patterns.

'Something's coming,' she warned, just as headlights flooded the studio's covered windows.

Multiple vehicles had surrounded the building. Armed figures emerged, led by someone whose corrupt patterns made Freya's heart stutter with recognition.

Thomas stepped into the light, but he was not the Thomas they knew. The Baobhan Sith before them was a masterwork of Agnes's corruption. His familiar features remained, but his markings—once a subtle harmony of silver and shadow—now writhed with righteous fire. She'd taken everything that made him Thomas—his gentle wit, his fierce loyalty, his capacity for joy—and burned it away, replacing warmth with zealotry. But worse than the physical changes was the look in his eyes. Where love for James had once shone, there was only hollow certainty, a fanatic's unshakeable faith. He had been converted.

They stared at him from the safety of the studio. Greer remembered how he'd been in the Dark Vault, stealing kisses from James between customers. How his markings would brighten whenever James entered the room, how their love had given hope to others of their kind. To see him now, transformed into a weapon against everything he'd once held dear, was almost unbearable.

Dior's fingers found Greer's in the darkness, squeezing tight. They both knew what Thomas's presence meant. Agnes wasn't just attacking their sanctuaries—she was claiming their own, turning love into a weapon more deadly than any blessed iron. The war had become personal in a way that even centuries of persecution hadn't prepared them for.

'No,' Dior whispered. 'Oh, love, what has she done to you?'

Freya stood between her lovers, their markings glowing in the darkness. Outside, Edinburgh burned. Inside, they prepared to face one of their own, transformed by Agnes's corrupting touch into a weapon against all he once loved.

The war for souls had begun.

And no one would emerge unchanged. But they would not surrender, Freya vowed silently, they would fight for him, for James, for every soul Agnes had twisted to her hateful purpose. They would fight for their right to exist, to love, to choose their own destiny.

Chapter Fifty-Six

The Viper's Den

Far across the city, in a sanctuary that had once been a haven, Mànas surveyed the remnants of his order. The attack on the Dark Vault had shaken them, revealing the hidden rot within his ranks. He had dealt with the traitor swiftly and brutally, but the damage was done. Trust, once absolute, was now a fragile thing, easily shattered.

He looked at the faces of his remaining lieutenants, their expressions cagey. He knew what they were thinking. *Could they trust him? Could they trust each other?*

'Agnes has made her move,' he said, his voice low and dangerous, the sound vibrating through the room. 'She has shown her hand. And now, we will show her ours.'

He slammed his fist on the table, the force of the blow cracking the ancient stone. 'We will find the rest of her spies. We will cleanse our ranks. And then,' his eyes, burning with a cold fury, met each of theirs in turn, 'we will make Agnes pay for what she has done.'

'What about the alliance?' one of the lieutenants dared to ask. 'Freya's plan?'

Mànas's lip curled into a sneer. 'The alliance is a tool, nothing more. A means to an end. We will use it as long as it serves our purpose.' He paused, a far-away look in his eyes. 'But we will not be bound by it. We are Baobhan Sith. We do not bow to humans, no matter how powerful their gifts.'

He turned back to his lieutenants, his eyes burning with a cold, dark fire. 'We will find Thomas,' he said. 'And when we do, Agnes will pay. We will make her regret the day she ever dared to challenge us.'

He raised his hand, his dark markings pulsing with power. 'We will adapt,' he vowed. 'We will learn from our mistakes. We will become stronger, more ruthless, more cunning than she could ever imagine.'

'We will survive,' he whispered, more to himself than to them. 'And we will prevail. By any means necessary.'

The order responded with a roar of approval, their fear momentarily forgotten in the face of their leader's fierce determination. But as Mànas looked at their faces, he knew that the true test was yet to come. The war had begun, and no one, not even him, knew how it would end.

He turned away from them and walked towards the window, his gaze fixed on the burning city below. The patterns, he knew, held the key to their survival. But they also held the potential for their destruction. He had to find a way to use them, to harness their power, before Agnes could twist them to her own ends.

And he had to do it quickly. Before everything he had built over the centuries crumbled to ash around him. Before his own order turned against him. Before Thomas was lost to them forever.

Chapter Fifty-Seven

A Weapon Forged

Freya stood between her lovers, their markings bright against the growing darkness. Ahead was Thomas, transformed by Agnes's corrupting touch. He and Agnes's crusaders hadn't stayed to fight, but instead turned and left as though they had been on reconnaissance. But they would be back, that was certain.

'We have to stop him,' Dior said. 'Before he comes again.'

'We will,' Greer said, her hand resting on the hilt of her dagger. 'But we need a plan. We can't just rush in blindly.'

Freya closed her eyes, reaching for the patterns, letting them guide her. She saw Thomas, his energy signature twisted and corrupted, but still faintly there, a flicker.

'He's not just a weapon,' she said, her voice filled with a sudden realisation. 'He's a key. Agnes is using him to track us, to find our weaknesses.'

'Then we need to cut him off,' Dior said, her nail lengthening. 'Sever the connection.'

'No,' Freya said, shaking her head. 'The corruption is

deep. It's intertwined with his very being. If we try to sever the connection too abruptly, we could destroy him.'

'So, what do we do?' Greer asked. 'We can't just let him lead them to us.'

Freya opened her eyes, staring at the far wall of the studio, where a half-finished painting seemed to shimmer in the dim light. It was a portrait of Thomas, one she had started weeks ago, capturing his likeness, his energy, his essence, before the darkness had touched him.

'We fight fire with fire,' she said. 'We use the patterns against them. We remind him of who he is, of what he loves.'

'You think you can reach him?' Dior asked with an edge of scepticism. 'Even through Agnes's corruption?'

'I have to try,' Freya said. She moved toward the painting, her hand hovering over the canvas. 'The patterns remember everything. Even what we've forgotten.'

She closed her eyes, focusing her gift, channelling the energy of her markings into the painting, weaving a tapestry of light and shadow, of memory and emotion. She poured everything she had into it—her love for Thomas, her hope for redemption, her belief in the power of choice.

When she opened her eyes, the painting was glowing with a soft, silver light. It was more than a portrait. It was a beacon, a message, a lifeline.

'What is it?' Greer asked.

'A way to reach him,' Freya said. 'A way to remind him of who he is.'

'And if it doesn't work?' Dior asked.

Freya met her eyes, her own filled with a fierce determination. 'Then we fight. But we fight knowing that we did everything we could to save him. To save ourselves.'

Chapter Fifty-Eight

Into the Lion's Den

The chapel loomed against Edinburgh's night sky, its Gothic spires piercing the darkness like accusing fingers. Once a place of worship, now it was twisted by Agnes's corruption. What had once been holy ground now pulsed with wrong energy—patterns warped into weapons, sacred geometry turned into chains. The very air felt thick with it, a cloying sweetness that masked a deeper, more insidious taint. They were taking their fight to reclaim Thomas, for their very survival, to Agnes.

'The wards are strong,' Ròs murmured, her geometric markings dimming as she studied the defences. 'Blessed iron in the walls, corruption in the very stones.'

Greer felt Dior's hand slip into hers, both drawing and giving strength. Around them, their strike team waited in shadows—the best warriors from each order, chosen for this desperate rescue. Freya moved beside them, her own markings pulsing with a soft, silver light that pulsed against the corrupted energy of the chapel. She was their compass now, their guide through the treacherous currents of Agnes's magic.

❄

'I can feel him,' Freya whispered. 'Thomas. Agnes's work is dark, wrapped around him.'

'Remember,' Bethia said, her voice sharp and urgent, her spiral markings barely visible in the gloom. 'We just need to get inside. Freya's power will do the rest.' But as they watched, Freya shook her head, her brow furrowed in concentration.

'It isn't that straightforward,' she said. 'The patterns are too complex, too corrupted. We need to break through the outer layers first, disrupt Agnes's control before I can reach him.'

The first wave moved with shadow, a silent tide of vengeance. Ròs's Stone Order warriors struck the eastern wall while Bethia's Shadow Order created a diversion at the main entrance, their movements swift and precise. Their markings blazed silver against the darkness as they engaged Agnes's guards—enhanced humans whose eyes burned with righteous fire, their bodies fuelled by a corrupted power that made them stronger, faster, deadlier.

Greer, Dior, and Freya slipped through the chaos, following the path Freya had mapped in their minds, a labyrinth of energy and intent. The chapel's interior was a maze of corrupted sanctity—crosses that burned with unholy light, fonts filled with water that whispered of damnation. Each step was a desecration, a violation of everything they held sacred.

They encountered the first trap in what had once been the vestry. A blessed iron net dropped from above, designed to ensnare and burn, but they'd been warned by Freya's sight. Dior's nail sliced through the mechanism, a whisper of sound in the sudden silence, while Greer dealt with the guards who came running, her movements brutal and efficient. Freya, sensing a surge of corrupted energy, raised her hand, her markings flaring. A wave of pure power slammed into the remaining guards, throwing them back against the wall with bone-jarring force.

'Left,' Dior said, her nose twitching as she sniffed the air, her nostrils flaring as she caught a familiar scent. 'Thomas's blood—faint, but there.'

Freya nodded, her own senses confirming Dior's assessment. She could feel the faint, discordant pulse of Thomas's energy, a beacon in the darkness, a thread she could follow.

They fought their way through more corridors, moving in perfect synchronisation, a dance of death honed over centuries. Freya, now attuned to the flow of battle, anticipated attacks, her power lashing out to disarm or incapacitate opponents before they could even strike. It was as though she could see the fight as a tapestry of energy, each thread representing a life, a movement, an intention. And she was learning to reweave that tapestry to their advantage.

Back-to-back, they faced waves of Agnes's followers. These weren't just enhanced humans anymore—some showed signs of partial transformation, caught between humanity and something darker, their bodies twisted into grotesque parodies of Baobhan Sith.

A woman with burning eyes and iron-laced flesh came at them with desperate speed, her movements jerky and unnatural. Greer's nail found her throat, a swift, merciful strike, while Dior's strike took out her partner, her claws tearing through corrupted flesh. Freya, sensing a trap, pulled them both back just as a section of the floor dissolved into shadow, revealing a pit lined with sharpened stakes. They were learning to use her insights her ability to read the flow of energy, to anticipate danger. But more kept coming, an endless tide of righteous fury.

'She's waiting for us,' Greer said, healing a slash across Dior's arm with a touch, her own markings flaring with power. 'She wants us to reach Thomas. It's a trap.'

'Or an opportunity,' Freya countered, her gaze fixed on the far end of the corridor, where the energy patterns converged in a chaotic knot. 'She's drawing power from him, using him as a focus. If we can disrupt that connection...'

They found evidence of Thomas's presence—scraps of his clothing, drops of blood that told a story of resistance. Each trace led them deeper into the chapel's heart, where the corruption grew stronger, the air thicker, the patterns more twisted and malevolent.

The main sanctuary had been transformed. Where an altar had once stood, Agnes had erected a stark steel frame inscribed with burning sigils, a grotesque parody of sacred geometry. And there, suspended in its centre, held aloft by chains that seemed to writhe and pulse with a malevolent energy...

'Thomas,' Dior gasped, in a mixture of relief and horror.

He hung unconscious, wrapped in chains of blessed iron and dark bindings that seemed to suck the very light from the room. His markings flickered weakly, fighting against the corruption trying to claim them, a faint, silver pulse in the encroaching darkness.

'Right on time,' Agnes stepped from the shadows, elegant as ever in her designer suit, a queen surveying her conquered territory. 'I was beginning to think you'd miss the ceremony.'

Her followers emerged from alcoves and doorways,

surrounding them with weapons raised, a wall of corrupted flesh and righteous iron. But it was Agnes who commanded attention—power and hatred, surrounded her warping the very air they breathed.

❄

'Let him go,' Greer's voice carried centuries of authority, a command from one ancient being to another. 'This is between us.'

Agnes laughed, the sound like breaking glass, a chilling counterpoint to the silent tension. 'Oh, but he's crucial to everything. The perfect weapon—one of your own, turned against you. Once the ritual is complete, his very nature will become a blade to strike at the heart of your kind.'

She drew something from her jacket—a blade that gleamed with unholy purpose, its edge shimmering with a corrupt energy that made any nearby markings recoil. 'Shall we begin?'

The fight erupted without warning. Agnes moved with unnatural speed, her blade leaving trails of fire in the air, a dance of death and destruction. Greer, Dior and Freya moved as one, trying to flank her, but her followers pressed in, forcing them back, their enhanced strength and blessed weapons a deadly combination. Freya, anticipating their movements, lashed out with tendrils of energy, disrupting their attacks, creating openings for Greer and Dior to exploit.

'You still don't understand,' Agnes taunted as she drove Greer back with a series of brutal strikes, her blade a whirlwind of fire and iron. 'This was never about him. It was about proving what you really are—creatures of darkness pretending at civilisation.'

Dior snarled, her nails extending as she launched herself at Agnes, a blur of motion and fury.

❋

Freya, sensing an opening, focused her will, drawing on the patterns that connected them all. A surge of power flowed through her, strengthening Dior's attack, momentarily disrupting Agnes's flow.

But the zealot was ready. She caught Dior's strike on her blade, using the momentum to throw her into a column, the impact shaking the very foundations of the chapel.

'Your time is ending,' Agnes continued, her eyes blazing with righteous fire. 'The world is waking up to the monsters in their midst. And when they see what you've made of Thomas...'

A crash from above interrupted her speech. Glass rained down as more figures dropped into the sanctuary—Ròs and Bethia's forces, finally breaking through the outer defences, their markings blazing like falling stars.

But Agnes merely smiled, a cold, triumphant expression that sent a chill down everyone's spines. 'Perfect,' she said. 'Witnesses to the beginning of the end.'

The battle for Thomas's soul—and perhaps the soul of their entire kind—had begun.

Chapter Fifty-Nine

The Price of Love

James's heart hammered against his chest as he slipped through the chapel's side entrance, legs trembling with each careful step. The sounds of battle echoed off ancient stone—blessed iron clashing against supernatural power, screams of rage and pain bouncing off vaulted ceilings. But all he could focus on was his thundering pulse and the promise he wore on his ring finger, a shining circle of silver.

Thomas stood in the centre of the chaos, but wrong—so terribly wrong. The familiar silver markings that James had traced countless times with reverent fingers now writhed with darkness, corrupted by Agnes's influence into something twisted and cruel. The sight made James's stomach clench. This wasn't his Thomas, who smiled softly in predawn light and whispered promises against James's skin. This was something else, something broken.

The ring hung heavy against his heart, warm from being pressed so close to his skin for so long. James touched it through his shirt, remembering the night Thomas had given it to him at the Dark Vault. How Thomas's hands had trembled as he'd slipped it onto James's finger, how his voice had caught when he'd said those words that changed everything: *Love is a choice. One we make every day.*

James had worn the ring on his finger since Thomas had given it to him. Now its weight felt like destiny. Getting Thomas back was all that mattered. Everything else—the blessed iron glinting in corrupted hands, the very real possibility of death—felt distant, unimportant compared to the need to reach the man he loved.

His fingers trembled as he worked the ring from his finger. The fear tried to choke him—fear of failure, fear of death, fear of losing Thomas forever to this darkness. But beneath the fear burned something stronger—love, pure and fierce and freely chosen. Every day, every moment, even now as Thomas snarled with alien rage, James chose him.

'Thomas!' The name tore from his throat, raw with emotion and desperation.

The fighting seemed to pause as all eyes turned to him. Thomas's corrupted markings pulsed with Agnes's power as he turned, lips pulled back in a snarl that broke James's heart. But underneath that darkness, James saw something flicker—a recognition, a fighting spirit that Agnes hadn't quite managed to extinguish. His Thomas was still in there, still fighting.

James's hands shook as he finally freed the ring. 'Remember what Freya told us,' he called out, forcing his feet to move forward despite every instinct screaming at him to run. 'Love freely given is the only power strong enough to break corruption.' He held up the ring, letting it shine. 'And this was given with the purest love I've ever known.'

Each step closer felt like walking through deep water, his body fighting against the waves of wrongness emanating from Thomas's corrupted form. But James kept moving, kept talking, his voice growing stronger with each word. 'Remember that night at the Dark Vault. Remember when you put this ring on my finger. Remember what you said.'

Thomas's markings flickered, darkness warring with familiar silver. James pressed forward, hope blooming in his chest even as fear tried to strangle it. 'I'm still choosing you, Thomas. I'll always choose you. No corruption, no power, no force in this world or any other can change that.'

He was close enough now to see the war in Thomas's eyes—corruption fighting against recognition, hatred against love. James held out the ring, his heart hammering so hard he thought it might burst. 'Come back to me,' he whispered. 'Choose us again.'

James pressed the ring into Thomas's palm closing those corrupted fingers around the silver band. 'Remember the night you gave it to me. Remember how your hands shook. Remember how you said love was a choice we make every day.'

He held Thomas's hand between both of his own, the ring a burning point of contact between them. 'Every fibre of you loves me, Thomas. Every mark, every pattern—they're not meant for hatred. They're meant for this. For us.'

His voice dropped to a whisper, intimate despite the chaos around them. 'And I love you. All of you. The darkness and the light. I choose you, Thomas. I'll always choose you.'

Thomas's markings flickered, corruption battling against recognition as James's words, his touch, his freely given love began to break through Agnes's control. The ring pulsed with warmth between their joined hands, carrying years of shared moments, of chosen love, of promises kept even in darkness.

Then bright, brilliant hot pain filled his chest.

❄

Thomas watched James approach through a haze of righteous fury, Agnes's corruption burning through his veins like holy fire. Her power tried to twist James's familiar face into something demonic, something that needed to be cleansed. But the ring—his ring—caught the light, and memory pierced through corruption like a blade through flesh.

The Dark Vault. James behind the bar, nervous but determined. The way his eyes had lit up when Thomas finally worked up the courage to offer the ring. The weight of promise in that simple band of silver. *Love as a choice, made new each dawn.*

'Remember that night,' James was saying, his voice steady despite the fear Thomas could smell on him, could almost taste. 'Remember how your hands shook. Remember every promise we made.'

The ring pressed into Thomas's palm, warm from James's skin, from being held so close to his heart. Memory flooded back—mornings spent pushing the edges of dawn just to share a few more moments, nights when James's blood and pleasure sang through Thomas's veins, quiet moments between when just existing together felt like a miracle.

Agnes's scream of rage shattered the moment. 'No!'

Thomas saw the blessed iron blade flash in slow motion. Saw James's decision not to move, not to save himself. Saw the exact moment James chose love over survival, his eyes never leaving Thomas's face as Agnes's corruption found his heart.

'Keep choosing love,' James whispered as he fell, blood bright against his shirt. 'Don't let her take what we had.'

Thomas wrenched his wrists free, the ring crushed into his palm, and the corruption in his markings burned away, replaced by an anger so profound it threatened to shatter reality itself. As James crumpled to the ground, Thomas caught him, pulling him close and cradled his dying body in his arms.

'No,' he breathed, pulling James closer, as if he could somehow push the life back into him through sheer force of will. 'No, please. I choose you. I choose you. Don't leave me.'

But James's eyes were already dulling, though his smile remained—soft and sure even in death. Then his lover's body went slack, the ring falling from Thomas's grip, as he scrambled to bring their two hearts together to share James's final breath.

Agnes stepped back, satisfaction warring with something like doubt on her face. She hadn't expected this—hadn't expected freely given love to prove stronger than her righteous power. Her followers shifted uneasily, sensing the change in the air as Thomas's markings blazed with a fury born of love and loss.

The ring pulsed once with power older than any corruption—the power of love freely given unto death. Thomas grabbed it and felt it resonate through his transformed markings, through his very soul. James's sacrifice had burned away Agnes's corruption, but it had tempered something new in its place.

Thomas lifted his head, his transformed markings now fierce as arctic wind and twice as merciless. Agnes and her followers took another step back, suddenly uncertain in the face of his grief-forged rage.

'Run,' he snarled.

They ran.

Thomas gathered James closer, the ring pressed between their hearts, and let his anguish shake the very foundations of Agnes's corrupted chapel. The grief would come later—the hollow emptiness, the endless nights, the memories that would both sustain and torture him. But for now, there was only this—the weight of James in his arms, the warmth leaving his body, and the knowledge that love, freely given and chosen unto death, had saved him.

Even if the price had been everything that mattered.

Chapter Sixty

A Vow of Vengeance

The chapel fell silent, save for his own ragged breathing. He cradled James's body, fingers tracing the corruption spreading from the blessed iron wound. The man he loved grew colder with each passing moment, the light in his eyes already dimmed to nothing.

His markings pulsed erratically, silver light fracturing with his grief. He felt Greer and Dior standing back, their own patterns dimmed in sympathy, knowing this loss would change him forever. But it was Freya who stepped closer, drawn by the raw agony emanating from him. He could see her reaching out with her gift, trying to understand the patterns of his pain, his very soul, shattering under the weight of his grief.

'Such weakness,' Agnes's voice cut through the silence. 'This is what comes of playing at humanity. Of pretending you're anything but monsters.' She moved forward, her designer heels clicking on the sacred stone. 'He died believing in love. How... quaint.'

Thomas's head snapped up. His markings flared with

sudden, terrible intensity, the air around him crackling with power. The grief in his eyes hardened into something darker, colder.

'You,' he said. 'You did this.'

'I showed him the truth.' Agnes's smile was razor-sharp. 'Showed him what happens when mortals dance with demons.'

He laid James's body down with infinite gentleness. When he stood, his movements had changed, becoming more predatory, more inhuman. 'I'm going to tear you apart,' he said softly. 'Piece by piece. Slowly.'

He launched himself at her with savage speed, his nail extending into a lethal point. His attack caught her off-guard—she barely managed to block his first strike. His fury made him stronger, faster, his markings blazing with unrestrained power.

But Agnes recovered quickly, meeting his rage with practiced skill. 'Yes,' she purred as they fought. 'Let the monster out. Show everyone what you really are.'

Greer moved first, catching his arm before he could strike again. Dior flanked him from behind, both women struggling to contain his fury.

'Thomas, stop!' Greer shouted. 'This isn't the way!'

He fought against their restraining grip, snarling with inhuman rage. It took both women's full strength to hold him back, to keep him from throwing himself at Agnes again.

He felt Freya's presence, her gift reaching for his fractured patterns. She projected memories into his mind —James's laugh, his smile, the quiet moments they'd shared. She wove these images into the raw energy of his grief, a soothing balm against the jagged edges of his pain. For a moment, he stilled, his rage momentarily receding as he saw, through Freya's power, the echoes of his lost love.

'Don't let her take what we had,' James's final words echoed in his mind, now amplified by Freya's gift, guiding him forward. The darkness receded slightly, leaving behind exhaustion and bone-deep grief.

'She's twisting your pain,' Freya said softly, her voice a gentle counterpoint to the raging storm within him. 'Don't let her use your love for James to fuel her hatred.'

He let out a scream, a pouring out of his anger, then said, 'I won't lose myself,' his voice steadying. 'But I will destroy you, Agnes. Not with blind rage. With purpose.'

But when he looked up, Agnes was gone.

He felt Greer and Dior exchange worried looks, but they released their hold. He stood straighter, embracing the full power of his transformed nature while holding onto that last thread of humanity James had given him.

'We'll help you,' Dior offered carefully. 'But not like this. Not through mindless vengeance.'

He nodded, but his eyes remained cold. He was already withdrawing from them, wrapping himself in solitude and resolve.

He watched as they began tending to the wounded, preparing to leave before Agnes could rally more forces. The chapel bore testament to their battle—broken glass, blessed iron scars, blood both human and Baobhan Sith.

He caught his reflection in a shattered window. His markings had changed, becoming something darker, more savage. He barely recognised himself.

But perhaps that was fitting. The Thomas who had loved James with pure human devotion was dead. This new creature, forged in loss and rage, had a different purpose.

He turned away from the others, his markings pulsing

with a dark promise. In his clenched fist he held the silver ring.

'I will end her,' he whispered to James's memory. 'Whatever it costs. Whatever I become.'

His markings flared one final time—not silver now, but something deeper. More dangerous.

The vow had been made.

Chapter Sixty-One

The Dawn of Reckoning

Dawn painted Edinburgh's sky in shades of blood. A chapel burned against the sunrise, black smoke mixing with the red light until it seemed the heavens themselves were on fire. In the streets below, chaos reigned. Sirens wailed their endless warning as emergency vehicles tried to navigate streets clogged with fleeing civilians and debris from the previous night's battle.

The first videos began appearing on social media within minutes. Shaky phone footage captured silver markings blazing against darkness, enhanced humans moving with impossible speed, and blessed iron leaving trails of corrupt fire through the air. Each new post spread faster than the last, impossible to contain or explain away.

Thomas emerged from the burning chapel carrying James's body, his movements mechanical, his markings pulsing with erratic grief. The corruption from the blessed iron had spread through James's flesh, leaving dark veins like a map of loss across his skin. Thomas's arms ached with the weight, but he couldn't bear to let anyone else carry this burden.

‘Thomas,’ Greer said softly, reaching for him. ‘Let us help—’

‘Don’t.’ His voice cracked on the single word. James deserved to be carried by the one who loved him most. The one who had failed to protect him.

He felt Dior close, protective but not touching, understanding there was no comfort for this kind of pain. They watched his markings flicker between silver and something darker, knowing this loss would reshape him into something new. Something dangerous.

He felt Freya move beside him, her own markings dimmed with sorrow. She reached out, her fingers tracing the air near his heart, a silent offering of empathy, a shared understanding of loss that transcended words.

Around them, Edinburgh woke to a changed world. A young mother stumbled from her tenement, clutching her children close as she stared at the impossible scene before her. An elderly man stood frozen in his doorway, a pint of milk forgotten at his feet. A group of students lowered their phones, their faces pale with the realisation that this was no elaborate hoax.

‘This isn’t possible,’ Thomas heard them whisper, watching silver markings dance across a Baobhan Sith’s skin. ‘This can’t be real.’

But it was real. All too real.

The first news van arrived just as he carried James into a nearby sanctuary—an old bookshop whose owner was one of their own. The reporter, a young woman, tried to maintain professional composure as she described scenes that defied explanation.

‘We’re getting reports of what appears to be... supernatural activity in central Edinburgh,’ she said, as an enhanced human crashed through a window behind her. 'Authorities are advising residents to stay indoors...'

More media arrived. Cameras captured everything—the burning chapel, the fleeing civilians, the silver-marked beings moving with inhuman grace through the chaos. Each new image stripped away centuries of careful hiding, of subtle misdirection, of living in the shadows.

Inside the bookshop, he laid James gently on a chaise longue, arranging his limbs with infinite care. The shop's owner, an elderly woman named Margaret, watched from the doorway, tears tracking down her weathered cheeks. Freya knelt beside him, her hand hovering over James's still form. He saw her searching for any signs of life, even the smallest glimmer, fragmented or fading, but there was none.

'I remember when he first came to the Dark Vault,' Margaret said softly. 'So young, so full of life. He never feared us.'

Thomas's markings pulsed with fresh grief. 'He should have,' he said. 'Fear might have kept him alive.'

Outside, the chaos grew. Police tried to establish cordons, but how do you contain the uncontainable? How do you control powers that defy natural law? Their radios crackled with panicked reports: 'Subject displaying unusual abilities...' 'Multiple casualties from some kind of energy weapon...' 'Request immediate backup at...'

The television in Margaret's shop flickered, every channel suddenly showing the same feed. Another emergency alert lit up everyone's mobile phones. The sight of Agnes Lasair filling their screens, elegant in a tailored suit that cost more than most people earned in a month. Her eyes held that subtle gleam of righteous fire that Thomas had come to hate.

'Citizens of Edinburgh,' she began, 'what you've

witnessed tonight is a manifestation of the evil I have been trying to protect you from.'

Thomas's hands clenched into fists. He felt Freya's hand on his arm, a calming presence. He could feel the storm of grief and rage within him, a tempest threatening to break free.

He heard Freya speaking. 'She's twisting it. Turning his death into propaganda.'

Chapter Sixty-Two

Agnes's Message

Freya watched Agnes appear on the shop's television, her designer suit immaculate despite the chaos she'd unleashed. Even through the screen, her presence made Freya's markings contract painfully, responding to the corruption that surrounded her like a toxic halo. But beneath the pain, Freya focused, determined to decipher the patterns, to understand the strategy woven into Agnes's twisted design.

'Citizens of Edinburgh,' Agnes began, 'what you've witnessed tonight is a manifestation of the evil I have been trying to protect you from.'

Behind Agnes, footage began to play. Freya recognised scenes from tonight's battle, but twisted, edited to show only violence without context. A Baobhan Sith feeding, the camera lingering on extended nails and silver markings, but not showing the willing donor. Thomas fighting Agnes's enhanced humans, but cut to make him appear the aggressor rather than someone desperate to save the man he loved.

'For centuries,' Agnes continued, 'these creatures have

preyed upon us. They seduce with promises of pleasure, feed upon our blood, corrupt our very souls.' Her eyes seemed to burn through the screen, and Freya's gift retreated, the patterns scattering like startled birds. It wasn't just the visual image, but the intent behind it—a carefully crafted manipulation designed to incite fear and hatred.

More footage played—carefully selected scenes that painted the Baobhan Sith as monsters. She recognised Greer in one clip, her markings blazing as she fought off an attacker. But Agnes's editing made it look like unprovoked violence against an innocent human rather than defence against an enhanced follower wielding blessed iron. Freya focused, pushing past the initial shock, trying to analyse what her gift would reveal from the footage.

'Some of you have already fallen victim to their corruption.' Agnes's tone softened with faux sympathy. 'They've made you complicit in your own degradation, convinced you that their hunger is love, their corruption is liberation.' She paused, letting her words sink in. 'But the Righteous Assembly offers you salvation.'

The camera pulled back, revealing Agnes standing in what appeared to be a command centre. Enhanced humans moved purposefully in the background, their eyes glowing with that terrible fire. Banks of monitors showed scenes from across Edinburgh—proof, in Freya's eyes, that she'd planned this revelation carefully.

'Look at what they truly are,' Agnes commanded as new footage began to play. These scenes were different—manipulated by Agnes to show the Baobhan Sith as demons rather than beings of compassion. Their markings appeared twisted, their feeding portrayed as violence rather than communion. Freya's gift showed her the truth beneath the manipulation—how Agnes had taken their natural ways and corrupted them through her lens of hatred. Each image was a lie, but a convincing one, designed to play on humanity's deepest fears. She could see fear spreading outwards from the broadcast, infecting the city like a virus.

'But you need not live in fear,' Agnes continued. 'The Righteous Assembly stands ready to defend humanity. We have developed weapons, techniques, enhancements that allow us to fight these abominations on equal ground.'

The footage changed again, showing her enhanced followers in action. But rather than revealing their true nature—humans twisted by corrupted power—the images portrayed them as holy warriors, their burning eyes presented as divine fire rather than evidence of corruption.

'Join us,' Agnes urged. 'Help us cleanse our city—our world—of this plague. Those who stand with us will be granted the power to protect themselves and their loved ones. Those who oppose us,' her smile cut like blessed iron, 'will be considered their allies.'

Her perception blurred, the shop's familiar lines dissolving into a chaotic web of silver threads. Each thread pulsed with Agnes's words, spreading outward like ripples in a pond, turning from the usual soft white of human thought to the harsh, coppery red of manipulated fear. She could see the connections, feel how they resonated with the ley lines, carrying the corrupted energy far beyond Edinburgh. She could almost see the country's energy grid, feel the pulse of its fear, hear the whispers of its growing anger.

'Even now, these creatures plot against us,' Agnes was saying. 'They gather their forces, prepare to strike from the shadows as they have always done. But we will drag them into the light. We will show their true nature. And we will end their reign of darkness forever.'

The broadcast cut to scenes from cities across the world

—other unnatural communities being exposed, other battles beginning. Agnes had orchestrated this perfectly, ensuring that when the truth emerged, it would be perverted to follow her narrative.

'The time has come,' Agnes declared, her voice rising with religious fervour. 'Stand with us, or stand with them. There can be no middle ground in this war.'

The screen went black, but the damage was done. Through the shop's windows, she could see people gathering in the streets, their phones held high as they shared Agnes's message. Fear turned to anger, anger to purpose, exactly as Agnes had planned.

She felt a surge of despair, a chilling premonition of the chaos to come. A spark of defiance ignited beneath it. Agnes might control the story for now, but she could see the underlying patterns, the threads of truth that still connected them to humanity. There was still a chance to fight back, to show people a different path.

'She's playing on their fear,' Freya said. 'Twisting their perception. But we can counter it. We can show them the truth.'

Margaret switched off the television with trembling hands. 'All these years,' she whispered. 'All these years of keeping secrets, of careful balance...'

'Gone,' Freya finished quietly. 'She's burned it all down.'

She turned to Greer and Dior, her markings pulsing with a new resolve. 'We need to reach out,' she said. 'To the humans who still see us, who still understand. There are signs of empathy, of connection, still woven into this city. We need to find them. Amplify them.'

She could see this was only the beginning. Agnes's broadcast had lit a fuse that would explode across the world.

The patterns showed her possibilities branching out like cracks in reality—each one darker than the last.

The war for Edinburgh's soul had begun. But she feared it was already too late to stop what Agnes had set in motion. Everything was changing, patterns breaking and reforming.

And through it all, Agnes's corrupted fire spread.

Chapter Sixty-Three

The World Responds

Freya watched the world tear itself apart. The patterns of society—invisible bonds that had held people together for centuries—were unravelling before her eyes. Markings that had once connected humans and the Baobhan Sith in delicate webs of mutual need now twisted and snapped like burning threads. She could see the fear spreading like a contagion, feel the hatred simmering beneath the surface, taste the bitter tang of betrayal on the air.

On George Street, a woman who'd been a willing donor for years now backed away from her Baobhan Sith friend, Agnes's words echoing in her mind. 'All this time,' she whispered, years of intimacy corrupted in moments by fear. 'What you've been doing to me...'

Phones buzzed with alerts: 'REMAIN INDOORS. STATE OF EMERGENCY DECLARED.' But it was too late for containment. Social media exploded with shaky footage of the supernatural—or unnatural world as Agnes called it—revealed, some calling for understanding, others for blood.

Her gift showed her the city's connections fracturing into chaos. Outside Waverley Station, tourists abandoned their luggage and fled as a follower pursued a young Baobhan Sith through the crowd. Her markings pulsed with terror—she couldn't have been more than sixteen when she was turned.

Margaret's weathered hands clutched her phone. 'They're mobilising the army. Special forces deploying to 'contain the unnatural threat.''

A helicopter thundered overhead, its searchlight cutting through the smoke from the burning chapel. Police radios crackled with confusion: 'Multiple reports of civilians with unexplained abilities...' 'Suspect displaying silver markings, approach with extreme caution...' 'Command, please advise protocol for...'

But while authority figures floundered, Agnes's followers moved with terrible purpose. They appeared on every street corner, offering blessed iron and promises of power to frightened humans. Their eyes burned as they spread their gospel of fear.

Margaret turned up her radio. The BBC World Service reported similar scenes unfolding across the globe. In London, Paris, New York—anywhere unnatural communities had hidden, Agnes's revelation was shattering centuries of careful secrecy.

She pressed her hand against the window, her markings reacting to the waves of fear and hatred radiating through the city. She could see how Agnes's corruption spread from person to person, turning neighbour against neighbour, friend against friend.

Outside a cafe where the Baobhan Sith had peacefully fed for generations, a crowd gathered with makeshift weapons. The owner—who had knowingly served both human and Baobhan Sith clientele for decades—now locked his doors and drew crosses on the windows with shaking hands.

'We need to do something,' Freya said. The patterns spoke of how quickly things were deteriorating. Every minute, more humans embraced Agnes's twisted narrative, their fear hardening into murderous purpose.

Greer stepped to her side, her own markings pulsing with a controlled fury. She caught Freya's hand, their fingers interlacing. 'We will. But we need to be smart about this.'

Dior moved to the other side of the shop, watching the television where Agnes's face still dominated the screen. 'She's planned this for years,' she said. 'Every move, every speech, designed to maximise chaos and division.'

A scream drew their attention. An older Baobhan Sith she recognised from the Dark Vault stumbled into view, clutching a blessed iron wound. The woman's markings flickered weakly as she sought refuge but doors closed in her face. Humans who had known her, served her, perhaps even loved her, now turned away. The woman's eyes met hers through the window. Recognition flickered—another of their kind, a potential saviour. Freya ran towards the door. She had to save her. But before she could get there, a follower emerged from the shadows. The blessed iron blade fell with terrible precision.

Freya felt the woman's patterns shatter, her death sending ripples through the web that connected them all. Another light extinguished, another soul lost to Agnes's crusade.

Margaret's voice was choked with tears. 'They're hunting us. After all these years of living together, they're hunting us like animals.'

Ròs appeared surprisingly calm amidst the chaos. 'Not all of them.' She'd entered the shop silently, along with Bethia, their markings dimmed in the low light. 'There are still humans who remember the old ways. Who understand the balance.'

Bethia nodded, her spiral markings pulsing faintly. 'We saw them, even as we fought our way here. Small acts of defiance. A shopkeeper hiding a wounded order member. A doctor tending to injuries without reporting them.'

'They need a rallying point,' Freya said, her mind racing, her gift showing her the fragmented patterns of resistance, the potential for a counter-movement. 'Something to show them they're not alone.'

But it wasn't that simple. Her gift showed her other patterns forming—smaller, but burning bright with defiance. A human doctor quietly treating supernatural wounds in a basement surgery. A police officer warning the Baobhan Sith about upcoming raids. A network of resistance taking shape in the shadows of Agnes's new world construct.

Not everyone had embraced hatred. But would it be enough?

There were more questions, more possibilities branching into darkness. Agnes's corruption spread like cancer, turning Edinburgh—turning the world—into something unrecognisable.

The city she had known, had loved, was dying. And what would rise from its ashes remained to be seen.

A noise from the back of the shop made them all turn. Thomas stood in the doorway, his markings pulsing with dark purpose as he watched the chaos unfold. His transformation was progressing—grief and rage reshaping him into something new. Something dangerous.

'We should get to the Vault,' he said, his voice hollow,

devoid of its usual warmth. 'See what can be salvaged. Help those who made it out.'

'No,' Freya said, shaking her head It's too dangerous. Agnes will be watching for any organised response. We need to think bigger. Wider.'

Greer's gaze was fixed on the burning city outside. 'She's right. This isn't just about Edinburgh anymore. It's about the entire world.'

'Then we make a stand. Here. Now. We show them that we won't be hunted. That we won't be broken,' said Dior.

Thomas's voice cut through their discussion. 'They're organising hunting parties. I can hear them coordinating. Police scanners, social media, WhatsApp groups—humans teaching each other how to kill us.' He held up James's phone—the screen which once held little more than pictures of them together now bore rallying cries for humans to join the crusade.

Margaret switched channels on her television. Every station showed the same scenes of chaos, but each with its own spin. Some called for calm, for investigation, for understanding. Others demanded immediate action against the 'unnatural threat.'

The BBC's coverage was clinical, almost surreal in its attempted objectivity: 'Reports continue to emerge of supernatural activity across the UK. The Prime Minister has convened an emergency COBRA meeting...'

Sky News took a harder line: 'The general public are advised to avoid all contact with suspected unnatural entities. The Home Office has established a hotline for reporting suspicious activity...'

But it was the smaller, local stations that truly showed

the city's transformation. Edinburgh Live streamed footage of people barricading their homes, of crowds gathering with makeshift weapons, of centuries-old alliances crumbling in minutes.

Her gift showed her the deeper emotions beneath the chaos. Fear spread like an infection, turning even rational minds toward darkness. But there was something else too—something in the way Agnes's corruption moved through the city's energy.

'It's not random,' she said suddenly, pressing her hand against the window. 'Look—the patterns of hysteria, they're being... directed. Like someone's conducting an orchestra of fear.'

Freya could see how Agnes's followers positioned themselves at key points throughout Edinburgh. Each enhanced human acted as an amplifier, broadcasting waves of terror and hatred that resonated with the city's natural ley lines.

Margaret breathed, understanding dawning. 'The ley lines. They're using our own power networks against us.'

'We need to disrupt the flow,' Freya said, her mind racing. 'Create counter-frequencies. Show them that there's another way.'

A commotion outside drew their attention. A group of humans had cornered a supernatural being—not a Baobhan Sith, but something older, its patterns speaking of earth and stone. The humans wielded blessed iron and righteous fury, but they were disorganised, uncertain.

Then one of Agnes's followers appeared. His eyes blazed as he raised his hands, and she felt the patterns shift. The humans' fear crystallised into purpose, their movements becoming coordinated, lethal. The ancient being didn't stand a chance.

'We need to warn the others,' she said, reaching for her phone. But communications were becoming difficult. Social media platforms were being flooded with Agnes's message, drowning out any attempt at organising resistance.

Dior shook her head. 'It's not enough. We need to do more than just react. We need to take the fight to Agnes.'

Ròs's arms were crossed, her geometric markings pulsing slowly. 'And how do you propose we do that? She has the city, an army, and now, apparently, the ability to turn our own kind against us.'

She looked at the faces around her—Greer, her steadfast protector; Dior, her fierce and passionate lover; Ròs and Bethia, seasoned leaders of ancient orders; even Thomas, his grief a raw, burning ember. They were all looking to her, to her gift, for answers.

'We fight her with the one thing she doesn't understand,' Freya said, her voice gaining strength, her markings blazing with conviction. 'Love. Connection. The very things she's trying to destroy.'

She stepped forward, raising her hands. The patterns on her skin pulsed with light, casting intricate shadows across the room. 'We create a new pattern,' she continued. 'A pattern of hope. Of resistance. Of everything she's trying to burn away.'

The others watched, mesmerised, as she began to weave the energy around them, her movements guided by an ancient knowledge that now flowed through her veins. It was a dangerous gamble, a desperate attempt to turn the tide. But as they stood together in the heart of a city on fire, it was the only chance they had.

She showed them sparks of hope: humans sheltering their Baobhan Sith friends, secret networks forming, acts of quiet defiance against the rising tide of hatred. In the financial district, a banker who'd fed the Baobhan Sith for years now used his influence to create safe houses. In the university, professors who'd long studied folklore began preserving records, protecting knowledge that Agnes's followers would surely try to destroy. Small rebellions, but significant. Each one created patterns of resistance that might, given time, grow into something stronger.

But time was not on their side.

'They're moving on the Dark Vault,' Thomas said suddenly, his markings flaring with alarm. 'Agnes's people—they know where all our sanctuaries are.'

'Have we heard from Maeve?' asked Greer.

'I've tried but there's no answer.' Dior shook her head. 'I don't want to believe the worst...'

Through the window, more military vehicles rolled past. Special forces teams deployed with equipment they couldn't possibly understand, preparing to face enemies they weren't ready to fight. Above them, news helicopters circled like vultures, broadcasting Edinburgh's transformation to the world. She saw the city's future splintering into countless possibilities. In some, understanding eventually prevailed. In others, the war escalated until nothing remained but ashes and hatred. But in every future, one thing remained constant: this moment, this day, had changed everything. The old world of shadows and secrets was gone forever.

Margaret asked a quiet question. 'So what do we do?'

'We fight,' Freya said simply. 'Not with blessed iron or righteous fire, but with truth. With love. With every weapon they don't expect us to have. And we start,' she continued, 'by showing them what we're truly fighting for.'

The patterns shifted again, showing her glimpses of what such a fight might cost. But they also showed her something else—something Agnes, in all her righteous fury, had forgotten.

Hope was its own pattern. And even in darkness, it could burn bright enough to light the way forward.

If they survived what was coming.

Chapter Sixty-Four

Freya's Vision

The vision struck without warning. One moment, Freya stood in Margaret's shop, watching Edinburgh tear itself apart; the next, she was drowning in patterns. Silver light exploded behind her eyes, reality fracturing into a thousand possible futures, each one more terrible than the last. She tried to focus, to control the flood of information, but the sheer scope of Agnes's plan threatened to overwhelm her. It wasn't just about power or control. It was about something far more fundamental, far more terrifying.

Greer caught her as she stumbled, but the contact was distant, unimportant. The patterns demanded all her attention, pulling her deeper into their revelations. She saw Edinburgh burn. Not just with physical fire, but with Agnes's corrupted energy, spreading through the ley lines like poison through veins. The castle, Arthur's Seat, every sacred site that had anchored magical power for centuries—all transformed into focal points of hatred and fear. The patterns shifted, showing her London. Paris. New York. Agnes's influence spreading across the globe like a cancer, turning humans against Baobhan Sith, and their counterparts in every city, every nation. But it was more than just violence. She saw how Agnes's power corrupted reality.

'Freya?' Greer's voice seemed to come from very far away. 'What do you see?'

She couldn't answer. The patterns were too intense, too demanding. They showed her humans being enhanced by Agnes's power, their natural patterns twisted into weapons. But the corruption went deeper than physical transformation. It reached into their souls, turning love to hatred, compassion to cruelty. She saw Thomas, consumed by grief and rage, becoming something terrible. His markings would darken until they were as black as pitch, his compassion for humanity burning away until nothing remained but vengeance. In some futures, he destroyed Agnes, but the cost was always his own soul.

The patterns spiralled outward, showing her decades, centuries of possible outcomes. In one, Agnes's victory was complete—a world purified by righteous fire, where anything *unnatural* had been burned away, leaving only cold, sterile uniformity. In another, the war between humans and the Baobhan Sith never ended, hatred passing down through generations until no one remembered why they fought. Worse were the futures where Agnes's corruption became complete. The patterns showed Freya how the zealot's power would grow, feeding on fear and hatred until she became something beyond human or supernatural—a being of pure, corrupted energy, reshaping reality.

'It's not just about destroying us,' Freya gasped, the words torn from her throat, the visions threatening to consume her. She fought to control them, to focus, to find a thread of hope in the chaotic tapestry of possibilities. 'She wants to rewrite everything. Change the very nature of reality.'

Through the patterns, she understood at last what they'd been trying to tell her. Agnes wasn't just seeking revenge. She was trying to undo creation itself, to burn away everything she saw as corrupt and rebuild it in her own image. The patterns showed her how it would work—how each act of violence, each surge of hatred, each moment of fear fed Agnes's power. The zealot had found a way to tap into something older than the Baobhan Sith curse, older than humanity itself. She'd discovered how to corrupt the very energy that bound reality together.

'Freya!' Greer's voice finally penetrated the vision, anchoring her. She felt Greer's hands on her face, felt Dior's presence close by, their patterns helping to steady her.

'Come back to us.'

She opened her eyes to find herself on the shop floor, her markings blazing, casting shadows on the walls. Her whole body trembled with the weight of what she'd seen.

'We have to stop her,' she whispered. 'Not just for us, not for the people we love but for everyone.'

'Tell us,' Dior urged. 'Show us what you saw.'

Freya reached for them. She showed them everything—past, present, possible futures, spiralling out like deadly fractals. When it was done, they sat in stunned silence. Outside, Edinburgh continued its descent into chaos, but it seemed small compared to what was coming.

'How?' Greer asked finally. 'How do we fight something like this?'

Freya's gift showed her one last pattern—faint, difficult to grasp, but real. A possibility they hadn't considered. A way to turn Agnes's own power against her, to use the very corruption she wielded to undo what she'd built. But the cost...

'We have to remind her,' Freya said slowly, the pattern becoming clearer. 'Not just of what she was, but of what everything was. Before hatred, before corruption. We have to show her the original patterns.'

'And how do we do that?' Dior asked.

Freya's hand went to her throat, where the silver brooch Glicia had given her pulsed with ancient power.

'We go back to the beginning. To where it all started.' She looked up at her lovers, knowing what she was asking might destroy them all. 'We have to take her to Pittenweem. Where the first curse was cast. Where the patterns were first corrupted.'

Greer drew in a sharp breath. Even after all these centuries, the name of that Fife coastal village carried weight. The place where righteous hatred had first turned love into a weapon, where the original curse had transformed their kind forever. The vision's echoes still rippled through her, showing her how this choice, too, could end in disaster. But they had to try. Had to fight. Because if they didn't, Agnes's corrupted fire would consume everything. And what rose from those ashes wouldn't be worth saving.

The patterns shifted again, showing Freya visions of Pittenweem as it had been centuries ago. Not the tourist-friendly fishing village it was now, but a place of fear and zealotry, where the first burning had twisted natural magic into a curse. The patterns there had never truly healed. The corrupted energy still lingered in the stones, in the earth itself, waiting. Agnes would be drawn there, whether she knew it consciously or not. Her power resonated with that ancient hatred.

'It's still there,' Freya said. 'The original corruption.

Like a... like a wound in reality that never healed. Agnes has been feeding from it without even knowing, drawing on that first act of hatred that created the curse.'

'We swore we'd never return,' Dior said softly. Her markings emanating with old pain, old memories.

'You were there? When they turned on Agnes?' Freya asked, though she already knew the answer. The patterns showed her Dior and Greer's presence that night, their desperate attempt to save her from the flames.

'We all were.' Greer's tone carried centuries of guilt. 'We should have stopped it. Should have seen what was coming. We never thought they would go that far.'

The vision pulled Freya deeper, showing her that terrible night in perfect detail. She saw the accusations, the betrayals, the moment when righteous hatred had transformed natural feeding into a curse. She felt the agony of that corruption, how it had spread from villager to villager turning their sacred bonds into weapons.

'Agnes is recreating it,' Freya gasped as understanding struck. 'Not just using the corruption—she's trying to remake that first moment. To spread it across the whole world.'

Freya saw how Agnes's power formed a dark mirror of that ancient night. But where the first curse had been born of human fear and misunderstanding, Agnes's version was calculated, deliberate. She meant to corrupt not just the Baobhan Sith and their likes, but reality itself.

'If she succeeds...' Freya couldn't finish the thought. The patterns showed her that future too clearly—a world where Agnes's righteous fire burned everything back to ash, where she could rebuild creation according to her twisted vision.

'Then we stop her,' Dior said firmly. 'We use Pittenweem's power against her. Turn her own corruption back on itself.'

But the patterns showed Freya the cost of such an attempt. To tap into that ancient power, to try to heal such old wounds—it would require sacrifice. The kind of sacrifice that irrevocably changed lives.

'The patterns there... they still remember everything. Every death, every betrayal, every moment of hatred and fear. If we go there, if we try to use that power...'

'We risk becoming what Agnes already is,' Greer finished quietly.

Freya nodded. The vision was fading now, but its implications remained clear. They had a choice to make—risk everything on one desperate gamble or watch Agnes's corruption spread until nothing remained of what they loved. The patterns offered no easy answers, no guaranteed path to victory. But they did show her one truth that gave her hope: love, freely given, was still the strongest magic they possessed. It had saved her during her transformation. Perhaps it could save them all. If they were willing to pay the price.

They would have to be careful. Strategic. Agnes would expect them to run, to hide, to fight back with desperate violence. She wouldn't expect them to strike at the very root of her power. The vision faded completely, leaving Freya exhausted but certain. They had a chance—small, costly, but real. But even in the face of such darkness, Freya held onto one truth: love was a power Agnes could never comprehend, a weapon she could never wield.

Chapter Sixty-Five

The Price of Memory

The hidden depths of the Crimson Sanctuary, the last Baobhan Sith refuge which remained intact, were where Thomas knelt beside James's body, arranging him on the ancient stone altar with gentle precision. His fingers traced the links of the silver chain he wore, each a memory of their time together, and like the ring, a symbol of their bond.

On his first night working at the Dark Vault, James had dropped glasses because he was too busy watching Thomas with fascinated eyes. Their first kiss in the storeroom, James tasting of whisky and fearless curiosity. The morning James had given him this very chain, saying, 'So you'll always find your way back to me.'

Now, the chain felt like iron against his fingers. The blessed iron's corruption had laced its way across James's skin, but his face remained untouched. Almost peaceful, if Thomas didn't look too closely at the wound.

'He wasn't supposed to be there,' Thomas whispered to the empty room. 'He was supposed to be safe.' His voice cracked on the last word. 'I was supposed to keep him safe.'

The sound of his fist hitting the stone floor echoed through the vault. Again. Again. Until Dior caught his bloody hand in hers.

'He chose this,' she said softly. 'He chose you. Every day, knowing the risks.'

Thomas looked at her, his eyes dark with something beyond grief. 'Then his choice killed him.'

Through her gift, Freya watched Thomas's patterns fracture and reform. Each new configuration was darker than the last, grief transforming him into something she barely recognised. His markings, once bright silver, now pulsed with shadows that sucked life from the room.

'I should have saved him,' Thomas said. 'I should have been faster, stronger.'

Greer moved to touch his shoulder but stopped when his markings flared with warning.

'James made his choice,' she said softly. 'He chose love over fear. Chose you over safety.'

'And look what it got him.' Thomas traced James's cold cheek with trembling fingers. 'Look what love is worth in Agnes's new world.'

Dior leaned against the sanctuary wall, her own markings dim with grief. She'd known James longest, had been the one to hire him at the Dark Vault. Had watched him fall in love with Thomas, despite knowing the dangers of their world.

'He knew the risks,' she said. 'From the first night he saw Thomas feed, he knew. But he stayed anyway. Loved anyway.'

Thomas's laugh was a broken thing. 'And now he's dead *anyway*.'

Freya's gift showed her the patterns of James's last moments—his desperate attempt to save Thomas, the blessed iron finding his heart, his final words of love. But more than that, she saw how his death had changed something fundamental in the fabric of their world. This wasn't just loss. In killing James, Agnes had done more than take a life—she'd created a weapon. Thomas's grief would reshape him into something deadly, something driven by the same kind of righteous fury that powered Agnes's own corruption. Unless...

'Show me,' Freya said suddenly. 'Show me how you met him. Show me what Agnes tried to destroy.'

Thomas looked up, his eyes dark with pain. But after a moment, he nodded. His markings shifted, letting Freya's gift read the patterns of memory. The memory hit Freya like a wave—the Dark Vault two years ago, Thomas walking in during James's first shift behind the bar. She saw through Thomas's patterns how James had smiled, nervous but unafraid, even after a Baobhan Sith had fed too roughly nearby.

'He dropped three glasses that night,' Thomas said, his voice softening with memory. 'But he never flinched. Never looked away. Just kept working, kept smiling, like serving drinks to creatures of darkness was the most natural thing in the world.'

More memories flowed—their first kiss in the vault's storage room, James laughing as Thomas tried to explain the complexities of Baobhan politics. Their first feeding, James offering his throat with complete trust. Small moments, precious moments, now turned to ash by Agnes's hatred.

'He saved me,' Thomas whispered. 'Not just at the end. Every day. Every moment he chose to stay, to love something society said was a monster...'

His markings flickered violently, grief warring with rage. Freya saw the patterns struggling to stabilise, caught between what Thomas had been and what Agnes's corruption was turning him into.

'And now Agnes wants to make me exactly what they always feared we were.' He ran a hand over his nail, watching it lengthen, becoming as black as pitch. 'Maybe she's right. Maybe that's all we can ever be.'

'No,' Dior said. 'That's what she wants. To prove her lies were the truth all along. To make us into the monsters she claims we are.'

Greer moved closer, her own markings responding to Thomas's pain.

'James believed in better. Believed in you. In us. Even at the end—'

'The end,' Thomas snarled, surging to his feet. 'When blessed iron was burning through his heart, when Agnes's corruption was turning his blood to poison—he still tried to save me. Still loved me. And what good did it do? You are telling me this is love winning?' He stared at Freya, desperate for an answer as though she had the key to making sense of James's sacrifice.

The sanctuary's shadows deepened as Thomas's power flared. Freya saw his patterns trying to twist into something darker, something born of pure vengeance. But underneath, James's love still anchored him, still fought against the corruption.

'Show them,' Freya said softly. 'Show them how he died. Not just the end—show them what he fought for.'

Thomas stared at her for a long moment. Then his markings shifted, letting them all see those final moments in the chapel. James, already wounded, breaking free of his restraints. His desperate run toward Thomas. The blessed iron blade meant for Thomas finding James's heart instead. But more than that, they saw what Freya's gift had shown her—the patterns of James's sacrifice. How his love had momentarily disrupted Agnes's corruption, had given Thomas a chance to resist her influence. Even dying, he'd fought not just with courage, but with an understanding of what his death might mean.

'He didn't just die for you,' Freya said, understanding blooming. 'He died to show you what Agnes can never understand. That love freely given is stronger than any righteous fury.'

Thomas touched James's cold hand. 'Then why didn't it save him?'

'Because this isn't the end,' Dior said quietly. 'This is just the beginning. James knew that. Knew what his choice might mean.'

'He left you a weapon,' Freya said. 'Not hatred or vengeance, but something Agnes can never corrupt. Something pure.'

Thomas's markings pulsed with confusion. 'What are you talking about?'

'His love,' Greer said softly, understanding dawning. 'Not just the memory of it—the actual pattern of it. Show him, Freya.'

Freya stepped forward. Using her gift she took Thomas's hand.

'Look,' she said, guiding his awareness to the patterns that grew when Thomas touched James's body. 'See what he left you.'

The patterns shimmered into visibility—not just the dark corruption of blessed iron, but something else. Something that glowed with a light neither silver nor fire. The pure pattern of James's love, crystallised in his moment of sacrifice. All of it flowed into Thomas's body.

'He knew,' Freya explained, feeling the truth of it

unfold. 'Maybe not consciously, but some part of him knew what his death could mean. Every moment of love between you, every willing sacrifice, every free choice—it's all there. A pattern Agnes can't twist because it was freely given.'

Thomas's hand trembled in hers. 'But what good is it now? He's still dead. She still won.'

'Did she?' Dior moved closer. 'Look at what his death prevented. You were nearly lost to her corruption. His sacrifice gave you back yourself.'

'And gave us something more,' Freya added. 'A key, maybe. A way to fight corruption with willing sacrifice instead of righteous fury. James might have saved us all.'

The sanctuary seemed to hold its breath as Thomas absorbed this. His markings still pulsed with grief and rage, but something else sparked beneath—a determination beyond vengeance.

'He always said love was a choice,' Thomas said. 'Every day, every moment, choosing to love despite everything the world said about us.' He looked down at James's peaceful face. 'Even at the end, he chose love over fear.'

'Then honour that choice,' Greer said. 'Not with hatred. Not with revenge. But with the same kind of love he gave you—freely chosen, freely given.'

Freya watched Thomas's patterns shift again, finding a new configuration. Not the pure silver of before, not the corrupt darkness Agnes had tried to force on him, but something new. Something tempered by grief but strengthened by love.

'She'll expect me to come for revenge,' he said, touching James's cheek one last time. 'To become the monster she always claimed we were.'

'Then surprise her,' Freya said. 'Show her what James

showed you—that love freely given is the one thing her hatred can't corrupt.'

Thomas stood, his movements carrying a new purpose.

'He needs to be laid to rest properly,' he said. 'Not here in darkness. Somewhere the sun can find him.'

The words carried weight—the Baobhan Sith traditionally kept to shadows, but James had loved sunlight. Had loved watching Thomas navigate the edges of day, testing the limits of what their love made possible.

'I know a place,' Dior said softly. 'Above Duddingston Loch. The sunrise over Arthur's Seat... he used to go there sometimes.'

Freya's gift showed her the spot through James's lingering patterns—a quiet place between light and shadow, where a human who loved darkness and a creature of darkness who loved a human had sometimes met in dawn's grey hours.

'Agnes will be watching the usual places,' Greer warned. 'The traditional grounds...'

'Good,' Thomas said. His markings had settled into that new configuration—grief and love forging something neither silver nor shadow. 'Let her watch them. Let her wait for a vengeance that won't come.'

He lifted James's body with infinite gentleness. The blessed iron's corruption had stopped spreading, leaving its dark lace pattern like a final mark of Agnes's hatred. But it hadn't touched his face, hadn't marred the peace there.

'I need to do this alone,' Thomas said. Then, seeing their concern, he added: 'Not for vengeance. For love. For the choices he made. The choices I'm making now.'

Freya saw the truth in his words. This wasn't the first step toward darkness—it was a reclamation. A way to honour James's sacrifice without letting it become what Agnes intended.

'We'll wait here,' she said, understanding. 'The patterns will watch over you.'

Dawn was approaching as Thomas carried James from the sanctuary. Freya saw possibilities branching outward. In some, grief still turned to vengeance. In others, love forged new paths through darkness. But in all of them, James's sacrifice had changed something fundamental.

The sun had risen when Thomas returned. His markings pulsed with spent emotion, but the darkness Agnes had tried to infect in him seemed diminished. Freya saw how the act of laying James to rest had shifted something in Thomas's patterns—grief crystallising into purpose rather than vengeance.

'He's where he should be,' Thomas said simply. 'Where light and shadow meet.'

No one asked for details.

'Agnes will come for us,' he said, his voice steady now. 'She'll expect us to scatter, to hide. To let grief and fear drive us apart.'

'Then we do the opposite,' Greer said. 'We stand together. We fight not with hatred but with what James showed us—that love freely given is stronger than any corrupted power.'

Chapter Sixty-Six

The Cobblestones of Gyles

The cobblestones of the Gyles were slick with pre-dawn mist as Dior walked along Pittenweem's harbour edge. Four centuries had passed, but some things remained unchanged: the creak of fishing boats against their moorings, the salt-heavy air, the way shadow gathered in familiar corners. Freya walked beside her, her senses attuned to the echoes of the past, the lingering energy that clung to the ancient stones. Greer and Thomas followed, their presence a silent strength in the gathering dawn. She stopped at a weathered doorway, its stone frame worn smooth by generations of hands.

'This was home,' she said softly. 'Before everything.'

Freya moved closer, her gift reading the patterns layered in the stone. Greer's fingers found Dior's, intertwined with practiced ease.

'My hands were always raw back then,' Dior continued, lost in memory. 'Salt and fish scales, day after day in the curing yard. I'd scrub them until they bled before church, trying to get the smell out.' She smiled faintly. 'Never quite managed it.'

'I noticed,' she heard Greer say from behind her. 'That first Sunday. You were sharing my hymnal, and I could smell the sea on your hands. But underneath that...'

Greer squeezed Dior's fingers.

'Lavender. You'd tried so hard to be proper for church.'

Dior led them along the harbour wall, past the spot where the curing yard had stood. 'I saw you every Sunday, you know. The tailor's daughter, so clean and educated. You'd help the minister with his letters while I gutted fish. Different worlds.'

'Until that morning in October.' Greer's voice carried centuries of tenderness. 'When there weren't enough hymnals to go around.'

'It was cold,' Dior said. 'I remember that. The first real bite of winter coming in off the sea. I was late to service - had to help land a catch at dawn. Slipped into the back pew, thinking I'd stand like usual. But then -'

'I saw her trying to peer at someone else's book,' she heard Greer say, and Dior smiled, remembering. 'And I just... moved. Slid over. Held my hymnal between us.'

A soft laugh escaped Greer's lips. 'My father would have been mortified. The tailor's daughter, sharing space with a fishwife.'

'Our fingers brushed when we turned the page.' Dior's markings pulsed with the memory. 'Just for a moment. But it felt...'

'Like touching sunlight,' they said together, an old shared phrase.

They walked on, past the old marketplace where Greer's father's shop had stood.

'We found excuses after that,' Dior said. 'I'd volunteer to clean the kirk. You'd suddenly need to deliver mended clothes to the harbour.'

'Little moments,' she heard Greer add. 'A shared smile across the marketplace. A brush of hands passing in the street. I'd watch you in the curing yard, the way you moved, so strong and sure.'

'And I'd find reasons to walk past the shop,' Dior admitted. 'Just to hear your voice reading scripture to your father's customers.'

They reached the ruins of the old priory where they'd first kissed. The stones were weathered now, nearly gone, but the patterns remembered.

'It was raining,' Dior said, touching the ancient wall. 'We were sheltering here after cleaning the kirk. You had... what was it?'

'Lavender again,' came Greer's gentle reply. 'I'd bought it at the market, thinking of you. You laughed when I showed you, said it was foolish to waste money on such things.'

'Then you kissed me.' Dior's voice softened. 'Right here, with the rain coming down and the sea-wind in our hair. Nothing dramatic. Nothing special. Just...'

'Love,' she heard Greer finish, the word a soft sigh in the quiet morning air.

❄

Thomas hung back, giving them space with their memories, but Dior watched as he touched his chest where James's ring hung. Some grief remained untouched by time. He watched the interplay between the three women, his gaze lingering on Dior's form as she shared her memories. The way her hands moved when she spoke, the subtle shifts in her markings that betrayed her emotions—he knew them all. He had spent years studying her every nuance, learning the language of her body as fluently as his own. She taught him how to be human. But now, there was a new layer to her, a depth he hadn't seen before. Freya's presence had changed her, changed them all. The young artist had unlocked something within Dior, a vulnerability that had been buried beneath centuries of pain and carefully constructed defences. He saw how she looked at Freya, a mixture of tenderness and a hint of something else... something that mirrored his own complex feelings for the woman who had so profoundly altered their world.

He thought of James, of the easy way he had loved, the way he had accepted them all without question. James, who had seen the darkness in Thomas and still chosen to stay. James, who had believed in a future where love could conquer even the most ancient of hatreds. A wave of grief, sharp and unexpected, washed over him. He closed his eyes. The memory of their last moments together replayed in his mind, a broken record of pain and loss. He forced himself to breathe, to focus. James wouldn't want him to fall apart. He would want him to fight, to survive, to find a way to honour his sacrifice.

❄

'We were careful,' Dior continued, more for Freya's understanding now. 'Meeting in shadows, in hidden corners. A touch here, a kiss there. Moments stolen between our regular lives. I still gutted fish. She still helped her father. We went to church, did our duties. Just two women who'd found something beautiful in a hard world.'

'Until that storm,' she heard Greer say quietly, the words heavy with remembered pain. 'When your husband returned early.'

Dior's markings flickered with pain.

'We thought we had time. Privacy. Just once, we wanted to love each other in daylight.'

They began climbing the worn path toward Gallows Hill, where the mist still clung in patches.

'The whole town turned out,' Dior said. 'To watch our shame. My husband with his whip, Greer's father turning away. Neighbours we'd known all our lives picking up stones.'

'But not Agnes,' she heard Greer add softly, a note of confusion in her voice.

Dior stopped, her hand resting against the damp stone wall.

'No. Not Agnes. She just... stood there. Watching. Then throwing stones. But Agnes kept her hands empty at her sides.'

'That's why they turned on her later,' Greer explained to Freya. 'When the crops failed. When the fishing was poor. They remembered how she'd held back that day. Started whispering that maybe she was complicit in our 'sin.''

'She paid for that small mercy,' Dior said. 'That one moment of... not understanding, exactly. But recognition, maybe. Of something she saw in herself.'

Through Freya's gift, they saw the patterns of that day—not just the violence and hatred, but that single still point in the storm. Agnes, standing apart, her hands empty while chaos raged around her.

'The curse wasn't just about punishment,' Dior explained, her eyes on the horizon where storm clouds gathered. 'It was about turning love itself into a weapon. Making pleasure into poison. Taking what was pure between us and twisting it into something that would mark us forever.'

'But they didn't understand,' she heard Greer say fiercely from behind her. 'Even as the curse took hold, even as it changed us, it couldn't change what mattered. We chose each other. Keep choosing each other.'

'Every day,' Dior whispered. 'Every moment. Like breathing. And Greer, no matter what happens you must never doubt that.' She pulled Greer into a tight embrace.

They reached the summit of Gallows Hill, where pre-dawn painted the harbour below in shades of pearl and steel. Dior watched fishing boats dance their ancient rhythm against the tide, remembering other dawns, other choices.

'Agnes lost everything too,' she said quietly. 'Not just that day, but in the months that followed. Her moment of mercy marked her. The whispers started—why hadn't she thrown stones? What unnatural sympathies did she harbour? When the fishing failed, when sickness came...'

Dior's markings pulsed with old understanding. 'They needed someone to blame.'

'They burned her,' she heard Greer say. 'It was born not just of hatred, but of regret for that one moment of compassion.'

Freya's gift revealed the intricate weave of patterns—how that single act of restraint had shaped centuries of Baobhan Sith history.

'She chose hatred after that,' Freya said. 'To prove she wasn't what they accused her of being.'

'No,' Dior corrected gently. 'She chose hatred because she couldn't bear the alternative. Because that moment of recognition, of seeing herself in us... it terrified her more than any fire.'

Thomas moved closer, his own patterns reflecting new understanding.

'Like James,' he said softly. 'Choosing love despite knowing the cost.'

'But Agnes chose the opposite,' Dior said. 'And that's why her power corrupts so deeply. Because every act of hatred is really just...'

She stopped, the truths still sharp after centuries.

'An act of self-hatred,' she heard Greer finish. 'For that one moment when she couldn't bring herself to throw stones.'

The wind picked up, carrying salt-laden air and memory. Below, Pittenweem began to wake—not so different from that morning centuries ago when two ordinary women dared to love in daylight, and one woman dared to show mercy.

'That's why it has to end here,' Dior said. 'Where it all began. Not with hatred or vengeance, but with truth. The truth she's been running from for four hundred years.'

Freya watched Dior's patterns shift and settle into new configurations. Something was changing—not just memory anymore, but purpose taking shape.

'She'll come here,' Dior said. 'Not just because we're here, but because part of her has been trying to get back to this hill for centuries. Back to that moment when she couldn't throw stones.'

'To prove she can now?' Thomas asked.

'To face what she couldn't face then.' Dior moved to the spot where the posts had stood. 'That she saw herself in us. That under all her righteous fire, she still does.'

Greer stepped closer to Dior, concern threading through her patterns. 'What are you planning?'

'What needs to be done.' Dior's voice was quiet but certain. 'To end what started here.'

The sun crested the horizon, painting Pittenweem in

shades of possibility and warning. They had preparations to make, but first, Dior needed them to understand one last thing.

'Remember,' she said. 'When everything happens. Remember we were just ordinary women who chose love. That's what Agnes could never accept—not our power, not our survival, but that we were brave enough to choose what she couldn't.'

Thunder rolled across the North Sea, though the storm was still distant. Below, Pittenweem stirred to life, unaware of the powers gathering above. Dior watched it all, her markings pulsing with a specific design Freya's gift couldn't quite decipher.

'We need to prepare,' she said, finally turning from the view. 'There isn't much time.'

She met their gazes, one by one. Thomas, his grief a raw wound. Greer, her steadfast loyalty a beacon. Freya, her gift a fragile hope in the gathering darkness.

'What's the plan?' Freya asked.

Dior's smile was a faint, fleeting thing, but it carried a weight of centuries. A hint of the woman she'd been before righteous fire had twisted the world.

'I'm going to show Agnes what she refused to see,' she said. 'I'm going to make her remember.'

'Remember what?' Thomas pressed, his voice tight with a need to understand, to control. 'What good will that do now?'

Dior turned to him, her markings pulsing with a light that pushed back shadows. 'Because that's where the pattern broke,' she said softly. 'That's where the corruption took root. And that's where we have a chance to heal it.'

'Heal it?' Greer's voice was sharp with disbelief. 'After everything she's done?'

'Not for her,' Dior said, watching the town below. 'For them. For us. For everyone Agnes's hatred has touched.'

She looked back at Freya, her markings shimmering with a purpose that went deeper than vengeance, deeper even than justice.

'You said it yourself, Freya,' she continued, her voice gaining strength. 'Love freely given is the strongest call. I'm going to remind her what it means to choose love,' she said. 'Even when it costs you everything.'

Freya, watching the patterns shift and settle around Dior, finally understood. This wasn't just about stopping Agnes. It was about redemption. Not just for Dior, but for every soul trapped in Agnes's web of hatred.

'She can't be allowed to release the seventeen.'

But was it too much of a risk? At best it was a desperate plan born of centuries-old pain and a love that had defied even death. Dior was ready to face the past. And in doing so, she might just change the future.

Chapter Sixty-Seven

Before the Storm

Freya watched dawn break over Pittenweem as her lovers and Thomas prepared the site. Her gift revealed layers of power building—old magic in the stones meeting new purpose, centuries of pain and memory crystallising into something potent. She could feel the history pressing down on them, a tangible force that seemed to hum in the very air. But it was Dion's patterns that caught her attention. They'd shifted since sharing their history, becoming more complex, harder to read. When she tried to focus on them directly, they seemed to slip away, like trying to catch smoke. There was a new intensity to them, a sense of purpose that both intrigued and worried her.

'The storm's building,' Greer said, looking out over the water where dark clouds gathered. She stood on Gallows Hill's summit, marking points in the earth with her nail. Silver light followed her movements, creating a web of power that resonated with the site's ancient energy.

Thomas worked the perimeter, his new patterns—born from James's sacrifice—interacting in a new way with the old magic. Every few minutes he'd stop, and touch where

James's ring hung on the silver chain, then continue with increased intensity.

More Baobhan Sith arrived as morning deepened. Ròs and her people moved like shadows through the town's narrow streets. Bethia's followers took positions on the harbour walls. Each group added their power to the growing web, but kept their distance from the hill itself. They all understood—what was coming belonged first to those who'd started here.

But something was wrong with Dior's markings. Freya had never seen them move quite this way—like they were preparing for something, rearranging themselves into new configurations. When Dior thought no one was watching, her fingers would trace patterns in the air, rehearsing movements that made no sense.

'The old chapel stones,' Dior said suddenly, pointing to a tumbled wall. 'We need them in a circle.'

Freya helped her move the weathered blocks, noting how Dior placed each one with precise care, as if following a design only she could see. Their hands met on the last stone, and Freya felt something pulse through Dior's patterns—resolution, grief, and something deeper she couldn't quite name.

'Dior—' she started.

'Just being thorough,' Dior smiled, but her thoughts, Freya could tell were elsewhere. She squeezed Freya's hand once, hard, then moved to help Greer with the boundary markers.

More signs of the coming confrontation appeared as morning wore on. Ravens gathered on Pittenweem's rooftops, drawn by the building power. The fishing boats stayed in the harbour despite the clear weather, their crews sensing something wrong in the air. Dogs barked at empty corners where patterns twisted too tight.

Ròs appeared beside Freya. 'We're getting reports from Edinburgh,' she said quietly. 'Agnes's followers are moving. All of them. Like a tide pulling back before a tsunami.'

'She's gathering her power,' Freya replied, watching Dior arrange candles in a pattern that made her gift recoil. 'Building to something big.'

'Bigger than we thought, maybe.' Ròs nodded toward the horizon where the storm clouds grew darker. 'That's not natural weather. She's pulling energy from everywhere, corrupting it as she draws it in.'

'Tell me what you see,' Freya said to Ròs, her eyes still on Dior. 'In her patterns. Am I imagining...'

'No.' Ròs's geometric markings pulsed with unease. 'They're changing. Like they're preparing for something. Something final.'

A gust of wind scattered the candles Dior had so carefully placed. She reset them with methodical precision, her movements almost ritualistic. When Greer approached to help, Dior shook her head, keeping her lovers at a distance.

'She was the first, you know,' Ròs said. 'The first one Agnes reached out to before all this happened.' She paused, watching Dior work. 'There's power in that kind of recognition.'

Thunder grew closer now. The storm clouds had taken on an unnatural copper tinge, reflecting the corrupted power Agnes drew into herself. Below, in Pittenweem's streets, humans hurried inside, shutters closing against the approaching darkness.

Bethia materialised from shadow, her spiral markings shifting with unease.

'My people spotted her advance guard. Enhanced

humans moving through Earlsferry, more powerful than we've seen. She's been saving her strongest weapons for this.'

'How long?' Freya asked.

'Hours. Maybe less.'

Dior had finished with the candles, her hand trailing along the ancient stone. Freya saw how the patterns responded to her touch—not just remembering anymore, but awakening. As if centuries of trapped power recognised something in Dior's altered markings.

Bethia's advance scouts brought more reports—entire villages emptying as Agnes passed through, humans either fleeing or falling under her influence. Those who joined her underwent immediate transformation, their patterns corrupted by her power until they became extensions of her will.

'She's building an army,' Thomas said, watching the growing line of burning eyes approach through the gloom. 'Using their fear to make them into weapons.'

'No,' Dior said again, still facing the harbour. 'She's building a wall. Between herself and what she really fears.' Her markings flickered with something Freya couldn't read. 'She always did need other people's hatred to hide from her own truth.'

Lightning cracked directly overhead, and in its flash, Freya saw Dior's patterns clearly. The sight made her breath catch. They weren't just changing—they were preparing to unravel.

'Dior,' she started, understanding beginning to dawn. 'What have you—'

'Freya.' Dior turned finally, and her smile carried centuries of love. 'Trust me. Please.'

Before Freya could respond, new movement caught

their attention. Agnes's advance forces had reached the outskirts of St Monans. Even at this distance, Freya could see how their enhanced strength had grown. They moved like predators, blessed iron glinting in their hands. But it was Agnes herself who dominated the scene. She seemed to pull the storm down around her like a cloak, corruption spreading outward with each step. The earth itself recoiled from her touch, patterns twisting into wrongness in her wake.

'She's stronger than before,' Ròs said, her geometric markings sharp with concern. 'Too strong for a direct confrontation.'

'That was never the plan,' Dior said quietly. She placed a hand on the stone circle one last time, and Freya felt ancient power respond. 'Some battles can't be won with strength.'

The storm clouds settled over Pittenweem, turning morning back to darkness. Only Dior's candles still burned, their flames unnaturally steady in the rising wind. Each one marked a point in her mysterious pattern, though even Freya's gift couldn't decipher its purpose.

'We should join the others,' Greer said, watching Agnes's army draw closer. 'Present a united front—'

'No.' Dior's voice was gentle but final. 'This ending started with us. With choices made on this hill.' She turned to Greer, touched her face with infinite tenderness. 'With love that survived even when they tried to stone it out of us.'

Freya saw the moment Greer understood—saw her patterns flare with desperate denial.

'Dior, don't—'

'Listen,' Dior said, including Freya in her gaze now. 'Both of you. Whatever happens next... remember what I told you. About ordinary women making extraordinary choices.'

Before either could respond, Agnes's power swept through Pittenweem like a tide of corruption. Windows shattered, stones cracked, centuries of built-up magic twisting under her influence. Only Dior's careful preparations held firm, her candles burning steady in the chaos.

'Time to take positions,' Ròs called. The others moved with practiced efficiency, forming defensive lines around the hill.

But Dior remained still, watching Agnes's approach with an expression Freya had never seen before—not fear or defiance, but something closer to recognition.

'Some fires,' she said softly, 'can only be fought with the truth they're trying to burn away.'

She squeezed their hands one final time.

'It's about choosing. Even when the choice costs everything.'

Greer surged forward, understanding dawning in her patterns.

'No! Whatever you're planning—'

But Freya caught her arm, she knew the inevitability of what was coming.

'It must be,' she said softly, though each word cost her. 'Look at her markings, Greer. We know what she's preparing to do.'

'There has to be another way!' Greer's voice cracked with four centuries of love and fear.

'There isn't,' Dior said gently. 'You know there isn't. This started with a choice on this hill. It has to end with one.'

She stepped into the circle of candles, her markings pulsing with that strange, pure light. Greer fought against

Freya's grip, but they both knew—some choices had to be made alone.

Agnes stopped at the hill's base. Her corruption rolled upward in waves of twisted power, but couldn't cross the boundary of Dior's candles. For a moment, the two women regarded each other across centuries of pain and possibility.

Then Agnes smiled. Righteous fire filled the world.

The final confrontation was about to begin. And Dior faced it with the same quiet certainty she'd once faced stones and whips and hatred—knowing that sometimes the greatest power lay not in magical gifts or ancient curses, but in the simple, unwavering strength of a human heart that dared to choose love, even when that choice might mean the end of everything.

Chapter Sixty-Eight

The Choice

Dior stood in her circle of candles as Agnes climbed Gallows Hill, righteous fire burning in her wake. But even through the corrupted patterns, Dior could see traces of the woman she'd known—in how Agnes's fingers still fidgeted when she was nervous, and how she held herself too straight when uncertain.

'Hello, Agnes.' Dior kept her voice soft, intimate against the rising storm. 'This day has been a long time coming, hasn't it? We should have done this sooner.' She watched Agnes's throat work, swallowing back whatever immediate retort had risen. 'But I was too busy running.' A sad smile touched Dior's lips. 'I'm sorry. I'm here now.'

Agnes raised her hands, power crackling around her. But Dior saw how her fingers trembled slightly, how the corruption in her patterns wavered. 'Look upon the corrupted ones!' Agnes called to her followers, but her eyes never left Dior's face. 'See how they mock us with their unnatural existence! Their perversion of God's natural order!'

The followers snarled their approval, blessed iron

flaring to life in their hands. Agnes's own blade stayed sheathed, though her hand strayed to its hilt several times as if seeking reassurance. Her righteousness felt rehearsed, a speech given too many times to still ring true.

'We never used to be like this, you and me, did we?' Dior kept her voice gentle, meant only for Agnes. She saw how the other woman's shoulders stiffened at the intimacy of her tone. 'We shared kindnesses you and me. Little intimacies.'

Agnes's fingers twitched against the dagger's hilt, her rhetoric faltering. A muscle jumped in her jaw—the same tell she'd had centuries ago when fighting against something she wanted.

'Do you remember?' Dior's words lingered in the air between them. She took a careful step forward, watching how Agnes's patterns responded to her proximity—fighting between corruption and recognition. The day you brought me water in the curing yard? No one else noticed how long I'd been working, but you did.'

Agnes's eyes flickered—just for a moment—to Dior's hands, as if remembering them raw and bleeding from the salt. Her own fingers uncurled from the dagger's hilt, a gesture so slight only Dior noticed.

Behind Agnes, her followers shifted restlessly, blessed iron glowing red in the storm light. But Dior saw how Agnes held them back with the slightest tension in her shoulders—the same way she used to stand between Dior and judgment in the marketplace.

'You used to find reasons to pass the curing yard,' Dior continued, her voice carrying memories of salt air and forbidden glances. 'Bringing messages that could have waited.' She watched Agnes's throat work, saw how her corrupted patterns stuttered at each remembered kindness.

'Your hands would shake when our fingers brushed over coins or cloth.'

'Silence!' Agnes's power crackled, but Dior saw what others couldn't—how the flames curled away from her, unwilling to harm.

'The day my hands were splitting from the salt,' Dior pressed gently, taking another step. The candles' light caught Agnes's face, showing shadows of the woman she'd been. 'You found me behind the cooperage. Remember? You'd been watching, hadn't you? Counting the hours I'd worked, seeing the pain I tried to hide.'

Agnes's breath hitched. Her followers' chants died away, sensing something changing in the air between the women.

'You didn't lecture about sin or duty.' Dior extended her hand, palm up, exactly as she had that day. 'You had tallow in your pocket, soft from the warmth of your body. You'd brought it for me, hadn't you? Been carrying it, waiting for the right moment?'

She could almost feel Freya and Greer's concern from the hilltop, but she ignored it, knowing this was a conversation that had to happen alone. This was a confrontation that had been brewing for four hundred years.

'Your hands were so gentle,' Dior said softly, watching how Agnes's fingers twisted in her expensive suit jacket—the same nervous gesture from centuries ago. 'You worked the tallow into every crack, every salt-burned crevice. And you didn't stop when my hands were done, did you?'

A tremor ran through Agnes's corruption. Behind her, her followers shuffled uneasily, sensing their leader's resolve wavering. But Dior kept her focus on Agnes's face, on the war being waged behind those burning eyes.

'You kept holding my hand. Your thumb drawing circles

on my palm.' Dior took another step closer, close enough now to see Agnes's pulse jumping in her throat. 'We both pretended it was still about healing, but we knew. Standing there in shadow, the smell of tar and salt all around us... we knew.'

'Stop,' Agnes whispered, but her voice had lost its righteous thunder.

'The way you looked at me in church,' Dior continued, each word carrying the weight of centuries. 'Not with the others' judgment. Not with hatred. With need.' She saw Agnes's patterns flicker, corruption warring with memory. 'The same warring need and fear I saw the day they dragged us into the street—when everyone else had stones in their hands, but you... you kept yours empty.'

'Why?' Dior took another step closer. She could feel the barely contained rage from the top of the hill, but she ignored it, knowing this had to be between her and Agnes. 'Because you're afraid to hear how my heart would race when you entered the curing yard? How I'd find any excuse to stay late, knowing you'd walk past at dusk?' Her voice softened. 'How I'd dream of your hands, wake up aching for your touch?'

Agnes's breath caught, her corruption wavering, offering fleeting glimpses of the woman beneath.

'I used to watch you too,' Dior admitted. 'In church, while you prayed. The way sunlight caught your hair, how your lips moved over the words.' She saw Agnes's patterns pulse with recognition. 'I'd imagine those lips on my skin, your prayers becoming something else entirely.'

Agnes's followers shifted uneasily, but neither woman noticed. The air between them thickened, charged with centuries of unspoken desire.

'The tallow was just an excuse, wasn't it?' Dior's voice

dropped lower, intimate. 'You wanted to touch me as badly as I wanted your touch. When you held my hands that day... I nearly leaned in. Nearly kissed you right there in the shadows.'

'You never...' Agnes's voice shook. 'You were with her. With Greer.'

'Not before, I hadn't noticed her then. It was all you.' Dior said softly. 'I gave up hope because you were the minister's wife, it could never be, and I was afraid. But don't tell me you didn't feel it too. Don't tell me you don't feel it now.'

The blessed iron dagger appeared in Agnes's hand, its corrupted patterns singing for blood. She raised it high, power coiling, ready for the killing blow.

But Dior saw what the others couldn't—how Agnes's hand shook, how her patterns fought against themselves, how centuries of hatred warred with a single moment of remembered desire.

'I'm here,' Dior whispered. 'I choose to be here. To offer freely what we were both too afraid to take.'

She closed her eyes, hoping her sacrifice would be enough. For Greer, for Freya, for all of them, she would give everything.

She waited. For the blade to fall.

Chapter Sixty-Nine

The Breaking

Greer watched the silhouette of the blessed iron dagger against the candle flames, every muscle in her body screaming to intervene. Four centuries of loving Dior rooted her to the spot even as her markings blazed with protective fury. Her throat burned with unspoken pleas, with rage, with terror. This couldn't be how it ended—not after everything they'd survived, everything they'd built. Freya's hand found her arm, steadying her. Greer barely felt it. All she could see was Dior—vulnerable, offering herself to the woman who'd spent centuries hunting them. The candlelight painted them both in stark relief, making shadows dance across Agnes's face as she held the blade high.

Every instinct demanded Greer move, fight, save her lover from this madness. But she knew Dior too well. Knew that set of her shoulders, that quiet certainty in her voice.

The wind caught Dior's words, carrying fragments of intimate whispers that made Greer's chest ache with memories. She'd always suspected about Agnes, about the complicated history there. She had seen how Agnes watched Dior when she thought no one was looking. But Dior was her love and suspecting was different from knowing, watching it unfold, from seeing Dior deliberately awaken those ancient feelings.

'She knows what she's doing,' Freya whispered, though Greer heard the tension in her voice. None of them could be certain how this would end.

The dagger's shadow wavered against the flames, and Greer's markings flared with desperate energy. One surge of power, one moment of intervention—she could stop this, protect Dior as she had for centuries. But something in Dior's posture held her back. This was a choice. Like that day in the rain when Dior had first kissed her, knowing the risks, choosing love over fear.

Still, every breath felt like glass in her lungs as she watched the blade's shadow dance between them.

'Let me go,' she whispered to Freya, though they both knew she wouldn't move. Couldn't move. The candlelight caught tears on her cheeks. 'I can't just watch—'

'You have to,' Freya's voice cracked with shared pain. 'Look at her patterns, Greer. Look what she's doing.'

And Greer could see it—how Dior's silver markings reached for Agnes's corruption, not fighting it but embracing it. Like she'd once embraced Greer's pain, her fear, her need. The same fearless love that had saved Greer four centuries ago was now offered to their greatest enemy.

The storm gathered, pressing closer, making the candle flames dance wildly. Agnes's followers pressed forward, blessed iron gleaming, but their leader seemed lost in Dior's words, in memories of gentle hands and secret longings.

The dagger's shadow trembled.

Then fell.

The sound of blessed iron striking stone cut through the

storm's fury. And before Greer could breathe, before she could move, Agnes surged forward. Their kiss wasn't gentle—four hundred years of denial and desire exploded between them as Agnes seized Dior's face between her hands. Dior's fingers tangled in Agnes's perfectly styled hair, ruining its careful arrangement as she pulled her closer.

'Jesus Christ,' Ròs muttered somewhere behind them. 'Get them a room.'

Greer couldn't look away. Every kiss she'd ever shared with Dior flashed through her mind as she watched Agnes press closer, desperate and demanding. Dior's hands slid down Agnes's spine, pulling their bodies flush together. The corrupt fire in Agnes's patterns flickered, fighting against something older, something pure.

'This is blasphemy!' One of Agnes's followers raised his blade. 'This is corruption incarnate!'

But his words choked off as Agnes moaned into Dior's mouth, a sound of pure surrender that held no trace of righteous fury. Dior broke the kiss just long enough to breathe 'Yes' against Agnes's lips before claiming them again. Their markings began to pulse in sync—silver light fighting corruption, love battling hatred. Agnes's perfect suit was rumpled now, Dior's hands leaving trails of silver light wherever they touched.

'Stop them!' Another follower screamed. 'This is—'

'No,' Freya said, stepping forward, her own markings blazing with power. 'This is what they were always meant to be.'

The patterns twisted and reformed, corruption burning away like mist in sunlight. Agnes's followers staggered back as waves of energy rolled off the embracing women.

'The curse,' Freya whispered. 'Look at the patterns—they're resetting to what they should have been.'

Silver light exploded outward as Agnes gave herself completely to the kiss, to the love she'd denied for centuries. The candle flames surged toward the storm clouds, carrying patterns of transformation with them.

And in their light, everything began to change.

From their kiss, the transformation rippled outward. Greer watched Agnes's corruption dissolve wherever Dior touched her, replaced by silver light that sung. The storm above them twisted, copper-dark clouds shot through with new patterns that made Greer's ancient markings respond in ways she'd never felt before.

Agnes tore her mouth away, gasping, as her carefully constructed walls crumbled. But Dior held her close, whispering against her throat, 'Let it happen. Let it go.' Her lips traced Agnes's jaw, each kiss undoing centuries of hatred.

'Kill them!' A voice from the crowd. 'Stop this unholy—'

The blessed iron in their followers' hands began to change, the corruption eating itself away. Some dropped their weapons with cries of pain or fear. Others stood transfixed, watching their leader arch into Dior's touch as silver light consumed the last traces of righteous fire in her patterns.

'The original curse,' Freya's voice shook with wonder. 'It's unravelling. All of it.'

Greer felt it in her own markings—an answering surge of power that felt cleaner, purer than anything she'd known since that day on Gallows Hill. Around them, other Baobhan Sith gasped as their patterns began to shift.

'Bloody hell,' Ròs breathed. 'They're actually doing it. They're actually—'

Agnes cried out—not in pain but in release. All her

careful control shattered as Dior pressed their foreheads together, sharing breath, sharing power. Their markings blazed so bright Greer had to shield her eyes.

And in that light, everything they'd ever been began to transform.

The transformation moved through the gathered, unnaturals taking their rightful place as supernaturals. Greer felt her own markings respond, centuries of cursed energy reshaping itself into something that felt... right. Pure. What they should have been all along.

Above them, the storm exploded into silver light as Agnes surrendered completely. Her fingers traced Dior's markings with reverent wonder, learning patterns she'd watched but never dared touch. When she spoke, her voice carried no trace of righteous fire, only awe.

'I tried so hard to hate you,' she whispered against Dior's lips. 'Tried so hard to burn this out of me.'

'I know,' Dior's hands cupped Agnes's face, thumbs catching tears that glowed with transformed power. 'But love freely given can't be corrupted. Can't be burned away.'

Their followers scattered as the wave of change reached them. Some ran screaming into Pittenweem's streets. Others fell to their knees, blessed iron forgotten as they watched their enhanced powers dissolve into something different. Something true.

'The patterns,' Freya gasped, her gift overwhelmed by the cascading changes. 'They're becoming what they were meant to be. Before hatred twisted them. Before the curse.'

Greer watched Dior with her ancient enemy, her lover of four centuries, and finally understood. This wasn't about losing or sharing. This was about healing something broken so long ago none of them remembered what wholeness felt like. Until now.

As the silver light faded, Agnes and Dior remained entwined, their foreheads touching, sharing breath. Greer felt an ache in her chest—not quite jealousy, but something more complex. She was watching the woman she'd loved for centuries heal something so fundamentally broken.

'Well,' Ròs's voice cut through the stunned silence. 'That's one way to end a holy war. Though I'd have settled for just killing her. I suppose we should just be happy there was no burying your gays.'

'Look at the patterns,' Freya breathed, her hand finding Greer's. 'Not just theirs—everyone's. They're... remembering.'

She was right. The markings on every Baobhan Sith on Gallows Hill were changing, becoming something older, purer. Greer felt it in her own flesh—the curse's bitter edge dissolving into something that sang of protection rather than predation.

Agnes pulled back slightly from Dior, confusion replacing centuries of hatred in her eyes.

'What have you done?' Her voice shook. 'What is this?'

Before Dior could answer, a cry went up from the Righteous Assembly's followers. Their enhanced powers were fading, leaving them ordinary humans facing extraordinary change. Some fled down the hill toward Pittenweem's streets.

Through her grip on Greer's hand, Freya felt the patterns continue to shift and change. Old magic stirred in Pittenweem's stones, responding to whatever had been awakened on Gallows Hill. She caught glimpses in the transforming patterns—fragments of what they'd been before the curse, but nothing clear enough to name.

'The blessed iron,' someone called. 'Look at the blessed iron!'

The weapons that had burned with corrupted power faded, their righteous fire replaced by a faint orange blush creeping rapidly across the metal, like wildfire consuming dry grass. Tiny beads of reddish-brown erupted, multiplying in a frenzy. They merged, forming rivulets of decay that flowed across the iron's surface, etching deep grooves into its form. What had once been daggers seemed to shiver, to shrink inwards as the rust ate away at its edges. Flakes of iron, brittle and fragile, began to detach, then they crumbled into dust, being blown on the wind. Several of Agnes's followers dropped their disintegrating blades, backing away from what they couldn't understand.

Agnes herself seemed lost, one hand still curved around Dior's cheek, the other pressed to her own chest where corruption had burned for centuries.

'The fire,' she whispered. 'It's gone. But there's something else...'

'I feel it too,' Dior said softly. She looked to Greer, uncertainty flickering in her transformed markings. 'Like remembering something we never knew we'd forgotten.'

Greer watched new patterns appear she couldn't read. The ache in her chest deepened—not loss exactly, but change. Profound, irreversible change.

Above them, the storm began to break apart, copper-dark clouds giving way to pre-dawn light. But nothing felt finished. Everything felt like a beginning.

'The patterns keep changing,' Freya said, her gift struggling to interpret what she saw. 'Not just ours—everything. The stones, the air, even the boundaries between human and Baobhan Sith.'

Throughout Pittenweem, lights began flickering on as the town stirred. Humans drawn to windows and doors by some instinct they couldn't name. The remaining Righteous

Assembly followers huddled together, watching their leader stand transformed in Dior's embrace.

'I remember...' Agnes started, then stopped, frowning. 'No, not remember exactly. But I feel...' Her fingers traced one of Dior's markings, following its new configuration.

'Connection,' Dior finished quietly. She looked past Agnes to Greer, eyes full of meaning Greer couldn't quite grasp. 'Like before. Before fear turned it wrong.'

Ròs moved closer. 'Before what? The curse? The burning?' She reached out to touch the nearest blessed iron blade, then jerked back. 'It's not just dead. It's... refusing. Like it knows it was never meant to harm us.'

Thomas knelt to examine one of Dior's candles—still burning despite the wind, their flames now tinged with silver.

'Something's awakening,' he said. 'But what?'

No one had an answer. Not yet. They could only watch as dawn crept closer and everything they'd ever known continued to change.

'Guardians, perhaps,' Dior said. Freya met her gaze and nodded. 'Guardians.'

Agnes shifted in Dior's embrace, watching the light spread.

'I used to watch you there,' she said softly, as if speaking from a dream. 'In the curing yard. The way you'd move among the other women, touching shoulders, easing aches...' She frowned. 'You were healing them. Not just... not just their bodies.'

'Yes,' Dior said, understanding. 'And you'd bring water, tend to cuts and burns. Not because you had to...'

'Because I could feel what they needed,' Agnes finished. 'Before I learned to fear that feeling. Before I turned it into...'

The remaining followers of the Righteous Assembly stirred uneasily, watching their leader's certainty crumble. But something else was happening among them. Some had fallen to their knees, not in prayer or fear, but as if listening to something in the stones beneath them.

Freya's grip on Greer's hand tightened.

'The patterns,' she whispered 'They're not just changing—they're showing us what we...' She stopped, overwhelmed by what her gift revealed.

'What we were,' Greer found herself saying, though she didn't know where the words came from. 'What we're supposed to be.'

Silver light spread through Pittenweem's streets, touching stone, wood, water, and air. Each place it reached seemed to wake, to remember. Greer felt it most strongly near the old kirk, where she and Dior had first shared a hymnal—a pulse of something that spoke of connection, of bonds freely given and received.

'The patterns keep shifting,' Freya said, her voice hushed with concentration. 'But they're not random. They're forming... networks? Like veins carrying...' She struggled for the word.

'Life,' Agnes whispered. Her hand had found one of Dior's markings again, following its new path.

Down in the harbour, fishing boats rocked gently against their moorings as silver light played across their hulls. A few early-rising fishermen stood frozen on the quay, watching their town transform. One of them—an old man Greer recognised from earlier—reached out to touch the light where it danced on the water.

'My grandmother used to tell stories,' he called up to them, his voice carrying clearly in the pre-dawn stillness. 'About the old ones. The healers.'

Dior's breath caught. Her fingers tightened on Agnes's arm as another wave of change rippled through their markings.

'Not just healers,' she said. 'We were...'

'Guardians,' Thomas finished, the word seeming to come from somewhere deeper than memory. 'Of more than just flesh and blood.'

The old fisherman's voice seemed to break some spell. Others began speaking—fragments of stories passed down, half-remembered tales of what the Baobhan Sith had been before fear turned them to shadow.

'My great-grandmother spoke of them,' a woman called from her doorway. 'Said they were midwives to both body and soul.'

'Healers of the spirit,' another voice added. 'Before the kirk called it witchcraft.'

Agnes trembled in Dior's embrace. The change had started and nothing, nor no one, could stop it now.

Chapter Seventy

Guardians of the Dawn

A collective gasp rose from the gathered as the truth settled into their bones. It wasn't just a change in their markings, but a fundamental shift in their being. Freya felt it in the taste of the air, in the pulse of the stones beneath their feet, in the way her very soul seemed to expand. Her gift, usually a torrent of chaotic possibilities, now flowed with a clarity she'd never known. She saw the patterns not as tangled threads, but as a vibrant tapestry, interconnected and purposeful.

'We weren't just meant to feed,' she said. 'That was the curse's lie. The hunger, the violence—it was all a perversion.'

'Then what were we?' Thomas asked, his gaze fixed on the receding darkness, as if seeing something beyond the physical.

'Guardians,' Dior said, the word resonating with the weight of a forgotten truth. 'Of the boundaries between worlds. Of the flow of life.'

Agnes, still held in Dior's embrace, looked down at her

own transformed markings, her eyes wide with a mixture of awe and fear.

'I remember… fragments. Whispers in the back of my mind, even through all the hatred. The stories my grandmother used to tell…'

'Not just stories,' Greer said, stepping closer to Dior and Agnes. She felt it in her own ancient bones. A resonance deeper than memory. Her hand found Freya's, their fingers interlacing. A silent acknowledgment of the bond that had helped them all rediscover this truth. 'Memories. Passed down, hidden, distorted. But still there.'

'Guardians,' she echoed, the word a revelation on her tongue. She looked at Dior, at Agnes, then back at Freya. A dawning understanding of the tapestry Freya had begun to weave, not just for them, but for all their kind.

Ever the pragmatist, Ròs was already testing the limits of her transformed abilities. Her geometric markings pulsed, and the stones of the hill shifted under her will, forming a low wall, a natural amphitheatre.

'If we're meant to be guardians,' she said, 'we'll need to relearn how. And quickly.' She nodded towards the base of the hill. 'It looks like our defences are being tested.'

She was right. The Righteous Assembly followers who remained, though stripped of their enhanced powers, were not giving up. They had regrouped at the base of the hill, their faces contorted with fear and confusion, but their hands still clutching the now-inert blessed iron. They were fewer now, their numbers thinned by desertion and the unravelling of Agnes's power, but they were still a threat.

'They don't understand,' Freya said, her heart aching for the humans who had been so thoroughly manipulated. 'They're still trapped in Agnes's old story.'

'They were used as weapons,' Thomas said, his gaze

hardening as he watched the remnants of the Righteous Assembly. He touched James's ring, his jaw tightening.

'Pawns in a game they never understood,' said Greer.

'Then we need to show them a new one,' he said, turning his gaze towards the town below, where the first rays of dawn were painting the sky with hues of hope. A new narrative, Freya realised. One where James's sacrifice wasn't in vain. 'A better one.'

Bethia stepped forward, her spiral markings alive with newfound energy. 'We can't just expect them to accept this,' she said, her voice low and urgent. 'Centuries of fear don't just vanish overnight. We have to show them that we're different now. That we're not the monsters Agnes painted us to be.'

And as the light of the new day finally broke over Pittenweem, the transformed of Gallows Hill prepared to face whatever came next. Not as monsters or victims, but as something far older, far greater. Something the world had forgotten it needed.

'We have much to do,' Dior said, her gaze sweeping over the transformed faces around her. She gently disengaged herself from Agnes, though their hands lingered for a moment, a silent acknowledgment of the connection that now bound them.

'We need to reach out to the other orders, to the lone practitioners, to every being who has been forced into hiding.'

'And the humans,' Freya added. 'We need to show them that we're not their enemies. That we can coexist, that we can protect them.

Agnes spoke, her voice hesitant, uncertain.

'They'll never trust us. Not after everything...' She trailed off, her head bowed as she stared at her hands.

'They might,' Greer said, stepping up beside her former enemy, offering a small, tentative smile. She offered a small, tentative smile. 'If we give them a reason to. If we show them what we can truly be.'

'Guardians,' Ròs said, rolling the word around her mouth. 'It has a certain ring to it, doesn't it? Should we have badges?'

Thomas's gaze was fixed on the horizon, where the sun was now fully risen, bathing the world in a new light.

'A new beginning,' he said softly, more to himself than the others.

Freya stood between Greer and Dior, feeling the patterns around them shift and settle into a new configuration. A pattern of hope, of resilience, of a future where love, freely given, could heal even the deepest wounds. A future they would now have to build.

Chapter Seventy-One

The Weight of Love

The pre-dawn air carried salt and memory as Agnes stood on Gallows Hill, her transformed markings casting silver light across ancient stones. Behind her, footsteps approached—Dior's presence a physical ache in her chest.

'I can't stay here,' Agnes whispered, not turning around. 'Not after what I did. What I caused.'

'You don't get to run,' Dior's voice was gentle but firm. 'Not this time.'

Agnes heard two more sets of footsteps—Greer and Freya joining them. Of course, some conversations needed all voices, all hearts present.

'How do you bear to look at me?' Agnes asked, finally turning to face them. Her voice cracked. 'After everything I did? The lives I destroyed, the hatred I spread...' She gestured at the town below. 'I tried to burn love itself from the world, starting right here.'

'You tried to burn it from yourself first,' Dior said quietly. 'That's what I couldn't see back then—how much you were hurting yourself with every stone you didn't throw.' She paused, her gaze searching Agnes's face. 'And with every fire you lit afterwards.'

Agnes's legs gave way and she sank to her knees on the damp grass. Her markings pulsed with remembered pain—not righteous fire now, but pure grief.

Dior knelt beside her, her own markings flickering with a complex mix of emotions. She reached out, her fingers tracing the edge of Agnes's transformed patterns.

'I remember the day they burned you,' she said, her voice soft but heavy with the weight of centuries. 'The screams, the smoke... the way the light in your eyes went out, even before the flames touched you.'

Agnes flinched, her gaze dropping to the ground. 'I deserved it. For everything I did that followed.'

'No one deserves that,' Dior said firmly. 'No one deserves to be burned alive for who they love. Or for who they choose not to hate.'

'But the betrayals,' Agnes whispered, her voice raw. 'My husband, the minister, turning on me. My neighbours, the people I'd grown up with... They all wanted me dead.'

'And that pain,' Dior continued, her voice thick with understanding. 'That betrayal... it twisted something inside you. Turned your fear into hatred, your compassion into cruelty.'

Greer moved closer, her markings resonating with ancient understanding. 'You chose fear over love. We all did, in different ways. The difference was, you had the power to make others choose it too.'

'Hannah,' Agnes whispered, the name a fresh wound. 'James. All those enhanced humans I corrupted, convinced them hatred was holy...' She looked up at them through tears. 'How do I even begin to make amends? How do I carry the weight of so many destroyed lives?'

'Not alone,' Freya said, kneeling beside her. Her gift read the patterns of Agnes's pain, saw the genuine remorse cutting deeper than any curse. 'That's the first lesson. We carry these burdens together.'

'I don't deserve—' Agnes started, but Dior cut her off.

'This isn't about deserving,' she said, her voice firm. 'It's about choosing. Every day, every moment, we choose who we are. What we become.' She took Agnes's hands in hers. 'You chose hatred for four hundred years. Now you can choose something else.'

Agnes's markings flared with response to Dior's touch—not the corrupted fire of before, but something pure, something that sang of possibility.

'I feel everything now,' she whispered. 'Every bond I tried to break, every connection I poisoned. How do you stand it? This awareness of what we're meant to protect?'

'You learn,' Greer said softly. 'To use it as it was meant to be used. To heal instead of harm. To strengthen instead of sever.'

'But the weight of what I've done...'

'Will always be there,' Dior finished. 'As it should be. But it can drive you forward instead of holding you back. Each life you help heal, each bond you help strengthen—it doesn't erase the past, but it builds something new.'

Agnes felt the town stir below, felt the complex web of connections she'd once tried to destroy shift. Now she could sense their true purpose—not sins to be purged, but sacred bonds to be protected.

'Show me,' she whispered, through tears, but also determination. 'Show me how to be what I was meant to be. What we were all meant to be.'

Dior's hand tightened on hers. Greer and Freya moved

closer, their markings harmonising with a shared purpose older than hatred, stronger than fear.

'Together,' Dior said softly. 'We learn together.'

And as the sun rose over Gallows Hill, four women knelt in the damp grass—former enemies transformed by understanding, by freely chosen love, by the fierce determination to heal what had once been broken. It wasn't forgiveness, not yet. But it was a beginning.

Chapter Seventy-Two

Awakening

The visions came to Freya, sharp and vivid, cutting through the murk of the curse. Not predators hunting prey—she saw them as they'd been before: guardians of sacred bonds. The connection between Greer and Dior wasn't about hymns or holy books; it was about the raw, undeniable energy that flowed between two souls who recognised each other—a force as natural as the wind and tides.

'The markings,' she breathed, her gift revealing deeper truths. 'They're not brands of curse or corruption. They're maps.' Her fingers traced the edge of one of Greer's patterns. 'Maps of how souls connect, how energy flows between beings.'

More memories surfaced in the silver light—Agnes moving through Pittenweem's streets, feeling the hurts and hopes of her neighbours, drawn to heal rather than condemn. Dior in the curing yard, her touch carrying more than physical comfort. Greer, sensing the subtle energies that connected the villagers, the invisible threads of community that bound them together. She remembered her father's stories, not from scripture, but from the land itself—tales of the old ways, of beings who walked between the worlds, helping to maintain the balance.

'We fed,' Thomas said slowly, his markings shifting with new understanding, 'because shared blood, shared pleasure—they were ways to strengthen bonds, to keep connections pure and strong.'

'Until fear taught us to take instead of share,' Agnes said, her fingers trembling against Dior's skin. 'Until we forgot what the hunger was really for.'

Down in Pittenweem's streets, more humans gathered. The silver light touched them, too, awakening old memories passed down through generations. Stories of twilight healers, of sacred guardians, of beings who maintained the delicate web of human connection. Not stories of saints and churches, but of something older, wilder—something woven into the very fabric of the land, into the very bedrock of Fife.

'Look,' Freya said, pointing to the silver light playing across the harbour. Patterns emerged in the water—ancient lines of power that had always run through Pittenweem. Not just ley lines, but something more intricate: the web of human connection made visible.

'The fishing boats,' an old man called up to them. His voice, rough with age, carried on the morning breeze. 'My grandmother said they used to bless them. Not just for safety, but for...' He struggled, grappling with a memory older than himself. 'For keeping the crews bound together. For making sure they'd find their way home to those who loved them.'

The truth of his words resonated through Freya,

vibrating in her transformed markings. How many times had she sensed the bonds between fishing crews and their families? How long had she dismissed that awareness as just another aspect of hunger?

'It wasn't just about rituals,' Dior said softly, her gaze distant, remembering. 'It was about the energy that flows through everything. The connections between people, between the land and the sea, between the living and the dead.' She looked at Agnes, a question in her eyes. 'That's what you felt, wasn't it? Even then.'

Agnes's breath caught. 'I felt everything breaking. Not just... not just what was between us. But something older. Something vital.' Her voice shook, catching in her throat. 'So I chose to break myself instead.'

The silver light reached the old priory ruins, where Dior and Greer had first kissed. The stones seemed to sing with remembered purpose—not just shelter for sacred rites, but a place where bonds between souls had been strengthened, protected.

'The patterns,' Freya gasped, a new understanding taking her breath away. 'They're not just showing us what we were. They're showing us what we can be again.'

But before anyone could respond, a new change rippled through the air. The silver light that had spread through Pittenweem began flowing back toward Gallows Hill, carrying with it centuries of memory and meaning.

'Something's coming,' Ròs warned, her transformed markings flaring in warning.

The light gathered around them, condensing, intensifying, until they stood in a column of pure silver radiance. Everything they'd been, everything they could be, everything they were meant to be, crashed over them like a wave.

Understanding dawned at last. The curse hadn't just twisted their nature. It had made them forget what that nature was.

Until now.

Chapter Seventy-Three

A Tapestry Rewoven

The understanding brought with it a euphoria but it was short-lived because the light that had flooded Pittenweem began to change, taking on a darker hue that made Freya's stomach lurch. The patterns, moments ago vibrant, now flickered, their edges blurring. The transformation—it wasn't holding. She felt it in her bones.

'No,' she whispered, watching corruption seep back into their newly transformed markings like poison through veins. 'Something's wrong.'

Around them, the night erupted with screams as their people began to fall. Newly transformed Baobhan Sith dropped to their knees, clutching their heads, their silver markings flickering and dying like stars devoured by darkness. The curse wasn't just fighting back—it was consuming them.

Agnes staggered, her own transformation wavering. The connection she'd forged with Dior sparked and crackled, turning toxic. When Dior reached for her, the contact made them both cry out in agony.

'The curse,' Agnes gasped. 'It's older than us, deeper than us. We were fools to think—' She broke off, doubling over as corruption fought to reclaim her. 'Perhaps this is justice,' she murmured.

The town below erupted in chaos as their protective barriers shattered. Humans fled screaming into the streets. The sound of breaking glass and splintering wood echoed through the night.

'All those people,' Greer's voice was tight with strain as she fought her own battle against the resurgent curse. 'If we lose control now—'

'Everyone who can still stand,' Freya called out. 'Form a circle. Like calls to like. Pattern to pattern. Choice to choice.'

They moved through the chaos, those still strong enough to fight. Ròs and Bethia came first, their geometric and spiral markings harmonising despite their differences. Others followed—thirteen in all, a sacred number, a number of power and transformation. Freya saw how their transformed markings reached for each other, a desperate attempt to hold onto the light amidst the encroaching darkness.

'Whatever you're planning,' Ròs ground out through clenched teeth, 'do it fast. We're losing people.'

'It will hurt,' Freya warned them as they joined hands, completing the circle. 'Some of us might not survive.'

'Better to die free than live cursed again!' Bethia shouted against the building wind.

They stood on Gallows Hill where it had all begun, thirteen souls linked despite the agony of contact. At the centre stood Freya, Greer, Dior, and Agnes—the four who had started this transformation. Thomas completed their inner circle, his grief-forged markings providing a crucial anchor. His gaze met Freya's, and she saw not just pain in his patterns, but a fierce, unwavering resolve.

The corruption struck then, full force, trying to tear them apart. Greer felt it like acid in her veins, burning away the silver light, trying to poison their connection. The brooch at Freya's throat blazed colder, brighter, fighting against the darkness.

'The stone,' Glicia called. 'Now, child! Let it show them the way!'

Freya ripped the brooch from her throat, the ancient silver burning cold as sea-spray against her palm. The Elie Ruby at its heart blazed with an inner fire that danced between blood-red and twilight-black, just as it had that night in 1634. The Celtic knots around it writhed and shifted, no longer protecting but preparing to release their power.

'Whatever happens,' she heard Dior say through gritted teeth, 'know that this was worth it. That we were worth it.'

Energy surged through Freya's gift, showing her what needed to be done. With all her strength, she hurled the brooch into the centre of their circle. As it flew, she saw within the stone both sides of that ancient force—the hatred that had tried to destroy love, and the love that had refused to die.

The Elie Ruby struck the ground and shattered. Light exploded outward—not silver or shadow, but the deep, fierce red of a love that could outlast centuries. The garnet's final gift spread like dawn over the sea, its power speaking of choice and sacrifice, of love freely given and finally reclaimed. It ripped through their circle like a tide of pure transformation, burning away corruption, searing them down to their very souls.

Greer heard screaming and realised it was Freya joining

the others as the energy around them recreated them on a molecular level. She felt her hand in Freya's, squeezing so hard their bones ground together. Felt Dior's fierce love, Agnes's desperate hope, Thomas's grief-forged strength—all of it flowing together, becoming something greater than its parts.

The curse fought back, but the light from the shattered stone burned brighter, called to something in their transformed souls that remembered what they once were.

'Choose!' Glicia's voice cut through their shared agony. 'Choose what you will become!'

And in that moment of ultimate transformation, as pain threatened to break them, as corruption tried to claim them, as the very fabric of reality hung in the balance—they chose.

They chose each other. They chose love.

The light that exploded from their circle was like nothing any of them had ever seen. It swept through Pittenweem like a tsunami of raw energy, burning away corruption, healing bonds, transforming everything it touched. Those who had fallen rose again, their markings blazing with new purpose. The veils between the worlds thinned, shifted, became something anew that honoured both sides of their nature.

Silence fell over Gallows Hill. No one moved at first, their bodies trembling with aftershocks of transformation. The circle remained unbroken, their hands clasped so tightly they'd left marks on each other's skin. Everything felt raw, new.

Freya swayed, exhaustion making her bones feel hollow. But Greer's grip anchored her, and Dior's presence at her back steadied her. Agnes's markings pulsed in time with their own—not fighting anymore, but harmonising.

'Look,' Thomas whispered.

Where the brooch had shattered, molten silver spread across the ancient stones in an intricate weave. It spiralled outward, each line and curve telling the story of their transformation.

Glicia approached slowly, her own markings shimmering. She knelt to touch the silver, and vibrations rippled out from her fingers.

'The old magics remember,' she said. 'They remember what we were and what you've chosen to become again.' She looked up at them, her eyes bright. 'And they will not forget.'

In the town below, the chaos had stilled. Everyone stood frozen, staring up at Gallows Hill. The air was different—cleaner.

They held the circle until the sun fully crested the horizon, their transformed markings adjusting to this new reality. When they finally let go, some stumbled, their legs weak. Others sank to their knees, overwhelmed.

'We did it,' Freya whispered, full of awe. She looked at her newfound family. 'We actually did it.'

'I can feel everything,' Ròs whispered, her geometric patterns dancing with heightened awareness. 'The land, the sea, the connections between all living things...'

'It's what we were meant to feel,' Bethia replied, helping another transformed Baobhan Sith to her feet. 'Before the curse twisted our nature.'

Freya knelt beside the silver burned into the stone, her fingers hovering just above its surface. Guardians not just of human bonds, but of all sacred connections. Protectors of the delicate web that held their earth together. The pattern was a map, a guide, a promise.

'The humans,' Dior said suddenly, looking down at the town. 'They'll have seen everything.'

Indeed, people were already gathering at the base of Gallows Hill. But something was different in how they looked at the transformed beings now. There was still fear, yes, but also recognition. Ancient memories stirring in their blood.

'They remember too,' Agnes said softly. 'Not consciously, perhaps, but in their souls.'

Dior moved to the hill's edge. After a moment's hesitation, she began to descend toward the waiting crowd. To everyone's surprise, Thomas followed her.

'What are you doing?' Freya called after them.

'Showing them,' Dior replied without turning. 'Showing them we're not what they feared. We're what they forgot they needed.'

The humans drew back as Dior and Thomas approached, but didn't flee. A child broke free from her mother's grip, running toward them. Before anyone could stop her, she reached out to touch one of Dior's markings.

Instead of recoiling, the child pressed closer, her eyes shining with delight.

'It tickles,' she giggled, reaching for the light again.

The tension broke. Other humans stepped forward, hesitant but curious. Thomas began speaking, explaining what they'd witnessed. Dior demonstrated her gifts, showing how she could strengthen connections with just a touch.

'We should help them,' Freya said, watching the scene unfold. She felt a surge of protectiveness towards these humans. But when she tried to stand, her legs buckled.

'Easy,' Greer caught her, supporting her weight. 'You've given enough for now. Let the others do their part.'

Agnes touched the silver. 'It's really over, isn't it? The curse, the corruption...'

'That part is over,' Glicia said. 'But your true work is just beginning.'

She was right, Freya knew. Her gift showed her challenges still to come—those who would resist this change, those who would try to twist it to their own purposes. Mànas was still out there. And humans, for all their awakening memories, would need time to fully accept this new reality.

But looking down at Pittenweem, at the scene of transformed Baobhan Sith beginning to connect openly with humans, she felt only hope. They had broken not just the curse, but centuries of fear and division.

'What happens now?' Dior asked, voicing the question they were all thinking.

Freya met her gaze, then looked at Agnes, at Thomas, at the others. 'We rebuild,' she said. 'We reconnect. We protect. We'll face it together.' She leaned into Greer's body for support.

'Together,' Greer agreed, the word carrying the weight of promise.

The sun climbed, setting the silver alight. Around the circle, their markings flared in response, a silent chorus.

The curse was broken. Not with a fanfare, but a deep, resonant shift, like tectonic plates settling into a new alignment. They'd found their way back to something ancient and true, not a victory won, but a remembering.

Challenges remained, shadows still clung to the edges of Pittenweem, but they would face them together, their unity a bedrock, their transformation a compass. The future was unwritten, not a new tapestry, but raw, untamed land. They were no longer weavers of a predetermined fate, but pioneers. The journey stretched before them, not a neatly paved road, but a wild, overgrown path, and as they stood on that ancient hill, the sunrise a stark, beautiful promise, they knew they were ready to forge their way forward.

Then the news broke, sharp and sudden, like a crack of thunder.

Chapter Seventy-Four

Echoes of the Awakening

Freya stood in the gallery's back room, watching multiple news feeds play across the screens Thomas had installed. BBC News showed aerial footage of Pittenweem, the silver on Gallows Hill gleaming even from above. CNN ran shaky phone videos of their transformation, the light show impossible to dismiss as special effects. Al Jazeera interviewed witnesses, their stories remarkably consistent despite their different perspectives.

'The UN Security Council is convening an emergency session,' Greer said, looking up from her phone. Her transformed markings pulsed steadily as she read. 'The UK government's official statement is due within the hour.'

'The Huldufólk in Iceland have just made contact,' Ròs said suddenly, unable to contain her excitement. 'They've been fighting against geothermal exploitation in their sacred spaces. They want to know if we'll stand with them.'

'The what?' Agnes said, momentarily distracted from the news feeds.

'Hidden folk,' Dior said, her fingers dancing over her

own phone as more messages poured in. 'Their version of us. Every land has them—beings who are meant to protect the sacred bonds between people and nature.' Her markings pulsed with recognition. 'We don't just guard human connections.'

The screens showed evidence of this worldwide awakening. In Greenland, the Qivittoq had stepped from the shadows of legend to stand against Ronald Sump's mining operations, their otherworldly powers wielding the icy wrath of the ancient glaciers to halt the destruction. Transformed Baobhan Sith worked alongside them, their combined abilities forcing even the most profit-driven corporations to recognise the sacred nature of the land.

'Look at this,' Thomas said, bringing up footage from Lancashire, where an order had joined environmental protesters at a fracking site. Their transformed powers had revealed the deep damage being done to the land's energy networks. The company's equipment kept mysteriously malfunctioning, their workers overwhelmed by inexplicable feelings of connection to the earth they were about to destroy.

Similar scenes played out across every continent. The Kitsune in Japan standing against nuclear waste dumping. The Encantados in Brazil protecting the Amazon. The Djinn in Arabia safeguarding ancient aquifers from exploitation. Every land's guardians emerging from myth, their gifts transformed and renewed, working together to heal mankind's connection to the natural world.

'Look at social media,' Freya said, their attention drawn to another screen. The hashtag #SupernaturalAwakening was trending worldwide, accompanied by millions of personal stories. Humans sharing memories of encounters they'd previously dismissed. Ancient tales suddenly making new sense. A collective remembering of what the world had lost and might now regain.

A loud bang from the street made their heads turn. A group of enhanced humans—former followers of Agnes who had escaped transformation—were attempting to breach the gallery's defences. But before anyone could move to confront them, something remarkable happened.

The crowd of humans and transformed supernaturals who'd been peacefully gathered outside the gallery formed a line between the attackers and the building. They linked arms, their unity a more powerful defence than any supernatural barrier. Freya watched, her heart swelling with a mixture of pride and hope. This was the future she had envisioned, a future where humans and supernaturals stood together, protecting the bonds that connected them all.

'You see?' Dior said. 'They're already starting to understand. To remember what it means to protect connections rather than break them.'

The enhanced humans faltered, then retreated. They weren't ready to attack their own kind, even in their corrupted state.

'We need to help them,' Agnes said, watching them go. 'Those who were enhanced by my hatred—they're lost, confused. They need guidance to find their way back.'

A new alert flashed across the screens. Live footage from London showed a transformed Baobhan Sith standing on the steps of St. Paul's Cathedral, her markings visible to all as she calmed a frightened crowd with nothing but words and presence. The Archbishop of Canterbury stood beside her, his unlikely alliance a powerful symbol of bridges being built.

'The Americans want to register us,' Thomas said with a grimace, scanning diplomatic cables. 'The Chinese are claiming they've always known about us and want 'cooperation agreements.' The Russians...' He shook his head. 'Well, they're being Russian about it.'

'And our own government?' Freya asked.

'Surprisingly practical,' Greer said. 'They've already drafted preliminary legislation recognising our rights while establishing frameworks for integration. Having Thomas's connections in Parliament helped.'

Indeed, Thomas had been invaluable. His centuries of operating in human political circles, combined with his understanding of their true nature, made him the perfect diplomat.

More footage poured in from around the globe. A transformed Baobhan Sith worked openly in a Manchester hospital, her markings glowing softly as she helped strengthen the bonds between patients and their loved ones, easing pain and fear with her mere presence. In Paris, an order calmed a riot, turning anger into understanding. In Tokyo, they helped rescue workers locate survivors after an earthquake, their supernatural senses augmenting human technology.

'It's not just about feeding anymore,' Freya said, watching the world adapt to their presence. 'It's about healing. Protecting. Strengthening all the connections that make life possible.'

The media struggled to keep up with the scale of change. Every hour brought new revelations, new alliances, new understanding of what their transformation meant for everyone. Stock markets fluctuated wildly as corporations tried to understand the implications. Religious leaders issued statements ranging from condemnation to cautious acceptance.

But it was the environmental impact that captured most

attention. Satellite imagery showed the effects of their awakened powers—areas of environmental destruction beginning to heal as supernatural guardians reclaimed their ancestral roles. The Great Barrier Reef showing signs of recovery as water spirits worked to restore damaged coral. Deforested areas in the Amazon beginning to regenerate as the Encantados wove their magic.

'They're calling it the Great Remembering,' Thomas said, watching. 'Humans recovering ancient knowledge of how to live in harmony with the natural world, guided by transformed supernatural beings.'

A new alert caught their attention—footage from the Arctic where transformed Baobhan Sith worked alongside Inuit elders and their own supernatural guardians. They were literally holding back the effects of climate change, reinforcing ice sheets, protecting vital ecosystems.

'The Old Ones are awakening everywhere,' Dior said, watching the footage. 'Every culture's guardians, transformed and renewed, remembering their true purpose.'

But shadows remained. Reports came in of resistance, of those who refused to move forward.

'There will be conflict,' Greer said grimly, reading reports of anti-supernatural groups forming. 'Not everyone wants to remember what we truly are.'

'Then we show them,' Freya said. 'Not through force, but through truth. Through healing. Through protecting what matters most.'

As if in response, new footage appeared—a massive environmental protest in Canada where transformed beings stood alongside indigenous people to protect sacred lands from pipeline development. Their combined powers made machinery malfunction and caused workers to suddenly understand the deep connection between land and spirit that they were about to sever.

'The hunger's different now,' Agnes said softly, watching the scenes unfold. 'Not just for blood or pleasure, but for healing. For restoring what was broken.'

'For protecting what's sacred,' Dior said, her hand finding Agnes's. Their markings pulsed in harmony, no trace remaining of their centuries of enmity.

Outside the gallery, the sun climbed higher over Edinburgh, illuminating a city forever changed. Their transformation had broken more than just a curse—it had broken centuries of division, of fear, of humanity's disconnection from the sacred web of life.

Freya watched it all unfold, her heart filled with a cautious hope for a future where the Baobhan Sith, and all their transformed kind, could finally step out of the shadows and into the light.

Chapter Seventy-Five

The Exile's Choice

Greer stood outside the cottage, deep in the heart of the Cairngorms, the wind whipping at her hair. She could feel his dark energy pulsing like a corrupted heartbeat. Mànas. Once her ally, her leader. Now, an exile clinging to the shadows of a time that had moved on without him.

She pushed open the door, the ancient wood groaning in protest. Inside, Mànas sat hunched over a table strewn with crumbling texts, the flickering of a single candle cast distorted shadows across his face. He looked up as she entered, his dark eyes glittering with a mix of resentment and curiosity.

'Greer,' he said. 'What brings you to my humble abode?'

Greer moved closer, her silver markings pulsing softly in the gloom. 'I came to see you, Mànas. To talk.'

A harsh laugh escaped his lips. 'Talk? About what? Your glorious new mandate? Your betrayal of everything we once stood for?'

'It's not betrayal,' Greer said softly. 'It's growth.

Change. We've all had to adapt, to evolve. The world is different now.'

Mànas sneered, his dark markings writhing like angry snakes. 'Different? You mean weak. Soft. You've forgotten what it means to have power, to command fear and respect.'

Greer shook her head, sadness welling in her heart. 'No, Mànas. We've learned what it means to have purpose. To be guardians, protectors. To use our strength for something greater than ourselves.'

She gestured to the dusty tomes scattered around him. 'Look at you, hiding away in this forgotten corner, clinging to the past. Everyone is moving on, Mànas. It's leaving you behind.'

A flicker of uncertainty crossed his face, but it didn't last. 'I will not bend to your new ways,' he growled. 'I will not become a lapdog to the humans, a slave to their whims.'

'Then you will fade,' Greer said, her tone heavy with finality. 'You will become nothing more than a footnote, a cautionary tale. Is that what you want? To be remembered as the one who was too stubborn, too proud to change?'

Mànas was silent, the only sound the howling of the wind outside. When he finally spoke, his voice was low, almost lost beneath the storm's fury. 'I cannot be other than what I am, Greer. I will not change.'

Greer felt a pang of sorrow, of regret for what could have been. She had hoped, perhaps foolishly, that even Mànas could be reached, that the transformation could touch even his hardened heart. But looking at him now, seeing the darkness that clung to him like a shroud, she knew it was a lost cause.

'Then this is goodbye,' she said, turning to leave. 'I hope you find peace, Mànas. Even if it's only in memory.'

She left him then, alone in his crumbling sanctuary. As

she stepped out into the storm, she felt a weight lift from her shoulders. She had done all she could. The rest was up to him.

But deep down, Greer knew the truth. Mànas had made his choice, just as they all had. And in choosing to cling to the past, to the ways of darkness and division, he had sealed his own fate.

In a world that had chosen light, there could be no place for those who embraced the shadows. Change was the only constant, the only path forward. And those who refused to walk that path would inevitably be left behind, lost to the mists of time.

It was a harsh truth, but a necessary one. A reminder that the work of transformation, of growth, was never truly done. That they must always be willing to adapt, to evolve, to meet the challenges of a world in constant flux.

As Greer walked away from that lonely cottage, she said a silent farewell to the Mànas she had once known. The warrior, the leader, the dark king of a bygone age. He had been great once, in his own way. But greatness, she had learned, was not a static thing. It was a choice, a commitment, a willingness to change and grow.

Mànas had made his choice. And in doing so, he had consigned himself to irrelevance, to obscurity. A sad end for one who had once commanded legions, but a fitting one for one who had refused the call of a new dawn.

Greer turned her face to the wind, letting it dry the tears she hadn't realised she'd been shedding. Then, with a deep breath, she set her course for home, for the family and the purpose that now defined her. There was still work to be done, and she would not let the ghosts of the past distract her from the bright promise of the future.

Chapter Seventy-Six

Sanctuary

The penthouse above Freya's gallery was quiet, the pre-dawn stillness heavy with the aftermath of a storm. *We were the storm,* Dior thought, watching silver light dance across her skin, a testament to the change that had swept through them. Her markings, no longer a symbol of a curse, pulsed with a power she was only beginning to understand.

Freya stirred beside her, her own transformed patterns shimmering, a visceral reminder of the night on Gallows Hill. Of Agnes, their ancient enemy, becoming something... more. Dior traced the lines on Freya's arm, a map, a story, a language she was only beginning to decipher. They were different, a fusion of human will and the supernatural.

'They're beautiful,' Agnes said, a trace of wonder in her voice. She lay on Dior's other side, a tapestry of silver shadow.

Greer chuckled softly, tangled with them. 'Took you long enough to notice,' she said, her hand finding Dior's beneath the covers.

Four hundred years of hatred, fear, and burning righteousness. And now... this. Agnes, nestled amongst them, humming with the same transformed energy. It was surreal. It was terrifying. It was... exhilarating.

'How do you feel?' Dior asked, needing to understand the changes wrought in their ancient enemy.

Agnes's hand found hers. 'Like I've been living a lie,' she said, her voice cracking. 'Like I'm finally allowed to be who I am.'

Could she be trusted? Could someone who had dedicated centuries to their destruction truly change? Dior searched her own heart, her own transformed markings, for the answer. The markings there, once symbols of a curse, now pulsed with an energy of connection, of healing, of love. Could Agnes, touched by that same energy, truly embrace such a shift?

'It's the connection,' Freya murmured, eyes still closed. 'The patterns... they show us what we can be. Together.'

When Agnes had first touched Dior after her transformation, she had felt a sense of belonging, a rightness she hadn't known she'd been missing.

Greer shifted closer. 'We need to talk about what this means,' she said, low and serious. 'For all of us.'

'It means,' Agnes said, her voice gaining strength, 'that I have a lot to atone for.'

Dior searched her face for any sign of deception. But all she saw was a raw, vulnerable honesty. Agnes met her gaze, her eyes—no longer burning with righteous fire, but shining with a different light.

'I spent centuries trying to destroy you,' Agnes said, her voice catching. 'Believing I was serving a higher purpose. But all I did was perpetuate a cycle of hatred and pain.'

'We all made mistakes,' Dior said softly. 'We all let fear and anger guide us.'

'But you also did good,' Greer said, squeezing Dior's hand gently. 'Even before the transformation, you were changing, Agnes. Your followers, some of them, they weren't just filled with hate. They were searching for something more.'

'A twisted version of the truth,' Agnes said, a shadow of her old bitterness flickering across her face. 'But perhaps... perhaps it can be untwisted.'

Freya sat up, eyes shining with intensity. 'We have to understand the patterns,' she said. 'Not just ours, but theirs - the humans who followed Agnes. Their motivations, their desires, their fears. We need to see how their energies connect to ours, how they can be... redirected.'

'You think we can change them?' Greer asked, sceptical but not entirely without hope.

'I know we can,' Freya said. 'The patterns show me possibilities. It won't be easy, but it's possible. We can guide them, show them a different way.'

Dior felt a surge of hope. Hope for a future where they weren't defined by their hunger, by their curse. A future where they could use their powers to heal, to connect, to build rather than destroy.

But even as hope bloomed, a different kind of hunger stirred within her. A hunger that had been amplified by the transformation, by the merging of their energies. It was a need for connection, for intimacy, for a depth of feeling she had only ever glimpsed before.

She looked at Agnes, her markings mirroring her own. At Greer, her steady anchor. At Freya, whose gift had opened new doors. Whatever came next, they would face it together. Not just as lovers or allies, but as something new. Something more.

'We should connect,' Dior said, a desire beyond the physical thick in her voice. 'All of us. Together.'

Greer's eyes darkened. Freya's breath hitched. Even Agnes felt the pull.

Dior rose, pre-dawn light dancing on her markings. 'Not just blood,' she said. 'Not just flesh. But something deeper.' Her hand went to the collar of her robe. 'Other ways to connect. Other hungers to satisfy.'

'We were meant to be guardians of sacred bonds,' she whispered. 'Protectors of love in all its forms.'

Greer moved beside her. 'What are you suggesting?'

Dior smiled, a slow, sensual curve of her lips that held a promise. 'I'm suggesting,' she said, her voice dropping to a near whisper, 'that we remind ourselves what that truly means.'

She let her robe slip from her shoulders, the silk dropping at her feet. Her markings, fully visible now in the soft morning glow, pulsed with a life of their own, a silent invitation to explore the uncharted territory of their transformed desires.

Freya's breath caught in her throat as she took in the sight of Dior's naked body. The older woman was a masterpiece, her skin glowing with an ethereal radiance, her curves accentuated by the intricate patterns that danced across her flesh. It was a beauty that transcended the physical, a beauty that spoke of centuries of experience, of pain transformed into love that had endured beyond death itself.

Agnes, too, seemed captivated, her eyes fixed on Dior with an intensity that was both unsettling and strangely compelling. There was a hunger in her eyes, a yearning. It was the hunger of a soul that had been starved for centuries, finally given permission to feast.

'Come here,' Dior said. She held out her hands, one to Greer, one to Agnes. 'Both of you.'

Greer moved first, drawn by a force she couldn't resist. She took Dior's hand, her fingers intertwining with hers. The contact sent a jolt of energy through them both, their markings flaring in response.

Agnes hesitated for a moment, her gaze flickering between Dior and Greer. Then, slowly, she reached out and took Dior's other hand. The moment their bodies touched, the room vibrated.

Freya watched them, as her heart raced. She could feel the energy swirling around them, the raw, untamed nature of their connection. A bond that had been forged in the fires of hell itself.

And now, that shared connection was being offered to her.

'Join us,' Dior said. Her gaze met Freya's, and in her eyes, Freya saw an invitation, a promise, a challenge.

She didn't hesitate. She moved to stand before them, her body trembling. She looked at Greer, at the woman who had first shown her the beauty of the darkness. She looked at Agnes, at the woman who had once been their greatest enemy, now transformed into something... greater. And she looked at Dior, at the woman who had always been the still point in their chaos, the anchor that held them all together.

'Show me,' Freya said. 'Show me what we can be.'

Dior smiled. 'Happily,' she said.

Freya obeyed, closing her eyes and surrendering to the darkness. She felt their hands on her body, their breath on her neck, their lips on her mouth. She felt their markings pulse against hers, their energies merging, intertwining, becoming something new.

Greer undressed her slowly, deliberately, every brush of

her fingers against Freya's flesh sending shivers down her spine. Agnes traced patterns on her arms, her touch no longer that of an enemy but a lover. When Dior's mouth found hers, it was a claiming, a promise, a surrender all in one.

They moved together, a slow, sensual dance of bodies and souls. Dior's hands were everywhere, stroking, teasing, igniting fires that Freya had never known existed. Greer's kisses were deep, possessive, each one a brand upon her soul. Agnes, surprisingly, was the gentlest of them all, her touch a feather-light caress that somehow carried the weight of atonement.

Freya felt herself unravelling, coming undone in the best possible way. Every touch, every kiss, every whispered word stripped away another layer of her old self, revealing the raw, untamed power that now pulsed beneath her skin.

They tumbled onto the bed in a frenzy of entwined limbs and silken sheets. Dior pinned Freya to the mattress with the heated weight of her body. Greer and Agnes closed in from either side, their clever hands and hungry mouths working in unison, igniting fireworks of pleasure that stole Freya's breath and left her writhing with need

This was more than just sex. It was a communion, a merging of souls, a dance of dominance and surrender that surpassed the boundaries of the flesh. It was a taste of what they had been, of what they could be again. It was terrifying and exhilarating, painful and pleasurable, a maelstrom of sensation that threatened to consume her entirely.

Freya's fingers dug into Dior's shoulders as she rode her, wave after wave of pleasure coursing through her body. It was unlike anything she had ever experienced before, a euphoria that resonated in her very soul.

Greer's tongue traced the line of her throat, her touch

igniting a fire that spread through every nerve ending. Agnes's hands were on her breasts, kneading, caressing, her touch both gentle and demanding. And then Dior's mouth found hers, and Freya was lost.

She surrendered to the darkness, to the hunger, to the love that flowed between them like a river. She let them take her, shape her, transform her.

More than just her own liberation, it was a collective rapture—a simultaneous eruption of ecstasy that resonated through the very core of the penthouse. In that timeless, boundless instant, their passion fused into a unified whole, their energies intertwining in a cosmic dance. She felt their bodies shudder around her, their hearts beating in unison with hers.

And in that moment, as their bodies trembled and their souls intertwined, Freya knew that they had found the extraordinary. Something that hatred could never touch, something that would bind them together for eternity.

As the last tremors of release faded away, they lay tangled together, their bodies slick with sweat. The room was filled with a sense of peace, of completion, of a love that had been tested and found true.

They were not just lovers, not just allies, not just survivors—they were the guardians and their love was its foundation.

Chapter Seventy-Seven

Dawn's Promise

One year after their transformation, the gallery hosted a markedly different kind of exhibition. Freya's latest work dominated the main wall—a massive triptych chronicling their awakening. But unlike her earlier paintings of their kind, these pieces captured something deeper than just Baobhan Sith beauty. They showed the intricate web of connections that bound all living things—the sacred patterns their people were meant to protect.

The central panel depicted Gallows Hill, its silver still discernible within the ancient stones. But now it extended outward, linking to similar sites across the globe where other guardians had awakened: the Huldufólk's crystal caves in Iceland, the Qivittoq's glacial strongholds in Greenland—sacred spaces where the veils between worlds had thinned, permitting ancient powers to flow once more.

Freya studied the painting, her fingers tracing the lines that interconnected the various locations. It was a map, yes, but also a promise. A promise to every living creature that the old ways were not forgotten, but reborn.

'It's quite something,' a familiar voice said behind her. She turned to find Lord Simon McKay looking at the painting, his security detail trying hard to look professional despite their obvious fascination with the transformed Baobhan Sith mingling freely with the crowd. It had taken delicate negotiation, but Bethia had finally convinced him to accept the title, banking a favour she'd no doubt use when she next needed something passed through the House of Lords. He'd taken to the new role with surprising ease, though he still preferred 'Dr McKay' in private.

'Thank you for coming, Simon,' Freya said. 'I know your schedule is rather full these days.'

He smiled wryly. 'Hard to ignore an invitation from the beings who've revolutionised our understanding of reality.' His gaze moved to where Greer stood deep in discussion with environmental ministers from three continents. 'Though I must say, your people have made the transition remarkably smooth.'

Indeed, the past year had seen changes none of them could have predicted. The Dark Vault, now officially licensed and regulated, had become a model for similar establishments worldwide. Places where humans could safely experience supernatural connection, where bonds could be strengthened through willing exchange of blood and pleasure.

But it was their environmental work that had truly captured global attention. The Great Barrier Reef showed signs of recovery. Ancient forests began to regenerate. Even the Arctic ice was stabilising under their protection.

'The International Supernatural Relations Act passes its final reading next week,' Thomas said, joining them. His own transformation had deepened over the year, grief for James tempered into fierce purpose. 'Full recognition of our rights and responsibilities, balanced with proper oversight and protection for all parties.'

'And the Enhanced Human Rehabilitation Programme?' Lord McKay asked.

'Showing promising results,' Agnes said, appearing with Dior at her side. Their own relationship had become a symbol of what was possible—ancient enemies transformed by understanding and freely chosen love. 'Eighty-seven percent success rate in reversing the corruption. Those who choose to accept help, of course.'

In the months following Agnes's transformation, her former followers found themselves adrift, their enhanced powers fading and their sense of purpose shattered. Some, like those present at the gallery, tried to hold on to their hatred, lashing out in confusion and fear. But many others, faced with the reality of the changed world, began to seek a new path.

The Rehabilitation Program, spearheaded by Agnes herself, provided support and guidance for those willing to embrace change. It was a difficult process, undoing centuries of conditioning and prejudice, but slowly, progress was made. Former adherents learned to channel their passions into more constructive pursuits, finding new meaning in service to their communities and in fostering understanding between humans and supernaturals.

Not all chose this path, of course. Some, unable to let go of their hatred, retreated into the shadows, clinging to the remnants of their former power. They became a scattered resistance, a reminder that the old ways would not die easily. But they were a dwindling minority, their influence waning with each passing day.

Freya watched Agnes, noting the subtle changes in her patterns. The righteous fire was gone, replaced by a calmer, more centred energy. But there were still shadows there, hints of a darkness that might never be fully extinguished. A reminder that even transformation had its limits.

The exhibition hummed with energy as humans and supernaturals mingled freely. A transformed Baobhan Sith demonstrated her powers, showing how she could sense the bonds between people, how she could strengthen connections through willing exchange. Her markings pulsed, beautiful rather than threatening. Humans lined up to have patterns of their own tattooed over their bodies in reverence to the new bonds they had established. Imitation is the sincerest form of flattery.

As the exhibition buzzed, Dior and Greer took a moment to step up to the small podium near the gallery's centre. They had an important announcement to make, one that had been close to their hearts for a long time.

'If we could have your attention, please,' Greer said, her voice carrying across the room. The chatter died down as all eyes turned to them. 'We'd like to take a moment to remember someone very special to us, someone who played a crucial role in bringing us to where we are today.'

Dior took over, her voice thick with emotion. 'Hannah was more than a donor to us. She was a friend, a confidante, and a bridge between worlds. She gave her life to protect us, to give us a chance to become what we were meant to be.'

Greer nodded, her hand finding Dior's. 'In her memory, and in consultation with Lord McKay, we have established the Hannah Dunlop Memorial Scholarship at the University of Edinburgh. This scholarship will support students, both human and supernatural, who are dedicated to studying and promoting understanding and cooperation between our communities.'

A murmur of approval rippled through the crowd. Lord

McKay, standing near the front, nodded his head in solemn agreement.

'And tonight,' Dior said, 'we are proud to announce the first recipient of this scholarship. Sarah, could you please come up here?'

A young woman, her eyes wide with surprise and gratitude, made her way to the podium. Freya recognised her as the human who had witnessed their transformation in Pittenweem—the one who had reached out to touch Dior's markings with wonder rather than fear.

As Sarah accepted the award, shaking hands with Dior and Greer, Freya felt a swell of emotion. This was what their transformation was all about - not just changing themselves, but changing the very core of perception and understanding. Creating a future where humans and the Baobhan Sith could learn from each other, understand each other, and build something new together.

Hannah's legacy would live on, not just in their memories, but in the lives she continued to inspire. And as Freya looked around at the faces in the gallery - human and supernatural alike - she knew that this was just the beginning.

From day to day understanding grew. A group of medical professionals discussed the implications of supernatural healing with representatives from the NHS. Police officers learned from Thomas how to identify and handle the more sensitive situations of handling Baobhan Sith needs. Environmental scientists eagerly shared data on the accelerating recovery of damaged ecosystems under their protection.

But it was the everyday interactions that truly showed how much had changed. A human mother asking a Baobhan Sith to help her understand her teenage daughter's emotional state. A businessman seeking guidance on strengthening team bonds at his company. A grieving widow finding comfort in a Baobhan's ability to sense and preserve connections even beyond death.

Yet, even amidst the progress, Freya felt a tremor of unease. Her gift showed her the fragility of this new world, the fault lines that still ran beneath the surface. Not everyone embraced the change. Fear and prejudice still lingered, fuelled by those who clung to the old ways.

Near the gallery's entrance, Ròs and Bethia stood before a wall of screens, their unlikely partnership now the backbone of their new coalition. Their geometric and spiral patterns, once so different, now worked in perfect harmony as they coordinated with guardians worldwide. After centuries of rivalry, the Stone and Shadow Orders had united, their combined strength greater than either could have achieved alone.

'Reports from the Arctic,' Ròs said, her precise patterns rippling with satisfaction. 'The Qivittoq report that the ice is holding. The seals are returning to their ancestral breeding grounds.'

'The Amazon too,' Bethia added, her spiral markings dancing with equal pride. 'The Encantados have pushed back another illegal logging operation. The forest is beginning to heal.'

Behind them hung a photograph that captured the moment their alliance began – Freya studied the faces of those who had fought alongside them that night. So many had changed, transformed by the events on Gallows Hill. But some, she knew, were still struggling to find their place. And others, refused to move forward.

At the gallery's heart stood a smaller exhibition - a memorial to James. Photographs showed him at the Dark Vault, his smile bright as he mixed drinks, stole kisses from

Thomas between customers, and built bridges between human and the Baobhan Sith without even trying. The silver chain, holding James's ring still hung around Thomas's neck, as it always would.

Thomas paused before the display. 'He would have loved this,' he said softly. 'All of it. The changes, the connections, the hope.' His transformed markings, once born of grief, now pulsed with something deeper—purpose forged from loss, strength tempered by love.

'He saw it first,' Bethia said, joining him. 'What we could be. What we were meant to be. Even before we understood ourselves.'

'He chose love,' Ròs added, her usual sharp tone softened by respect. 'When everything said he should choose fear. That's why we honour him. Why we'll always honour him. He led the way.'

Freya felt a pang of sadness as she looked at the memorial. James's sacrifice had been the catalyst for so much change, but it was a change he would never get to witness. A bittersweet reminder that even progress had its price.

Freya felt Greer's arms slip around her waist as they watched their transformed world take shape. Dior and Agnes joined them, their markings pulsing in harmony. The four of them stood together, watching the future unfold through the gallery's windows.

'Do you ever regret it?' Agnes asked softly. 'Choosing this path? Knowing what it cost?'

'Never,' Dior said firmly. 'Every sacrifice, every scar - they're part of what makes us what we are now.'

'And what are we?' Agnes asked.

'Guardians,' Freya said. 'Protectors of the bonds that make life worth living. Between people, between communities, between humanity and the earth itself.'

'Love's warriors,' Greer added with a slight smile.

'Family,' Thomas said quietly, joining them.

Outside, Edinburgh's lights twinkled under a dark velvet sky. The city had changed, like everything else. Humans and the Baobhan Sith now walked its ancient streets openly, undivided and intertwined. The curse was broken. Love had won.

They had made a choice on Gallows Hill, a choice to embrace their true nature. Now they had to live with the consequences, to prove to the world - and to themselves - that they were worthy of the power they now wielded.

'It won't be easy,' she said, voicing the thought they all shared. 'There will be resistance. Setbacks. Pain.'

'But we'll face it together,' Dior added, her hand finding Freya's. 'As we always have.'

Agnes nodded, her transformed markings pulsing in agreement. 'We have a chance to build something new,' she said. 'Something better.'

Thomas looked at the memorial to James, his expression a complex mix of grief and determination. 'For him,' he said. 'For everyone we've lost. We have to make this new world worth the price they paid.'

Freya met their gazes, her heart full. They were a tapestry, woven together by love, loss, and a shared purpose. A family forged in darkness, now stepping into the light.

'Then let's get to work,' she said, a faint smile touching her lips. She looked at her family and smiled. Their story was far from over.

Consider leaving me a review?

I hope you've loved reading Blood Marks as much as I've loved writing it. If you've enjoyed this book, would you consider rating and reviewing it? Reviews are very important to authors and I'd be really grateful!

Leave a review on Amazon

Reviews are also welcome on Good Reads and Apple Books too.

Also by Ruby Scott

May I Call You Mistress?

Darkness of Desire

Mistress of Desire

Commitment to Desire

Rescuing Hearts

Evergreen

Hot Response

Love Trauma

Open Heart

Diagnosis Love

Trails of the Heart

Healing of the Heart

Inside Fighter

Seconds Out

On the Ropes

The Stranger Within Me

Strangely Familiar

No Way Out

Also by Ruby Scott writing as Frankie Duncan

First Comes Love

Love in Action

Her Christmas Escape

About the Author

Ruby Scott is the pen name of Susie Fleming, author of over twenty sapphic novels. She lives in a quiet Scottish village with her wife, Angie. An avid animal lover and traveller, she seeks out adventures that combine both passions – often leading to entertaining stories along the way.

Under her own name, Susie also writes the DI Viv Wylde crime thriller series for Coppers Publishing.

Acknowledgments

A huge thank you to Angie, my sounding board and bringer of common sense, wine and chocolate – you always know what I need.

To my wonderful support team: Lise, your designs are, as always, awesome. You finish what I start with such polish and make it visually gleam!

My editor, Em – it is always a pleasure... although sometimes I hide it well. I appreciate you. Thank you.

To my advance support group: each and every one of you is so very much appreciated. It's one thing to have an idea in your head, but knowing it translates into something readers want to invest their time in makes my heart sing. Thank you for your honesty – you pull no punches, and I wouldn't have it any other way.

Ruby Scott

www.rubyscott.com

www.ingramcontent.com/pod-product-compliance
Ingram Content Group UK Ltd.
Pitfield, Milton Keynes, MK11 3LW, UK
UKHW040752020725
6679UKWH00014B/93